KRISHNA'S MUSICIANS

Krishna's Musicians

Musicians and Music Making in The Temples of Nathdvara, Rajasthan

ANNE-MARIE GASTON

MANOHAR
2020

First published 1997
Reprinted 2019, 2020

ISBN 978-81-7304-161-7

Published by
Ajay Kumar Jain *for*
Manohar Publishers & Distributors
4753/23 Ansari Road, Daryaganj
New Delhi 110 002

Printed at
Replika Press Pvt. Ltd.

To

GURU PURUSHOTTAM DAS (1907-91)

Pakhavaji, Shri Nathji Haveli

and the Musicians of Nathdvara

Contents

10: FESTIVALS 215

11: THE FAMILY HISTORY OF GURU PURUSHOTTAM DAS 242

"If you find some mistakes, I beg your pardon; and if you find something useful, kindly grasp it and use it. By doing so you will make my efforts successful. That alone gives me satisfaction. Just as the swan can separate water from milk, my excellent readers, grasp the good and ignore the mistakes" (*Mridang Vadan* 1911 Pr.: 3).

Pakhavaji Ghanshyam Das 1869-1916
Shri Nathji Haveli, Nathdvara Rajasthan

Acknowledgements

This research was made possible by the co-operation and full support extended to me by many musicians and townsfolk in Nathdvara and in other centres of the Vallabha Sampraday. Among them, the late Pakhavaji Guru Purushottam Das, deserves particular mention. The debt I owe to him I can never repay. My knowledge of the *pakhavaj* began with practical training in the oral tradition with him. It was the care and dedication that he extended to me that prompted me to embark on this research. He assisted me at all stages and especially in my transformation from the practical to the sociological inquiry into the place of music and the musicians in Nathdvara. It was a great sadness for me that he died before this work was published.

In Nathdvara, my research would not have been possible without assistance from the Tilkayat of the Vallabha Sampraday, Shri Shri 108 Shri Govindlalji. Others who assisted me there in particular were Prakash Chandra Kumavat, and Sushil Paliwal.

Much additional impetus to undertake this research came from Joan Erdman and Karine Schomer who encouraged me to expand my chapter published in *The Idea of Rajasthan* (Schomer *et al.* 1994). Rupert Snell of the School of Oriental and African Studies, London, fuelled my enthusiasm, encouraged me to record events in which I participated and offered valuable suggestions. I am also very grateful to Andrew Topsfield, Assistant Keeper, Department of Eastern Art, Ashmolean Museum, Oxford and the official art historian of the House of Mewar, Rajasthan, who read an earlier draft and spent many hours with me discussing my research. Their insight and vision were an important influence on the final shape of the book and I thank them all for their generosity.

Some of the material included in this book formed part of my

D. Phil. for Oxford University, entitled "Continuity and Re-Creation: A Study of Two Artistic Traditions". I wish to express my gratitude to my thesis supervisor, Bryan Wilson, Reader in the Sociology of Religion, All Souls College, Oxford, for his assistance and encouragement, extended to me throughout the period that this work was prepared. In addition, this work would not have been possible without the trust and enthusiasm extended to me over many years by Professor Richard Gombrich (Boden Professor of Sanskrit, Oxford University) and his wife Sanjukta Gupta.

Others who read and gave useful comments on parts of this book were: Nik Allen, Joep Bor, Erica Claus, Nalini Delvoye, Robert Gottlieb, Stephen Inglis, Elaine Keillor, Mukund Lath, Tapan Raychauduri, Prem Lata Sharma, Salima Tyabji, Wim Van der Meer, and Richard Widdess. I thank them all.

For financial assistance, at various stages of my research, I am grateful to the Social Science and Humanities Research Council (SSHRC), Max Mueller Fund, Spalding Trust, Wolfson College, Oxford University, and ISTAR (International Society for Traditional Arts Research).

Amit Ambalal was very generous in allowing me to take photographs of his private collection of paintings that illustrate the various activities of the Vallabha Sampraday, and also in assisting me in my research in Ahmedabad.

The greatest encouragement came from my husband, Tony Gaston, an environmentalist with particular interest in Indian wildlife and ecosystems. He shares with me a respect and appreciation for artists trying to survive in our rapidly changing world. Both traditional artists and eco-systems can be viewed as endangered species, worthy of preservation. For that reason he is able to empathize with my complete involvement with the artistic traditions of India. It is this support that has sustained me. Much of our life together has revolved around participating in, and sharing the artistic riches of India.

Wolfson College, Oxford ANNE-MARIE GASTON
May 1995

Abbreviations

AP	*Aparna patrika*: dedication in the *Mridang Sagar*
BMJ	Banmaliji Haveli
Jiv	*Jivani*: family background section in the *Mridang Sagar*
MMJ	Madanmohanji Haveli
MS	*Mridang Sagar*
MV	*Mridang Vadan*
NNP	Navnitpriyaji Haveli
Pr	*Prastavana*: the preface in the *Mridang Sagar*
SNJ	Shri Nathji Haveli
VNJ	Vitthalnathji Haveli

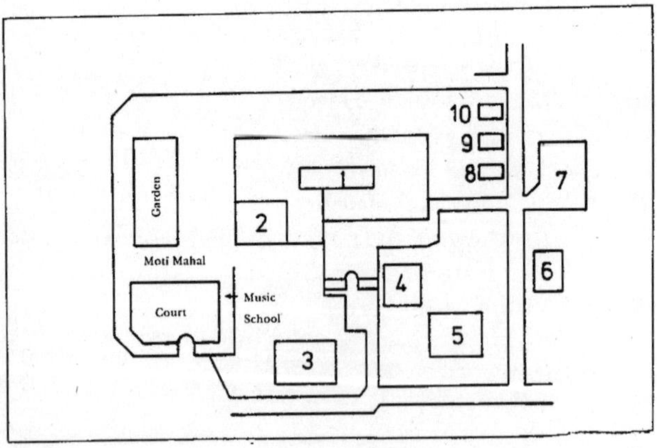

FIGURE 1: VALLABHA *SAMPRADAY HAVELIS* IN NATHDVARA

1. Shrine of Shri Nathji (*nij mandir*)
2. Navnitpriyaji Haveli
3. Dvarkadishji Haveli
4. Banmaliji Haveli
5. Madanmohanji Haveli
6. Gopallalji Haveli
7. Vitthalnathji Haveli
8. Kalyanrayji Haveli
9. Jamunaji Haveli
10. Govindrayji Haveli

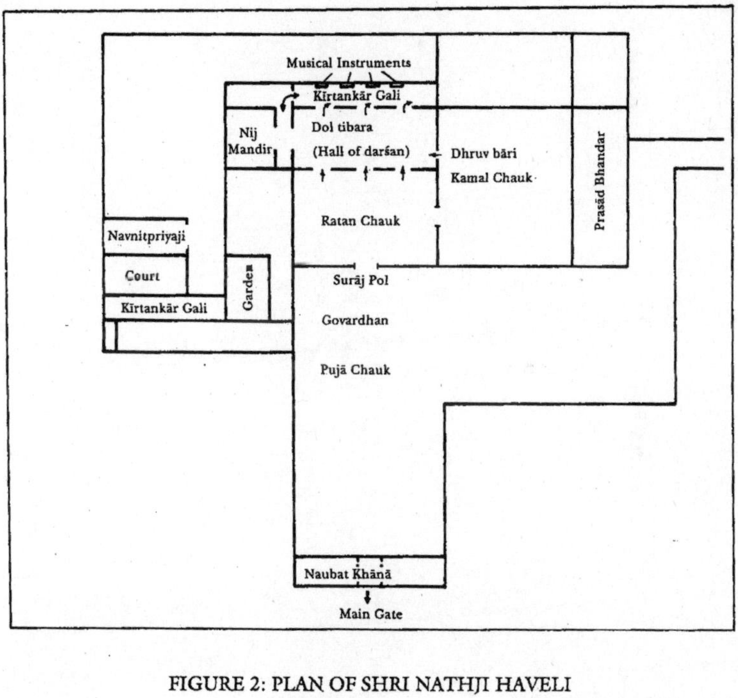

FIGURE 2: PLAN OF SHRI NATHJI HAVELI

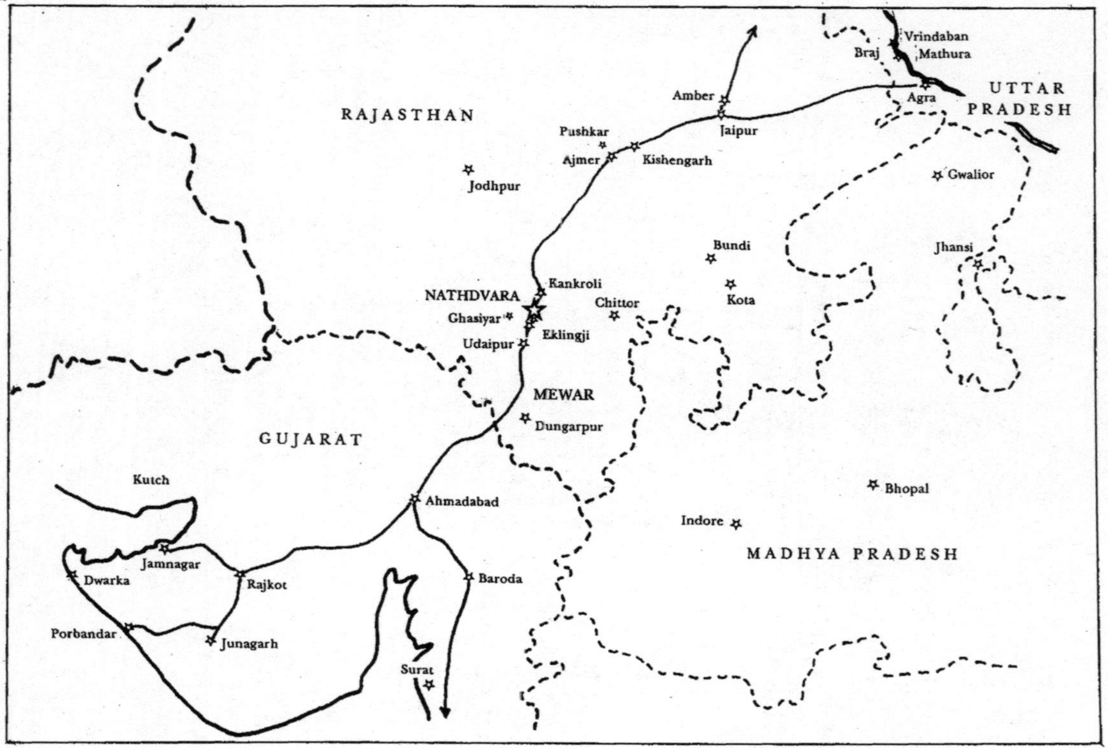

MAP OF LOCATION OF TEMPLES IN NATHDVARA

CHAPTER 1

Background

INTRODUCTION

Unlike contemporary artistic traditions in the West, many of the Indian arts continue to be heavily influenced by religion. Until recently, the situation was reminiscent of Europe before the Renaissance. Even today, the content of India's classical arts is taken largely from Hindu religious texts, and many current performance genres evolved from religious rituals. While the various genres of classical arts are now performed frequently in most of the large metropolitan centres, and the artists themselves are sent abroad as ambassadors of Indian culture, it is only in the twentieth century that they have adapted to the concert stage (Gaston 1983a: 297).

Initially the setting for classical performance arts shifted away from temples and other religious venues to the theatrical stage, film and television screens. In the 1980s there was a movement to reintroduce some remnants, or even large portions of the religious heritage that had been carried over into these secular contexts. In some cases, new religious rituals have even been introduced (Gaston 1991b). It may be difficult in some situations to distinguish the traditional religious heritage from recent accretions. In the wider context of the performing arts in India, this difficulty is aggravated by the increasing scarcity of arts still performed in their traditional contexts by hereditary specialists (Gaston 1983a, 1991a,d; Neuman 1980; Marglin 1985: 28-9). It is therefore of particular interest to examine an artistic tradition which exists in a temple context still largely unmodified by outside influences.

Although virtually all Indian performing arts trace their origins to religion, or have close ties with it, some are specifically devoted to presentation in religious contexts. Such sacred arts are usually the preserve of hereditary practitioners, many of whom are still supported by Hindu temples. One such hereditary group in north India is that of the hereditary musicians (*kirtankars*) who still serve in Nathdvara, Rajasthan, in the temples of the Vallabha Sampraday (sect),[1] also known as *pushtimarg*. Nathdvara is unusual in retaining a sizeable community of *kirtankars* whose profession it is to be involved full-time in the performance of temple music.

The study of *kirtankars,* as examples of a traditional artistic community, is not irrelevant to the present because the traditional arts of India remain a strong repository of indigenous classical culture. Moreover, although Indian artistic traditions are very diverse, they share certain fundamental characteristics: hereditary transmission, oral rather than written instructions and tight bonds between students and teachers, which allow generalizations among traditions.

My study of the Nathdvara musicians originated through my association with the late Pakhavaji Guru Purushottam Das (1907-91), a hereditary musician from Nathdvara. Members of Guru Purushottam's family had been drummers in Nathdvara for several generations and his relatives continue in this capacity. Through him, I got to know many other Nathdvara musicians, and other members of the temple hierarchy. My research began as a project to collect and record the drumming tradition of Guru Purushottam Das (Gaston 1983b). It soon became evident that to appreciate fully this tradition, I would have to study it in its context, during the religious rituals in the Shri Nathji temple. Gradually my orientation changed from studying the music of the *pakhavaj* to studying musicians and their environment. By profession I am a dancer, and have spent many years studying Indian classical dance in Madras, Delhi and in south India. Hence I was very familiar at the outset with many aspects of teaching and performing arts in India, and with the amazing depth and strength of the Indian classical traditions.

Indigenous musical traditions are not peripheral to modern Indian society, but form an integral part of it, in a manner hardly equalled elsewhere in the world. As Neuman comments: "The music culture of India is the only major system outside the West that has succeeded in maintaining its traditions largely unmarked by the West ... and that has also journeyed away from its cultural home to be welcomed elsewhere" (Neuman 1980: 17).

Understanding the sociology of hereditary north Indian musicians requires knowledge of their historical contexts. Given that the

Nathdvara musicians (*kirtankars*) are practising a traditional art, still in a very traditional way, it is fortunate that Guru[2] Purushottam Das possessed a copy of *Mridang Sagar*, a book written by his father Ghanshyam Das (1869-1911). As well as notated *pakhavaj* compositions it includes a brief history of their family, and of its association with the music of the temple.

Ghanshyam was a *pakhavaji*, a drummer who plays the *pakhavaj*, a two-ended, double conical-shaped drum with two heads. He was the third generation of the family to serve in the Shri Nathji temple in Nathdvara. His son, Pakhavaji Guru Purushottam Das, with whom I studied, followed in his footsteps. Guru Purushottam's book, on the music of the *pakhavaj*, *Mridang Vadan*, was published in 1982. Guru Purushottam's observations and reminiscences are other important sources for this study. I have used the material in these books to supplement my own interview material regarding the history of the musician community. The little historical information that exists for Nathdvara, principally that recorded in the *Mridang Sagar*, tends to support the continuity of the tradition; that what is done now is closely related to what was done before. A comparison of all available sources suggests that the music tradition of Nathdvara remains essentially unchanged in its social context, performance, and presentation, exhibiting simply a gentle decline in its prestige and in the remuneration of its exponents.

In the past, north Indian classical music was supported by two types of patronage: secular, in the form of royal courts and wealthy landowners; and religious, comprising temples in which classical music formed a part of worship. The music of the courts and temples was often similar in style and content, irrespective of the venue. Through the movement of musicians across the boundaries between the religious and secular, the music of temples and courts remained closely related. In the modern context, however, differences in function and venue have created divergences. While the secular tradition has found no difficulty in adapting to the changing realities of the twentieth century, the temple tradition has fared less well. There are now few places in north India where classically trained musicians are supported by temples; the temples of Nathdvara being an exception.

The Vallabha Sampraday was founded in A.D. 1494 by Vallabha.[3] All the temples of the Vallabha sampraday are called *haveli*, being modelled after the *haveli* or large manor house typical of the royal houses of Rajasthan. Although *haveli* is more precise, the term temple is often used interchangeably to describe a building that houses an image venerated by the Vallabha Sampraday. The Shri Nathji shrine in Nathdvara, Rajasthan is the most important centre of the sect (Barz 1976: 27).

The music played in the *havelis* is known as *haveli sangit*, or *pushtimarg bhakti sangit*. Today Nathdvara, particularly the Shri Nathji Haveli, is the main centre for this musical genre. Hence, essentially the music of the Shri Nathji Haveli defines what constitutes *haveli sangit*.

The Nathdvara temple complex, like many other great Indian temples, is a virtual living museum of culture. Given the conservatism exhibited in other ways by the rituals of the *sampraday*, I see no reason to think that there has been much change in the role of music and the manner of performance in the Shri Nathji Haveli over the past century. This book explores the role of the *kirtankars* as musicians and producers of some of the traditional arts of Nathdvara. It also examines the extent to which their survival depends on the continued existence of the temples. Some of the major festivals, the role of the arts in their celebration, and the way in which the present and past are inextricably interwoven into the cultural fabric of Nathdvara are described.

In studying the musicians of Nathdvara, I have treated the musical establishment of the town as an example of a traditional north Indian artistic community. It may be typical of the type of social organization common among artists in the past. Many features of the music and its associated arts in Nathdvara are no doubt unique to the town. Nevertheless, I believe that the Nathdvara tradition as it existed during nine visits that I made between 1981 and 1988, probably represents many features typical of musician communities associated with large temples or religious centres over the past few centuries.

In my research I concerned myself principally with the lives of the hereditary musicians of Nathdvara, and their role in its temples. I have highlighted the family of my teacher, Pakhavaji Guru Purushottam Das. The male members of his family can trace their musical lineage to the seventeenth century and their association with the Shri Nathji Haveli for four generations. I have looked at the celebration of some important festivals in the temple and described their special features. I have drawn some parallels with other *havelis* of the *sampraday*.

Paintings from the eighteenth to the twentieth centuries which record the events and celebrations of events in the temple are included as I observed that much of what occurs today is mirrored in them. I have not included theoretical analysis nor accounts in texts, as much of this has been covered by other scholars (Barz, Snell, Entwistle, Verdia, etc.). The written word does have a satisfying precision, in comparison with the imprecisions and contradictions of oral testimony. We have, however, no way of knowing how closely the written word may have mirrored reality in the past; and there is no reason to assume that it is any more accurate than the reminiscences of current practitioners and the records of trained observers. Because I am concerned mainly with the living tradition and what it can tell us about the past I have conducted my enquiries primarily by interviewing those involved and making observations on the context in which they performed their tasks. While I have consulted both the *Mridang Sagar* and *Mridang Vadan* for details about the family history and musical tradition of Guru Purushottam, this book is largely a participant-observer's view of Nathdvara's musicians in the 1980s.

THE TOWN, THE TEMPLE, AND SHRI NATHJI

The town of Nathdvara lies forty-five kilometres west of Udaipur, on the road to Jodhpur and Ajmer. The surrounding land is largely rocky uplands, part of the Aravalli range of hills, and is cut by a few narrow fertile valleys. Most of it has been deforested long since. Many of the inhabitants of the surrounding district are tribal people (Bhil and Mina). With a relatively low density of population in the surrounding areas and no importance as a distribution centre, the town owes its existence almost entirely to its temples and the resulting traffic of pilgrims. The temples in turn owe their attraction mainly to the presence of one particular deity, Shri Nathji, who is the presiding deity of the main temple in Nathdvara. The temples were built by the Vallabha Sampraday. Braj, where the sect was originally founded by Vallabha, remained its centre for nearly two hundred years before the image of Shri Nathji was transported to Mewar (1670-72), leading to the foundation of Nathdvara, and the building of the Shri Nathji temple.

SVARUP

Shri Nathji is but one of the forms of Krishna, identified in the broader framework of the Hindu pantheon as an incarnation of Vishnu. There are a variety of ways in which Krishna may be represented and each has a different name and shape. Added to the differences in outward appearance and nomenclature, is the innate character of the image; whether it is reputed to have been fashioned by an artisan or manifested fully formed. The three technical categories of images are: ***vigraha*** (individual form or shape, figure) ***murti*** (embodiment) and ***svarup*** (own form). ***Vigraha*** and ***murti*** are fashioned in the shape considered appropriate for the deity according to rules given in various texts; the image is later sanctified by invoking the divine to enter it. ***Svarup*** is not manmade, but appears fully formed as the embodiment of the deity. Shri Nathji in Nathdvara is an example of a ***svarup***, a divine manifestation of Krishna on earth, and not merely a likeness of him (Barz 1976: 28; Eck 1985: 34). There can be many ***svarups*** of different manifestations of Krishna; but of Shri Nathji there is only one embodiment, and he resides in Nathdvara (Eck ibid.; Entwistle 1987: 79). This makes Shri Nathji a very personal god. Devotees must come to make personal contact with him, perform tasks for him (***seva***) or give donations of cash or kind that can be used for his daily routine.

WORSHIP IN THE SHRI NATHJI HAVELI

Shri Nathji is worshipped in a manner appropriate to a living person. The daily rituals that surround Shri Nathji involve such mundane human activities as waking, bathing, dressing, eating, and enjoying music. As he is also a god, all of these activities are carried out with the pomp and splendour accorded to medieval kings. Shri Nathji is often referred to as ***Thakurji***, meaning "Lord"; a term used to refer to a feudal landlord, master or chief. This epithet is also used for other manifestations of Krishna (Entwistle 1987: 78).

As befits a royal personage, Shri Nathji resides in his own mansion or ***haveli*** (Commissariat 1938; ***Marg*** 1977a; Parmar 1987: 187-201). As he is also worshipped here the word ***mandir*** or temple is used interchangeably with ***haveli***. Within its high walls, the ***haveli*** is a fully functioning, self-contained estate with its kitchens, storage rooms, bathing rooms, etc. There used to be a garden as well but this has been built over.

SEVA/BHAKTI

In common with many other Krishna temples, worship in the Shri Nathji Haveli has two essential ingredients: *bhakti* or devotion to god, and *seva* or service. All work in the *haveli* is regarded as *seva* to Shri Nathji. Music, which has always been one of the most important components of the religious rituals of the Shri Nathji Haveli, is one form of *seva*. It is presented up to seventeen times a day. *Seva* of Shri Nathji must be performed with *bhakti*, and complete selflessness and humility, with obsessive attention to ensuring his comfort and maintaining his status as a manifestation of god on earth. *Seva* and *bhakti* are inextricably interwoven, neither can exist without the other. *Bhakti* gives the impetus and *raison d'être* for the various activities associated with the worship of Shri Nathji.

DARSHAN

There are appointed times when Shri Nathji's devotees may visit him daily. These occasions of visitation are known as *darshan* (literally, seeing). *Darshan*, implies not only that the worshipper observes the deity (or saint or another esteemed person), but that the deity transmits some part of his holiness to the beholder (Eck 1985: 6-7). Shri Nathji receives his subjects and imparts his divine grace during *darshan*, held at seven or eight specified times each day. This is the main form of congregational worship for the Vallabha Sampraday.

THE SPIRITUAL, HEREDITARY HEAD OF THE *SAMPRADAY*, THE *TILKAYAT*

The present spiritual head of the Vallabha Sampraday, the Tilkayat, Shri Shri 108 Shri Govindlal,[4] is a direct descendant of Vallabha. All of Vallabha's descendants, including the Tilkayat, are also called Maharaj. The title Maharaj was used from the time of Vallabha's son, Vitthalnath (A.D. 1516-86) (Motivala 1935; Barz 1976: 41). The title Tilkayat is reserved for the head of the *sampraday* and came into use later.

I have used the term "Maharaj" to refer to the religious leaders of the *sampraday* and "Maharaja" to refer to the secular rulers of the various Rajput states.[5] This is simply a convention adopted to clarify matters for my readers; in Hindi the words are the same. Another name by which all the heads of the *sampraday* are known is Gosvami.

"Ji", is an honorific suffix used in north India. To differentiate deities from persons, I have chosen to attach "ji" only to the names of deities and temples. After the names of members of Guru Purushottam's family, I have also omitted "ji" to make for easier reading. In quotations from the *Mridang Sagar* and *Mridang Vadan*, however, it remains. For eminent persons such as Tilkayats, Maharajs/Maharajas I have omitted "ji". I have adopted these conventions purely for clarification, because the names of many of the deities, Maharaj and other persons, are often the same. I have chosen to use the title Maharaj for a spiritual leader and Maharaja for a secular ruler.

The Tilkayat has his private apartments within the temple complex. Although the finances of the temple are administered by a temple board he continues to have both spiritual and temporal power. In practice the Tilkayat's 'sweet will' is a major force in the activities of the temple and town. From my own observations, the musical tradition survives in Nathdvara as a direct result of the continued support it receives from the temple, and in this matter particularly, the Tilkayat wields great influence.

LITERATURE

For a town of its size (22,000 persons, Jindel 1976), Nathdvara has attracted a surprising amount of attention from scholars, most of it focused on the religious arts. The presence of music in the Shri Nathji Haveli is mentioned in a number of earlier scholarly works but none deals in detail with the music and its role in temple ritual. Tod (1829) supplied the earliest account of Nathdvara in English, but as he did not gain entry to the temples, he does not mention music. Jindel (1976) gives the most accurate comments on the role of music in worship, although her remarks are cursory. Verdia (1982) mentions the musicians, not the context in which music was presented. Barz (1976) provides an excellent account of the historical background of the

Vallabha Sampraday and of the main composers of its musical tradition, known as the *ashtacchap*; but of the current practices of the Vallabha Sampraday or the context of music today he does not have much to say. The miniature paintings illustrated in Ambalal (1987) are invaluable as historical documents for showing where the music was played, and the type of instruments. However, he does not include comparisons with the present day situation. Skelton (1973), Maduro (1976), and Talwar and Krishna (1979), refer to the music only incidentally and concern themselves entirely with the artistic traditions of miniature painting, and the making of decorative cloths suspended behind images of the Vallabha Sampraday (*pichhvai*).

At several places I have drawn comparisons with the accounts of the practices and customs of the Vallabha Sampraday given in the writings of Karsondas Mulji (1865), who was a member of the *sampraday* from birth. His opinion of the *sampraday* remains controversial. Attacks on the Maharaj in his newspaper, *Satya Prakash*, led to a celebrated libel case. His book, *A History of the Sect of the Maharajas*, again was critical of many of their practices. Both had strong repercussions and undermined the influence of many of the Maharaj.

Growse's (1880) views, not entirely sympathetic towards the *sampraday*, were no doubt coloured by the Mulji case which was still very much in living memory: "Such being the revolting character of their theological literature, it is easy to understand why the Vallabhacharyas have always shown a great reluctance to submit it to the criticism of the outer world of unbelievers, who might not be prepared to accept such advanced doctrines..."

Partly as a result of such criticisms, there is, even today, a general reluctance on the part of the members of the *sampraday* to be forthcoming, as Pocock remarked:

> Although the sect appears to have passed its luxurious heyday in the nineteenth century it is still very large and influential. The present Maharaj and their followers are quite excessively sensitive to the reported delinquencies of their grandfathers; for this reason some are reticent about the doctrines and practices of the sect. I am understandably, very grateful therefore to the present incumbent of the Kankroli Haveli, Shri Vrajbhushanlalji Maharaj[6] who, to my mind, embodies the spirit of the Maharaj (Pocock 1972: 113).

Hein also referred to the Karsondas Mulji libel case as having consequences and impact far beyond the Vallabha Sampraday.

> The entire Krishna cult suffered greatly in the public eye, not because Krishna

devotees as a whole had been proved guilty of wrongdoing but because it had been necessary in the course of cross examination to lay the entire mythology and liturgy and ritual of the Gopala cult before the uninitiated westerner or westernized minds of India (Hein 1988: 11).

For my part, I received the full cooperation of the Tilkayat and his staff. An earlier first draft of this book was read by his highness and his staff kindly produced a page of typed suggestions for me to consider.

MRIDANG SAGAR (1911), *MRIDANG VADAN* (1982)

The existence of the *Mridang Sagar* gave me an unusual opportunity to provide a historical context for my study. Guru Purushottam was nine years old when his father, Ghanshyam, died. This tragedy was slightly alleviated by the fact that part of his ancestors' musical legacy, as it was played in the late nineteenth century, and some musical theory, had been notated by Ghanshyam in the *Mridang Sagar*. Some of this knowledge has been reconstructed by Guru Purushottam, but without the direct assistance of his father much material has been lost.

Even though much of the material in the *Mridang Sagar* is not used and may not be fully understood, this book and Guru Purushottam's own teachings, are still regarded by all the *Pakhavajis* in Nathdvara as the ultimate authority on the *pakhavaj* music of Nathdvara. The book includes both traditional *pakhavaj* compositions, common to all the *Pakhavajis* of Nathdvara, and special pieces unique to Guru Purushottam's family, some of which are attributed to particular composers. In addition there are numerous transcriptions of *pakhavaj* compositions and a description of contemporary *pakhavaj* terms. From the systematic recordings I have made, I can detect a considerable divergence between the *pakhavaj* music notated in the *Mridang Sagar* and that presently practised in Nathdvara. This illustrates how difficult it is to transcribe a tradition that is essentially oral. This material has been published elsewhere.[7]

The *Mridang Vadan* (MV) (1982), written by Guru Purushottam, repeats some of the material in the *Mridang Sagar* but also includes additional information from both contemporary and oral accounts concerning their more recent family history, and more *pakhavaj* compositions. He acknowledged that he received some help in its preparation from Bhagavat Upreti, one of his most accomplished *pakhavaj* students and a university lecturer. It is written in Hindi that is straightforward and easily comprehensible. On the other hand, the language in the *Mridang Sagar*, published in 1911, before Hindi was standardized, is much more difficult to comprehend.[8] For assistance in this I am grateful to Shri Dayal Chandra Soni, a retired Hindi teacher living in Udaipur. As both a Rajasthani and linguist he was familiar with the local Mewari dialect (Hiralal 1980). Shri Dayal said that Ghanshyam chose to write in Hindi because he saw it as the language of a learned person. He commented: "It is creditable that he has written this book. He was not educated. You can tell this from the number of grammatical mistakes. If you know Hindi in the local context then you can understand this book: the style, the mode. If you only have a dictionary it would not be possible to read it".

Despite these negative qualifications Shri Dayal acknowledged that the *Mridang Sagar* was an important book. It is very professionally presented, with a hard cover, clear print, and good photographs. Although Shri Dayal was a competent linguist and had spent his life in nearby Udaipur, he was unfamiliar with the musical terms, the oral history of Guru Purushottam's family and the sociological setting for the music, in particular the traditional practices associated with the Vallabha Sampraday. Consequently unravelling its contents would not have been possible without our collaborative efforts. My own familiarity with the practices in the temple acquired by attending many *darshans*, sitting with musicians during the pre-*darshan* periods, visiting their homes and spending many hours with each of them and their families gave me the supplementary material needed to interpret the contents of the *Mridang Sagar*.

Many of the musicians mentioned in the *Mridang Sagar* were known by the present musicians either personally or by reputation. The women of the families would often add their comments. The older women contributed experiences from both their natal and their married homes, so that the oral history that they imparted could, to some extent, be cross-referenced.

Ghanshyam, in the *Mridang Sagar* (MS Ap: 1), refers to James Tod (1829) as the source to consult for the history of Nathdvara and Rajasthan. For some of the events that affected Ghanshyam's relatives, Tod was actually present and I have followed Ghanshyam's advice and included Tod's observations where he comments on historical events that affected Ghanshyam's relatives. I have usually used Crooke's (1920) edition of Tod which is acknowledged as more accurate than Tod's unedited account with regard to dates and spelling. Guru

Purushottam and other musicians added to the recorded history with their own accounts of the oral history of their family. The miniature paintings of the period substantiate many of their comments and reinforce my own observations that the rituals and celebrations associated with the temple have remained largely unchanged.

The texts of both the *Mridang Sagar* and *Mridang Vadan* are mostly devoted to documenting the Nathdvara *pakhavaj* tradition. I have studied most of the compositions in the *Mridang Vadan* and made recordings of Guru Purushottam playing them. The *Mridang Sagar* gives a detailed description of contemporary *pakhavaj* terms for compositions and techniques of playing. It also provides transcriptions of numerous compositions for the *pakhavaj*, some of which are unique to Guru Purushottam's family. For that reason, the *Mridang Sagar* is an indispensable source concerning the *pakhavaj* music of Nathdvara, but is apparently not widely available outside Nathdvara.[9]

Information in the *Mridang Sagar* confirms the close connection between religious and courtly music by documenting the careers of musicians who performed in both situations. The movement of the musicians between these two centres of patronage provides a parallel for the origins and development of *haveli* music and its interconnections with the evolution of the courtly tradition of *darbari-dhrupad* (Srivastava 1980: 22). *Haveli* music is still an important part of temple ritual, not only in the Shri Nathji temple, but in most temples of the Vallabha Sampraday.

METHODS

In collecting material on the musicians and music of Nathdvara, and in particular on Guru Purushottam's life and music, I was conscious of the fact that it was not only Guru Purushottam and the musicians then employed in the Shri Nathji temple who were worthy of record, but rather the whole life-style and tradition of which they were a product which required recognition. Although this work describes a tradition that remains very much alive, it would be naive to assume that it is static and unassailable by outside forces. The history of Guru Purushottam's family, his musical tradition and the careers of the other temple musicians shed light on how context can influence performance as well as providing much information about the functioning of temple music traditions.

In the course of my investigations in Nathdvara I attempted to answer the following questions: what role does the music play in temple worship? Who are the musicians and how are they recruited? What level of commitment does the musical profession require and how do musicians earn their living? What is the current state of the Nathdvara musical tradition and what are its prospects? With reference to my teacher, Guru Purushottam Das, I have attempted to describe the impact of his family as well as his own contribution to Indian music. I have also included observations made in some of the other centres of the Vallabha Sampraday outside Nathdvara.

Except where I have referred to other authors, all of the information was obtained from personal observation or from local residents. Where my conclusions are similar to those of previous writers I have indicated our agreement. Like Maduro (1976) and Jindel (1976) I employed participant observation as my method. Because of the esoteric tendency of the Vallabha Sampraday, none of us were able to obtain significant written records from the temple. Other writers in a variety of disciplines have commented on the importance of recording an oral tradition and the path taken by participant observers.[10] The musicologist Ashok Ranade affirmed: "The variety of areas in which oral traditions remain active is sufficient to persuade social thinkers to take a close look at it. Oral tradition assumes greater importance in the Indian context because it is not confined to music" (Ranade 1984: 23).

My friend Joep Bor, a musician and musicologist (1986/7: 6-7), also believes in the importance of the oral tradition: "If one had to rely merely on the information provided by musical treatises, the history of the *sarangi* (a bowed instrument) could be written on a few pages and would remain incomplete ... the first step—and by far the most important one—was to learn the *sarangi* from a master.

Powers also commented on the problems associated with textual description of a performing art. For him, data drawn from texts can suffer from the disadvantage that at a certain historical distance it acquires a sanctity which may be misleading. "Furthermore, the nature of much of the material such as technical terms of performing practice and above all drum syllables makes the many contradictions in the sources for the *Natya Sastra* (written approximately fifth century AD) impossible to resolve" (New Grove 1980: 132).

Klostermaier's comments are also relevant with regard to the tendency to idealize when writing about India from a distance: "They settle down in some library and find enough books there by means which it can be proved.... Many a thing looks different when seen fro a European library—more beautiful, more pleasant, and more abstrac (Kolstermaier 1969: 47).

In the course of my work in Nathdvara I came to realise that tl major difficulty for my research did not lie in obtaining people cooperation, but in formulating questions that would elicit responsı on matters that they had always taken for granted and about whic they felt it unnecessary to elaborate. The workings of the academ mind are far removed from the everyday concerns of people in a temp town, especially artists whose work is at a subconscious level. As professional dancer, I believe that I may have been more capable tha most observers of understanding the issues that affect the lives artists, but even so I have to admit that my own experience is ve different from theirs.

Documenting the lives of the musicians and placing them in tl larger context of the functioning of the Vallabha Sampraday w something that I did not undertake until after I had considerab exposure, both to the *pakhavaj* tradition of Guru Purushottam and t the functioning of music within the Shri Nathji Haveli. I feel that th gives a particular weight to those instances where my observatioı corroborate those of others, because I approached the subject withoı preconceptions. In other words, I was not looking for verification particular elements, but had experienced the working of the *haveli* an many aspects of the *sampraday* prior to embarking on this inquir Later, during my reading, I was pleasantly surprised to find that shared many experiences with other writers.

I have not attempted to evaluate the traditional beliefs of tl Vallabha Sampraday, or their own accounts of their history.[11] Whatev the facts of the past, the traditions accepted by the people of tl Nathdvara are the reality for them and what they believe is more like to affect their attitude to current events than whatever may actual have occurred years ago. This is an account of the musician communi and their recent history. The broader sweep of events I leave for othe to verify.

NOTES

1. For lack of a better English equivalent, the word 'sect' is used here as equivalent to *sampraday.* The two are not entirely synonymous: a sect is a breakaway group whereas the Vallabha Sampraday has not broken away from mainstream Hinduism. Nevertheless, like a sect it is an exclusive group and its members have to be initiated (See Barz 1976: 40).
2. The term Guru refers to Purushottam Das as an accomplished musician and teacher. The term is also used to refer to a spiritual master.
3. Vallabha is often referred to as Vallabhacharya. The suffix *acharya* acknowledges him as a great teacher.
4. The number 108 is an auspicious number; therefore Shri 108 times is the most honorific title that can be given to someone. Shri Dayal, who assisted me in the translation of the *Mridang Sagar* said that he could remember his father writing to various persons at the beginning of the century addressing them as Shri Shri 5 Shri.
5. The rulers of these various states also had titles unique to their own state. For example the ruler of Mewar was referred to as Maharana; of Amber/Jaipur as Sawai; and of Dungarpur as Raval.
6. Vrajbhushanlal Maharaj was also very helpful to Dr. Eleanor Gadon (1984) when she was conducting her research on the *Balagopalastuti* manuscript.
7. Guru Purushottam's *pakhavaj* tradition was partially documented in my report submitted to the SSHRC (Social Science and Humanities Research Council), Canada 1982 and ISTAR (International Society for Traditional Arts Research), Amsterdam and New Delhi, 1984.
8. Hindi was not standardized until the early decades of the twentieth century. Shri Dayal stated that the main difficulties in translating this book were the long sentences, use of two subjects, and the mixing of words by joining some and separating others (Shackle and Snell 1990: 1-33).
9. Copies of both these books are to be found at Delhi University and in the Sangeet Natak Akademi, New Delhi.
10. Some other scholars who have taken the same approach to Indian music include Shankar (1968), Higgins (1973), Shepherd (1976), Sorrell (1980), Neuman (1980), Qureshi (1986) and Kippen (1988).
11. See Snell, Entwistle, Barz, Holly, and others.

Plate 1.1: Ghanshyam Das (c. 1911); author of the Mridang Sagar

Plate 1.2: Guru Purushottam with the author (Anne-Marie Gaston), 1982

Plate 1.3: The town of Nathdvara with the Aravalli hills in the background

Plate 1.4: The home of one of the ritual mukhiyas of the Shri Nathji Haveli, Nathdvara

CHAPTER 2

Nathdvara, Shri Nathji and the Vallabha Sampraday

NATHDVARA

Religious towns such as Nathdvara, have been important centres of music in the past, but their influence has declined with the rise of large metropolitan cities and the increased secularization of both the venues for music and the music itself. Despite all the changes that have occurred in India, a visit to Nathdvara is like stepping back in time. The old town nestles in a bowl of hills where a dip occurs in the ridge flanking the east bank of the river Banas. The town does not face the river, which is flanked on the Nathdvara side by steep bluffs, but rather looks eastward, with the lie of the ground, towards Udaipur. The town centre crowds around the sprawling compound of the Shri Nathji temple. The surrounding buildings are tall, like the temple walls, rising three or four stories. Down in the alley-ways that wind everywhere, the sunlight hardly ever penetrates. In winter people live out on the rooftops, where the slope of the hills gives most homes a fine panoramic view over the town. Bands of fearless black and white *langur* monkeys[1] bound from terrace to terrace, looking for unguarded food on rooftop kitchens. In the streets, cows, pigs and dogs forage energetically among the vegetable stalls and tea shops, threading among the bustling pilgrims.

Guru Purushottam must have anticipated my trepidation on visiting Nathdvara for the first time. His telegram in response to my first proposed visit read, "Proceed fearlessly". And so I did, through streets crowded with people, and through narrow lanes with whitewashed walls where paintings of decorated cows, beautiful milkmaids with pitchers on their heads, and ceremonial elephants, greeted me at every turn. In this respect, Nathdvara is not greatly different from many old Mewari towns. To appreciate the uniqueness of Nathdvara one must enter its temples, but this at first I was not permitted to do. I could only be granted that privilege by the Tilkayat.

This could have proved a major setback: if I was to be able to appreciate fully the role of the *kirtankars*, I would have to make observations in the temples which provide its essential context. Non-Indians were not usually allowed in the *havelis* of Nathdvara then. After some initial reluctance, I was able to meet His Holiness the Tilkayat, Maharaj Shri Shri 108 Shri Govindlal, through the good offices of Guru Purushottam. He granted me permission to visit the Shri Nathji temple, take *darshan* along with the devotees, and sit with the musicians before each *darshan*. Thus I was allowed to see and hear the music as it is presented to Shri Nathji.

The Tilkayat has always been very difficult for foreigners to meet. This is confirmed by Growse writing in the nineteenth century,

> In the official world he is barely known by his name ... he declines social intercourse with Europeans, even of the highest rank, so much so that when the Lieutenant Governor of these provinces visited the station in 1873 and being unaware of this peculiarity expressed in writing a desire to see him, the invitation was not accepted. The compliment was prompted by the Gosain's annual gift of a prize of rupees three hundred for the student who passes first in the general examinations for Calcutta University (Growse 1880: 268).

The Tilkayat personally conducted my initiation ceremony, which was very simple.[2] I was required to give a small donation, and while kneeling in front of the Tilkayat repeat after him, '*Shri Krishnah sharanam mama*', after which he presented me with some betel and a *tulsi* necklace (*kanthi*), which should be worn at all times.

The Tilkayat and other members of the *sampraday* seemed to accept that, although I had been initiated, my allegiance was not total and I would still remain interested in other faiths and in religion in general. They did not require that I denounce other paths or exhibit overt displays of devotion. It was enough that I attended *darshan*, and was interested in the day-to-day activities. Most importantly, Guru Purushottam, whose credentials within the *sampraday* were impeccable, was completely behind my work. This gave me credibility.

On the occasion of my first initiation in 1983, I was allowed to enter the Shri Nathji temple only once, at *Raj Bhog darshan*. The next year, I was initiated again, in the same way, by the Tilkayat's son and given free access to the temple. The second initiation was required because the documents that recorded the original ceremony could not be located. On both occasions the ceremony was performed in the evening around 8.30 p.m., one of the two specific times of day at which the Tilkayat is available to meet devotees (10.30-11.30 in the morning and 8.00-9.00 in the evening). Other pilgrims were present and made several small donations to the Tilkayat in cash or in kind. The atmosphere was always relaxed.

By virtue of having been initiated by the Tilkayat I was also granted access to the other two temples under his direct control: the Navnitapriyaji Haveli (which is in the same compound as the Shri Nathji temple) and Madanmohanji as well as five other Vallabha *havelis*: the Banmaliji, Kalyanrayji, Gopallalji, Jamunaji, and Govindrayji, even though they are administered by different families (see map and appendix).

For some time I was not allowed to visit the Vitthalnathji Haveli, the second largest *haveli* in Nathdvara, which is controlled by another spiritual head, Maharaj Kalyanray, and his two brothers, Shri Gokulotsav and Shri Devkinand. This family is also related to Vallabha and traces its descent to Govindray, the second son of Vitthalnath (1516-86) (Barz 1976: 55; Growse 1880: 262). Kalyanray and his two brothers do not live permanently in Nathdvara, but in Indore. They visit Nathdvara only for special occasions and when they are there they reside in their palace, located beside the Vitthalnathji Haveli. To visit this *haveli* I was required to get special permission directly from Maharaj Kalyanray. This was refused in 1983 but granted with no difficulty in 1985. I attribute this change of heart to the fact that Maharaj Kalyanray witnessed one of my dance performances for the Tilkayat a few months earlier and may have been convinced of my sincerity by its devotional content. I was therefore able to enter all the temples in Nathdvara at one time or another, as well as others affiliated with the Vallabha Sampraday in Porbandar, Junagarh, Jamnagar, Udaipur, Kankroli, Madras and Baroda. I observed the role that music plays in each one.

My dance recitals for the Tilkayat enabled me to obtain an insider's view of the position of artists in relation to the Tilkayat and the temple organization. I performed on two occasions for the Tilkayat at events which included numerous dance and music recitals. The first occasion was at his son's wedding in Mathura in 1972, when I danced as part of the ten-day celebrations. In 1985, on the occasion of his son's birthday and his grandson's *mundan* ceremony[3] he invited me to perform three styles of classical dance: Odissi, Bharata Natyam and Kuchipudi, in his palace, Moti Mahal, adjoining the Shri Nathji temple. This recital was presented along with those of other dancers and musicians on a stage specially built in the courtyard of the Moti Mahal. Some recitals of other artists were also held in both the large and smaller audience halls of the palace. These events illustrate the continuing tradition of including dance and music in the celebratory events associated with the Tilkayat's family as well as in the worship of Shri Nathji.

THE MYTHOLOGY AND ICONOGRAPHY OF SHRI NATHJI

Shri Nathji, the deity enshrined in the main *haveli* in Nathdvara, is represented in the posture of raising Mount Govardhan (*Govardhan dharan*), a feat celebrated throughout India by one of the main festivals of the Hindu calendar. The event is the central theme for many artistic expressions: music, poetry, dance sculpture and painting, in both the folk and classical idioms.[4] Govardhan is the name of a mountain in a general geographical area known as Braj which is sacred to Krishna.

The Govardhan legend is one of the oldest myths in which Vedic religious practices and the supremacy of Indra, the storm god, are challenged by Krishna, god incarnate living amongst peasant farmers (Sheth 1984: 30; *Harivamsa* 59. 1-30, 59. 56-63.13; *Bhagavata Purana* 10. 24-7). According to the *Bhagavata Purana*, in the autumn when the cowherds, according to their custom, wished to honour the rain god Indra, Krishna dissuaded them by arguing that, as cowherds, they were entirely reliant on the bounty of their animals. Consequently, he suggested that they worship their animals and the hills on which they grazed, making offerings to Mount Govardhan instead of to Indra. Krishna then, through his power (*maya*), became the mountain god and consumed the sacrificial offerings himself.

Enraged by this action, Indra sent a frightful storm, but Krishna lifted Mount Govardhan, and held it over the villagers and their animals to protect them. After seven days the storm ceased and Indra, recognizing Krishna as an incarnation of Vishnu, worshipped him.

Two aspects of this myth are especially significant for the Vallabha

Sampraday. The first is that Shri Nathji is the iconographic representation of Krishna holding up the mountain with his left hand. The second is the idea of Krishna eating the food (*anna*) that was placed on the mountain (*kuṭ*). This is celebrated once a year in a particularly grand and spectacular manner during the festival of Annakut which is one of the most important in Nathdvara (chapter 10).

VALLABHA (1479-1531)

The legend of Krishna raising the mountain predates the discovery of the image of Shri Nathji by at least a thousand years. According to the traditions of the Vallabha Sampraday the black stone image of Shri Nathji miraculously appeared in AD 1410, emerging from Mount Govardhan in the form of a bent arm stretched upward (Barz 1976: 22, 49). The inexplicable appearance of the image and its discovery by a local herdsman occurred sixty-nine years before the birth of Vallabha, the founder of the Vallabha Sampraday, in April-May, 1479.

I shall encapsulate briefly the traditions of the *sampraday* relating to Vallabha's career. There is relatively little historical record of Vallabha's life, and in any case for the devotee the facts are not important. For an objective evaluation of the historical facts on the life of Vallabha see Entwistle (1987). What is important is that the charisma of his person and teachings were sufficient to establish a following which remains a vital force within the fabric of Hindu philosophy.

The literature of the *sampraday*[5] records numerous miraculous phenomena associated with Vallabha's birth; the most important of these was the sudden and unexpected movement of the Shri Nathji image which brought it further out of the ground to reveal a face along with the uplifted arm. The coincidence of these two events was not recognized until much later as Vallabha was born far away from Braj, in a forest in Raipur district, Madhya Pradesh.

The son of Telugu brahmin parents, Vallabha spent his childhood in Banaras, studying Sanskrit and wandering with his parents to various holy centres. From a very young age Vallabha had shown interest and skill in debating matters of theological importance at Vaishnava shrines. In 1493 when Vallabha, at the age of fourteen, was on a pilgrimage to south India, Shri Krishna appeared to him and instructed him to go to Braj and reveal to the world that the image on Mount Govardhan was not just an image, but Krishna himself, a *svarup*, and as such should be highly venerated. Vallabha went to this spot, and one year later, "at midnight on the eleventh of the bright half of the moon of the month of *Shravana*" Krishna once again appeared and gave Vallabha the *brahmasambandha mantra* ('Shri Krishna *sharanam mama*'), the same *mantra* that is used today to initiate devotees into the *sampraday*. The next morning Vallabha initiated Damodardas, his close companion. This event in 1494 is generally regarded as the 'founding' of the Vallabha Sampraday. Both these events occurred in Braj, at Gokul on Govind Ghat (Growse 1883; Barz 1976: 27; Vaudville 1976, 1980; Toomey 1985, 1988; Das Shyam 1985).

Work started almost immediately on building a temple on the spot where the image was found and in 1520 it was completed. Worship continued undisturbed in Braj and the image was granted protection by the various Mughal rulers during the lifetimes of Vallabha and his son Vitthalnath (1516-86), who assumed the headship on his father's death. The descendants of Vitthalnath's seven sons remain the spiritual heads of the *sampraday*, the present Tilkayat tracing his lineage to the eldest, Giridhar. These descendants are the various Maharaj. The most influential are those who have inherited one of the seven important *svarups* which appeared miraculously to Vallabha in various places while he was on pilgrimage around India. All of these were passed on by Vallabha to his son Vitthalnath when he became the head of the *sampraday*. In 1577, ten years before his death, Vitthalnath distributed them among his seven sons. He gave the main *svarup*, Shri Nathji, another *svarup*, Shri Mathureshji, as well as their family deity, Navnitpriyaji to his eldest son, Giridhar. Navnitpriyaji is now considered to be of equal importance to the other *svarups*, increasing the number to nine (Barz 1976: 41, 54, 55).

Subsequent to the founding of the *sampraday*, Vallabha is reputed to have found numerous additional *svarups*. The traditions of the *sampraday* record that the Navnitpriyaji image was plucked from the river Yamuna while Vallabha was performing his ablutions; the Vitthalnathji image while he was bathing in the river Ganges, in AD 1516, the year in which Vallabha's son Vitthalnath was born (Barz 1976). Shri Nathji and three of the seven images distributed by Vitthalnath—Navnitpriyaji, Vitthalnathji, and Madanmohanji are installed in Nathdvara. Shri Nathji and Navnitpriyaji arrived in 1672 (Barz 1976) but the Vitthalnathji image, originally given to the second son, Govindray, did not reach Nathdvara until about two hundred years later, after spending 125 years in Kota and about 80 years in

Khammaur (Barz 1976). The most recent *svarup* to be installed in Nathdvara is Madanmohanji (Barz 1976). Originally given to Vitthalnath's youngest son, Ghanshyam, it later came into the possession of the wife of Fateh Singh, Maharana of Udaipur (r. 1884-1930). She presented it to the Tilkayat[6] along with lands and a cash donation of one lakh rupees for its maintenance (Barz 1976:55 ; Jindel 1976).

Although the Mathureshji image was also given to Vitthalnath's eldest son, Giridhar, it was installed at Jatipura, in Braj, and not taken to Nathdvara along with the Shri Nathji and Navnitpriyaji *svarups* (Growse 1876: 273; Barz 1976: 55; see photo). Shri Dvarkanathji, given to Vitthalnath's third son, Balkrishna, is now housed in Kankroli, about thirty kilometres from Nathdvara. The other *svarups* were given to Vitthalnath's remaining sons who installed them elsewhere in central and western India:[7] Gokulnathji is installed at Gokul, in Braj; Gokulchandramaji at Kamvan; and Balkrishnaji at Surat.

The successors to the sons of Vitthalnath, who have control over the nine main images by virtue of descent, have the power to initiate persons into the *sampraday*. While these images are the most venerated by the Vallabha Sampraday, sectarian literature records others that were found by Vallabha during his travels around India which, although not as important, bestow power on their owners to initiate and administer temples. The connection of other images with Vallabha is less direct (Das Shyam 1985).

Mulji, writing in 1865, noted that time there were then about sixty to seventy Maharaj dispersed throughout India. He estimated eight to ten in Bombay, fifteen to sixteen in Gokul, one or two each in Surat, Ahmedabad, Nagar, Kutch, Porbandar, Amreli, Jodhpur, Bundi, and Kota and two in Banaras (Mulji 1865: 45,100); the remainder must have been in other centres that he omitted to specify. In Chapter 12, where I describe some of the centres outside Nathdvara, we shall see that his estimate may have been too modest. Mulji also noted that Vallabha is said to have distributed more than thirty images under various forms and names, although the seven distributed to Vitthalnath's sons are the most respected (Mulji 1865: 100).

THE BRAJ-NATHDVARA CONNECTION

Braj, in Hindi is the derivative of the Sanskrit term *vraja*, which stands for an enclosure or station where cows are permitted to roam freely. It is appropriate therefore that the land of the cowherder Krishna

TABLE 2.1: THE SEVEN *SVARUPS*

Son	Svarup	*Location in 1987*
1. Giridhar	Shri Nathji	Nathdvara (Rajasthan)
	Shri Navnitpriyaji	Nathdvara
	Shri Mathureshji	Jatipur (Braj,[8] Uttar Pradesh)
2. Govindray	Shri Vitthalnathji	Nathdvara (Rajasthan)
3. Balkrishna	Shri Dvarkadeshji	Kankroli (Rajasthan)
4. Gokulnath[9]	Shri Gokulnathji	Gokul (Braj, Uttar Pradesh)
5. Raghunath	Shri Gokulchandramaji+	Kamban (Rajasthan)
6. Yadunath	Shri Balkrishnaji	Surat (Gujarat)*
Yadunath	Shri Mukundrayji	Varanasi (Uttar Pradesh)*
7. Ghanshyam	Shri Madanmohanji	Kamban (Rajasthan)
8. (Tulsidas	Shri Gopinathji	Dera Gazi Khan (Sind)**

Notes
* There is some uncertainty about which of these images is the original given to Yadunath (Barz 1976: 55).
** See Entwistle 1983 *The Rasamanakopada of Kevularama.*[10]
+ Details concerning the relocation of these images are given in Mulji 1865 and Entwistle 1987.

should be known as Braj. Vaudville discusses the establishment of Braj as a sacred area (Vaudville 1976: 195-213). The area has no specific boundaries; it has never been a self-governing political entity or state. Growse, in the Gazetteer of 1880, included Braj as part of the administrative area known as Mathura district. Most of Braj today is located in the modern state of Uttar Pradesh, with only a very small portion in the state of Rajasthan. The central towns in Braj are Mathura, Gokul and Vrindavan.

Braj is defined as that area which includes all the places of importance in Krishna's early life, his birthplace, specific spots where he revealed his miraculous powers during his childhood, his youth as a cowherder (*gopa*) and locations where he enjoyed romantic encounters with his beloved Radha and the other milkmaids (*gopis*). Krishna's adult life when he pursued more serious concerns as a wise statesman, was spent elsewhere. In the early days of the Vallabha Sampraday, Braj contained many centres of worship (Entwistle 1988: 14-18). Today there are fewer and it is only within the last one hundred years that three of the main images were returned to Braj. The emergence of Braj as a major pilgrimage area is of fairly recent origin (Vaudville 1976, 1980; Entwistle 1988). Nevertheless today it attracts thousands of pilgrims, in whose minds Brajbhumi represents the body of Krishna (Klostermaier 1969: 1).

The importance of Braj in the artistic life of India in both folk and classical traditions is very great. It is idealized in poetry, songs, miniature paintings and dance. The *Gita Govinda*, a twelfth century Sanskrit text, is perhaps the most celebrated literary source from which many classical arts draw their inspiration. Its poems form the basis for much choreography in Indian classical dance, and a frequent subject for paintings. Much of the imagery that we associate with Braj has its source in this classic which celebrates the love between Radha and Krishna. The third song is a description of spring:

> When the tender Malayan wind touches the lovely clove creeper, when the hut of the grove is filled with the sounds of the cuckoo intermingled with swarms of honey-making bees...[the wind] perfumes the woods with fragrant powders of pollen shaken from the slightly opened [flowers of] the jasmine creepers; here the wind which is like the breath of [the god of] love ... (Seigal 1978: 245-47).

However, on visiting Braj most people would have to agree with Entwistle (1987), that little of the countryside lives up to the poetic description (see also McDowell and Sharma 1987: vii-x): "There are no luxuriant forests lining the banks of the Yamuna, no profusion of exotic flowers, nor does the breeze bear the fragrance of sandalwood" (Entwistle 1987: 2).

But for the devotee, Braj is a state of mind, a vision of eternal youth and spring: "In Vrindavan he who has eyes can observe Krishna and Radha at their love play even today" (Klostermaier 1969: 1).

The importance of Braj gained momentum with the rise of devotional Vaishnavism (Entwistle 1988: 19).[11] To share Krishna's life, Braj is the place to visit. For the Vallabha Sampraday Braj is not only the physical spot where Krishna lived, but also the place where the image of Shri Nathji was found. The Shri Nathji Haveli in Nathdvara celebrates Krishna's life in Braj, outwardly as a child but with allusions to his adolescence. In Nathdvara, Braj is recreated on a small scale, with the names of certain locations in the *haveli* recalling some of young Krishna's more famous exploits in Braj.

Krishna is said to have engaged in "love sports" from the early age of seven. His youth was spent "sporting" with the milkmaids and cowherders in Vrindavan. Thus Vrindavan evokes joy. He left for Mathura never to return (Hardy 1983:7), and this instils pangs of separation (*viraha*). The physical place of Braj, in particular the forests and rivers, take on a personification in themselves. To be by the Yamuna or in the forest of Vrindavan suggests to the devotee having the potential to be with Krishna. The mere mention of one of the standard descriptive phrases associated with Vrindavan evokes pre-established metaphors and a plethora of poetic conventions.

Vaudville describes in detail the "rediscovery" of Braj as a pilgrimage centre in the sixteenth century, a phenomenon that coincided with the resurgence in north India of the *bhakti* tradition (Vaudville 1976: 186). Entwistle gives a detailed account of pilgrimage in Braj according to texts and describes the prescribed pilgrimage route. I visited some of these sites in 1985. For spectacle, the temples of Braj cannot compare with the great temples of south India with their fine sculptures. The southern shrines with their austere rituals provide a contrast to what occurs in Braj. Even in north India, the earlier temples, for example at Khajuraho and Bhubaneshwar, with their magnificent sculptures, far outshine anything created by the later *bhakti* sects. As a result, temples in Braj are visited mainly by pilgrims; foreign tourists, archaeologists and scholars tend to look elsewhere. Consequently, the volume of western scholarship associated with the temples of Braj has been relatively small until recently.

The connection between Braj and Nathdvara has never been severed and it is believed that each evening Shri Nathji returns to Braj by an underground tunnel, which links the two centres, returning before dawn to Nathdvara.

THE MOVE FROM BRAJ TO NATHDVARA

From the foundation of the Vallabha Sampraday in the late fifteenth century the political situation in central and western India was in constant flux. Rajput kings and princes fought each other as well as the Mughals and the Marathas. Despite the fact that the Mughal rulers in

Delhi numbered Rajput princesses amongst their wives, and there was widespread intermarriage between the ruling Rajput families, the region was in a state of perpetual turmoil. When Chittor, the capital of Mewar and one of the main fortifications in that area, fell to Akbar in 1568, Rana Udai Singh of Mewar was forced to flee and founded a new capital at Udaipur. Mewar would continue to be the most independent of the Rajput states with regard to the Mughals and later would be the only Rajput state confident enough to offer asylum to Shri Nathji (Richardson 1979).

From the beginning of Mughal rule the emperors controlled Braj. Akbar, Jahangir and Shah Jahan were either indifferent or well disposed towards the members of the Vallabha Sampraday. Akbar declared the position of Tilkayat to be hereditary, granted the Tilkayat Vitthalnath some lands, and is said to have donated the diamond in Shri Nathji's chin.

Various reasons are given for the departure of the image from Braj (Richardson 1979). The most popular is that in 1670, fearing the iconoclastic zeal of the emperor Aurangzeb, Vitthalnath, and hundreds of followers fled with the *svarups* of Shri Nathji and Navnitpriyaji (Tod 1978: I, 415-22). The records of the time are unclear as to the prominence of the *sampraday*, but the number of devotees must have been substantial, enough to attract the emperor's attention (Richardson 1979). Setting out for Chaupasni village near Jodhpur, they took an indirect route via Agra, Bundi and Kishangarh. They were continually on the move because none of the rulers of these states was willing to allow the image to reside permanently within their boundaries (Barz 1976; Entwistle 1987). Some of the original party decided to stay behind in Chaupasni, in particular, several musicians. They, however, maintained their connection with Shri Nathji; and several generations later some of them followed in his footsteps to find employment in the temples of Nathdvara.

Tod records that eventually the Maharana of Mewar offered asylum to the Braj devotees and sent troops to escort them safely to the borders of his territories. In 1670,[12] the image arrived in Mewar territory. It is possible that Maharana Raj Singh had intended that it be brought to the capital, Udaipur, but according to tradition, at a certain point on the journey the wheels of the cart carrying the image became stuck, perhaps attempting to cross the river Banas. This was taken as an indication of divine will, and the image remained near the village of Sinhar. The place was named Nathdvara, literally the gateway (*dvara*) of the lord (*nath*). The carts reputed to have carried the various images are still displayed in Nathdvara and are one of the main tourist attractions. Although these events appear fortuitous there is evidence from an earlier land-grant in 1665 that the *sampraday* had already acquired land close to Nathdvara. The real causes of the migration from Braj to Mewar were probably complex and may well have involved considerations other than security (Richardson 1979: 1-10). The followers of the *sampraday* attribute the removal of Shri Nathji[13] to Nathdvara to Shri Nathji's fondness for playing chess with a lady, Ajab Kunwar Bai, who lived in Mewar. According to sectarian accounts, it was at her suggestion that Shri Nathji left Braj to live in Nathdvara so that he could save himself the trouble of travelling back and forth (Entwistle 1987:110; Jindel 1976: 22).

THE VALLABHA *SAMPRADAY* AND THE HOUSE OF MEWAR

Maharana Raj Singh granted considerable land to Shri Nathji and the Tilkayats for the construction of temples, for grazing cattle owned by the temples and for other agricultural purposes. His generosity was probably influenced by the fact that his wife, Charumati, was a Vaishnava devotee. The original copper plate documenting the land gifts was lost, so the grants were again formalized in 1737 by Maharana Jagat Singh II and by Maharana Bhim Singh in 1809. Maharana Bhim Singh's generosity extended to giving the Tilkayats the freedom to levy taxes and settle disputes, and the town itself was exempted from paying duties on all foreign products imported there. Nathdvara and all the villages attached to it were also granted the right of sanctuary (Jindel 1976).

The grant of gifts of land, protection and privilege was not unconditional. Nathdvara was located in the fief of Dilvara, one of the many small principalities that owed their allegiance to the royal house of Mewar. For that reason the rulers of Dilvara (Thakurs) and Mewar (Maharanas) were entitled in some instances to exert their secular authority over the Tilkayats and intervene directly in the affairs of the *sampraday*. There are also examples of the Maharana disinheriting the hereditary Tilkayats.

The house of Mewar has never looked upon the Nathdvara temples as its personal property, unlike the nearby Shaivite temple of Eklingji which has been under the direct control of the royal family since the present temple was constructed in A.D. 1467 by Rana Raimal. Eklingji has particular significance for the Mewar rulers because it was constructed on the spot where in the eighth century their ancestor, Bapa Rawal, received a *linga* (aniconic form of Shiva) from a sage and then went on to conquer the great fortress of Chittor and establish it as the capital of the Guhilot dynasty (Tod 1829: 219). Eklingji, the phallic manifestation of Shiva is still acknowledged as the official ruler of Mewar and the Maharana serves Eklingji as his hereditary prime minister. Tod observed that when the ruling Maharana of Mewar was in the Eklingji temple, his authority superseded that of the priests, "The Ranas of Mewar, as the dewans, or viceregents of Siva, when they visit the temple supersede the high priest in his duties, and perform the ceremonies, which the reigning prince does with peculiar correctness and grace" (Tod 1829: 411-12).

Even today the Maharana makes weekly visits to the Eklingji temple, driving the thirty or so kilometres from Udaipur to Eklingji.

The Maharana has never enjoyed the same ritual privileges in the Shri Nathji temple that he enjoys in Eklingji. The hereditary Tilkayats have always had, and continue to have, precedence in the Shri Nathji Haveli. Interestingly, the main spiritual connection between the house of Mewar and the *sampraday* is not with its leader but with the Kankroli Maharaj. The present Maharana told me that he did so because his forefathers and all the royal family had looked to the Kankroli Maharaj as their spiritual Guru. The *haveli* at Kankroli is beside Raj Samund, a pleasure resort, illustrating the importance that the *sampraday* placed upon being closely aligned with royal power and patronage (see Richardson 1979).

Despite its royal connection, Eklingji, the much older and more established shrine, must have been affected by the arrival of Shri Nathji. In the beginning it may have suffered financially with the newer shrine of Shri Nathji attracting donations from devotees that previously would have been given exclusively to Eklingji. Today, however, Eklingji is a popular spot for both pilgrims and tourists. Its location halfway between Udaipur and Nathdvara makes it easily accessible particularly since it is a regular halting spot for buses carrying pilgrims between the two centres.

KRISHNA, SHRI NATHJI AND *BHAKTI*

His devotees believe that Krishna experienced prolonged incarnation on earth.[14] His mythology includes accounts of all stages of his incarnation: the baby, the child, the youth, the lover, and finally the mature statesman. Although the image of Shri Nathji represents the child Krishna raising Mount Govardhan, most of Krishna's other aspects are recalled in songs and artistic representations in the numerous crafts and decorative arts produced in Nathdvara. The most common themes include Krishna playing his flute surrounded by the milkmaids (*gopis*) in the groves of Vrindavan, dancing on the serpent Kaliya and playing with his friends the cowherds. Representations of these events in painting, sculpture and poetry provide potent stimuli for the devotees, helping them to recall and celebrate Krishna's various forms and miracles of divine power. They also serve to remind devotees that at each phase of his mythical life, Krishna must be approached differently. There are a variety of ways to gain Krishna's favour and all devotees yearn for the ultimate experience of ecstatic union with him (Hardy 1983).

The worship of two of Krishna's most important aspects, as the child and the youth, require the devotee to relate emotionally with one of the three important female figures in Krishna's life: his mother Devaki, his stepmother Yashoda,[15] or his mistress Radha. Those devotees who empathize with Krishna the child identify with the emotions of his mothers, Devaki and Yashoda, while those who find Krishna the youth more approachable, identify themselves with Radha. Both forms of devotion are based on the expression of love; but while the former involves the love that a mother feels for her child (*vatsalya*) the latter is through erotic or romantic love (*shringar*). Hardy (1983: 409) gives examples from the southern tradition of Krishna's erotic concerns while still a child. Inherent in the worship of Krishna is his elusiveness. His devotees must endeavour to coax and cajole him to grant his favour. Separation from him is the deepest form of suffering, *viraha*. The metaphor used is the state of a lovelorn maiden waiting in constant anticipation for the arrival of her beloved.

The important texts from which the devotees of Krishna draw their inspiration are the *Bhagavata Purana*—in which the tenth chapter is the ultimate authority—the *Harivamsha*, and *Vishnu Purana* (Sheth 1984). The commentaries on Vallabha's work are also consulted

(Entwistle 1987: 177), but the Vallabha Sampraday gives greater importance to concrete acts, or *seva*, and outward manifestations of devotion (*bhakti*), rather than to intellectual philosophical inquiry (Chatterjee 1981: 115-31).

In Nathdvara, most of the rituals associated with the worship of Shri Nathji centre on tending to Krishna's needs and whims. The head priest (*mukhiya*) acts on behalf of the devotee. His daily tasks mimic those performed by Yashoda, Krishna's stepmother. Shri Nathji is cared for from the very start of the day when he is gently woken by music, first of the *bin*, and then singing, at which time he is given a cup of milk, followed by his bath and adornment in beautiful clothes. This selfless concern is intended to give the devotee that same emotional satisfaction that a mother receives from looking after her child.

Krishna's devotees make donations so that he can be dressed in lavish costumes; they in turn experience delight when they behold him. The aesthetic pleasure (*rasa*) that a beautifully decorated image transmits to a devotee, evokes a feeling (*bhava*) within the beholder. *Rasa* and *bhava* are central to the religious experience of the Vallabha Sampraday.

Devotees even take pleasure in Krishna's self-indulgence. Krishna as Shri Nathji is given too much of everything and devotees take great pleasure in doing this. Perhaps the rationale for giving Shri Nathji so many sweets is that, like any other child, he expects them as a reward for allowing adults to dress him in heavy ornate costumes. No effort is spared to give him the best of everything. The explanation given by several devotees was that, if they did not cater to his every whim, he might behave like any other child and become bored and want to leave, or get into a bad temper and lose his adorable appearance. Devotees take great delight in his physical beauty and never seem to tire of either hearing or recounting his mischievous pranks. The child Krishna is the ideal, the one longed for by every Hindu family. Pocock asked the Maharaj of Kankroli the significance of worshipping a child, to which he responded:

> Well you know, supposing that we were to worship the Lord (Krishna) in his mature form as King, how should we dare to lay down the rules for him? We couldn't say to him "Now you are going to eat this and now you are going to wear that", and we certainly couldn't pack him off to bed at six o'clock in the evening (Pocock 1973: 114).[16]

The metaphor of the family extends to the *haveli* where Shri Nathji is housed. Devotees may visit it only at specific periods. At that time they take part in all its functions, much as visitors might behave in the homes of their relatives.

Mulji's description of a *haveli* could be applied generally to most *havelis*, a good indication that their architecture has not changed: "A Vallabhacharya temple consists of three successive compartments. The central one is larger and more open than the other two to accommodate the worshippers. One is the residence of the Maharaj, the other is dedicated to the worship of the image of Krishna" (Mulji 1865: 99).

The patriarch of the "family" is the head of the *sampraday*, the Tilkayat, and he receives all his children in his private apartments adjacent to the *haveli*. This convention is also observed by the other Maharaj in the other centres; meetings with several of them are discussed in chapter 12.

Shri Nathji blesses those who serve him; there is no evidence to suggest that he punishes. Many deities in the Hindu pantheon can be vengeful and must be honoured and placated in a variety of ways, often associated with ascetic practices such as engaging in severe physical austerities, abstaining from the pleasures of food and sex, or offering live animals as sacrifice. However, Shri Nathji rejects all of these practices. Instead, he encourages his devotees to lead a family life and relish all material comforts (Parekh 1943).

For members of the *sampraday*, affirming one's faith involves experiencing Shri Nathji's *darshan*. Shri Nathji is worshipped by making a donation in cash, kind or service (*seva*), which ensures maintaining his supply of sweets, finery and physical comforts. It is believed that when a devotee stands before Shri Nathji that person is privy to direct communication with him. Many devotees report Shri Nathji speaking to them (pers comm several musicians, taxi drivers, local photographer, and townsfolk). This is just one example of the ways in which his powerful presence is exerted on devotees.

RASA, BHAVA

When a devotee is moved by the beauty of Shri Nathji's dress and adornments (*shringar*), the *rasa* (literally flavour or taste) that is experienced creates *bhava*, feeling or emotion in the beholder. This state of mind, and those attributes considered suitable for particular states of mind, are integral to the theory of Indian aesthetics. The most important of the early aesthetic theoreticians, Anandavardana AD 850, and Abhinava Gupta AD 1000 interpreted *rasa* as a secular aesthetic experience: "It would thus seem that the *rasa* theory, instead of explaining religious emotionalism, deprives it of all its religious significance" (Hardy 1983: 560).

Hardy traced the transformation of the nine emotions (*nava rasa*) and their absorption into the religious *bhakti* traditions to the writing of Vopadev, of Maharashtrian origin in AD 1265. Vopadev referred to episodes from the *Bhagavata Purana*. Hardy noted that Vopadev's recognition of Krishna as "the container of the nine *rasas*" was the first indication of a new direction in the theory of *bhakti rasa*" (Hardy 1983: 561). Thus the groundwork was laid for Vallabha (1481-1533) who acknowledged *bhakti rasa* as the supreme experience and interpreted all *rasa* and *bhava* as religious, "When the mind and all senses have taken on the form of Bhagavan ... who (which) creates pure bliss, then alone one possesses *bhakti-rasa*" (Hardy 1983: 562).

Various means are used to transmit *bhakti rasa* and singing songs describing Krishna is one of the most important. The themes of these songs tie in with the various stages of Krishna's life.

ASHTACHHAP

Vallabha encouraged singing in the first Shri Nathji temple on Mount Govardhan that was completed in 1520, but it was not until the Tilkayatship of his son Vitthalnath (1531-86) that music was formally integrated as part of worship (Barz 1976: 50). Music has continued to be an important and indispensable part of the ritual. Sectarian literature records eight poet singers known as *ashtacchap*, as being instrumental in inspiring Vallabha to include musical offerings. Barz notes that their use of the vernacular Brajbhasa was a practical choice because it is a sister language to many of the other north Indian vernacular languages—Punjabi, Avadhi, Bhojpuri and varieties of Rajasthani (Barz 1976: 98). It enabled devotees to understand the songs unlike when Sanskrit was used earlier. The title *ashtachhap* (eight seals) refers to their names (seals) used in the last couplet of their poems. According to sectarian sources Vallabha initiated four of them: Kumbhandas[17] in 1500 (Das 1985: 269-73), Surdas in 1511 (Das 1985: 257-63), Krishnadas[18] in 1512 (Das 1985: 274-6), and Parmananddas in 1521 (Das 1985: 264-8), while Vitthalnath initiated four more: Nanddas, Govindsvami,

Chhitsvami[19] and Chaturbhujdas. Their compositions form the core of the devotional music used in the Shri Nathji Haveli. Each is considered the pre-eminent, though not the exclusive composer for one of the *darshans.*

Barz (1976) has translated the *vartas* or accounts from the lives of four of them (Surdas, Kumbhandas, Parmananddas and Krishnadas). Each preferred certain aspects of Krishna's life (*lilas*). Thus Surdas wrote mainly about *man lila* or Radha's jealousy and anger at Krishna's philandering, Kumbandas liked the "play" (*lila*) of Radha and Krishna in the *nikunj* forest—(*nikunj lila*); Paramanddas preferred Krishna's *lila* as a child (*bal lila*); and Krishnadas the circle dance (*ras lila*) of Radha and Krishna (Barz 1976: 103). The number eight is significant in the *sampraday*[20] and the importance of the poets has been sustained since its beginning. Scholars have recently challenged the association of three of the most famous—Surdas, Parmanddas, and Nanddas—with Vallabha (Hawley 1984: 25-8; McGregor 1984). However the continued importance of the *ashtachhap's* compositions is reflected in the fact that most of the townsfolk in Nathdvara can readily recall their names, an indication that the poetry of the music still holds very real significance for them. Most devotees can also identify which composer is considered appropriate for which *darshan*. Consequently the correspondence between certain *darshans* and certain poets has entered the previous literature and is often interpreted as fixed. In practice, however, the compositions sung for a particular *darshan* are not exclusively the work of a particular poet. Many of the songs sung in the Shri Nathji Haveli are by other composers but those compositions of the *ashtachhap* are still regarded as exceptional in their literary and devotional merit.

The *ashtachhap* poets composed out of religious fervour wishing to recount and share the ecstasy they experienced in their devotion. Barz comments on their attention to the smallest detail in preference to describing mythological events. Their poems filled a niche that had been created by the contemporary resurgence of the Vaishnava *bhakti* movement,[21] which ensured that they were widely disseminated (Barz 1976; Bryant 1978; Srivastava 1980; Hardy 1983). Although the *Bhagavata Purana* is written in Sanskrit, the *ashtachhap* composed in Brajbhasa, the vernacular because it was thought to be more appropriate to praise Krishna in the language of his childhood home (Barz 1976: 97). This is in contrast to Vallabha who wrote in Sanskrit, considered more suitable for a learned *acharya*. "The day of the vernaculars was dawning—the epoch of classical religious literature was more or less closed. Brajbhasa was also related to many of the north Indian languages: so it was relatively easy for these devotees to follow the poems" (Parekh 1943: 108).

THE *BHAGAVATA PURANA*

At the same time that worship in vernacular languages, of which Brajbhasa was only one, was introduced, the *Bhagavata Purana*, a Sanskrit text spread from the south into north India.[22] This text had a profound influence on the content of the music and the art of the Vallabha Sampraday (Gadon 1984). The stories in the *Bhagavata Purana* evoked such devotion (*bhakti*) to Krishna that schools of thought emerged which considered Krishna not just as an *avatar*[23] of Vishnu but the supreme Lord (Gonda 1963:115-87; Misra 1971; Vaudville 1976, 1980).

The *Padma Purana* gives an excellent definition of a Krishna devotee (*bhakta*): "One should regard oneself as a beautiful girl (there) in the eternal Vrindavan among them (the *gopis*), endowed with an attractive figure and youth, to be a wanton girl... imagining oneself like this, one should serve Krishna there" (Hardy 1983: 565).

The problems of a male *bhakta* realizing a woman's emotion are discussed by Hardy (1983). He also suggests the reason the *gopis* exemplify the highest form of *bhakti* is that they were willing to sacrifice their honour.

There are numerous examples of men serving the deity and identifying with feminine emotions. This practice is exemplified by illustrations of Shri Nathji dressed as a bridegroom wearing a *sehra* or bridegroom's crown. In a painting from the first quarter of the nineteenth century, Gosvami Purushottam of Kankroli is officiating, "this special *manoratha* performed by Purushottam expresses the devotion of a beloved for a lover" (Ambalal 1987: 116/155). Another painting, from the same period represents Maharaj Giridhar with his shawl over his head like a sari and wearing female bracelets. According to members of the *sampraday*, to better express the love (*madhurya*) that he felt for Shri Nathji he identified with Krishna's mother Yashoda by letting his hair grow. Once he missed going to the *haveli* for Shri Nathji's *darshan* because he was combing his long hair and he atoned by having his head shaved (Ambalal 1987: 111,154).

CONCLUSION

It is important to understand the basis for devotion in the Vallabha Sampraday if we are to understand the place of music in Nathdvara. The distinctive form of worship practised by the *pushtimarg* can be seen to derive primarily from the belief in the image of Shri Nathji as a living entity. Because he is really God incarnate, and because in this particular incarnation he is a child, he requires certain types of offering which must be provided in a literal manner; no mere symbolism suffices. The food, the drink, the fine ornaments and toys, and the music must all be physically present. In addition, to understand the significance of certain festivals and practices, it is necessary to bear in mind the particular iconography of Shri Nathji, which refers principally to the lifting of Mount Govardhan.

Historical factors, especially the relocation of Shri Nathji from Braj to Nathdvara, have had profound consequences for the present structure of the *sampraday*. Nathdvara is much closer than Braj to Gujarat, where most of Shri Nathji's devotees reside today. Although the town supports a few small temples devoted to other Hindu deities, the Vallabha Sampraday essentially constitutes the entire religious focus of the population. There are no other competing Vaishnava sects, and although there may be some competition among the various branches of the *pushtimarg*, worship is very similar in all of them. This exclusiveness, the relatively backward area in which the town is situated, and the lack of close connections to major cities, have combined to maintain a highly traditional society in the face of the changes wrought almost universally elsewhere by modernization.

NOTES

1. See Klostermaier's (1969: 8) description of the monkeys in Vrindavan. Monkeys are a common feature in most pilgrimage centres.
2. Mulji 1865: 120-1 describes the initiation ceremony. See also Growse (1883: 285-8) and Schaffer (1987). The latter was initiated into the *pushtimarg sampraday* in Jatipura.
3. Ambalal 1987: 72 recounts some of the special activities that have been arranged for life-cycle events of the Maharaj of the Vallabha Sampraday.
4. Early examples of classical sculpture date to the time of the Guptas, (4th-6th cent. A.D.), and Pallavas (Mahaballipuram 7th-8th cent. A.D.) (Williams 1982:81,147; Harle 1974:63) and it is still a popular theme with present day

traditional artists; two examples are the Orissan *Pat* paintings (Das 1982) and *Kalamkari* painting on cloth (Sethna 1985).

5. The *Shri Acharya ke Prakatya ki Varta* gives accounts of events of Vallabha's life and the *Baithak Charitra* gives the events associated with Vallabha's travels around India (Barz 1976: 103).
6. Although no date is given for this event it would have been sometime after A.D. 1884.
7. See Entwistle 1983 who describes the 8th *gaddi*.
8. The events surrounding the removal of the Shri Mathureshji image from Braj to Kota and its return to Braj are discussed in Entwistle 1987: 223.
9. Karsondas Mulji (1865: 43); Gokulnath (1552-1641) gathered up traditional texts known as *vartas*. Four of them are translated in Barz 1976. Gokulnath is also credited with writing several texts, the most celebrated being the *Siddhanta Rahasya*.
10. Tulsidas, who was nicknamed Lalaji, was an adopted son of Vitthalnath. Tulsidas spread the *pushtimarg* in the Punjab and Sindh. The *svarup* in the possession of his descendants is not equal in status to the seven listed (Entwistle 1983: 11). In 1948 the descendants of Tulsidas brought the manuscript, *The Rasamana ke pada of Kevalarama* to the Shri Gopallalji Mandir in Vrindaban.
11. The four main traditions in Vaishnavism and their numerous sub-sects are discussed by Hardy (1983) and Entwistle (1987).
12. Ambalal 1987: 24 includes a portrait of Damodar (1655-1704) also known as Bade Dauji who was the head of the sect at that time and who brought Shri Nathji from Govardhan to Nathdvara.
13. This was not the first time that Shri Nathji had been moved. Earlier he had been moved to Gantholi and Mathura (Entwistle 1987: 110).
14. Another example would be Rama.
15. The birth of Krishna involved the replacing of the embryo in the womb and the switching of children at birth (O'Flaherty 1975). Devaki, Krishna's real mother, of all the figures in Krishna myths, "resembles the human *bhakta* most clearly: full of love for Krishna and longing to see him and all his deeds and to be in physical contact with him, both [i.e. the *bhakta* and Devaki] have to content themselves with hearing about them and imagining them" (Hardy 1983: 433).
16. Pocock (1973) interpreted the acceptance by the sect of the child Krishna as their main object of worship as acceptance of *maya*, the play of illusion in the apparent world.
17. Kumbhandas is said to have been ten years older than Vallabha. He was a farmer, father of another of the *ashtacchap*, Chaturbhujdas (Entwistle 1987: 166).
18. Krishnadas, a Gujarati, was the manager of the first Shri Nathji temple in Gokul (Entwistle 1987: 166).
19. Chhitsvami is said to have been a Chaube brahmin (Entwistle 1987: 166).
20. Eight companions of Krishna, eight *sakhis* of Radha, eight periods of daily

worship, eight *gaddis* of *pushtimarg*, eight syllables of the *matra* to initiate one into the sect (Entwistle 1987: 166).

21. Entwistle 1987: 166-73 lists the other *sampraday* founded at this time.
22. The *Bhagavata Purana* is regarded as a southern text (Hardy 1983).
23. One of the best examples of this is a song, '*pralaya payodi*' in the *Gita Govinda* in which the ten incarnations of Vishnu are described. In this song the ninth incarnation is the Buddha and after the complete song is sung there is a brief salutation to Krishna as supreme over all the other incarnations (Siegel). I had never thought about this until once the narrator for one of my dance recitals a Krishna *bhakta* was distressed to find that Krishna had been omitted as one of the ten incarnations of Vishnu. He felt that there had been some mistake in my translation, and was insistent that we remove Buddha, despite the fact that I assured him there was a coda at the end of the song declaring the supremacy of Krishna.

Plate 2.1: Udaipur Painting: Maharana Amar Singh visiting Eklingji (c. A.D. 1700-05) (reproduced by permission of the Ashmolean Museum, Oxford)

Plate 2.2: Kankroli, Dvarkadishji's guest house in Nathdvara attached to the Shri Nathji Haveli

Plate 2.3: A painting of Vallabha embedded with stones

CHAPTER 3

The Maharaj

The title of Maharaj effectively conveys the full force of the sway, influence and secular power of the hereditary leaders of the *sampraday*.[1] Like Krishna, they also have the appellations Gosvami (Lord of the Cows), and Gosain. Vallabha and his descendants are regarded as manifestations of Krishna on earth and it is considered appropriate for the Maharaj to be worshipped in the same manner as the various *svarups* of the *sampraday*:

> The God Krishna is worshipped by its members in the form of images, and in the form of their gurus, the so-called Maharajs. The Maharaj is considered by a great many of his followers as an incarnation of God, as god incarnate according to Hindu notions (Dr John Wilson in Mulji 1865: 141).

> Besides the adoration of the image, worship is performed to the Maharaj himself ... In one of the apartments of his residence the Maharaj during the time that divine honours are paid to him, seats himself in a raised seat. The Bhattias, Banias, Lohanas, the Multanes and other persons are the followers of this religion and are known as *sevaks*, or servants. All of them, rich and poor, adore him by saluting his feet (Mulji 1865: 141).

Some authorities elevated the Maharaj to a position above god and recommended worshipping him as a means of receiving rewards in the next life.

The promised reward for this (worship of the Maharaj) is the highest heaven, whereas the mere worship(per) of God enter(s) an inferior paradise (Mulji 1865: 85).

As god incarnate the Maharajs exerted considerable influence over the lives of their followers.

> Since the Maharaj exercise such unlimited spiritual authority over their adherents, it follows that they should possess considerable temporal influence

and power. Great personal respect is paid to them; they are invited to sumptuous entertainments by their votaries, are constantly in the receipt of valuable and choice presents, are consulted on most matters of importance, and their sway over society is considerably great (Mulji 1865: 144).

ARRIVAL AND DEPARTURE OF THE MAHARAJ

The Maharaj have always been very mobile. No doubt they realized the importance of personal contact. Vallabha's travels are documented in the *Chaurasi Baithak* and the spots that he visited are venerated. It appears that his son Vitthalnath's travels were even more extensive (Barz 1976; Shyam Das 1985).

Although the Maharaj appear to like travelling, devotees prefer to have one permanently in residence so that their presence and advice is always available. Bombay today has more Maharaj than any other centre and probably supports more *havelis* than any other city in India. The present Tilkayat could be said to live permanently in Bombay, visiting Nathdvara for the major festivals of Divali, Dussehra and Annakut. This was not always so, and Mulji records the incentives given to the Maharaj Gokulnath to attract him from Surat to Bombay so that his devotees could have easier access to him.

... in 1811 when Gokulnathji Maharaj, the ancestor of Jivanji,[2] came to Bombay, all the Vaishnavas of the island of Bombay collecting in a body, requested his Holiness to settle permanently with his family 'for the purification of their souls', offering, at the same time, to build a temple for him, and to make arrangements to meet his expenses in connection with the temple (Mulji 1865: 145).

For present day Maharaj, the attractions of Bombay are many. This commercial capital of India is home to many members from the trading communities who form the bulk of the members of the *sampraday*. In addition, within the past sixty years, the cultural life of Bombay and other urban centres has held attractions for the Maharaj who may find their provincial homes less exciting. Also, Bombay is well connected by rail, air and bus to Gujarat, which facilitates movement to places where most of their followers reside.

Large numbers of devotees attend the comings and goings of the Maharaj between their numerous *havelis*, which may be yet another incentive for them to travel so much. In Junagarh, in 1988, I witnessed the departure of Maharaj Kishore Chand from his *haveli*. About two hundred and fifty devotees were present. I waited within the walled compound of Moti Haveli for two Dodge cars of the 1940s vintage to arrive. The atmosphere breathed excitement and expectancy as we waited for the Maharaj and his wife to leave their apartments and be whisked off to the train. The ladies present sang, reminiscent of the milkmaids (*gopis*) singing farewell to Krishna leaving Vrindavan. Not only are the Maharaj incarnations of Krishna but, as we have seen, many of their activities and the manner in which devotees respond to them are intended to mirror those of Krishna and his interaction with the *gopis*.

Before leaving, the Maharaj blessed those devotees who came forward. This took so long that his departure was considerably delayed. However, a call had been made to the station to alert the railway authorities that they were expected to delay the departure of the train. Times do not change. Mulji described the attention given to these peripatetic Maharaj: "When a rumour reaches a city that a Maharaj is approaching, a large throng of devoted followers go forth to meet him, and, forming themselves into a procession, he enters the town with great pomp and jubilation" (Mulji 1865: 144).

SEVA OF THE MAHARAJ

Performing *seva* for the Maharaj is an honour sought after by both rich and poor: "The most influential and rich members of the sect think it no degradation to perform the most menial offices in his service" (Mulji 1865: 144).

A painting of a Vaishnava devotee massaging the legs of one of the Maharaj gives us some appreciation of the importance of service (*seva*) to them. There is no indication who commissioned the painting; most probably it was the devotee himself who wished to record his meritorious act (Ambalal 1987: 120-1, 156). Devotees who made a substantial donation, or persons of high social status would be treated with deference both on entering the temple and in meeting with the Maharaj: "All of them, rich and poor, adore him by saluting his feet ... and for a short time after these devotions the rich or influential are accommodated in the hall, while persons of moderate means are left to shift for themselves" (Mulji 1965: 105).

THE SACRED FOOD OF THE MAHARAJ

The sanctity of the person of the Maharaj is reflected in the tradition of eating the remains of his meals, known as *jutha*. *Jutha*, as well as half masticated *pan supari* (betel nut and various other substances wrapped in a betel leaf), were sought after by devotees as particularly holy, because the Maharaj is identified with Shri Krishna himself. With this analogy, *jutha* could be equated to *prasad*, or the sanctified remains of Shri Krishna's meals:

> The remnants of the Maharaj's meals called *juhtan* (sic), are preserved, being considered very precious, and can be had on formal application by any Vaishnavas who desire to eat them. In private banquets and caste feasts, given with the Maharaj's permission, these impure remnants are first served, and are eaten as though they were ambrosia! The *pan-supari* (leaf and betel-nut) which the Maharaj throws out after chewing, is called ogar, and is collected and preserved to be distributed to males and females who take great pleasure in chewing it over again (Mulji 1865: 107).

Mulji was not impressed with this tradition. Nor were some of my Indian acquaintances who were not members of the *sampraday*, but who observed devotees anxious to eat *jutha* during a social function attended by a Maharaj in Jaipur in 1987. I myself have never been offered *jutha*. After meetings with a Maharaj I have always been given a large bundle of betel nut wrapped in leaves, and in some instances a huge package of food which comprised mainly sweets, probably from among those which had been offered to the deity (*prasad*).

SECULAR ACTIVITIES OF THE MAHARAJ

An important secular activity of the Maharaj was as defender of Shri Nathji and the other *svarups*. The Maharaj had to be prepared to fight if they were to maintain control of their territory. They had to be good horsemen, and if circumstances required, good fighters. Dauji II/ Damodara II, a Tilkayat of the nineteenth century is illustrated mounted on horseback ready for battle (Ambalal 1987: 65). In this case it was during the disruption caused by the Marathas. Before battle the *svarups* were removed from Nathdvara, first to Udaipur and later to Ghasiyar, for their safety. Tod described the Tilkayat and his army:

> Damodara accordingly made the tour of his extensive diocese at the head of

four hundred horses, two standards of foot and two field pieces. He rode the finest mares in the country, laid aside his pontificals for the quilted ***dugla***, and was summoned to matins by the kettle drums instead of bell and cymbal" (Tod 1829: 572-3).

Tod knew of the Tilkayat's identification with Krishna and drew parallels with Krishna's ability to reveal his warlike nature. Krishna had taken part in the great wars of the *Mahabharata*, and this had not meant any conflict between his religious and secular roles: "In this he [the Tilkayat] only imitated Kanhaiya (Krishna) who often mixed in the ranks of battle ... covered with a helmet, the shaven crown, his conduct and character are amenable and unexceptionable" (Crooke 1920: 643).

WOMEN IN THE *SAMPRADAY*

Tod commented that it was the custom for the Maharaj to have one wife and no harem (Crooke 1920: 642). This was in contrast to other rulers of the period. Krishna, the religious model for the Maharaj had two wives: Rukmini and Satyabhama; Radha is variously described as either his mistress or his wife. A parallel in the sexual mores of Krishna and that of the Maharaj shocked many: "The highest ambition of his (The Maharaj) followers was to become a *gopi* and sport eternally with Krishna in heaven, an ideal which degenerated into gross eroticism" (Bhagowalia 1980: 179).

In Mulji's day (1865) the women of the Tilkayat's family and those of the various Maharaj observed ***purdah***: "One end of the building, known as the ***zenana khana*** (seraglio) is occupied by the Maharaj's wife and daughters who never appear in the sight of men: their residence is considered sacred and only the ***sevakis*** (female worshippers) have permission to enter it" (Mulji 1865: 105).

I did not have an opportunity to meet the wife of the Tilkayat or those of any Maharaj. I did, however, meet the two daughter's-in-law of the present Tilkayat, who co-incidentally were both named Rajeshwari. I had performed Bharata Natyam and Odissi as part of the wedding celebrations of the elder son Rakesh. His bride came from a highly placed Vallabha Sampraday family of Tamil Nadu. The second son, who married the daughter of the Maharaj of Kankroli, had a 'self-arranged' marriage; the couple expressed the wish to marry after meeting at some family gathering and secured their families' approval.

The daughter-in-law from Tamil Nadu had a college education. Her daughter was attending a school attached to a convent in Bombay. She also reported that many of their family had settled in the United States and abroad. All my meetings with these womenfolk were in the presence of a mixed group of devotees and there did not appear to be any concession to purdah.

On those occasions when the wives and daughters of the Maharaj take *darshan* in the *havelis* of the *sampraday* they enter the area known as *manikota*, with their husbands and the priests, and it appears that they can go as close to the image as the men. The circling of the *arati* lamp, however, appears to be reserved for males; I have never seen women do it.[3] Neither have I seen it in any paintings. Wives do accompany their husbands in the ritual best described as 'playing with Krishna'—pushing the cradle, and shaking rattles during the celebrations for the Nandotsav festival which recalls the birth of Krishna. On these occasions, they do not pull the end of their saree (*palu*) over their face but sit naturally and in full view. The only manifestation of purdah in the *haveli* was for the wife of the Tilkayat Govindlal. I saw her only in the distance, passing through the temple. Her maidservant and other temple employees called out that she was about to pass by, and on cue, various strategically placed curtains were pulled across gateways and intersections so that she could pass unseen.

MUSICAL ACCOMPLISHMENT OF THE MAHARAJ

Many of the Maharaj and members of their families have not only supported musicians but have taken more than a passing interest in studying and performing *pakhavaj*, vocal and instrumental. Their musical accomplishments include several styles of vocal music (*haveli sangit*, *dhrupad dhamar* as well *khyal* and *thumri*), instrumental music (*bin*, *sitar*, *sarod* and violin) and the percussion music of the *pakhavaj*. I mentioned the three Maharaj brothers, Gosvami Kalyanray, Gosvami Gokulotsav,[4] and Gosvami Devkinand who are in charge of the Vitthalnathji Haveli, Nathdvara and for whom I danced. Their *pakhavaj* teachers included Chunnilal, the father of a concert *Pakhavaji* of repute, Lakshminarayan Pawar, as well as Lakshminarayan's other teachers.[5] They have also studied vocal (*khyal*, *dhrupad-dhamar*) violin[6] and *sarod*.[7] Most of their musical training, which is of the classical variety, has been in Indore[8] where they stay for more than half the year in the Shri Govardhannathji Haveli. They spend a great deal of their time both studying and performing music. I have heard the eldest of them, Maharaj Kalyanray, play *pakhavaj* in the Shri Nathji Haveli during the *mundan* celebration of the grandson of the present Tilkayat in 1985. I met the three Maharaj on two occasions and they showed great interest in music as art, as well as part of *darshan* celebrations. Kalyanray presented me with three volumes of *haveli sangit* compositions that he had compiled for use in the Vitthalnathji Haveli.

ARTISTIC PATRONAGE BY THE MAHARAJ

From Ghanshyam's account in the *Mridang Sagar* it would appear that music and artistic concerns have been particularly important for several Maharaj, in particular the then (mid-nineteenth century), Maharaj of Jamnagar, Shri Brajnath, who is described as having: "a great passion for the art of music" (MS Jivani: 4; MV: 3).

When Maharaj Brajnath visited Nathdvara in 1854 he was accompanied by a *pakhavaji*, Aditram, and their presence sparked off a music conference discussed in chapter 11 (MS Jivani: 4; MV: 3). Like his ancestors, the father of the present Maharaj of Jamnagar was keenly interested in music. He took a personal interest in the upbringing of one of the *kirtankars*, Manaklal, whose father and uncles continue to be employed as musicians in the various Nathdvara *havelis*.

Ghanshyam acknowledged that the Kankroli Maharaj,[9] Shri Balkrishna(lal) (1868-1917) read his book, the *Mridang Sagar*, prior to publication, and said that it was "praiseworthy and fit to be published" (MS:Pr. 2). The accompanying text gives some insight into the personality and contribution of Balkrishna Maharaj and to the artistic life of the *sampraday*.

> Balkrishnalalji was a man of taste. Once while he was in Varanasi in 1888, during the spring festival of Budhva *mangala* he managed to see that all the people who attended the festival were dressed in pink, and paid all the expenses incurred by them for the dyeing of their clothes. People in Varanasi still remember this colourful event.
>
> He wrote poems using the pen name of Krishna and Kahna and participated in the plays by the drama troupe founded by him with the help of his friend, Bharatendu Harish Chandra, a noted Hindi poet writer of that time. Many

paintings and photographs of aesthetic and historical importance preserved in the Kankroli Maharaj collection were collected by Balkrishnaji (Ambalal 1987: 160).

There is a portrait of Balkrishna Maharaj illustrated in Ambalal (1987: 146-7,160). It shows the Maharaj seated between his two sons. All of them are wearing saffron robes, that appear to be silk, pearl earrings and choker pearl necklaces, as well as other necklaces of assorted jewels. Even today, the dress of many of the Maharaj approximates that worn by Balkrishna in the painting as my meeting with various Maharaj confirmed (chapter 12). The cost of publishing the *Mridang Sagar* was borne by the Tilkayat, Govardhanlal, whom Ghanshyam described as "patron and art lover... an ornament in the line of Vallabha" (MS: Pr. 2). Certainly the assistance of the Tilkayat and possibly the next most important Maharaj, that of Kankroli, would indicate that they were interested in Ghanshyam's endeavour, and no doubt musical endeavours in general. Such patronage, although diminishing, is still very important for the survival of the musical tradition within the *sampraday*.

MISUSE OF POWER

Since the Vallabha Sampraday was founded there have been two memorable occasions in which Tilkayats have been deposed. In 1876 Rana Sajjan Singh (r. 1874-84) exiled the Tilkayat Giridhar (1843-1903) to Braj, installing Giridhar's elder son, Govardhanlal (1862-1934) in his place (Karsondas Mulji 1865; Entwistle 1987). In 1933 Maharana Bhopal Singh (r. 1930-55) removed the Tilkayat Damodarlal (1897-1934) after less than a year in office, replacing him with his son, the present Tilkayat, Govindlal (born 1928), at that time a minor. On several occasions devotees have questioned the supremacy of the Tilkayats in both religious and secular areas. Sometimes they were able to bring about reduction in the power of the various Maharaj. The activities of many of the present musicians at the time of the removal of the Tilkayat Damodar are described in chapter 7.

With so many Maharaj the odds were good that some among them would tend to abuse their powers. In addition to the Karsondas Mulji case (1865), there is also mention of misconduct by the Maharaj of

Manvi, in Kutch, who allegedly robbed various towns with the help of several Muslims. The then British Resident in Kutch refused to allow him to return (Mulji 1865: 155). This must have been sorted out at a later date as the *haveli* there, by all accounts, was flourishing in the 1980s. There is also a report of a Maharaj being flogged by the Portuguese and another being imprisoned at Jalnapatan, at that time an independent principality (Mulji 1865, appendix 10).

CONCLUSION

I have met the different Maharaj only in rather formal situations, usually briefly, and I did not have sufficient contact with any of them for them to drop their customary public persona. It is hard to treat people normally when others are prostrating before them and presenting them with gifts. I have noted what others have said on the subject of the leaders of the Vallabha Sampraday because their comments have contributed to the popular perception of the Maharaj.

Most of the Maharaj that I approached found some time to speak to me, despite many demands on their time. Because my interest lay mainly in the music and its role in the sect, almost all of my conversations with them revolved around music. In this field they appeared to be remarkably knowledgeable, with a surprisingly high proportion of actual practitioners. Especially noteworthy was their predilection for the *pakhavaj*. To understand a preoccupation with *haveli sangit* is relatively easy as these songs form part of the textual basis of the *sampraday*; not so their attraction to a percussion instrument like the *pakhavaj*. Throughout India, drumming is generally regarded as a rather low-status occupation; drummers usually have a position subordinate to vocalists and instrumentalists. Krishna is sometimes shown in miniature paintings playing a drum— and this might provide a connection—but he is far more often shown with the flute, for which the Maharaj show no particular enthusiasm. Whatever the reason, the interest of the Maharaj has secured a firm place for the *pakhavaj* in the music of the *sampraday*. This interest may also explain the high regard that was exhibited by the Tilkayats towards the family of Pakhavaji Guru Purushottam, with their acknowledged mastery of the instrument (chapter 11).

NOTES

1. Tod confirms this; "The present pontiff Damodara ... in addressing him verbally or by letter is styled Maharaja, or great prince" (Crooke 1920: 642).
2. Jivanji Maharaj was the Maharaj about whom Karsondas Mulji wrote in his paper, *Surya Prakash.*
3. Crooke (1920) noted that during the early nineteenth century the seventh *svarup* was the property of a woman. Entwistle (1987: 183) records the service of the deity being organized by the elder daughter until her brother came of age. The mother of the present three Maharaj of the Vitthalnathji Haveli, Nathdvara, administered it after her husband died and her sons were still minors. A *haveli* in Baroda is presently controlled by a woman, Gabila Betiji, sister of the present Tilkayat. She is said to have a large following in London and the USA. There are several women who are heads of *havelis*; presumably, where a woman is the head of a *haveli*, she is given the privilege of circling *arati.* The circling of *arati* was one of the main duties of the *devadasis* in the temples of south India.
4. There is at least one CD available of Gosvami Gokulotsav.
5. These included Krishna Das, Banatwala Bhurhanpur and Sivnarain Govindraj Veda.
6. The violin was introduced to India from Europe some time in the eighteenth-nineteenth century. It seems to have had more success in southern India. It has never become part of temple music traditions either in north or south India.
7. Their vocal teacher was M.A. Golvakar from Indore. Their violin teacher was Jagdish Chandra Vedi and their *sarod* teacher Pradeep Chaterjee, a Bengali who lives in Bombay.
8. See Burghardt (1976).
9. The *Balagopalastuti* was produced under the patronage of Balkrishna, a Maharaj of Kankroli (Gadon 1984); Shyam Das (1985) acknowledged the present Maharaj of Kankroli, Vrajbhushanlal, for assistance in publishing his book *Chaurasi Baithak.*

Plate 3.1: The three Maharajs of the Vitthalnathji Haveli Nathdvara 1985.

FROM LEFT TO RIGHT: Shri Devkinand, Shri Kalyanray and Shri Gokulotsav. They were photographed in their palace attached to the Vitthalnathji Haveli.

Plate 3.2: Some Maharajs of the Vallabha Sampraday

CHAPTER 4

Worship in the Haveli

DARSHAN

Shri Nathji's devotees share his daily routine by visiting him at specific times. These occasions are known as *darshan* (literally 'seeing'). On these occasions the deity transmits some part of his holiness to the beholder (Eck 1985: 6-7). All the activities in the Vallabha Sampraday temples at Nathdvara revolve around preparing the various images for *darshan* and honouring them with objects of aesthetic pleasure. *Darshans* in the Shri Nathji Haveli are the most widely attended. Devotees go to see and be seen by Shri Nathji's crescent-shaped eyes. Luminous and white, their black pupils gaze downward. They appear to be made out of mother of pearl and are very striking. They emphasize that he watches over his devotees as they take shelter beneath Mount Govardhan which he holds aloft in his left hand.

Shri Nathji is said to be eleven years and sixty days old. As he is a child, the ceremonies prior to *darshan* are modified to suit his age, but as he is also a god, other rituals of a more adult nature are also observed. Thus, he is presented with toys, which are intended to amuse him, but when he goes to bed a situation suitable for 'love sports' is created.

The worship involves a detailed re-creation of his day-to-day life in Braj, where he was born and brought up. Shri Nathji must be woken, dressed, entertained, fed and finally lulled to sleep. All these activities, although carried out in a literal manner, include ritual components which maintain the traditions of previous centuries, long buried by time and modern innovations in the outside world. Worship centres around presenting Shri Nathji with delicious food, decorating him in opulent clothes and singing songs in his honour.

All the activities in the *havelis* revolve around preparing the *svarups* for *darshan* and honouring them with pleasurable objects and experiences. *Darshan* preparations for Shri Nathji are the most lavish and serve as a model for other *havelis*. The *havelis* in Nathdvara are normally open seven or eight times a day; in some other centres the opportunity for *darshan* is less. The importance of *darshan* has been central to developing and sustaining all artistic traditions associated with the *sampraday*. Hereditary specialists are in charge of producing these components and carrying out the various tasks. They are assisted by volunteer devotees (*sevavalas*).

SEVA

In the context of the Vallabha Sampraday, *seva*, literally service, is any type of work performed for the comfort of the deity. As Shri Nathji is both a deity and a royal person, *seva* has extensive forms. Objects of aesthetic pleasure are generally produced by specialists, who are usually hereditary artists. All work of the *haveli* is regarded as *seva*, which is to be offered with devotion (*bhakti*) without a sense of personal gain. *Seva* has been organized into various departments which specialize in producing the finest objects for Shri Nathji. They are clearly defined, and over the years have become standardized.

Each department has a director (*mukhiya*) who ensures quality control. There are permanent employees in each department with their specializations though devotees volunteer for much of the routine work. The sheer volume of work during festival days, when much food and elaborate preparations must be completed, calls for many extra hands. Activities include cutting and chopping vegetables, stringing flowers, trimming betel leaves, etc. (Jindel 1976: 113-20). Devotees work in whatever department needs them for any particular day. As these volunteers are in contact with the articles that will later be offered to Shri Nathji they must follow the same bathing procedures described below for the priests. The running and functioning of the temple is largely dependent upon the *seva* performed by townsfolk as well as pilgrims. The elaborate celebrations are important in attracting pilgrims, who in turn make substantial donations to support Shri Nathji. Music, poetry, perfume, rich food, jewellery, and various forms of decoration such as painting, elaborate wall hangings (*picchvai*), embroidery,—all confirm the *sampraday's* commitment to the arts. These arts trace their origin to various regions of India. The original connection with Braj is very much in evidence; other regions such as Gujarat and Rajasthan continue to exert an influence on the manner in which religious objects are made. These arts—which may be visual, edible or musical, are driven by the need to make a "good show" in the royal presence of Shri Nathji.

DARSHAN ROUTINE

Most of the townsfolk of Nathdvara attend at least one *darshan* daily; pilgrims, having come for this specific purpose, try to attend all of them. To attend those *darshans* at the Shri Nathji temple, let alone those at the less important shrines, is a full-time task. The first *darshan* of the day begins anytime from 4.30 to 6 a.m., earlier in winter than in summer. In explanation of this somewhat surprising practice, it is said that when the days are shorter the child Krishna goes to bed earlier and gets up earlier. Other *darshans* are fairly evenly spaced up to about 7 p.m. with a break of a few hours in the early afternoon for Shri Nathji's siesta.

Each *darshan* is representative of one of Shri Nathji's daily activities, highlighted with appropriate ritual objects. At *Mangal* his devotees greet him just after he has awakened; in winter he appears wrapped in a quilt (*razai*), and in summer covered with a diaphanous cloth. At the next *darshan*, *Shringar*, he appears in the fine clothes that he will wear all day. The dress worn is appropriate to the season, with great attention given to detail (Talwar and Krishna 1979: 9-10,133). Each *darshan* includes some visual symbol—particular toys and implements—by which Shri Nathji's activity during that *darshan* may be identified. Thus, at *Gval darshan* he is shown with a stick and cows as he leads the cattle off to graze. Shri Nathji has his main meal of the day at *Raj Bhog*, the fourth and most elaborate *darshan*. This offering becomes sanctified food (*prasad*), part of which is later given to the temple employees as payment (*neg*) for their service to the deity (Khare 1976: 25). At *Shringar* and *Raj Bhog* Shri Nathji is honoured as a prince while *Gval* recalls his peasant origins in Braj.

The duration of *darshans* is flexible, depending mainly on how long the preparations take (see Table 4.1). On festival days, such as Divali, unusually elaborate preparations are made for *Raj Bhog*, generally considered the most important of the eight *darshans*. The huge number of devotees wishing to take *darshan* on festival days necessitates keeping the shrine open considerably longer, by two or more hours. On such occasions, *Gval*, the *darshan* between *Shringar* and *Raj Bhog*, is performed privately by the priests; it will not be open to the public. An extended *Raj Bhog darshan* usually results in *Bhog* and *Arati* commencing late or being combined. *Shayan darshan* is closed for six months of the year, during the hot season, when Shri Nathji sleeps out of doors (Jindel 1976: 67).

Because of uncertainty concerning the timing of *darshan*, particularly on festival days, when the preparations are more elaborate, pilgrims have to be alert and ready to rush to the temple. *Darshans* are announced over loudspeakers and the *naubat*, *naqqara* (drums), and *shahnai* (reed instrument), are played from the room above the main gate. This room is popularly known as *naqqara khana*, though *naubat khana* would be more correct since the playing of *shahnai* and *naqqara* is known as a *naubat* ensemble.

The *svarup* is decorated by priests, with only the first four priests (*mukhiyas*) allowed by the Tilkayat to touch the image (Jindel 1976: 117). According to the second *mukhiya* of the Shri Nathji Haveli, before the priests report for duty, they must bathe within the temple and exchange their clothes for clean ones, which remain within the temple. The bathing takes place in a special area about four feet square. Hot water from a pot is poured "like a shower" while they are still fully clothed. Soap is not used. The bather must wear wooden sandals and his feet must not touch the ground; if they do he must bathe again. He then puts on the temple clothing, spreading his wet clothes to dry on bamboo poles. Each person is allotted two bamboo poles for his clothes. Bathing is also compulsory for the servants and *sevavalas* who handle the cooking or touch the articles that will later be offered to Shri Nathji. Anyone of them who leaves the temple must bathe again on re-entering.

GAINING ENTRY INTO THE *HAVELI*

Guards are very much in evidence. Armed guards are posted at all entrances. Until about 1986 they carried flintlock muskets with fixed bayonets; now they have switched over to bolt action rifles, also with fixed bayonets. They have considerable discretion about whom to allow into the temple. Just because one has been in before does not mean that a second entry will be allowed. When I first began to visit the *haveli* it took some time to gain the acquiescence of all the guards, who were accustomed at that time to preventing non-Indians from entering. Whenever I had trouble I could usually appeal to someone from the musician community who would vouch for me.

The guards are found at the three main entrances: just inside the large gate that leads to the Tilkayat's private apartments, on both sides of the main gate, and at the back entrance in the lane (*gali*) opposite the Vitthalnathji Haveli. There is a barracks near the high school playing fields but those on duty in the Shri Nathji Haveli sleep in a recess behind the large gates after they have been locked for the night. I used to see them when leaving after my *pakhavaj* class in the music school, which often continued after the temple was otherwise closed. In addition to these soldiers, others are usually to be found lounging around or sleeping in the corridors of the *haveli*. Jindel (1976) noted that several Maharajas who were members of the Vallabha Sampraday, such as the Maharaja of Kota, had made some of their soldiers available for the Tilkayat as part of his army.

In addition to the soldiers who form the Tilkayat's bodyguard, there is a second class of guards in the *haveli*. These are known as *jhapatiyas* and their main function is crowd control. Like the soldiers, they also keep an eye open for persons who should not be in the temple, such as Muslims, untouchables,[1] and foreigners. Unlike the soldiers, who have military uniforms and are paid a salary, some *jhapatiyas* are volunteers, and their work is considered *seva*; others receive payment in kind (*neg*). *Jhapatiyas* wear the regular dress required for temple employees which consists of a Rajasthani style of *kurta* or shirt (*angarkhi*) and a lower garment tied at the waist (*dhoti*).

VISITING THE VARIOUS DEPARTMENTS

Bona fide pilgrims usually make the rounds of the various departments to marvel at the richness and opulence in the preparations. Such visits are often facilitated by hiring a professional guide or by gaining help from a temple employee. Many temple servants, including the musicians, supplement their income by guiding pilgrims. I visited the different departments on numerous occasions, and at various times, but always accompanied by either a musician or another temple employee. Gaining entry on non-festival days is not a problem; but on festival days, because of the intense activity, the sheer volume of work and the numerous *sevavalas* working on the elaborate preparations, it was sometimes impossible. Guards are usually everywhere, especially on festival days.

I found it most interesting to visit the departments just before *Raj Bhog darshan* when the greatest amount of activity was in progress to prepare for the most elaborate *darshan* of the day. Most townsfolk would be there and the atmosphere was industrious, but happy and joyful. Workers seemed to enjoy their tasks and took pleasure in producing articles of beauty for Shri Nathji. Those arranging flowers, for example, took pains to attain perfection in their work, often pausing to consider if one particular flower matched the one beside it and if the arrangement was symmetrical. Some jobs could be done by both sexes, while others were strictly regulated. Many of the local inhabitants would be there and there was little doubt that the daily contribution made by the local women was essential to the functioning of the *haveli*. I was closest to the musicians' families, and I could not help but be impressed by their energy and devotion in performing *seva*. The family of Ramchandra (*haveli* singer in the Shri Nathji Haveli) was particularly active in this respect. I visited their home in 1986, after *Raj Bhog darshan* at about 1 p.m. He was well into his seventies and his wife was in her sixties. He had just returned from the temple where he had been singing and sometimes playing the *pakhavaj* since 7 a.m. His wife was also at the temple doing household chores such as cleaning and chopping vegetables and sweeping floors. After five hours of working in the *haveli* for Shri Nathji, both of them set out to cook their own midday meal from scratch, again washing, cutting and preparing vegetables. What was more remarkable was that, after a brief nap, by 4 p.m. Ramchandra would certainly be back in the temple for another two hours of singing and possibly playing the *pakhavaj*, and his wife usually returned also to help with various tasks. Such *seva* by the older women from the musician community was commonplace. I saw one of the wives hard at work soon after an operation for cancer. Another widow of one of the former head singers never missed a day; her radiant face remains embedded in my memory. In most instances the burden of their own household was taken over by daughters-in-law and granddaughters. I was nevertheless much impressed by the apparent energizing effect of *seva*, in contrast to the drudgery of the household tasks left to the younger women.

WAITING TO ATTEND *DARSHAN*

While the image is being prepared, the devotees wait in the outer courtyard (*kamal chauk*). The more privileged—those who have made a sizable donation to the temple (in 1983 it was approximately three hundred rupees or more)—wait in the inner courtyard (*ratan chauk*). Admission to *ratan chauk*, which allows prior entry to the *darshan* room, may also be obtained through the goodwill of employees who help the favoured ones past the soldiers who guard the entrance. In some instances this may also involve private financial transactions.

In addition, if one is especially privileged, as I was, it is possible to wait in *kirtankar gali*, literally the musicians' lane. This is a hallway about four yards wide that stretches the full length of the *darshan* room. It is called *kirtankar gali* because it is there that the musicians sing during the pre-*darshan* period, wait before going in for *darshan*, and store their instruments. It is also the area through which devotees exit after *darshan*.

ENTERING THE *DARSHAN* HALL (*DOLTIVARI*) WITH DEVOTEES

The devotees enter the *darshan* hall via *ratan chauk*, with the women entering the door at the front, and the men through the two doors behind. There is usually a long queue and much jostling as the time of *darshan* approaches. The atmosphere is electric with anticipation. As soon as noises signal the unbarring of the doors, the crowd is on its feet and pressing for the doors. At first, the three purple wooden doors between *ratan chauk* and the *darshan* room are unlocked and thrown open. The same procedure follows for the steel bars behind them. This sets off a chain reaction. The privileged, who are already in *ratan chauk*, rush into the *darshan* room, while those previously held behind the outer doors, of which there are two sets, stampede through to join the queue. This ensures that they will be in the second wave of pilgrims that enter. As the doors open, the *jhapatiyas* cling to the door jambs or jump up on the bars that divide the public area from the room in which Shri Nathji is housed (*mani kota*). These bars hold back the pilgrims and prevent them from surging to where the musicians stand.

Position is crucial if one is to see what is going on. It is useful to go in with a preplanned idea as to where one will stand.

The floor in the *darshan* hall is a series of wooden steps, about six inches high and about thirty-nine inches deep. To some extent this helps in viewing, but the uneven surface can make balance precarious.

I always tried to make a point of keeping clear of the bar which separates the area where the musicians stand from the *darshan* hall. On one occasion, I was pushed up and over it, rather like a champagne cork being forced out of a bottle. Another time I nearly had my ribs crushed. I was also close to being knocked out once, when from the back of the *darshan* hall, an excited devotee threw a coconut for Shri Nathji; it did not quite clear the crowd, scraping my head in flight. That said, I have seen the old and infirm and infants in arms all taking *darshan* under these turbulent conditions, but none of them have been hurt. Although the crowd looks like a football scrum, there is actually more consideration given to others than it appears. Also, bars divide the chamber into sections, which serve to break any concentrated surge to the front.

The present custom is to allow only women to enter via the door closest to the image. Inside the *darshan* hall, a steel bar divides their section from the men's. Mulji, writing in the last century, describes the situation prior to this division: "Many men have intruded for vicious and immoral purposes and assault the modesty of females with impunity. The crowd is so dense that, in extraordinary occasions, females are totally denuded of their slight and loose clothing in the crush" (Mulji 1865: 104).

While today a few men may be admitted to the front row so that they might get a better view, I have never seen the type of behaviour Mulji described.

Within seconds of the *darshan* hall opening, it is full of a seething mass of people pressing against each other. I have seen women remove their silver anklets, as a precaution against theft. I removed my head scarf, before entering the *darshan* area, for fear it might be tightened round my neck, as the crowd would pull, push and grab onto anything for leverage in an effort to get a better view of Shri Nathji. Children are lifted up onto shoulders, and the old and infirm are carried or supported. Jindel's (1976) and Mulji's experiences were very similar:

The Vaishnavas, with their wives and daughters, having previously assembled in the passage, the door is opened, the crowd rushes to enter, crying out, Jaya!, Jaya! to prevent the doors from being closed. The noise and confusion are immense. No time must be lost, for in ten or twenty minutes the doors are again closed. It is impossible all can get into the small room at once, and the weaker of the crowd have to await their turn to enter (Mulji 1865: 103).

It is the *jhapatiyas* task to retain order, prevent devotees from being trampled on, and keep the crowd moving. This is achieved by flipping long strips of cloth. A slight snap at the shoulder signals that it is time to move on (see also Jindel 1976: 95-6). In earlier times, the *jhapatiyas* may have been more violent:

To accelerate the devotion of those who have got in, and to induce them to make room for other devotees who are anxiously waiting outside, one of the guardians of the temple mounts upon a rail, with a thick black cord in his hand to whip them along. Many of the devotees receive a very severe beating; and it has happened that an eye has been lost, or other severe permanent injuries inflicted (Mulji 1865: 103).

Mulji's description may not have been typical, even at that time. Two mid-eighteenth century paintings figured by Ambalal (1987: 98, 99) appear to illustrate white strips of cloth being used by the *jhapatiyas*, just as we see today, and not the whips described by Mulji.

In other *havelis* of the *sampraday* where I have taken *darshan*, such as those in Porbandar, Junagarh, and Baroda, the devotees still rush to enter, but once in, everyone moves in a direction, and at a pace, that seems to be known to all. Such orderly behaviour is not typically seen in the Shri Nathji Haveli. It seems that in the smaller centres all the devotees know each other, and there is more consideration for others present. Also they know exactly what they are going to see. By contrast, in the Shri Nathji temple many of the devotees are visiting pilgrims who may come only once a year or even once in a lifetime; and they wish to maximize their *darshan* period. Details of *darshan* in the other *havelis* are given in chapter 12.

I would have to agree with Mulji that most *darshans* are similar, except for festival days when there are embellishments: "Upon all these occasions the ceremony is much the same, consisting of little more than waving a light, and presenting flowers, perfumes and food to the image by the priests" (Mulji 1865).

Other than looking at the image and making a personal prayer, there is no communal worship. Mulji commented on this:

The votaries, on beholding the image, or its lustrous embellishments, do nothing but repeat the name of the idol or Thakurji (Shri Nathji) several times, with a variety of protestations and obeisances. This is the worship. There is no established ritual for general use, nor any prescribed form of worship (Mulji 1865).

The ritual activities performed by the priests, which can be seen during *darshan*, are simple, straightforward and literal: the presenting of a mirror so that Shri Nathji is able to admire himself, the removal of the flute from his hands prior to taking rest. The elaborate bathing, dressing and eating rituals are performed only by those select priests who have sufficient ritual status; the general devotee is not privileged to see these activities.

Mulji noted that the Maharaj entered *mani kota* before *darshan* opened for the public, and when it was opened he circled an open flame (*arati*) in front of Shri Nathji:

> Previous to the opening of the division of the temple where the image of the idol is placed, the Maharaj takes his stand near the image. Here, after the entrance of the votaries, he occasionally swings the image or waves before it a small metallic lamp, in which burns a light fed by clarified butter (Mulji 1865: 103).

While this sometimes occurs, in my experience it is more common that the only persons in place at the start of *darshan* are the musicians, and one or two priests. The Maharaj appeared to enter whenever they wished; their presence was not obligatory at all *darshans*. The Tilkayat, or one of his sons, usually arrived after the *darshan* was well under way, just in time for the circling of *arati*; he usually stayed on until the Shri Nathji *darshan* was closed before moving on to the nearby Navnitpriyaji Haveli, where he also performed *arati*.

The timings of *darshans* at the two *havelis* were roughly co-ordinated to allow the devotees to take *darshan* of both *svarups*. Thus, the *darshan* at the Navnitpriyaji Haveli opened after the *darshan* at the Shri Nathji Haveli was well under way; and closed later. On festival days there was much pomp and ceremony as the Maharaj and his sons, the visiting Maharaj, and other relatives, moved in procession between the two *havelis*.

Mulji's description, given above, and miniature paintings of *arati*, recall a technique used in the theatrical presentations of Krishna's life, known as *Ras Lila*. In *Ras Lila*, the curtain opens, revealing all the principal characters in place, rather like a *tableau vivant*. This may have been more common formerly, and it is possible that since Mulji's days there has been some change in the timing of events during *darshan*.

MUSIC AT *DARSHAN*

Mulji was one of the few to remark upon the presence of musicians at *darshan*:

> Upon the door of the temple being opened, the musicians and songsters placed there commence a succession of lascivious chants, descriptive of Krishna's amorous sports with the *gopis*. These choristers and musicians occupy a place opposite the image and the Maharaj, but behind[2] the worshippers who throng through the open intervening space (Mulji 1965: 105).

Although I frequently entered the *darshan* hall with the main body of devotees from *ratan chauk*, I could not be sure of getting close to the image or being able to observe the musicians properly when I took this route. On those occasions when I waited for *darshan* while listening to the music played in *kirtankar gali* I entered directly from there. This ensured me an excellent view.

In *kirtankar gali* the musical instruments are either hung on the wall or locked in special cupboards which also contain the musician's turbans, song books and some of the payment in kind (*prasad*) that they receive from the temple. Hanging on the wall are: four *bins* (stringed instruments), two to four *pakhavajs* and eight pairs of *jhanjh* (cymbals played only on festival days). Interspersed between them are paintings of the child Krishna.

While outside the temple, throngs of devotees wait for *darshan* to open, in *kirtankar gali*, the musicians play and sing enthusiastically. During this pre-*darshan* period they sit informally and engage in what in popular music would be called a 'jam session'. The public is not allowed in, but visiting musicians, usually from other Vallabha Sampraday *havelis* or professional musicians visiting Nathdvara, are admitted. For these pre-*darshan* periods I sat with the musicians in *kirtankar gali*. When unaccompanied *bin* was played, the *binkar* did it in the *darshan* room, where he was the only musician admitted. I could observe him by peeping through the bars separating *kirtankar gali* from the *darshan* room.

When *darshan* commences, the musicians have only a few seconds to pick up their instruments enter through the door on the right side of Shri Nathji, to their positions in front of the *svarup*. I used to enter the *darshan* room simultaneously through the doors that normally provide the exit after *darshan*. I was often assisted by the *jhapatiyas* and soldiers who pulled me in and made sure I had a good position in the front row.

The music begins just as the devotees rush into the hall. If visiting musicians wish to sing during *darshan*, they must obtain permission for this honour from the Tilkayat; those who are granted it must wear the required dress of *angarkhi*, *dhoti* and turban. Only male musicians sing in the *darshan*.

The musicians stand roughly three to four feet away from the image. They do not touch it, or anything that will be offered to it. Therefore, unlike the priests and *sevavalas*, they are not required to bathe within the temple. But before reporting for duty they must bathe at home. This only needs to be done once a day. This rule, which also governs the devotees who wish to enter the temple, is a general practice for entering Hindu shrines.

The musicians usually stand on both sides of the image with the head *kirtankar* closest. I saw a variety of arrangements and concluded that the actual arrangement was flexible. Most of them stand, except for the harmonium player and *Pakhavaji*. Guru Purushottam always sat to play, but Shyamlal, who was younger, would often stand, with the drum slung from a cord around his neck (for an illustration in painting see Talwar and Krishna 1979: 21, plate I). The *sarangi* player either sat or leaned against the wall with one knee raised supporting the instrument. Although he was officially employed to play the *sarangi*, he did not always do so. I have seen him on numerous occasions seated, playing the harmonium and singing. He was also an accomplished *bin* player. He played for me in his home but I had never heard him do so in the *haveli*. Likewise the *Binkar* did not always play the *bin*, instead he very often sang. Most of the musicians had a variety of musical skills.

FESTIVAL MUSIC

For a normal *darshan* I have only seen a single *pakhavaj*, *sarangi*, *bin* and harmonium played, but on special festivals, such as *Holi*, *Chhapan Bhog* and *Divali*, I have heard two or three *pakhavajs* played simultaneously. On such festival days there are usually visiting musicians from other temples also playing at *darshan*. The *Pakhavajis* sit facing the image; the rest of the musicians stand in a line on both sides of it.

If the *darshan* period was particularly long, not all the musicians stayed for the entire musical presentation. Generally all of them were present for the first half of the *darshan*. This happened for example, in the case of the *Chhapan Bhog* celebrations, the festival at which Shri Nathji is offered fifty-six varieties of foodstuffs, which sometimes lasted for one and a half hours (Talwar and Krishna 1979: 140; Vaudville 1980).

The musicians usually finished playing well before *darshan* was over. They could not, however, leave the temple as they had to play again while preparations were under way for the next *darshan*. Consequently they stood in *kirtankar gali*, pressed against the wall cradling their instruments, to avoid the devotees on their way out. Alternatively, they hung their instruments on the wall and walked around the temple. When the doors in front of the image were shut, signifying the completion of *darshan*, all except musicians had to vacate *kirtankar gali*. Removing stragglers was a function of the *jhapatiyas* and the entrance door to *kirtankar gali* was guarded either by one of them, or by a soldier. The guards on duty had the discretionary power to grant access to *kirtankar gali*. Needless to say, their cooperation was essential to my work.

Within about five minutes of *darshan* being closed the musicians re-assembled in *kirtankar gali* to play there at pre-*darshan* while the priests attended to preparing Shri Nathji for his next *darshan*.

While music is played for practically every *darshan*, for the devotees, it is drowned out by their ecstatic shouts, pushing and jostling. Many devotees are unaware that music is being played. I first realized this when a research scholar at my college in Oxford who was also an initiate in the Vallabha Sampraday remarked: "How can you study the music in the Nathdvara temple? I have taken *darshan* and did not hear it or notice any musicians."

The music during *darshan*, may last anywhere from five minutes to several hours. The folding of the cloth on which Shri Nathji stands is the signal for the music to end; at that point the musicians usually walk off. *Darshan* may continue for another half hour. The priests may make several attempts to close the *darshan*, but they are usually stopped each time by fervent pleas from the crowd.

THE STAGING OF *DARSHAN*

Darshan, as presented in the Shri Nathji Haveli, is a theatrical event as well as a religious one. The rituals which surround the *svarup* are only a small part of the proceedings. To the average pilgrim they are somewhat irrelevant, because he hardly gets to see much of them. The rush is certainly intense, but it is also somewhat orchestrated to help to intensify the religious fervour. The fact that there is no exact and predictable time of opening certainly heightens anticipation, keeping people on edge while waiting. Once inside the *darshan* hall, it is possible to be almost physically overcome when in the centre of the crowd that sways back and forth, and sideways.

The *jhapatiyas*' conduct seems to be critical to the organization of *darshan*, and to the devotees behaviour. It appears that, although there are generally recognized rules that govern the access of devotees to different parts of the *haveli* at various times, there is also some latitude for interpretation by individual *jhapatiyas*. Hence, devotees who are sufficiently importunate, or sufficiently liberal, can obtain special concessions, and feel themselves privileged. Such uncertainty about the outcome of attendance at a particular *darshan*, along with the special effects introduced from time to time, and the general unpredictability of schedules, heightens peoples awareness of the event, and may help to maintain enthusiasm.

The considerable number of musicians maintained in the Shri Nathji Haveli stresses the importance that is placed by the *sampraday* on the presentation of *haveli sangit*. Yet the circumstances of *darshan*, with the shouting and pushing and general hurly-burly, seem to make the quality of the music somewhat irrelevant. This situation contrasts with practices in some Krishna temples in Braj, where *bhajans* are played among the congregation and the songs can be clearly heard. Such performances seem to add substantially to the devotional atmosphere.

In Nathdvara the music would seem to have little effect in creating the mood for devotees, unlike some other aspects of the *darshan* "theatre". Some devotees are not aware of it at all. Moreover, more music is played during the pre-*darshan* periods, when it cannot be heard by devotees, than during *darshan*. I am forced to conclude that the offering of *haveli sangit* in the Shri Nathji and other *havelis* is largely of ritual significance. Nevertheless, the popularity of *haveli sangit* is becoming widespread. Well known singers such as the late Bhim Sen Joshi and others are adding them to their repertoire. Local vendors have begun to offer cassettes of *haveli sangit*, which is a recent innovation.

Much of the food offered to the deity is likewise unseen by those taking *darshan*, but it is subsequently sold as *prasad* and hence furnishes significant income for the *haveli*.

NOTES

1. Untouchables are generally not allowed in the temple. Swami Agnivesh attempted to have this ban lifted in 1988. The current situation appears to be that technically untouchables may enter the temple.
2. The practice today is for the musicians to stand in front of the worshippers. Probably he actually means in front of the worshippers. See diagram for the position of ***mani kota***.

TABLE 4.1: *DARSHANS* IN THE SHRI NATHJI HAVELI

Darshan	*Time* (approximate)	*Activity*	*Music*
pre-*Mangal*	03.45	awakened eating	*bin* unaccompanied, conch is blown 2 songs sung by *Binkar* and/or *Kirtankar Mukhiya* unaccompanied
Mangal	04-05.00 winter 05-06.00		*Ashtachhap*: Parmananddas 1-2 songs *Kirtankar Mukhiya* and *Binkar* summer sing unaccompanied (30-40 min)
pre-*Shringar*		bathing dressing	all musicians except *Binkar*, in *kirtankar gali*, 2-3 songs at the same time as the *Binkar* plays in the *darshan* hall
Shringar	07-07.30 (10 minutes)	fully dressed	*Ashtachhap*: Nanddas 1 song, all musicians
pre-*Gval*		eating	1 song, accompanied, followed by *bin* accompanied by *pakhavaj*
Gval	08-09.30 (10 minutes)	leading cows to graze	*Ashtachhap*: Govindsvami 1-3 songs

Darshan	*Time* (approximate)	*Activity*	*Music*
pre-*Raj Bhog*		bringing lunch	*bin* and *pakhavaj*
		setting the table	*pakhavaj*
		eating	4 songs
		chewing pan	1 song
		removing food	6 songs
Raj Bhog	10-11		*Ashtachhap*: Kumbhandas
		lunch finished	1 song
REST			
pre-*Utthapan*		walking	conch is blown
		eating	*bin* unaccompanied one song unaccompanied sung by *Binkar* or *Kirtankar Mukhiya*
Utthapan	15.15-16.45 (10 minutes)	awakened	*Ashtachhap*: Surdas *Binkar* and *Kirtankar Mukhiya*; 1 song is sung, sometimes *Binkar* plays, no accompaniment
pre-Bhog chewing pan		eating	*bin*, unaccompanied 1 song

TABLE 4.1 (CONTD.)

Darshan	*Time* (approximate)	*Activity*	*Music*
Bhog	16.00-16.15 (10 minutes)	afternoon meal	*Ashtachhap*: Chaturbhujdas; *bin*, *sarangi* and *pakhavaj* or all musicians sing 1 song
pre-*Arati*		eating	all *kirtankars*
Arati or *Sandhya*	17.00-17.30 (30-45 min)	leading cows home	*Ashtachhap*: Chhitsvami; 1 song, all home. *kirtankars*
pre-Shayan		undressing drinks milk evening snack	2 songs 1 song
Shayan	18.00-19.00	putting Shri Nathji to sleep	*Ashtachhap*: Krishnadas
		love making	1 song by *kirtankar mukhiya* or *Binkar* with *tanpura*
		falls asleep	*bin* unaccompanied, played under *dhruvari*

Notes: All the pre-*darshan* music takes place in *kirtankar gali* except during pre-*Shringar* when the *Binkar* plays in the *darshan* hall alone. All music during *darshan* is played in front of *mani kota* except after *Shayan* when the *bin* is played under *dhruvari*.

Plate 4.1: Darshan Hall, Doltivari

A summer festival is being celebrated in which the hall is filled with water. Pilgrims usually enter the doors on the left and leave via the doors on the right. From a painting in the collection of Amit Ambalal.

Plate 4.2: Mangal in summer, mid-nineteenth century

The painter illustrates the actual ***darshan*** on the upper left while the other segments of the painting are intended to illustrate a "feeling" behind the ***darshan*** and some of the rituals. Shri Nathji is awakened with a conch and the singing of the ***kirtankars***, playing the ***tanpura***, and the ***gopis*** or milkmaids. Vallabha "with the tenderness of a mother" lifts the thin sheet which has covered Krishna that night. Krishna is depicted in three locations: lying down, seated on his father Nanda's lap, beside the image of Shri Nathji, and as Shri Nathji, wearing a thin cloth. After Shri Nathji has finished a snack of dry fruit and sweets, a flute is placed in his hands. The belief is that he will then enjoy the company of his beloved Radha, known as Swaminiji. This picture is in the collection of Amit Ambalal (1987: 24).

Plate 4.3: Mangal in summer
(mid-nineteenth century; detail of Plate 4.2)

Plate 4.4: Navnitpriyaji

A bronze image of Navnitpriyaji of the type bought by pilgrims for the shrines in their home.

Plate 4.5: Shri Nathji's Darshan

The ***darshan*** of Shri Nathji is depicted. One Maharaj is performing ***arati*** and musicians are accompanying the ***darshan*** activities. This painting is in the private collection of Amit Ambalal.

CHAPTER 5

The Venues and the Instruments

AREAS IN THE *HAVELI* WHERE MUSIC IS PLAYED

Music is played regularly in several parts of the Shri Nathji Haveli. Four such spots are in the inner temple: in front of the *nij mandir* that houses the deity, in *kirtankar gali*, in *doltivari* and in *kamal chauk* underneath *dhruvari*, a small window reputedly aligned between Shri Nathji and the north star. Music is also played at the entrance to the *haveli* and in the *naubat khana* above the main gate. In other designated areas music is played less frequently. Thus, during the months when *Shayan darshan* is closed to the general public, the musicians play in *patal ghar*, a lane parallel to *kirtankar gali*. I heard music played there on several occasions, once I attained the status of being considered an honorary musician. When *Shayan darshan* is open to the public the musicians play in their usual spot, in front of the *nij mandir*.

On festival days, such as Holi and Divali, music is played throughout the *haveli*, in places such as *ratan chauk*, and on the terrace in front of the Navnitpriyaji shrine. The garden behind the palace was also a popular spot, particularly during the month of Phalgun when the arrival of spring is celebrated. In 1987, a building was erected on this site.

THE *NAUBAT/NAQQARA KHANA*

A *naubat/naqqara khana*[1] forms part of the palaces and forts of important Mughal and Rajput families. In the Shri Nathji Haveli it is a room about twenty-five by ten metres, above the main gateway and open on both sides, so that music played within can be heard both inside and outside the temple. The presence and continued use of the *naubat khana* remind us of the temporal powers of the *sampraday*, and emphasize the nature of the *haveli*, as distinguished from a regular temple. Here the *naqqara*,[2] *mardal*, *tali*, *karnal* (the long horn usually associated with festivals in the Himalayas) and *shahnai* are stored. Music is played in the *naqqara khana* daily before *Raj Bhog darshan* (10:30-11.30 a.m.) and before *Shayan darshan* (6.30-7.30 p.m.), to call the devotees to worship (Jindel 1976: 50).

Music from the *naubat khana* summons the worshippers, generates excitement and focuses attention on the temple and its celebrations. It is a constant reminder to the townsfolk and pilgrims that episodes from Krishna's life are being re-enacted. Music played in the *naubat khana*, more than twice a day, indicates that a festival is being celebrated, and continuous music indicates that it is a very important festival. On Janmashtami, Krishna's birthday, music is played from 4 a.m. to midnight and culminates in the blowing of the *karnal* to announce Krishna's birth. During *Nandotsav*, held the next day, devotees gather to share the joy of the birth of Krishna with his father Nanda. The music continues from 8 a.m. to 11 p.m. The celebration of Radhashtami, the birth of Radha calls for music to be played from 4 p.m. to 11.30 p.m. During *Divali*, music is played prior to all *darshans* and continues throughout the day, from 5 a.m. to 10 p.m. During *Annakut*, music in the *naubat khana* is played at night, a time at which it is not usually heard, beginning at 6 p.m. and continuing until midnight or later.

CATEGORIES OF MUSICAL INSTRUMENTS

Most accounts of musicians, musical instruments and music, look nostalgically at the past as a time when artistic traditions and artists were regarded with reverence. Ghanshyam's comments written in the *Mridang Sagar* at the turn of the century are no exception, and could just as easily have been written today.

Very little progress can be seen of the old arts in the present time. The old arts are not making any progress (MS. Pr: 1).

Ghanshyam acknowledged that this was one of the motivating forces behind recording his family's oral tradition. His book is mainly a compilation of drumming material. Ghanshyam does not generally mention where, and why, the music was played. He does, however, attempt to establish his musical credentials by referring to "old books", in particular the *Sangit Ratnakara* (thirteenth century), from which he adopts the same four categories for classifying[3] musical instruments:[4] *tata* ("stretched") or string instruments, such as the *bin* and *sarangi*, *avanadhda* ("covered") or drums, such as the *mridang* or *pakhavaj*, *shushira* ("hollow, tubular") or wind instruments, such as the flute, *ghana* ("metal"), and brass instruments that are struck, such as a bronze plate, *tala*, bell, *jhanjh* or cymbals (MS.Pr:1). Ghanshyam concluded that the most important was the *avanaddhu* category and the most important instrument within it the *pakhavaj/mridang*. This is not surprising considering his vocation!

Ghanshyam did not list the instruments that were played in the *haveli*, or the particular occasions on which they were used. Nor did he give any systematic account of the music. The anecdotal material in the *Mridang Sagar*, however, although sparse, gives us some insight into the life and career of a professional musician's family. His observations augment the reminiscences of the present musicians and the visual records of musical gatherings and associated events to be found in the miniature paintings and photographs of the *sampraday* and royal courts (Ambalal 1987; Topsfield 1980).

INSTRUMENTS PLAYED IN THE *HAVELI*

Certain instruments are played inside the *haveli*, as part of the *darshan* celebrations. These performances usually take place in *mani kota* and *kirtankar gali*. During festivals or special events, music may be played elsewhere in the *haveli*. Some instruments are played only on these occasions. Each instrument is played only in a particular context and only in a particular place in the *haveli*. All the instruments played in the *haveli* precincts or in the *naubat khana* are the property of the temple and remain in their respective places. The instruments played within the temple precincts cannot be interchanged with those played in the *naubat khana*.

STRING INSTRUMENTS

Within the Shri Nathji Haveli, three string instruments are played regularly: *bin*, *sarangi*[5] and *tanpura*. The *bin*[6] and *tanpura* are played by plucking, and the *sarangi* by bowing. The *bin* has immovable frets, the *sarangi* does not have frets. The *tanpura* acts as a drone. The strings of the *sarangi* are made of gut, those of the *tanpura* and *bin* of wire.[7] All these instruments are made of wood. The *bin* has two large gourds, which act as resonators; these are connected by a wooden neck. The *sarangi* is made out of a single hollow piece of wood with the body, neck and peg box clearly distinguishable. The *tanpura* is fashioned out of wood and includes a gourd and a stem. Miniature paintings and sculptures confirm that the shape of all these stringed instruments has not altered since the sixteenth century when music was first introduced as part of the ritual of the Vallabha Sampraday.

BIN[8]

The *Mridang Sagar* claimed that Nathdvara was notable for its *bin* tradition. The ritual importance of *bin* in the Shri Nathji Haveli, remains considerable. This was confirmed when, on several occasions I saw it being plucked in the most perfunctory manner. *Bin*, unaccompanied, is played in the *haveli* four times a day. These performances are not public. They are designed to create a soothing atmosphere for Shri Nathji to undergo the transition from, and to sleep. These occasions are the period when Shri Nathji is wakened in the morning (pre-*Mangal darshan*); the period before *Shringar darshan*; the period before *Bhog darshan* in the early afternoon after his afternoon nap; and during *Shayan darshan*, when he goes to sleep. At these four times the *Binkar* plays solo and is alone except for the priests who are attending to Shri Nathji's needs at that time. *Bin* accompanied by *pakhavaj*, but without vocal support, is played during pre-*Raj Bhog darshan*, when Shri Nathji eats his midday meal. *Bin* and *sarangi* accompanied by *pakhavaj* are played when Shri Nathji enjoys an afternoon snack.

The *bin* has a long and intimate association with the *dhrupad-dhamar* style of Hindustani music. Previously the *bin* used to accompany the *dhrupad* style of singing; it is only recently that the *bin* has become a solo instrument (Deva 1987; Van der Meer 1980). It appears that the Nathdvara tradition, where *bin* is used both solo and as accompaniment, is a hold-over from earlier times, representing a tradition extinct elsewhere. Probably the *bin* was much more common and adapted to a wider variety of occasions than today. Miniature paintings[9] and drawings of the eighteenth century depict the *bin* accompanying

Kathak dance (Hardgrave and Slawek 1988/89). Although I have never heard it played on such occasions, it is part of the orchestral accompainiment for a Kathak '*nautch* dance' in a drawing done in Calcutta the eighteenth century (Hardgrave and Slawek 1988/89: 85). The *bin* is no longer used to accompany dance. Instead other stringed instruments, such as the *sarangi*, *sarod*, *sitar*, and harmonium, provide the melodic accompaniment. Miniature paintings also depict the *bin* being played by Hindu and Muslim saints (Bor 1987).

During *darshan* the *bin* may be played seated or standing. If the session is long the musician usually sits. But if the *darshan* period is relatively short, or if a "heavy rush" of pilgrims is expected the *Binkar* stands and plays with the gourd across his shoulder. Standing might be considered a mark of respect for the person being played to, but it appears that the length of the concert, rather than the audience, determines whether the *Binkar* sits or stands. Matu Binkar is depicted seated playing the *bin* in the Shri Nathji Haveli on the occasion of the solar eclipse in 1883 (Plate 11.3; Ambalal 1987: 134,158). When I photographed two *Binkars* in Nathdvara: Vallabhdas the present *binkar* of the Shri Nathji Haveli, and Amritlal, employed as the *sarangi* player in the Shri Nathji Haveli but who also plays the *bin*, both chose to play seated.

SARANGI

Although Ghanshyam makes no reference in the *Mridang Sagar* to the *sarangi*, both the family histories of resident musicians and miniature paintings document the use of the *sarangi* in the Shri Nathji Haveli (Ambalal 1987: 134, 158), before 1911. His omission is particularly puzzling, for the miniature painting of the solar eclipse mentioned above identified Ghanshyam's father, Shankar playing the *pakhavaj* and Devkishan playing *sarangi*. Further evidence that the *sarangi* was very much a part of the Shri Nathji Haveli tradition is provided by two surviving photographs. One *circa* 1911 (plate 7.3), includes Guru Purushottam at about eight years of age; it shows a *sarangi* player, identified as Parasuram, a Palival brahmin. The other photograph, plate 7.8, *circa* 1932, depicts Gokuldas (*kumavat, jalandhara* division), at that time the *sarangi* player of the Shri Nathji Haveli, playing for the *Ras Lila*. The present *Binkar* in the Shri Nathji Haveli, Vallabhdas and his brother, Pannalal, who is the *haveli* singer there, are Gokuldas' sons; neither pursued *sarangi*. No doubt the reason why Vallabhdas studied the *bin* was because he was adopted by his father's elder brother, Jamnadas, who was the *Binkar* in the Shri Nathji Haveli. Many of the musicians employed in the *havelis* of Nathdvara at the time are shown with their instruments accompanying the *Ras Lila* presentations. The antiquity of the *sarangi* and its association with temple and folk music has been extensively documented by Bor (1987).

TANPURA[10]

The *tanpura* is used solely as a drone. *Tanpuras* vary in size, some being three and one half feet or less, which makes them reasonably portable. The larger ones have a more resonating sound. They usually have four strings, some have five or six. The instrument is played by plucking with the side of the fingertips. Although no great skill is needed, some practice is required to produce an even sound. The *tanpura* is the ideal drone instrument because "not only are the notes vibrant with harmonies, which greatly assist the intonation of the singer or instrumentalist, but they are lasting" (Sorrell 1980: 44).

Although several *tanpuras* are kept in *kirtankar gali*, I saw them being used only occasionally. I was told that they were used either solo or to accompany songs during pre-*Mangal* and pre-*Utthapan* periods, when Shri Nathji is being awoken or lulled to sleep. At these times only the musician on duty is allowed in the *darshan* room, while priests and other officials wait on Shri Nathji. No additional stringed instruments are played during festivals or in the *naubat khana*.

WIND INSTRUMENTS

Four instruments of the wind variety are associated with music in the Shri Nathji Haveli: harmonium, conch (*shank*), *shahnai* and *karnal*. The harmonium and conch are played inside the *haveli*, the *shahnai* and *karnal* in the *naubat khana*. The harmonium and *shahnai* are played daily; the *karnal* only for festivals. Except for the conch[11] and the harmonium, which is a relatively recent instrument (Bor 1987), wind instruments have not played an important part in *darshan*.

FLUTE

The flute is Shri Nathji's instrument and symbol. During *darshan* the image is presented with only a symbolic flute represented by a stick; it is placed in, or removed from Shri Nathji's hand according to the particular activity in which he is engaged during each *darshan*. Taking the flute from Shri Nathji's hand and laying it down symbolizes that he is sleeping (Jindel 1976). Curiously, real flutes are never played in the Shri Nathji Haveli. The musicians gave various explanations for the flute not being part of the *haveli* ensemble:[12] that the flute is the instrument to be played only by Krishna, that its sound is too soft to be heard when played as part of ensemble music; that it is only recently that the flute has achieved the stature of acceptance as a classical concert instrument. The third explanation appears the most plausible.[13]

HARMONIUM

The one wind instrument that is used inside the temple is the harmonium. The instrument was not invented until the 1800s in Paris (Bor 1987) and may have joined the ensemble of the *haveli* within the last hundred years. It is not shown in any of the pictures figured by Ambalal (1987), which range in date up to the end of the nineteenth century.

SHAHNAI AND *KARNAL*

In the *naqqara khana* the *shahnai* is played daily. On festive occasions a large horn, the *karnal* is blown. The *shahnai* is a small double-reed instrument, somewhat akin to a miniature oboe. Although played daily in the *haveli*, it is generally regarded as a festive instrument. Miniature paintings and present-day custom confirm that both royal celebrations—births, weddings and martial victories—and weddings for the common man have adopted the *shahnai* as the festive instrument par excellence (Sorrell 1980: 35). In southern India, the *nagasvaram*,[14] a similar reed instrument, serves the same function as the *shahnai*. The *shahnai* can also be used as a drone when accompanying another *shahnai*.

THE DRUMS OF THE *HAVELI*

The *pakhavaj*, once known as the *mridang* ("having one part of clay" New Grove 1980: 133), is now made of wood. It is the only drum played regularly inside the *haveli*. Another drum, the *daff* is a festive instrument and is played only occasionally, such as during Holi, the festival of spring. In the *naubat/naqqara khana* three drums are played: *naqqara*, *dhol*, and *dhumsa*. These are discussed later.

There is reference to the *mridang* in the *Natya Shastra* (fifth century A.D.). Probably both the north Indian *pakhavaj* (as the *mridang* later came to be called) and its southern counterpart, which is still called *mridangam*, can be traced to the drum described in the *Natya Shastra*. However the *pakhavaj* tradition has altered considerably since then and to think of the present tradition as unbroken is unrealistic. Many authors have noted differences between drum material described in the *Natya Shastra* and the later text the *Sangita Ratnakara* (thirteenth century A.D.). The continued evolution of a living tradition is emphasized by the fact that in 1982 none of the *pakhavaj* players in Nathdvara, including Guru Purushottam, could understand, or play, all of the material in the *Mridang Sagar*. This was after a period of less than seventy years since its publication![15]

Drums are divided according to their shape, how they are played, and whether or not they are tuned. The three shapes represented amongst those played within the Shri Nathji Haveli are: barrel, kettle and framed. The *pakhavaj* and *dhol* are of the barrel variety, the *naqqara* and *dhumsa* of the kettle variety and the *daff* of the framed variety. Only the *pakhavaj* is finely tuned, tension being adjusted by means of wooden wedges inserted under the thongs connecting the drum heads at either end of the drum. The pitch on the other drums is adjusted by heating the leather, which increases the tension on the heads. The *pakhavaj* is played with both hands; the *daff*, *naqqara*, *dhol* and *dhumsa* are played by beating with one or two sticks, held in the hand.

PAKHAVAJ

The *pakhavaj* historically has accompanied both music and dance. It is played in religious ritual of the Vallabha Sampraday; the *khol*, another barrel-shaped drum made of clay, accompanies the devotional congregational singing of another Vaishnavite Sampraday founded by Krishna Chaitanya (1485-1533) which flourished in Braj at the same time as the Vallabha Sampraday (Barz 1976: 31,106). The Chaitanyaites, who used the *khol*, were active in Calcutta. This could account for these observations made in the eighteenth century that playing the *pakhavaj* was mainly to accompany dance:

The *pakhavaj* is seldom heard at the feasts or ceremonies of religion, but it is in frequent use at private entertainments, especially in *nautches*, where it often serves for accompanying (Hardgrave and Slawek 1988/89: 40).

The *pakhavaj* is a double-conical-shaped drum with the greatest girth (*kumbha*) at about one-third of its length from the left hand end. It has two heads covered with skin. Although it differs from the more commonly used north Indian drum, the *tabla*, both in construction and technique of playing, most *Pakhavajis* have studied, and play, some *tabla*. They may even earn their living by teaching *tabla* as today this drum has more varied applications (Misra 1985: 35-6). As noted, Shyamlal, the *Pakhavaji* in the Shri Nathji Haveli, is also employed as the official *tabla* teacher in the music school. Guru Purushottam also taught *tabla* as well as *pakhavaj*. Ghanshyam also combined expertise in both *pakhavaj* and *tabla*; the *Mridang Sagar* described him accompanying *sitar* which he probably did on the *tabla*. The *tabla* dominates north Indian music and is the main rhythmic accompaniment for Kathak dance, as well as several classical and semi-classical vocal styles: *khyal*, *thumri* and *dadra* and the instrumental music of the *sitar*, *sarod*, flute and *sarangi*. The *tabla* is now so ascendent that few *tabla* players find it necessary to learn the *pakhavaj*. Most of the Nathdvara musicians had some rudimentary skills on the *tabla*. But since the *pakhavaj* is still an important instrument in the temples of Nathdvara, it was essential that they had sufficient skill to play it for *darshan*.

Most of the well known *pakhavaj* players in the 1980s were Hindus (Guru Purushottam Das, Raja Chatrapatisingh, Gopal Das, Ayodhya Prasad, Pagal Das, Ramji Sakharam).[16] The *tabla* in contrast, while it has famous exponents from both Hindu and Muslim communities, has Muslim families in the majority (Shepherd 1976; Kippen 1988). Traditionally *Pakhavajis* have been afforded greater respect and status than *tabla* players. A historical explanation may be found in the intimate association of *tabla* with dance and the *tawaif*[17] tradition. The *pakhavaj*, though it has been an important percussion instrument for Kathak dance recitals, is less intimately associated with the dance.

Tabla and *sarangi* are a fixture of daily dance practice and cannot be dispensed with, whereas *pakhavaj* is an extra embellishment. Most miniature paintings of dance, however, include both a *tabla* and a *pakhavaj*. In the modern context of concert performances *tabla* players, who are often famous soloists, are accorded equal, or almost equal status, with the musicians that they accompany. The nature of solo *pakhavaj* playing is generally more controlled, and less flamboyant than the *tabla*. Consequently, with some exceptions, *Pakhavajis* have not yet been accorded the "star" attraction and billing sometimes given to skilled *tabla* players.

PAKHAVAJ DURING *DARSHAN*

During *darshan* in the Shri Nathji Haveli, I observed that the *pakhavaj* was usually played standing. It was slung from the neck or upper back to hang horizontally across the body just below waist level. This permitted the *Pakhavaji* to carry the *pakhavaj* with him and begin playing immediately upon arrival in front of the *nij mandir*. Miniature paintings provide numerous illustrations of playing the *pakhavaj* in this fashion as well as a pair of *tabla* strapped to the body at waist level so that the player is mobile. However, in the concert situation today, both *pakhavaj* and *tabla* are usually played seated on the ground, most often cross-legged, as with all Indian musical instruments. The *pakhavaj* rests horizontally in front of the musician or in his lap. The main use of the *pakhavaj* in the Shri Nathji Haveli is as accompaniment during fourteen of the seventeen occasions on which music is presented. *Pakhavaj* is not normally played solo in the temple, but only to accompany *haveli sangit* or *bin*.

THE EIGHT *PAKHAVAJ'S* IN THE SHRI NATHJI HAVELI

In the *Mridang Vadan*, Guru Purushottam describes some of the *pakhavajs* kept in the Shri Nathji Haveli. The largest, oldest, and most venerated, is the *meghnad*, named after the rumbling of thunder which accompanies the black clouds (*megh*) of the monsoon. While being played, it usually rests on a wooden stand that reaches up to the waist of the performer (MV: 5). The *meghnad pakhavaj* is a festival (*utsav*) instrument. Guru Purushottam reported that it was the custom for it to accompany the music for ten to fifteen minutes during *Raj Bhog darshan*, on those occasions when Shri Nathji is honoured with a *tilak* painted on his forehead. According to Guru Purushottam this occurs during at least ten festivals: Janmashtami, Rakhi Bandhan, Pavitra Ekadasi, Divali, Dussehra, Bhai Bij, Mahaprabhu ka Utsav, Gosain ka Utsav, Annakut and Sarat Purnima.

The *meghnad* is one of eight named *pakhavajs* kept in the Shri Nathji Haveli. All except two (the *meghnad* and *bhandar*) are wrapped in cloth and hung on the wall in *kirtankar gali*. The fingering and technique for playing all of them is the same.

The *Mridang Vadan* gives the measurements in both feet and a less precise term "fingers". The *meghnad* is two feet in circumference, the right hand head measures twelve fingers across and the left hand head, fourteen fingers across. The *meghnad* is reputed to have been looted from a Mughal camp, by a devotee of Shri Nathji who later donated it to the *haveli*. If this story is true, it must be at least two hundred and fifty years old. According to Guru Purushottam it was allowed to deteriorate, but it has been repaired and is now in good shape. The third *pakhavaj* is referred to as the *nal*.[18] It is made of teak and is almost three and one half feet long, and about one and one half feet wide, at its broadest point; the head on the right side is twelve "fingers" across and the head on the left fourteen "fingers" across, the same as the *ghan garaj*, another *pakhavaj* considered to be important. The fourth *pakhavaj*, "screw wala", was presented to the *haveli* by an *acharya* or religious person, from Galata, near Jaipur. It derives its name from the metal screws that are used to adjust the tension in the heads. All other *pakhavajs* are adjusted by means of wooden blocks and leather thongs. In that respect it looks more like a *nal* than a *pakhavaj*. "Screw wala" is slightly smaller than the others with a circumference at its widest spot (*kumbha*) of one foot, the right side measures ten fingers across and the left twelve fingers across. There are two *pakhavajs* known as Baroda Wala, because they were presented by one of the Gosains of Baroda. They are somewhat smaller, and are made of *khaira* (*Dalbergia sissu*) wood. Likewise, "Ahmedabad Wala" was presented to the temple by a Gosain from one of the *havelis* in Ahmedabad. The smallest instrument is *Misri Wala* (the sweet one). As its name suggests, it is considered to produce the sweetest sound and measures about a foot at the *kumbh*. The head on the right side is eight fingers across, and the left is ten fingers across. As the total number of *pakhavajs* comes to eight, we are once again reminded of the significance of the octad, recalling the *ashtachhap*, the eight poet singers of the *sampraday* and the eight musicians of the Shri Nathji Haveli.[19]

For the *darshans* that I attended, the three most frequently used *pakhavajs* were the two from Baroda and *misri Wala*. These are all similar in size to a conventional *pakhavaj* and may be preferred because they are more easily portable than the large festival instruments. I was able to measure them, but not allowed to measure the *meghnad*, which is much larger. I was, however, able to photograph an old *meghnad pakhavaj* that had been retired from temple service and was being kept in a private home.

NAQQARA, DHUMSA AND *DHOL*

Three drums are played in the *naubat/naqqara khana*: *naqqara*, *dhumsa* and *dhol*. The *naqqara* and *dhumsa* come from the military tradition having been used by both the Mughals and Rajputs. They were usually carried into battle while mounted on elephants and horses and used to both inspire and rally the troops. The *dhol*, a semi-classical instrument is generally featured in miniature paintings of dancers and musicians. All the drums played in the temple premises may be played as solo instruments but only the *pakhavaj* is played in art music. The *dhol* is a two-ended drum, similar in shape to a small *pakhavaj*, but with symmetrical ends, and no *shyahi* (black spot). This drum is used throughout north India to accompany folk music and *bhajans*. I did not see it used in Nathdvara and it seems to be less important than the *naqqara* and *dhumsa* in the music of the *naqqara khana*. The latter two drums are both conical, or hemispherical in shape, the skin of the *naqqara* being about eighteen inches in diameter, and the *dhumsa* about twice as large. Both are played with two sticks, the *naqqara* being used generally in pairs. The combination of *naqqara* and *shahnai* is known as *naubat*, hence the orchestra is also referred to as the *naubat khana*. This combination of instruments is very common throughout north India and is played at the entrance of the Shri Nathji Haveli at particular times to announce certain *darshans*. For centuries it has been used for the celebration of marriages and festivals. The Emperor Akbar, in the sixteenth century, kept a celebrated *naubat* which included twenty pairs of *naqqara* (Deva 1987: 68). Once two *dhumsa* were strapped on either side of an elephant and rallied the troops during war. Today they are played to summon devotees on festival days in addition to the *shahnai* and *naqqara*.

DAFF

The *daff* is a festive instrument that is played inside the *haveli*. It is regarded as the simplest of drums, having a circular loop of wood or metal covered with skin on one side. Often small cymbals are attached around the edge of the circular loop so that it looks somewhat like a tambourine (Deva 1978,1987). According to Gosvami (1961: 309) this type of drum originated in Arabia. It is played by beating on the skin with the fingers of the right hand while intermittent strokes are executed with a stick (Hardgrave and Slawek 1988/89: 40).[20] In Nathdvara the *daffs* used are about one metre in circumference.

The *daff* is almost synonymous with spring and is frequently featured in miniature paintings of the celebration of spring which climaxes in Holi. It also forms an integral part of Holi celebrations in Braj according to Growse (1874). In Nathdvara both the specialists who play the *daff*, and the songs they sing are known as *rasiyas*. The *daff* is frequently referred to in devotional poetry.

METAL PERCUSSION INSTRUMENTS

The fourth category of instruments, the *ghana* type, may all be regarded as festive instruments as they are normally played for special celebrations. *Ghana* instruments are made of metal and are struck. Several are spherical such as the *jhanjh* and plate (*timile*). The former are two circular pieces of metal about ten inches in diameter that are held in either hand and struck against each other. These are played in the temple, at certain *darshans* during specific months and for certain festivals. *Jhanjh* are struck together while the plate (*timile*) is struck with a piece of wood. The *jhanjh* are played inside the *haveli* while the plate is played in the *naubat/naqqara khana* during festivals, in particular during the celebrations of Janmashtami, Krishna's birthday.

HAVELI SANGIT, BIN AND *PAKHAVAJ* TRADITIONS IN NATHDVARA

Historically, Nathdvara is renowned for *haveli sangit*, *bin* and *pakhavaj* (MS, MV). We must therefore conclude that the other two instruments presently played in the Shri Nathji temple, *sarangi* and *harmonium*, were introduced later. Neither is mentioned in the *Mridang Sagar* despite the fact that a painting dated at 1883 (Ambalal 1987: 134) illustrates a *sarangi* being played during *darshan* as well as a *tanpura*. While *sarangi* and *harmonium* are today very much a part of the regular musical offerings, in the context of the musical traditions of the *sampraday* they are recent innovations. They are versatile instruments for accompaniment and may have entered the temple tradition because of the interchange between musicians summoned by the Tilkayat to perform in his palace for his pleasure and the practice of visiting musicians presenting their art to Shri Nathji.

Musical accompaniment for *dhrupad-dhamar* was originally provided by the *tanpura*, *bin* and *pakhavaj*. The *bin* is generally no longer used to accompany *dhrupad* or *dhrupad-dhamar*. The Dagar family, which includes *Binkars*, as well as vocalists, may however occasionally include the use of *bin* as accompaniment in a vocal recital. The solo *bin* tradition is continued by the Dagar family among others.

Haveli sangit, as performed today, presents a curious mixture of conventions that are no longer followed by the *dhrupad-dhamar* tradition. *Bin*, once used to accompany *dhrupad*, still accompanies *haveli sangit*, but so do *sarangi* and harmonium. The latter two instruments are also used to accompany *khyal* and light music. The Shri Nathji temple is one of the few temples that still includes a *Binkar*, *Pakhavaji*, *Sarangiya* and harmonium player on their roster of musicians in active service. The recent introduction of *sarangi* as accompaniment to *dhrupad* during the annual *dhrupad melas* was considered by Prem Lata Sharma to be an innovation. Bor (pers. comm.), on the contrary believes that this was reviving an old tradition and *sarangi* was previously used to accompany *dhrupad*.

In the same illustration from Ambalal, mentioned above, the singers are not shown playing cymbals (*jhanjh*); one appears to hold a palmleaf manuscript while another, in the back row, is holding a conch. There appears to be eight musicians in all, joined by other persons privileged to sit in the *darshan* room. Ambalal (1987: 102) also illustrates musicians playing for *Shringar darshan* on a summer's day. Here a

Pakhavaji and a *Binkar* are playing with two singers, one of whom appears to be holding *jhanjh*. The pictures suggest that there has been little change in the complement of eight musicians in the Shri Nathji Haveli over the past century.

The *pakhavaj* is still the percussion instrument used to accompany both instrumental and vocal rendering of *dhrupad-dhamar* and *haveli*. Since the mid-eighteenth century there has been a steady decline in its popularity. This eclipse is linked to the increasing popularity of the vocal genres, *khyal*, and *thumri*, and the instrumental music of *sitar* and *sarod*. The *tabla*, which is better suited to accompany these forms (Wade 1971), is also currently used to accompany music played in the temples in Vrindavan (Wade 1979:113). The predilection of some of the Maharaj for the *pakhavaj* has already been referred to, and may be a major reason why the instrument has persisted in the music of the *sampraday*.

CONCLUSION

The instruments played inside the compound of the *haveli* are completely separate from those played in the *naubat/naqqara khana*. The different parts of the temple (near *nij mandir*, *kirtankar gali*, and throughout the temple compound) and the *naubat khana*; all have their own instruments that are specific to each venue, including some that are used daily and others used only for embellishment at festivals. These differences for both daily and special events appear to derive from the fact that the music of each situation originated from a different source. The music inside the temple owes its purpose and function to the *bhakti* cult and has its origins in Braj. The music at the entrance of the temple in the *naubat khana* seems to have originated as martial music and derives from practices of the royal houses of Rajasthan. Generally speaking, it is true to say that the temple instruments represent those typical of the art music of earlier centuries—this applies particularly to the *pakhavaj* and *bin*. Instruments only recently popularized for classical performance (flute and *shahnai*) are absent inside the temple, as are other instruments considered to be "recent" innovations, in particular the *sitar*. A miniature painting dated at 1883 and illustrated in Plate 11.3 (and also by Ambalal (1987: 134) includes a musician identified as Rancchor Sitariya, son of Devkishan Sarangiya. He is playing a stringed instrument with a single gourd. However, the position in which the instrument is being held and the way in which it is being plucked suggest that he was playing a *tanpura*. As he is identified as a *Sitariya* he no doubt played a *sitar* outside the *haveli*. Even today musicians play several instruments and assist in *darshan* and pre-*darshan* periods in a variety of musical capacities.

The most interesting features of music in Nathdvara, are the use of *bin* and *pakhavaj* and *haveli sangit*. The *bin* and *pakhavaj* have a long history in both secular and religious contexts. One of the unique features of *haveli sangit* is that it combines elements of classical music with the style of popular religious music. The music of Nathdvara presents a fertile field for musicological analysis.

NOTES

1. See Bailey 1980; Nath 1987:137 for photographs of a *naubat khana*.
2. Uma 1990: 216 notes the use of the *naqqara* in south Indian temples.
3. These four categories are also used in an earlier Sanskrit text, the *Natya Shastra* fifth century A.D.; Deva 1975:97-9).
4. The Western terminology for these various categories of instruments is: chordophones (*tata*), membranophones, aerophones (*shushira*) and idiophones (*ghana*) (Fox-Strangeways 1914).
5. Uma (1990: 212) notes that in Tamil Nadu a *sarangi* is played in the temples at Tirunelveli, Tenkasi and Kutralam. Hereditary musicians known as *oduvars* sing and accompany themselves on the *sarangi*.
6. Uma (1990: 212) notes that the *vina* is played in the Shrirangam Temple in Shrirangam Tamil Nadu during the Eksantha *puja*.
7. Strings of early instruments were not of metal but of spun grass (*murja*) or animal sinew (Deva 1977: 81).
8. See Fowke in S.M. Tagore 1965: 129-33.
9. Banerjee (1986: 2) includes an illustration from the Bundi Court dated at the seventeenth century. A man is dancing in the Kathak style in front of the Raja accompanied by a woman playing *pakhavaj*, another woman playing the cymbals, and a man playing the *bin*. All the musicians are standing, a practice that was followed until recently in several styles of dance including Kathak and Bharata Natyam (Gaston 1991a).
10. Rich Hindus in eighteenth century Calcutta kept a *tanpura* "as an object of luxury which they expose frequently in their best rooms" (Hardgrave and Slawek 1988/89: 14).
11. The *shankh* is the notable exception to the general brahmanical prohibition against the use of wind instruments" (Hardgrave and Slawek 1988/89: 10).
12. Another reason might be that the saliva produced when playing the flute is

polluting. A picture of a brahmin playing the flute by blowing it from his nostrils is illustrated in Hardgrave and Slawek 1988/89.

13. Some examples of professional Hindustani flautists are Pannalal Ghosh, Raghunath Seth, Hariprasad Chaurasia, Devinder Murdeshwar and G.S. Sachdev. See also Sorrell 1980: 35.
14. See Sankaran 1990: 33-40.
15. New Grove 1980: 132, *Natya Shastra* translated by Ghosh: chapter 33.
16. See Misra 1985: 35-6 for details about Pandit Sakharam's life.
17. See Bor (1987) for further elaboration on the stigma attached to certain instruments because of their association with the dancing traditions. It is curious that although the *pakhavaj* is played for dance the instrumentalists who play it have never suffered the same opprobrium as *tabla* and *sarangi* players.
18. *Nal* is also the name of another type of drum, which can be confusing.
19. The significance of the number eight for *darshans*, *ashtachhap*, *pakhavajs* etc is explained further in Entwistle 1987.
20. Hardgrave and Slawek 1988/89: 57 illustrate an octagonal *daff* from Rajasthan known as a *dampha*.

Plate 5.1: Vallabhdas, Binkar, Shri Nathji Haveli (1985)

Plate 5.2: Amritlal, Sarangiya, Shri Nathji Haveli (1985)

Plate 5.3: The Meghnad Pakhavaj

This ***meghnad pakhavaj*** is no longer played in the Shri Nathji Haveli. It is now kept in a private home. Pyarelal is seated behind.

Plate 5.4: Lord Vitthalnathji in his garden pavilion mid-eighteenth century

The image of Vitthalnathji is in a separate temple in Nathdvara. Here a garden has been created by decorating it with plantain leaves. The musicians are standing facing each other. There is a *Pakhavaji* and three *jhanjh* players. Usually the musicians sit in this area. The Maharaj of the Vitthalnathji Haveli stands on the left and is holding the lamp for *arati*. The presence of at least four Maharaj suggests that one may be the Tilkayat. The *jhapatiyas* hold strips of cloth with which they strike the pilgrims if they wish them to move on or they become unruly. I celebrated the spring festival (Holi) in Nathdvara in 1985. In this painting the dress, the arrangement of the figures, and the ambience in which spring is celebrated in Nathdvara are captured. This painting is from the collection of Amit Ambalal 1987: 98,152. He writes: "Devotees welcome this (a blow from a *jhapatiya*) as they believe that a *jhapat* striking them rids them of sin."

CHAPTER 6

The Music of the Nathdvara *Havelis*

The Nathdvara musicians stated that *haveli sangit* was closely related to the art music form, *dhrupad-dhamar*. It is generally accepted that both *haveli* and *dhrupad-dhamar* evolved from an earlier musical form, *prabandha* (Deva 1974: 47, Sharma 1970b), and both share many musical characteristics. Nevertheless, *haveli sangit* is a religiously inspired genre in which enthusiasm and devotion are more important than musical intricacy. As a result, *haveli sangit*, as performed in the temples of Nathdvara is simpler and more straightforward than *dhrupad-dhamar*.

Dhrupad-dhamar is undergoing a renaissance and interest in it is considerable both in India and abroad. In the arrangement and presentation of concerts it is modernizing. The new wave of interest has also led to notation of the music (Srivastava 1980).

DEVELOPMENT OF *DHRUPAD-DHAMAR* AND *HAVELI*

Raja Mansingh's court at Gwalior (1486-1525) is remembered as an important musical centre in the development of north Indian music (Te Nijenhuis 1974: 84; Van Der Meer 1980: 31). It was there that important musical changes that had been taking place coalesced and the *dhrupad-dhamar* style emerged. The dissemination of the court genre of music, *darbari-dhrupad*, was given considerable impetus by a major political event in the history of India. In 1526, Raja Vikramaditya, son of Raja Mansingh of Gwalior, joined forces with Ibrahim Lodhi at the battle of Panipat. They were defeated by the Mughal, Babar. The Gwalior court disintegrated. Its associated musicians were forced to find other patrons and they dispersed all over north India, taking with them their music, in particular the *dhrupad-dhamar* genre. Some went to temples and ashrams at various religious centres such as Vrindavan and Mathura; others sought royal patronage in both Hindu and Mughal courts.

Dhrupad drew enthusiastic support from the Mughal emperors. The most famous of all *dhrupad* performers and composers, Miyan Tansen (*c.* 1520-95) had Akbar (1556-1605) as his patron. Mughal patronage continued under Jahangir (1605-27), Shah Jahan (1627-58), and Aurangzeb (1658-1707), generally regarded by historians as being intolerant of the arts, gave patronage to several leading musicians.

The Vallabha Sampraday was founded in this political and artistic climate incorporating music as part of the ritual (Barz 1976; Bennett 1983). The *sampraday* had close links with both Hindu and Mughal courts. Commencing with Maharaj Vitthalnath, the life-style of the head of the sect was intended to reflect the same grandeur and refinement of its secular counterparts. *Dhrupad* would have been probably performed for the personal entertainment of the head of the *sampraday*.

The formal setting provided by the royal courts, with their lavish patronage and discerning audiences gave the impetus for *dhrupad-dhamar* to develop greater complexity. Audiences devoted their full attention to the appreciation of the music (Wade 1979: 159-69). This is contrasted to the present situation in the Shri Nathji Haveli, presumably unchanged from earlier times, where music is only one of several forms of devotional offerings taking place simultaneously. The *haveli sangit* tradition that remains today is confined to performance mainly in a religious context (Srivastava 1980: 22-6).

Both *dhrupad* and *haveli* songs are generally in *Brajbhasa*, (Srivastava 1980), a dialect of Hindi which, through its association with the mythology of Braj as Krishna's birthplace, became an important literary dialect from the fifteenth to the nineteenth centuries. *Brajbhasa* still exists as the spoken vernacular of Braj. The word *dhrupad* is the Hindi derivative of the Sanskrit, *dhruvapada*, *dhruva* in this context meaning structured, fixed or rigid, and *pada* a word or syllable. The name *dhrupad* is indicative of the importance of its literary content. Present-day *haveli sangit* gives even greater importance to the text (Srivastava 1980). As it is concert presentations of *dhrupad* tend to emphasize the musical content with a greater elaboration of the *raga*.

The text in *dhrupad* songs is more varied than in *haveli* songs, most of which recount episodes in the life of Krishna. It is a fundamental belief of the Vallabha Sampraday that all beings have the potential for a unique experience with Krishna (Barz 1976: 87-90). First, however, they must be receptive and believe that the stories which surround his mythology and are recorded in the texts are a result of divine inspiration. The poetry in the songs awakens this potential by helping devotees to visualise themselves as actually participating in the life of Krishna. Language and music create the scene and the listeners are transported to the sacred land of Braj (Barz 1976: 98-100). On the rare occasions when the musicians in the employ of the Nathdvara *havelis* perform outside, they recite the text of the song before it is sung, so that the audience can savour the poetry and its metre.

Though *dhrupad* and *haveli sangit* share the same rules, the latter does not include all the components demanded by *dhrupad*. In a *dhrupad* performance there are two distinct sections: *alap*, which is sung to meaningless syllables, without rhythmic accompaniment, and *dhrupad*, the text or composition, which is set to a *tala* and accompanied by percussion, normally on the *pakhavaj*. Although the word *dhrupad* strictly refers only to the composition, virtually all modern performances include a prolonged *alap*, so that it has become common to refer to the entire exposition, including the *alap*, as *dhrupad*.

The late Zia Mohinuddin Dagar (1934-89) (pers. comm.), a recognized exponent of the instrumental style of playing *dhrupad* on the *bin*, was adamant that *haveli sangit* was not *dhrupad-dhamar*. He based his objection on the lack of systematic development of musical ideas (*raga*) in *haveli sangit*. Likewise solo *bin* recitals, as performed in public today, derive from a court tradition which is unlike that of the present *Binkars* in Nathdvara.

The Dagar family to which Zia Mohinuddin belonged were aware that temple music in the hands of trained musicians could be of as high a standard as art music. They did not think that Guru Purushottam was devaluing his skill by accompanying *haveli sangit*, even though such songs might call for little skill. Guru Purushottam himself noted that *haveli sangit* was often presented without rhythmic complexity. He attributed this to the musicians' lack of musical training, not to lack of potential in the *haveli sangit* genre.

RAGA[1]

Understanding Indian music depends upon being conversant with two concepts: *raga* and *tala*. *Raga* has been loosely defined as a musical idea; its essence is that it must embody a certain atmosphere, which is achieved by the treatment, and use of certain intervals and notes (Van der Meer 1980: 5). According to Van der Meer there are fifty to seventy well known *ragas*, and two hundred that are heard from time to time; after a great deal of digging one might come up with five hundred.

The number of *ragas* with which a musician is familiar is less important than the depth and understanding with which he expounds them. It was said, for example, about Bhimsen Joshi, one of the most famous north Indian vocalists:

> It is well known that he (Bhimsen Joshi) has a limited repertoire and likes to confine himself to four *ragas*. His answer is that ... "these *ragas* suit my temperament and style of singing. Each time I sing them, I approach them with fresh inspiration. So the varieties I create are always different. Then where is the question of repetition?" (Sehgal 1989: 87).

Even amongst those *ragas* that are heard regularly their distinguishing features are sometimes subtle.

Raga has no English equivalent. Though the word is often roughly translated as "scale", it is much more than that. The musician-scholar Nazir Jairazbhoy, has defined the *raga* concept as containing five main elements: scale, ascending and descending line, translucence, emphasized notes and register, intonation and obligatory embellishments (Jairazbhoy 1971: 45). Because many of the characteristics of particular *ragas* are complex and subtle, they are hard to learn from written instructions. The *raga* system may be a major reason why Indian classical music is still, for the most part, an oral tradition. Certainly, the subtleties required to produce Indian music appear to defy complete codification.

The songs of *haveli sangit* are usually sung to a prescribed *raga* and *tala* suggested by the composer. In addition, the collective song books used by the Nathdvara musicians recommend the relevant *darshan* for each song. Two of the many factors that determine when a *raga* will be performed in classical Hindustani music are, the time of day, and season of the year. Within the context of the ritual during which *haveli sangit* is sung, the time and season are important considerations, not only for the music, but also for other things such as decoration, food and the physical comforts given to the deity. *Haveli sangit* conforms to the same aesthetic considerations that determine *ragas* in the classical styles of *dhrupad-dhamar*, but neither the manner in which the *ragas* are rendered, nor their names correspond to current classical Hindustani music (pers. comm. Mukund Lath). It may be that the

Nathdvara tradition diverged gradually from the main stream of Hindustani music over the centuries of comparative isolation. It is equally likely that some or all of the differences are due to the preservation in Nathdvara of archaic forms now superseded elsewhere. The subject calls for further musicological research.

As the *raga* used for a particular song is prescribed by the composer, the *ragas* used in *haveli sangit* depend on the choice of song. Certain *ragas* were considered suitable for particular *darshans* but these varied according to the musician I consulted. No one was able to tell me exactly how songs were selected. I was left with the impression that there were no fixed rules and that the *Kirtankar Mukhiya* exercised considerable discretion.

For the period of 20-7 December 1983 I obtained a complete record of the first songs sung for each *darshan* (Table 6.1). More than sixty compositions by twenty-four different composers were sung. A little over half (thirty-five) were compositions attributed to the *ashtachhap*, although none composed by Kumbhandas (the prescribed composer for *Raj Bhog*), or Nanddas (prescribed for *Shringar*) were sung. Only four of the songs were by the composer considered appropriate to that particular *darshan*; two by Chhitsvami during *Arati*, one by Krishnadas during *Shayan* and one by Chaturbhujdas during *Bhog*. Essentially the choice of composer seemed random with respect to the particular *darshan* (Table 6.3). The variety of songs and composers makes it clear that the musicians do not simply repeat a small number of favoured songs, but explore extensively within the repertoire of the *sampraday*.

Among the *ragas* to which the songs were set, nearly one quarter were in *raga sarang*, which was the dominant *raga* at *Raj Bhog* and *Utthapan*. The next most common were: *Raga Bhilawal* which was used for *Mangal*, *Shringar*, and *Gval*, although on only four days; *Raga Asaveri*, used for *Shringar*, *Gval* and *Raj Bhog* and *Raga Kanhara*, used for *Mangal*, *Arati* and *Shayan*. Other *ragas* were not used more than five times. *Raga Naiki*, used only three times, was only employed for *Shayan*.

TALA

Tala is a structured metric cycle. All compositions sung or played to percussion accompaniment are set to a specific *tala*. In both *dhrupad-dhamar* and *haveli sangit* the rhythmic accompaniment is provided by the *pakhavaj* which usually maintains a single *tala* throughout the four musical divisions of *sthayi, antara, sanchari* and *abhog* (Te Nijenhuis 1974: 81; Van der Meer 1980: 30-49). These sections will include the poetry or *pada*. Each section is completed within one or more rounds of the *tala* to which it has been set.

The musical characteristics of *dhamar* and *dhrupad* are so close that the style is often called *dhrupad-dhamar*. The term *dhrupad* is used in a broad sense to include compositions in a variety of *talas*, the most popular today being 12 (*chau*) (P.L. Sharma 1988) and to a lesser extent 10 (*jhap* and *sulphakta*) and 8 (*adi*) (Te Nijenhuis 1974: 80). *Dhamar* is sung exclusively in 14 beats (*dhamar tala*).

Despite the assertions of the musicians that *haveli sangit* and *dhrupad* are closely related, there is considerable difference in the use of different *talas*. Classical *dhrupad* favours *chau tala* over other rhythms, whereas *haveli sangit* favours songs in various *talas*: *rupak* (7), *dhamar* (14), *charchari* (10) and *adi* (8). I analyzed the *talas* used for *haveli sangit* in the Shri Nathji Haveli during the week of 20-7 December 1983 (Table 6.1). Only one was in *chau tala*, the preferred *tala* for *dhrupad*, while most (75 per cent) were in *dhamar* (14) or *rupak* (7). In *dhrupad-dhamar*, *dhamar tula* is used only for *hori-dhamar*. *Rupak tala*, being in seven beats, is very similar in structure. The co-incidence between the *talas* used in *haveli sangit* and those used in *hori-dhamar* may not be accidental.

The poetic content of *dhrupad* is varied and includes songs in praise of various deities as well as secular themes (Srivastava 1980; Wade 1979: 161-7). *Dhamar* usually describes the love sports of Krishna. It is particularly popular during the festival of Holi, and is often called *hori-*(*holi-*)*dhamar*. *Haveli sangit* chooses themes which centre around the exploits of Krishna, both as a child and a lover. It seems that songs in seven, or its multiples, are particularly appropriate to the theme of Krishna.

ALAP

A *raga* is rendered beginning with *alap*, which has no predictable metre and no formal rhythmic cycle (*tala*). Unhampered by the text of the song, or any pre-composed musical pattern, it introduces the *raga*, allowing it to unfold in a leisurely manner. In a *dhrupad* performance, *alap* is essential and precedes the text (the true *dhrupad*). It can be as long as, or longer than, the rhythmic rendering of the text (Srivastava 1980:47,50). The Dagar family's style of *dhrupad* features *alap* which is much longer than the structured section of the song. The late Fayazuddin Dagar explained the concept of *alap* in his tradition: "The *alap* of *dhrupad* is distinguished from *alap* of other forms in several ways. It is very long in terms of the length of the entire composition. It is in fact treated, not as the introduction to the composition, but as its focal point" (Joshi 1989: 63-64).

Alap starts in slow tempo in the lower octaves and gradually moves into the middle and upper registers. It develops a recognizable metered pulse before it arrives at the structured composition, the *dhrupad*.

The music sung in the Nathdvara Havelis contains little or no *alap*. According to the Nathdvara musicians, the lack of a lengthy *alap* is the chief structural difference between *dhrupad* and *haveli sangit*. The latter, as performed in the temples of Nathdvara, usually begins with a very short *alap* lasting about eight seconds, before proceeding immediately to the actual poetry. On those occasions when the *alap* is longer it generally occurs in the middle of the song, as a manifestation of ecstatic outpouring. This practice is often followed when *haveli sangit* is sung in the concert situation.

PERFORMING *HAVELI SANGIT*

Because *alap* is short for *haveli sangit*, *pakhavaj* accompaniment is played virtually throughout the piece. When *haveli sangit* is presented in a concert, rather than a temple setting, a longer *alap* precedes it with the same rules as for *dhrupad* being followed. In October 1982, when several musicians from Vrindavan visited Nathdvara on pilgrimage, they held a musical soiree with the resident musicians. The venue was great hall beside the Shri Nathji temple and part of the Vallabha cottage *dharamsala* complex. An extensive *alap* was then presented with typical *haveli* songs. It would thus appear that the length and development of *alap* is determined more by the situation than by the demands of the music itself. Some of the musicians at least are capable of delivering a fairly lengthy *alap*. They simply do not sing it in the *haveli*, where the lyrics are paramount over the *raga*.

ACCOMPANYING *HAVELI SANGIT*[2]

Ghanshyam wrote: "The *tala* structure is the same for singing and drumming, the singer informs the drummer where to be careful ... when the singer raises his voice that is the most difficult time for a *Pakhavaji*" (MS Pr:5).

He was probably referring to vocalists becoming so engrossed in their music that they failed to adhere to the *tala*. Ghanshyam also gave a few hints for accompanying musicians. In particular, at the beginning of the piece a *Pakhavaji* should begin to accompany vocal by playing the combination of three basic sounds (*aksharas*), "dhe na na ka". Ghanshyam also suggested specific compositions (*peshkar*) especially suitable for accompaniment. After completing pieces of the *peshkar* variety, the *Pakhavaji* should then increase the rhythmic density by playing the combination of sounds "dhe na na ka" at one and a half times the former speed, but maintaining the same *laya* (underlying rhythm). This is known as *de'orhi* (Kippen 1988: 207). It is essential that the time taken for one cycle of the *tala* remains the same. At the beginning of the next *tala* cycle (*sam*), the *Pakhavaji* should increase the rhythmic density to double the original speed (*dugan*); and at the next *tala* cycle, to three times the underlying speed (*tigun*). This is to be followed by another type of fixed composition (*paran*), played first three times the original tempo (*tigun*), and then four times the original tempo (*chaugan*).

Ghanshyam was disparaging of the situation regarding musicians and accompanists: "The singer and the drummer no longer put effort into this [rehearsals]" (MS Pr: 5). One consequence of this was a lack of coordination between musicians. He describes, in a surprisingly irreverent manner, the activities of certain accompanists:

> ... striking *thap*[3] [or *thapi*, a particular stroke of the right hand] whenever the singer sings 'a'. The *Pakhavaji* watches the singer's mouth and then does *thap* when the singer sings 'ham'. But suppose the drummer does not beat the drum at *sam*, then he waits for the whole thing to be repeated and the next time he does it (Ms Pr: 5).

Blaming both the musician and the *Pakhavaji* for this hit and miss approach to accompaniment, Ghanshyam remarked: "both of these people deceive the listeners and are not honest". He lamented that the public was partly to blame because it did not demand professional integrity: "many players and singers have done this [practised conscientiously] ... others have not and this does not seem to affect the number of concerts they have" (MS Pr: 5).

Ghanshyam does not give a clear outline of how best to proceed and build up confidence when attempting to accompany singers and instrumentalists. He concludes rather abruptly: "Only this much will I write." It appears that much is left to the percussionist to adapt and modify set rhythmic compositions (*paran*, *peshkar*) and combinations of sounds (*aksharas/matras*). The overriding principle is that the end result should be aesthetically pleasing to the ear.

I analyzed a considerable amount of music that I had recorded of *haveli sangit*. I concluded that in practice it was uncommon for Guru Purushottam, when accompanying either vocal or instrumental music, to play fixed *pakhavaj* compositions. The only occasion on which he might choose to do this was when the vocalist or instrumentalist repeated certain sections (*sthayi* or *antara*) of the composition without elaboration. The predictability of the music allows the *Pakhavaji* to play pre-arranged compositions, embellishing and improvising on their rhythmic structures.

It is often difficult to differentiate between what is improvised and what is from the fixed repertoire as much of the music and drumming involves reorganizing previous patterns (Sorrell 1980). At this time the *tala* structure is very clear, freeing the *Pakhavaji* to play long sequences that would be too complicated when he is called upon to adjust to the demands of the singer. The spontaneous nature of the drumming here is termed *upaj*. The general guidelines for *upaj* are that the drummer must play in the *tala* of the piece and anticipate when the singer will end on *sam*. Guru Purushottam translated *upaj* as "idea or imagination", as here the *Pakhavaji* must exercise all his creativity. The drummer as musician is challenged; he must be sensitive to the nuances of the music while still being sufficiently in control of the *tala*. As the singer approaches a crescendo, the *Pakhavaji* must create a rhythmic sequence that will culminate with that of the music. This is done by increasing the rhythmic density and repeating a particular pattern three times. The technical term for this is *tihai*. Much of the initial training centres on memorizing *tihais*; from this comes the ability to manipulate them on the spot. *Upaj* cannot be taught directly but certain combinations lend themselves to improvisation. At first these are reproduced by rote and then, with practice, particular phrases may be added or taken away as desired.

Although the singers generally allow their accompanists a short segment to demonstrate their skills, in concert performances of *dhrupad* such periods of time are relatively short compared to those given to the exposition of the *raga*. The overall time in which the *pakhavaj* is actually played during a recital of *dhrupad-dhamar* is generally no more than one-third of the total performance. In *haveli sangit* the *Pakhavaji* accompanies for a much larger proportion of the time.

The relatively short duration of the percussion accompaniment in *dhrupad-dhamar* does not diminish the importance of a good accompanist, as the *Pakhavaji* must respond to the music rhythmically and inspire the singer. Anticipation is the key when accompanying.[4] In a performance there is cooperation between the vocalist and the drummer for the first part of the improvisation. To generate excitement, false endings can be thrown in by the vocalist, which the drummer is expected to follow. Because of the nature of the music no performance situation reproduces exactly *pakhavaj* lessons that are taught. Lessons are intended only to give mastery over correct sound production, *tala*, *laya*, and acceptable combinations of drum syllables.

CONCLUSION

My investigations into the music presented in the Shri Nathji Haveli indicated that it is not nearly as formalized as one might expect of ritual music. The texts of the songs, of course, are fixed and recorded in song books which are kept by the *kirtankars*. The choice of songs for particular *darshans* is, however, not dictated entirely by considerations of composer or *raga*. Nor is it simply that the choice has narrowed down to a small range of familiar songs. There was no indication that the musicians had any special expectations, or that they might be able to anticipate what was to be sung next. Clearly the *darshan* involved, the season, and the occurrence of festivals, had significant influence on the choice of songs. But within these constraints there appeared to be considerable latitude. Like most other events occurring within the *haveli* there was an element of inexactitude and spontaneity about the songs.

The range of composers used is very large, with twenty-four represented in a sample of sixty songs sung in one eight-day period. The compositions of the *ashtachhap* are important, but by no means dominant, in the repertoire. The most uniform feature of the music was the dominance of *talas* in 7 (*rupak*) and 14 (*dhamar*). These rhythms were generally presented in a sprightly, rather than sedate manner, making them a suitable format for the very enthusiastic renderings which were characteristic of the singing. The music seems appropriate for a sect which emphasizes an optimistic outlook without recourse to penance or asceticism.

TABLE 6.1: *RAGAS, TALAS*, AND COMPOSERS OF *HAVELI SANGIT* IN THE SHRI NATHJI HAVELI RECORDED IN DECEMBER 1983.

Darshan	Time	*Raga*	*Tala*	Composer
		TUESDAY, DECEMBER 20,1983.		
Mangal	03.45-04.15	Bhairav	*	+Parmananddas
Shringar	07.00-07.20	Dhanashri	Adi(8)	+Parmananddas
Gval	Did not take place due to preparations for *Chhapan Bhog* at *Raj Bhog*			
Raj Bhog	12.30-13.30	Sarang	Charchari(10)	Krishnadas
Utthapan	16.15-16.30	Sarang	Dhamar(14)	Manikchand
Bhog	17.15-17.40	Nat Kalayan	Rupak(7) Dhamar(14)	Sagundas ++Chhitsvami
Arati	*BHOG* and *ARATI* were combined into one *darshan*)			
Shayan	19.15-19.30	Behag	Dhamar(14)	Vagdhish
Shayan was not open for the public until Dec. 27,1983				
		WEDNESDAY, DECEMBER 21, 1983		
Mangal	05.15-05.30	Ramkali	Dhamar(14)	+Surdas
Shringar	06.45-07.00	Bilaval	Dhamar(14)	Madhodas
Gval	08.15-08.30	Sarang	Dhamar(14)	Madhodas
Raj Bhog	10.00-10.45	Sarang	Charchari(10)	Vishnudas
Utthapan	15.45-16.00	Sarang	Charchari(10)	Vallabhdas

Darshan	Time	*Raga*	*Tala*	Composer
Bhog	16.15-16.30	Sarang	Rupak(7)	Madhodas
Arati	17.00-17.30	Kalayan	Dhamar(14)	++Chhitsvami
Shayan	18.45-18.55	Naiki	Rupak(7)	Vitthaldas
		THURSDAY, DECEMBER 22,1983		
Mangal	05.00-05.15	Bilaval	*	+Chhitsvami
Shringar	06.50-07.10	Devgandhar	Rupak(7)	+Chaturbhuj
Gval	08.00-08.15	"	"	"
Raj Bhog	10.00-10.30	Sarang	Dhamar(14)	+Chhitsvami
Utthapan	15.45-16.00	Sarang	Dhamar(14)	+Chhitsvami
Bhog	16.05-16.25	Gauri	Adi(8)	+Chhitsvami
Arati	16.55-17.30	Nat	Rupak(7)	Sagundas
Shayan	19.00-19.10	Kanhara	Dhamar(14)	++Krishnadas
		FRIDAY, DECEMBER 23, 1983		
Mangal	05.00-05.30	Bilaval	*	+Krishnadas
Shringar	06.50-07.10	Bilaval	Dhamar(14)	Sagundas
Gval	08.00-08.15	Bilaval	Dhamar(14)	+Surdas
Raj Bhog	10.10-10.45	Asavari	Dhamar(14)	Manikchand
Utthapan	15.45-16.00	Sarang	Dhamar(14)	Haridas
Bhog	16.15-16.30	Dhanashri	Rupak(7)	Hari-jivan
Arati	17.00-17.30	Kanhara	Dhamar(14)	+Chaturbhuj
Shayan	19.10-19.20	Yaman	Dhamar(14)	Navallal

Darshan	Time	*Raga*	*Tala*	Composer
		SATURDAY DECEMBER 24,1983		
Mangal	05.15-05.45	Devgandhar	Dhamar(14)	+Chaturbhujdas
Shringar	07.00-07.15	Bilaval	Dhamar(14)	+Krishnadas
Gval	08.00-08.20	Bilaval	Dhamar(14)	+Surdas
Raj Bhog	10.15-10.45	Sarang	Charchari(10)	+Krishnadas
Utthapan	15.30-15.45	Sarang	Charchari(10)	+Krishnadas
Bhog	16.10-16.30	Gauri	Adi(8)	+Chhitsvami
Arati	17.15-17.40	Yaman	Dhamar(14)	Govinddas
Shayan	19.10-19.20	Kanhara	Dhamar(14)	+Chhitsvami
		SUNDAY, DECEMBER 25, 1983		
Mangal	05.10-05.35	Ramkali	*	Vitthalesh
Shringar	07.00-07.15	Asavari	Dhamar(14)	+Parmananddas
Gval	07.55-08.15	"	"	+ "
Raj Bhog	10.05-10.50	Sarang	Charcari(10)	Vishnudas
Utthapan	15.45-15.55	Sarang	Charchari(10)	Manikchand
Bhog	16.15-16.30	Gauri	Dhamar(14)	Nija-Jan
Arati	17.00-17.30	Kanhara	Dhamar(14)	Haridas
Shayan	19.00-19.10	Naiki	Rupak(7)	Vitthaldas
		MONDAY, DECEMBER 26,1983		
Mangal	04.45-05.10	Ramkali	Rupak(7)	+Krishnadas
Shringar	06.45-07.00	Ramkali	Adi(8)	Askaran

Darshan	Time	*Raga*	*Tala*	Composer
Gval	08.00-08.15	"	"	"
Raj Bhog	10.00-10.45	Asavari	Rupak(7)	Dhandhi
Utthapan	15.45-16.00	Sarang	Dhamar(14)	+Parmananddas
Bhog	16.15-16.30	Nat	Rupak(7)	++Chaturbhujdas
Arati	17.10-17.40	Adana	Rupak(7)	Narayanadas
Shayan	19.00-19.10	Kanhara	Dhamar(14)	+Parmananddas
		TUESDAY, DECEMBER 27, 1983		
Mangal	05.00-05.30	Kanhara	*	Shribhatt
Shringar	07.00-07.30	Asavari	Adi(8)	+Govinddas
Gval	08.00-08.15	Asavari	Dhamar(14)	+Surdas
Raj Bhog	10.10-10.40	Sarang	Dhamar(14)	Rasik
Utthapan	15.30-15.45	Sarang	Dhamar(14)	+Parmananddas
Bhog	16.00-16.15	Dhanasri	Rupak(7)	Mukund
Arati	17.05-17.20	Nat	Rupak(7)	Vishnudas
Shayan	19.00-19.10	Naiki	Chau(12)	+Chhitsvami

One song was recorded for each *darshan*. For the pre-*Mangal* and post-*Shayan* periods, the *bin* was played solo.

* = no *pakhavaj* accompaniment; + = an *ashtachhap* composer

++ = the *ashtachhap* was the recognized composer for that *darshan*

TABLE 6.2: ANALYSIS OF COMPOSERS, *RAGAS* AND *TALAS* IN MUSIC PERFORMED IN THE SHRI NATHJI HAVELI (20-27 DECEMBER 1983)

Composer	Frequency	
Aksaran:	1	
+Chaturbhuj	5+	(the *ashtachhap* for *Bhog Darshan*)
+Chitsvami	9+	(the *ashtachhap* for *Arati Darshan*)

Composer	Frequency	
+Govinddas	2+	(the *ashtachhap* for *Gval Darshan*)
Haridas	2	
Harijivan	1	
+Krishnadas	7+	(the *ashtachhap* for *Shayan Darshan*)
Mandadas	1	
Manikchand	3	
Mukund	1	
+Nanddas	1+	(the *ashtachhap* for *Shringar darshan*)
Narayandas	1	
Nijajan	1	
Navallal	1	
+Parmananddas	7+	(the *ashtachhap* for *Mangal Darshan*)
Rasik	1	
Sagun Das	3	
Shri Bhatt	1	
+Surdas	4+	(the *ashtachhap* for *Utthapan Darshan*)
Vagesh	1	
Vallabhdas	1	
Vishnudas	1	
Vitthaldas	4	
Vitthalesh	1	
Total number of composers	24	

Ragas played and their Frequency	
Adana	1
Asaveri	6
Bhairav	2
Bihag	1
Bilaval	7
Devgandhar	3
Dhanashri	3
Gauri	3
Kalayan	2
Kanhara	6
Naiki	3
Nat	4
Ramkali	5
Sarang	15
Yaman	2
Total *ragas* played	15

Talas	
Adi or Tin (8 or 16)	6
Charchari (10)	7
Dhamar (14)	29
Rupak (7)	13
Chau (12)	1
Total number of *talas*	5

N.B. Some discrepancies between these tables is accounted for by the fact that not all information could be obtained for every song.

TABLE 6.3: ANALYSIS OF *ASHTACHHAP* COMPOSITIONS IN RELATION TO THE *DARSHANS* IN WHICH THEY WERE PERFORMED

Ashtachhap	*Darshan*							
	Mangal	Shringar	Gval	Raj Bhog	Utthapan	Bhog	Arati	Shayan
Parmananddas	1*	2	1		2			1
Nanddas		*						
Govinddas		1	*					
Kumbhandas				*				
Surdas	1		3		*			
Chaturbujdas	1	1	1			1*	1	
Chitsvami	1			1	1	3	1*	
Krishnadas	2	1		2	1			1*

* *Darshan* for which this is the recognized composer

NOTES

1. See Te Nijenhuis 1974: 1-12 for reference to description of *raga* in early texts.
2. For further examples of *pakhavaj* accompaniment for *dhrupad* see Van der Meer 1980: 222-47.
3. *Thap* refers to the stroke known as *thapi*. This is the most important stroke on the *pakhavaj* and is usually played to emphasize a point in the music such as *sam*. It marks a coming together of the vocal and percussion music.
4. See Van der Meer 1980, for some simple combinations suggested by Guru Purushottam.

CHAPTER 7

The Musicians

THE MUSICIANS OF NATHDVARA

With one exception, all the musicians employed by the Nathdvara temples during the 1980s were born in the town. Although a few travelled occasionally to other centres to perform, either in temples, in public, or on All India Radio, only Guru Purushottam had become a recognized artist of national stature. The status of musicians in Nathdvara has not undergone the changes that have been observed by Higgins (1976) with regard to classical musicians in Madras: "... a respectability that leads to the recruitment of musical specialists from a wide variety of backgrounds" (Higgins 1976: 4). Nevertheless, one or two prominent vocalists elsewhere in India have recently added *haveli sangit* to their repertoire and this should help to raise the status of the form. As *haveli* music is essentially a genre specific to a certain setting, the musicians are not making the same claims as Karnatic musicians: "Many carnatic[1] musicians wished to say that their music was equal to the western, capable of being international, available to the world. But this meant admitting that music was essentially something technical, something to be learned by anyone willing to apply himself" (Nettl 1985: 7).

Because of the emotive quality of the songs and the necessity of appreciating the subtle nuances in Krishna's life the poetry in *haveli sangit* remains tied to its cultural context. Krishna is praised in song all over India, but the music of the Nathdvara temples remains distinct. It has evolved to provide a specific effect, as part of a tradition that has continued in comparative isolation for many generations of hereditary specialists.

THE MUSICIANS WHO PLAY IN THE *HAVELIS*: THE *KIRTANKARS*

The musicians who play within the *haveli* during *darshan* are known as *kirtankars*. They appear to have no links by marriage, either with the musicians in the *naubat khana* or with personnel of the military band. Those *kirtankars* who were in active service in the Nathdvara *havelis* during the 1980s belonged to seven families closely interlinked by marriage. Aside from musicians, these families included watch and clock repairers, tailors, makers of *picchvai* and other decorative objects (*shringar*, *mukut*), building contractors, stenographers and farmers; several of the younger generation included college graduates, medical doctors, teachers and businessmen. The group exhibits tendencies common to Indian society as a whole, with increasing educational attainments and a diversification of employment.

While there are seven divisions of *kirtankars* (Table 7.1), they belong to only two communities: *kumavat* and *brahmin*. Six of the families are *kumavat*.[2] The sole *sanadhya brahmin* family traces its origins to Braj, as does one *kumavat* family. The other five *kumavat* families are of Rajasthani origin. The *sanadhya brahmins* remain separate; the *kumavats* intermarry, irrespective of their geographical origin. One example of *kumavat* intermarriage is Guru Purushottam's daughter, Radha. Guru Purushottam's ancestors come from Jaipur, Rajasthan (Das 1911: 1-5). Damodar, Radha's husband is a *Brajvasi*.[3] Their son, Prakash has recently married a Rajasthani from Jaipur whose family, though *kumavat*, has no connection with music.

Brajvasis from the one division of *kumavats* (*jalandhara*) and the *sanadhya brahmins* trace their origins to various villages in Braj such as Gantholi (Entwistle 1987: 144) and Karahla/Karahala (Growse 1874; Hein 1972: 224; Entwistle 1987). Their ancestors arrived in Nathdvara at its foundation. There are examples of more recent immigration as well. Kisanlal, a *sanadhya* (*haveli sangit*, NNP), whose family had lived in Nathdvara, was brought up in Braj and returned to Nathdvara to seek employment. The family of Mathuradas (*kumavat* from the *Parihar* division), the former *Kirtankar Mukhiya* of the Shri Nathji temple, also arrived at a later date, from Chaupasni, Rajasthan, where he and his relatives had been serving in the *haveli* of the *sampraday* (Jindel 1976: 95; Verdia 1982: 50). Mathuradas' two sons, Ramdas and Amritlal, were employed in the Shri Nathji temple—Ramdas as *Kirtankar Mukhiya*, succeeding his father, and Amritlal as a *sarangi* player.

TABLE 7.1 THE SEVEN DIVISIONS OF *KIRTANKARS* (SEE ALSO APPENDIX)
KUMAVATS (SIX DIVISIONS)

From Braj (One Kumavat Division)

1. Jalandhara (from Gantholi, Braj, U.P.)
   Shri Nathji Haveli:
      Asst. *Kirtankar Mukhiya*: Tolaram
      Haveli sangit: Pannalal
      Binkar: Vallabhdas
   Navnitpriyaji Haveli:
      Kirtankar Mukhiya: Damodar
      Haveli sangit : Kanhayalal II,
   Vitthalnathji Haveli:
      Kirtankar Mukhiya: Radhakrishna to 1984, then Bhanvarlal II

Rajasthani (five *kumavat* divisions)

2. Vanavadia (Rajasthan)
   Shri Nathji Haveli:
      Pakhavaji: Shyamlal
      Haveli sangit: Ramchandra

3. Kakatiya (from Jaipur, Rajasthan)
   Shri Nathji Haveli:
      Honourary *Pakhavaji*: Guru Purushottam Das
   Navnitpriyaji Haveli:
      Pakhavaji: Sohanlal

4. Mandalia (from Jaipur, Rajasthan)
   Shri Nathji Haveli:
      Harmonium: Mulchand
      Haveli sangit: Brijlal

5. Parihar (from Chaupasni Rajasthan)
   Shri Nathji Haveli:
      Kirtankar Mukhiya: Ramdas
      Sarangi: Amritlal

6. Devatval (from Jodhpur, Rajasthan)
   Navnitpriyaji Haveli:
      Haveli Sangit : Bhanvarlal I
   Vitthalnathji Haveli:
      Pakhavaji: Daulal

Sanadhya Subdivision of Brahmins

7. Sanadhya (Karela, Braj., UP)
   Navnitpriyaji Haveli:
      Haveli Sangit: Kisanlal

POLLUTION RULES GOVERNING THE *KIRTANKARS'* MUSIC

Everyone who enters the *haveli* must strictly observe pollution rules. Pollution affects all devotees, but for those who serve in the *haveli* it can have financial implications. They receive no remuneration when they are forced to be absent during periods of pollution. It is of utmost importance for the musicians to be aware of their relationship by marriage, as pollution in the extended family directly affects their ability to work in the *haveli*. As most of the musicians are closely related, a death in one family can seriously upset the daily routine.

I became aware of the importance of pollution rules for the *kirtankars* when, on the morning that I was granted permission to take my first *darshan*, at *Raj bhog*, Ganeshlal, a member of the *jalandhara* division of *kumavats*, died of a heart attack during the first *darshan* of the day, *Mangal*. Although Jindel (1976) reported that when a death occurred inside the temple, it was closed for purification, no closure occurred on this occasion. I was able to take *Raj bhog darshan*, but the musical offering was limited as very few musicians were unaffected.

To understand the ramifications of pollution after Ganeshlal's death, we must examine not only his family tree (*jalandhara*, division) which included both *vanavadia* and *kakatiya* divisions, but his wife's family tree. The musicians explained pollution as it affected them:

> After marriage a girl changes her sub-caste [in this instance *vanavadia*] and most of her impurity is tied to that of her husband [in this instance *jalandhara*]. When a married girl's father dies, only she and her husband are polluted for three days, but not their children. Pollution occurs only in relation to the girl's father and mother, not her brothers and sisters. Her brothers and sisters are, however, affected by the pollution restrictions that she brings with her husband's family. The implications of impurity are much more extensive in relation to her husband's family.

The deceased Ganeshlal's wife was the daughter of Guru Purushottam's sister (*kakatiya*) and Mannalal (*vanavadia*). She had two brothers among the *kirtankars* in the Shri Nathji Haveli: Ramchandra, *haveli* singer and Shyamlal, *Pakhavaji*. Neither could take up their duties as they were part of the wife's immediate family. Pollution also applied to their children. Shyamlal's son Balkrishna, though he had a reasonable command over the *pakhavaj* could not substitute for his father because of the effect of pollution. The paternal cousins[4] of the deceased: Damodar (*Kirtankar Mukhiya*) and

Kanhaiyalal (*haveli sangit*) were also excluded from working in the Navnitpriyaji Haveli; so was Damodar's son Prakash, who played *pakhavaj*.

With the musicians who belonged to the *jalandhara* and *kakatiya* divisions unable to perform, the number of possible substitutes in Nathdvara was severely depleted. Guru Purushottam was also marginally polluted through the female line: the deceased's mother-in-law was his sister. Substitutes, therefore, had to be called from as far away as Baroda and Bombay. Such eventualities demonstrate not only the importance attached by the temple hierarchy to ritual pollution, but also the absolute necessity of having appropriate music during *darshan*.

Although pollution is important, there are examples where the rules have been overlooked at the discretion of the head of the *sampraday*. For instance, there is a traditional account of one of the original *kirtankars*, Kumbhandas, who sang in the first Shri Nathji Haveli, established by Vallabha. When Kumbhandas' son died, Vallabha allowed him to take *Mangal darshan* during the period of ritual pollution, even though this was quite irregular:

> Gosainjee [Vallabha] showed him this favour, although he was considered unclean, since he well knew the pangs of separation that Kumbhandas would feel if he did not see the image ... During this period of separation Kumbhandas composed songs of agony (Parekh 1943: 143,145). Kumbhandas is included as one of the *ashtachhap*.

KIRTANKAR MUKHIYAS

Each temple has a head musician (*Kirtankar Mukhiya*), who is highly regarded, and receives additional remuneration on account of his added responsibility. *Kirtankar Mukhiyas* are appointed by the spiritual head of the temple and are traditionally chosen from among the singers. The musicians report that selection is based on seniority, but in practice, it is apparent that other factors, come into play such as their father's position, their talent, and the Tilkayat's own preference.

Kirtankar Mukhiyas decide which songs are to be sung in the *haveli* and coordinate the music. They usually hold the song book and sing louder than the others to co-ordinate the singing. The other musicians appear to know many of the songs by heart, although they may occasionally require some reminding. The *Kirtankar Mukhiya* is in charge of granting leave and making sure the required number of musicians are present. Each musician may take fifteen days' paid holiday a year. In each case the *Kirtankar Mukhiya* will authorize the leave only after the musician concerned has appointed a substitute. The temple pays the substitute's salary. Other than this sanctioned leave, if musicians do not report for work—including for reasons of ritual impurity—they are not paid.

Instead, their payment for that day goes to whoever takes their place.

RASIYAS

Haveli sangit is sung by *kirtankars.* There is another genre of songs, the *rasiya*; those who specialise in it are known as *Rasiyas.* Originally from Braj, they are the repository of this style, which is sung once a year. The songs, which are heavy with erotic content, are still a part of Holi celebrations in both Braj and Nathdvara, and provide a direct link with Braj culture (Growse 1874; Hein 1972). *Rasiyas* are not in the permanent employ of the temple; they are called upon to sing during the month of Phalgun (February-March) in which the festival of Holi occurs. At other irregular times, too, *rasiya* songs are sung in the shrines of Shri Nathji and Navnitpriyaji and throughout the *haveli.* In the Shri Nathji Haveli usually only hereditary *Rasiyas* play the *daff*, the drum that is special to this type of song. In March 1985, however, in the Navnitpriyaji Haveli, two sons of that temple's *Kirtankar Mukhiya* often performed this function (see also Jindel 1976: 159).

MUSICIANS OF THE NATHDVARA *HAVELIS*

The number of musicians employed varies between *havelis.* In 1988 there were five *haveli* singers in service in the Shri Nathji Haveli, four in the Navnitpriyaji Haveli, and one in the Vitthalnathji Haveli. They play the *jhanjh* (cymbals) during festivals and other specific occasions. The *jhanjh*, struck vigorously according to the *tala* of the song, gives the music a lively quality that does not accord well with pre-*Mangal*, *Mangal*, or *Shayan darshans*, when the mood is intended to be tranquil. For that reason *jhanjh* are not usually played for these *darshans.* Each *haveli* also has one *Pakhavaji.* The Shri Nathji Haveli is unique in that it employs separate harmonium, *sarangi* and *bin* players. The *Binkar* here is required to play the *bin* daily: first thing in the morning while waking the deity, before *Mangal darshan*, and the last thing at night while putting him to sleep (*Shayan darshan*). This makes his hours of work the longest of all. Except on these two occasions, at other *darshans* the *binkar* sings *haveli* songs. Three or four of the other musicians have also received instruction on the *bin*. In the Vitthalnathji and Navnitpriyaji Haveli, the *Kirtankar Mukhiya* combines his duties with playing the *bin*.

Many of the musicians have worked at various times in more than one of the Nathdvara Havelis, including the Vitthalnathji which is administered separately. Occupational succession is a common form of recruitment; several recent replacements have involved sons following their fathers. There are numerous examples of families losing a post, usually because no son has been given musical training; or the normal successor is not old enough to take over. For example, Guru Purushottam was too young when his father died to assume his father's position as *Pakhavaji* in the Shri Nathji Haveli. It appears that Guru Purushottam did not regard regaining his family prerogative as a foregone conclusion; it is possible that the incentive provided by the loss of the position was partly responsible for his attaining a high level of skill. Whether it was his expertise, or the disposition of the Tilkayat to reinstate a representative of the hereditary family, that enabled him to recover the post is unclear.

HEREDITARY CONNECTIONS AMONG THE NATHDVARA MUSICIANS

MUSICIANS OF THE SHRI NATHJI HAVELI (SNJ)

The musicians of Nathdvara stated that there should be eight musicians, to correspond with the number of *ashtachhap*, plus one *Pakhavaji*. During 1983-88 this tradition was still in effect in the Shri Nathji Haveli, the only temple where the actual musicians and the total number employed remained unchanged. If we include Guru Purushottam, whose post was honorary, then all the divisions of the *kumavats* except *devatval* were represented in this *haveli*. There were no *sanadhya brahmins*.

The *Kirtankar Mukhiya* was Ramdas (*parihar* division), who was married to Parvati, the sister of Mulchand the harmonium player (*mandalia* division). Ramdas' grandfather, Krishnadas had sung in a *haveli* in Chaupasni; his father Mathuradas had left Chaupasni for Nathdvara to become, eventually, the *Mukhiya* of the Vitthalnathji temple.

Ramdas' predecessor as *Mukhiya* in the Shri Nathji Haveli had been Raghunath, father of Tolaram (*jalandhara* division), who was now assistant *Kirtankar Mukhiya* there. In 1987, Ramdas' brother Amritlal had been employed as a *sarangi* player in the Shri Nathji temple for forty years. Tolaram's nephew, Bhanvarlal II had succeeded his father Radhakrishna (*jalandhara* division) as the *Kirtankar Mukhiya* of the Vitthalnathji Haveli after Radhakrishna's death. Thus these two *kumavat* families from the *jalandhara* and *parihar* divisions have alternated in the post of *Mukhiya* of the Shri Nathji and Vitthalnathji temples between them. As Tolaram is currently serving as assistant *Kirtankar Mukhiya*, he may eventually succeed Ramdas. If that happens, the *Mukhiyas* of both these temples will come from the same family in the *jalandhara* division. Tolaram and Shyamlal (*vanavadia* division, Pakhavaji SNJ) are married to sisters, Kishibai and Khemibai whose father Jaikrishna (*jalandhara* division) had been a singer in the Navnitpriyaji temple.

The other singers in the Shri Nathji temple were Brijlal, Pannalal, Ramchandra and the Binkar Vallabhdas. Pannalal and Vallabhdas were the sons of Gokuldas; *jalandhara* division, singer and *sarangi* player in the Banmaliji Haveli which no longer employs a *sarangi* player. Vallabhdas was officially adopted by Gokuldas' eldest brother, Jamnadas, who had been the *Binkar* of the Shri Nathji Haveli and was taught *bin* by his adoptive father. He is currently the only *kirtankar* with an official appointment as a *Binkar* in the temples of Nathdvara.

Ramchandra was first employed as a singer in the Shri Nathji temple in 1981. Earlier, he had been the *Pakhavaji* from 1957, replacing Guru Purushottam while the latter was in Delhi. In 1981 his younger brother, Shyamlal succeeded him as *Pakhavaji*. Their father Mannalal had been the *Kirtankar Mukhiya* of the Shri Nathji temple and his career had overlapped that of Guru Purushottam. Mannalal had married Guru Purushottam's eldest sister Sundar, thus Shyamlal and Ramchandra were Guru Purushottam's nephews.

Mulchand was employed as the harmonium player in the Shri Nathji Haveli; he also sang and was the *pakhavaj* teacher in the music school attached to the temple. His father, Parmananddas (*mandalia* division) had been *Pakhavaji* in the Shri Nathji temple for about a year (see Table 11.1) and he reported that his grandfather, Devkishan had also been employed in the Shri Nathji Haveli. Ambalal (1987: 158) illustrates a miniature painting dated 1883 which includes Devkishan playing *sarangi*. Although Mulchand was three years older than Guru Purushottam, Mulchand's mother, Haribai, and Guru Purushottam's first wife, Gulab, were sisters, daughters of Tikamdas (*devatval* division). Pakhavaji Tikamdas had also been a student of Ghanshyam, Guru Purushottam's father. Mulchand's father, Parmananddas, on the death of his first wife Haribai married Guru Purushottam's older sister Chandra.

Shyamlal was employed as the *Pakhavaji* in the Shri Nathji Haveli, and as the *tabla* teacher in the temple music school. Although Shyamlal was the only official *Pakhavaji* in the Shri Nathji Haveli, four other *Pakhavaj* players performed there regularly: Guru Purushottam,

TABLE 7.2: MUSICIANS EMPLOYED IN THE SHRI NATHJI HAVELI (SNJ)

Kirtankar Mukhiya:	Ramdas, born 1908 (*parihar*) (elder brother of Amritlal, *sarangi*, SNJ)
Haveli sangit: (Assistant *Mukhiya*):	Tolaram, born 1927 (*jalandhara*) (uncle of Bhanvarlal II, *Kirtankar Mukhiya*,VNJ)
	Ramchandra, born 1918 (*vanavadiya*) (elder brother of Shyamlal, *Pakhavaji*, SNJ)
	Pannalal, born 1927 (*jalandhara*) brother of Vallabhdas, *Binkar*, SNJ)
	Brijlal, born 1904 (*mandalia*) (brother of Mulchand, harmonium, SNJ)
Sarangi:	Amritlal, born 1925 (*parihar*) (brother of Ramdas, *Kirtankar Mukhiya*, SNJ)
Harmonium:	Mulchand, born 1905 (*mandalia*) (brother of Brijlal, singer, SNJ)
Bin:	Vallabhdas, born 1943 (*jalandhara*) (brother of Pannalal, singer, SNJ)
Pakhavaj:	Shyamlal, born 1928 (*vanavadiya*) (brother of Ramchandra, singer, SNJ)
Honorary *Pakhavaji*:	Guru Purushottam, born 1907 (*kakatiya*)

Prakash Chand, Mulchand (harmonium Shri Nathji Haveli) and Ratanlal, Mulchand's younger brother. Both Mulchand and Ratanlal had studied *pakhavaj* with their father, Parmananddas. During the period of my study, Ratanlal was earning his living as a watchmaker in Bhilvara, about one hundred kilometres distant but was a frequent visitor to Nathdvara and played *pakhavaj* and *bin* often in the Shri Nathji Haveli.

MUSICIANS OF THE NAVNITPRIYAJI HAVELI (NNP)

During the period 1981-88 the Navnitpriyaji temple employed four singers and a *Pakhavaji*. Damodar (*jalandhara* division), son-in-law of Guru Purushottam, was the *Kirtankar Mukhiya*, who succeeded his father Channulal to the post. In 1984, his youngest brother, Kanhaiyalal II, was appointed as a singer; he also taught music in the music school attached to the temple.

Before his appointment to the Navnitpriyaji Haveli, Kanhaiyalal II had been working as the sole musician in the Madanmohanji Haveli

TABLE 7.3: MUSICIANS EMPLOYED IN THE NAVNITPRIYAJI HAVELI (NNP) IN 1989

Kirtankar Mukhiya:	Damodar, born 1926 (*jalandhara*) (son-in-law of Guru Purushottam, elder brother of Kanhaiyalal, singer, NNP)
Haveli singers:	Bhanvarlal I, born 1920 (*devatval*) (father of Daolal, Pakhavaji VNJ, first cousin of Shyamlal, Pakhavaji SNJ and his brother Ramchandra)
	Kisanlal, born 1943 (*sanadhya*) (recently arrived from Braj, related to Tikamdas; also worked in the VNJ)
	Kanhaiyalal II, born 1943 (*jalandhara*) (appointed in 1985, youngest brother of Damodar)
Pakhavaj:	Sohanlal, born 1948 (*kakatiya*) (related to Guru Purushottam through Khem, Guru Purushottam's paternal great uncle)

(up to 1982). In 1982 he was given the post of *haveli* singer in the Navnitpriyaji Haveli. This post had been previously held by Pyarelal (*devatval* division). Pyarelal was transferred to the Madanmohanji Haveli, but took exception to the transfer which was considered a demotion, both in status and salary (reduced from four hundred rupees to two hundred rupees). He was able to refuse to work there because he was not dependent on his temple earnings since his shop, located just inside the first gate of the Vitthalnathji temple, and dealing in religious articles, provided his livelihood.

Sohanlal (*kakatiya* division) family has a very close connection with the Navnitpriyaji temple; he has been the *Pakhavaji* in the Navnitpriyaji temple since his father, Narayanlal died in 1982. Narayanlal had been a singer in the same *haveli* before he was hired as a *Pakhavaji* and his father Vitthalnath, had also been a *Pakhavaji* there. Vitthalnath's father-in-law had played the *bin* in the same temple, a post that is no longer filled. Sohanlal was also related to Khem, Ghanshyam's uncle, who first started collecting the material for the *Mridang Sagar*.

MUSICIANS OF THE VITTHALNATHJI HAVELI (VNJ)

In January 1984 the Vitthalnathji Haveli employed three musicians: the late *Kirtankar Mukhiya*, Radhakrishna (*jalandhara* division), had a stroke and was temporarily replaced by his son, Bhanvarlal II who also took over his father's post as *haveli sangit* teacher in the music school. After his father's death, in 1988, Bhanvarlal II was appointed as the *Kirtankar Mukhiya*.

In October 1983 Daulal was the *Pakhavaji*, but in January 1984 he was often employed as a singer in the Navnitpriyaji Haveli replacing his father, Bhanvarlal I (*devatval* division).

TABLE 7.4: MUSICIANS EMPLOYED IN THE VITTHALNATHJI HAVELI (VNJ)

Kirtankar Mukhiya:	Bhanvarlal II, born 1953 (*jalandhara*), (son of late Radhakrishna (1923-1988) who held this post until 1985
Haveli sangit:	Kisanlal, born 1943, (*sanadhya*), related to Tikamdas, singer. Also employed in the NNP.
Pakhavaj:	Daulal, born 1953 (*devatval*), son of Bhanvarlal I, singer NNP

MUSICIANS EMPLOYED IN OTHER *HAVELIS* IN NATHDVARA

The Madanmohanji (MMJ) *haveli* is under the direct control of Shri Shri Maharaj Govindlal. During 1981-87 there was only one full-time musician, who was required to sing, and play *jhanjh* and *pakhavaj* simultaneously. Up to 1983 this was Kanhaiyalal II (*jalandhara*). The position then passed to Pyarelal (born 1943, *devatval*) and in 1986 to Kanhaiyalal I (born approx. 1904, *jalandhara*). Plate 7.6 shows Kanhaiyalal I playing *pakhavaj*, *jhanjh* and singing in the Madanmohanji Haveli.

The Banmaliji (BMJ) *haveli* is funded by Maharaj Masilu Baba, who lives in Porbandar, Gujarat where the main *haveli* under his control, the Ranchorji Haveli, is situated. In the Banmaliji Haveli (BMJ), as in the Madanmohanji Haveli, only one musician was employed, to sing and simultaneously play *jhanjh* with one hand and *pakhavaj* with the other. In 1986 Brijlal II (*jalandhara*) occupied that post. When I took *darshan* at the Banmaliji Haveli, Tolaram (*jalandhara* division, *haveli sangit* SNJ), came in to worship and sang with the rest of us standing in the designated *darshan* area. No doubt this happens often, as he and his son run a shop in the covered market just outside the temple.

AGE OF THE MUSICIANS

In 1988 the oldest musician was Mulchand, eighty-three years of age. The youngest were Daulal and Bhanvarlal II, both thirty-five years of age. Out of the seventeen musicians who were in the regular employ of the temples, twelve were sixty, or over. In the most prestigious temple, the Shri Nathji, the *Binkar*, Vallabhdas, the *Binkar*, was forty-five, four of the musicians were in their sixties, two in their seventies, and two in their eighties, as was the honorary Pakhavaji, Guru Purushottam. In the Navnitpriyaji Haveli two of the musicians were in their forties and two in their sixties. The three musicians of the Vitthalnathji Haveli were all under fifty. The difference in age distribution amongst the three temples presumably reflects the fact that, as they rise in seniority, musicians tend to shift to the Shri Nathji temple.

The senior musician, the *Kirtankar Mukhiya*, was not necessarily the oldest. In the Shri Nathji Haveli, Ramdas was eighty, and the assistant *Kirtankar Mukhiya*, Tolaram, was sixty-one. In the Navnitpriyaji temple, Damodar was sixty-two, younger than another *haveli* singer, Bhanvarlal I, and in the Vitthalnathji Haveli the *Mukhiya*, Bhanvarlal II was one of the youngest musicians employed in the Nathdvara temples. There is clearly an element of family prerogative in the appointment of *Kirtankar Mukhiyas*.

THE MUSICIANS OF THE *NAUBAT/NAQQARA KHANA*

There are eight musicians employed in the *naubat khana*: five *shahnai* players and three drummers who play *naqqara*, *dhumsa*, and *dhol*. The head *shahnai* player, Shankarlal, was the youngest, aged thirty-two; he was appointed to the post by the Tilkayat. All the musicians inherited their posts, their fathers having played the same instruments. They themselves had learnt with their fathers. On several occasions, when I visited the *naubat khana*, I found other non-musician temple servants assisting by playing a simple beat on the *dhol*. During the cool months, a fire was usually smouldering on the stone floor in the centre of the room to heat the drum heads in order to tune them.

The musicians who play in the *naubat khana* are a separate group from those performing in the inner temple. The two groups do not intermarry, nor does one group learn the music of the other. One exception was Amritlal, the present *sarangi* player in the Shri Nathji temple, who learnt his instrument with Dayaram, the father of Bansilal, who now plays *shahnai* in the *naqqara khana*. Dayaram also played *shahnai* and worked in the *naubat khana* in the Shri Nathji temple, while as a *sarangi* player he played for the dancing girls (*tawaifs*) in the court of the Maharana of Udaipur.[5] Dayaram taught *shahnai* to his son Bansilal. The tradition that music is played in the *naubat khana* is presumably Rajasthani in origin. All the musicians who worked there in 1982-89 lived in Sirnar, the village on the outskirts of Nathdvara which existed before the town was founded. They said that playing in the *naubat khana* had been a family tradition dating from the building of the Shri Nathji Haveli in Nathdvara. It seems likely, therefore, that the custom of having a *naubat khana* was adopted by the temple after the installation of the image at Nathdvara. By contrast, many of the musicians who play inside the *haveli* during *darshan* trace their ancestry to both

Rajasthan and Braj, from where Shri Nathji migrated.

By caste, the musicians who play in the *naubat khana* of the Shri Nathji Haveli are known as *dholis*. Shankarlal, the *Mukhiya*, stated that they are allowed in the Shri Nathji Haveli only on five occasions: during the festivals: Holi, Nandotsav, Annakut and Divali, and after a solar eclipse. Temple musicians however, reported otherwise. They said that the musicians of the *naubat khana* are not allowed in the temple, except on the day after Holi, which they referred to as *dhol* day. They also reported that the family who repair drums in Nathdvara was similarly unable to take *darshan*; whenever a *pakhavaj* had to be repaired the repairer worked in *govardhan chauk*, the first courtyard on entering the temple.

I asked Shankarlal the reason for his exclusion from the *haveli*. He explained it as the Tilkayat's policy; the Tilkayat felt that allowing the *naubat khana* musicians to attend *darshan* would disrupt the music in the *naubat khana* because the music has to be played at regular intervals from the *naubat khana* to announce *darshan* and it usually continues until *darshan* is closed. Nevertheless, the fact that the *naubat khana* musicians made no attempt to attend *darshan*, even when they were not required to play, presumably relates to a tradition based on their caste.[6]

TABLE 7.5 : THE MUSICIANS OF THE *NAQQARA KHANA*

Instrument	*Community*	*Name and Other Data*
Shahnai	Chauhan	Shankarlal, *Mukhiya* also *naqqara* Nareshchandra son of Bansilal Bansilal, also teaches music in Boys Higher Secondary School
	Pamar	Ruplal (also *mardal*, plays in Bhil Lok Mandal Band) Brijlal
Karnal		Narayanlal
Naqqara	Asvar	Mohanlal*
Dhol	Sheshodiya	Mohanlal* II (father was Pratha, also played the *dhol*)

*Note: There are two Mohanlals employed in the *naubat khana* and several *kirtankars* employed in the various *havelis* also with the name Mohanlal.

THE BAND OF THE TILKAYAT'S BODYGUARD

Another group of musicians in Nathdvara is the band of the Tilkayat's personal bodyguard. The presence of a bodyguard and a military band emphasizes the secular power of the Tilkayat and his family. The military band is an important musical presence in the town, but performs outside the temple mainly during festivals and on other ceremonial occasions, such as the arrival and departure of visiting *svarups* and other religious leaders. The band includes sixteen musicians, who play most of the instruments to be found in a regular military band: trumpet (2), clarinet (1), euphonium (3), alto horn (1), circle bass (1), large and small tubas, a large bass drum, and several smaller kettle drums. Trombones and french horns are not represented. The band has the same eclectic repertoire that is heard from Hindu wedding bands: military music, western pop music, and Hindi film songs. The same band can be hired for private marriage celebrations.

On the occasions on which it plays it does so marching through the streets of the city, accompanied by the rest of the soldiers carrying guns, with fixed bayonets. These weapons are with them at all times while on duty guarding the three entrances to the temple. The military band, along with the soldiers, and the huge spikes embedded in the temple gates at the right height to deter elephants from ramming them with their heads, are reminders of the insecurities of the past. Even today the large doors of the *haveli* are locked after seven in the evening, after which time entry is restricted to a very small door approximately three feet high by two feet. The bodyguard and the band signifies the royal status, personal power, and wealth still held by the Tilkayat. The music played today by the military band is of recent origin, and is played throughout India.

VISITING MUSICIANS AND DANCERS

Professional musicians and dancers come to Nathdvara for two reasons: to entertain the Tilkayat in his private apartments, or as a personal pilgrimage, made either specifically for this purpose, or as a slight detour while travelling from one engagement to another. Singing, playing instrumental music or dancing in front of the image by visiting artists always takes place just before *Shringar darshan*. It requires permission from the Tilkayat. The usual procedure is to play or dance in the Tilkayat's palace beforehand and then personally to request him for the honour of doing so before Shri Nathji. This is rationalized by saying that only the very best can be offered to Shri Nathji and it is the Tilkayat, as connoisseur in matters both temporal and spiritual, who passes judgement.

There appears to have been a well-established tradition of music and dance being performed by visiting artists in the various *havelis* and in the private apartments of the many Maharaj of the *sampraday*. Mulji in 1865 described the occasions and the dancers: "... sometimes when there are marriages and such occasions, dancing and singing go on in the temples; but not in the part where the idols are kept. Prostitutes are invited on such occasions to dance in the temple" (Mulji 1985, appendix 4).

He also observed that the same dancers performed in the temple for the Maharaj and other patrons of high social status.

> The dances take place in the house [of the Maharaj] on one side, and sometimes in the compound of the temple. All the *nach* dancers in Bombay are prostitutes. *Nach* dances are frequently given by respectable persons on occasion of the celebration of marriages and other events (Mulji 1865, appendix 5).

When Govardhanlal, the grandfather of the present Tilkayat held the post, Damodarlal, the father of the present Tilkayat, maintained a Kathak troupe for his personal pleasure. The troupe remained in Nathdvara for several years and also performed in the Shri Nathji temple. Hamsa, a Kathak dancer from Almora, was Damodarlal's favourite. The arrangement of the photograph (plate 7.7) confirms that Damodarlal publicly acknowledged his relationship with Hamsa.

When Damodarlal (1887-1936) succeeded his father, Govardhanlal (1862-1934) as Tilkayat, he continued his affair with the dancer, to the great consternation of the people of Nathdvara. Eventually they drove the Kathak troupe from the city. Some *kirtankars*, however, sheltered members of the troupe in their homes, despite threats of physical violence by local people. Guru Purushottam hid Balmukund, with whom he had made some study of the *tabla*; and Pannalal, at present *haveli* singer in the Shri Nathji Haveli, gave refuge in his home to the troupe's harmonium player, Shyamlal. Subsequently, responding to requests from the citizens of Nathdvara, the Maharana of Udaipur, Fateh Singh, forced Damodarlal to abdicate in favour of his son Govindlal (born 1928), the present Tilkayat, who was a minor then

(1933). From all accounts, Damodar's affair with Hamsa was only one of several reasons for his ouster.

Guru Purushottam reported that Hamsa thereafter lived in a fashionable area of New Delhi (12 Prithviraj Road), as well as in Old Delhi. When Guru Purushottam went to Delhi to play on All India Radio he recalled visiting her and the deposed Tilkayat.

Besides Hamsa, the troupe included a male Kathak dancer, Mohan. When the troupe disbanded, Mohan moved to Delhi where he taught Kathak privately. Guru Purushottam often stayed with him when he went to Delhi. The Kathak troupe also included a singer from Braj, Tikamdas (*sanadhya*), not to be confused with Guru Purushottam's father-in-law Pakhavaji Tikamdas (*kumavat*, *devatval* division), who stayed on in Nathdvara. Tikamdas the singer trained both his sons, Balkrishna, who was blind, and Sundarlal (Table 7.1, see Appendix). Balkrishna was subsequently employed as a *haveli* singer in the Navnitpriyaji temple and also learnt *tabla* with Guru Purushottam. Sundarlal although trained in *haveli sangit*, left Nathdvara and returned to Braj, where he took a job in the government. Later Balkrishna gave up his job in the Navnitpriyaji temple and joined his brother in Braj where he taught Sundarlal's son, Kisanlal. Kisanlal returned to Nathdvara about five years ago and is currently employed as a *haveli* singer in the Navnitpriyaji temple. The fact that Tikamdas, one of the troupe's singers and a *Brajvasi*, stayed on to work in Nathdvara may have been related to the fact that his family was from Karahla, the town in Braj from which many of the original musicians migrated. His family was the last *kirtankar* family to become established in Nathdvara. The Braj/Nathdvara connection has existed from the foundation of the town.

The conduct of the *kirtankars* in the confrontation over the Kathak troupe is a little surprising, considering that they were all local people. Whereas the townsfolk threatened physical violence against members of the troupe, the resident musicians were willing to protect their fellow artists and later kept in touch with them. On both counts they presumably risked the opprobrium of some townsfolk. This suggests a strong professional bond within the community of artists, extending beyond the boundaries of Nathdvara, and suggests that they saw themselves as musicians first and foremost.

Visiting musicians form an important component of the artistic life of Nathdvara. Their performances bring a new stimulus to the existing system. Guru Purushottam learnt *tabla* with two of them. Resident musicians do not seem to be troubled by jealousy of the visiting musicians, no doubt because their posts are largely hereditary and they therefore do not feel threatened. I have noticed myself that visiting musicians and dancers are welcomed by the resident Nathdvara musicians. Apparently, resident musicians do not consider themselves court (*durbar*) musicians for the Tilkayat.

The main function of the Kathak dance troupe was secular, as it was maintained primarily for the Tilkayat's pleasure. Nevertheless, Guru Purushottam and the other musicians of his generation recalled that it was an accepted practice for Kathak to be performed in the *haveli* between the first *darshan*, *Mangal*, and the second, *Shringar*. Although the Shri Nathji Haveli and other temples of the Vallabha Sampraday have never employed professional dancers (*devadasis*), as was the custom in southern India (Kersenboom 1987; Gaston 1991a), the practice of singing and dancing continues when visiting artists are available.

An artist who is invited by the Tilkayat to perform for him is treated as a guest and is usually given remuneration in cash and in kind for the performance. Whereas the pre-*Shringar darshan* performance is donated as part of the artist's personal *seva*, there is no ambivalence on the part of the artist over accepting payment, even though the Tilkayat himself is regarded by many as an extension of Krishna. In 1985, a vocalist and her musicians from Bombay were not paid immediately after their evening performance. The next morning they drew attention to this by camping outside the Tilkayat's offices protesting loudly about such treatment of artists. They were recompensed several hours later.

This occasion in 1985 marked the *mundan* ceremony of the Tilkayat's grandson, for which there were many dance and music concerts. I also danced for these festivities. My performance for the Tilkayat was in the evening in the same room in his palace in which I had been initiated; the one in which he receives his devotees. Other performances were held in the courtyard of the temple, below the rooms used by the music school. There, a stage was erected about 5 feet high and 25 feet square. A canopy was put on top, and microphones and lights set up. Uma Sharma gave a Kathak recital, Konkana Banerji sang, and other artists were also presented here. All of the recitals were held in the evening after dark.

On the evening of my recital I dressed in one of the guest houses where I was staying. There were the usual electricity cuts, always a challenge, especially when putting on make-up. Another unforeseen problem was the difficulty in locating fresh flowers, after the temple had been closed for the night and all the flower sellers had dispersed. Fortunately I was able to dispatch a friend who rode off on his bicycle to the Hanuman temple near Lal Bagh, some distance out of town, where many of the flower sellers live. A special order was prepared, which I must say was exquisite.

Although I was looking forward to the performance, I was uncertain about walking through the town dressed in my Odissi dance costume, heavily laden with silver jewellery. I carried my bells so as not to attract attention. At about nine o'clock, by which time it was fully dark, I was escorted by several music students and friends of the *kirtankars* who were in charge of the visiting artists. I wrapped a shawl around me, pulling it over my head and peeped out as we threaded our way through a crowd that had gathered to celebrate a local wedding. The military band played film music and lights were provided by petromax lamps held aloft.

We reached the back door to the temple, its huge elephant-deterring spikes looming sinisterly over our heads. By now it was firmly locked. Pushing open the tiny inner door, we bent down and stepped into the first courtyard, now deserted except for lights in Moti Mahal shining behind coloured glass windows. We left our shoes with the guards, many of whom had bedded down for the night in the narrow passage way of the gate, and walked across the courtyard. The sky was clear and the stars provided sufficient light. At the end of the courtyard we passed another soldier who was leaning against the wall and climbed the narrow stairs, first past the large durbar hall, lined with portraits of previous Tilkayats and paintings of Krishna. The round glass lamps, the fixtures on the walls, and the few pieces of furniture all echoed the Victorian period during which it was constructed. We continued on upstairs to emerge into the Tilkayat's private apartments.

A large crowd had assembled, waiting in expectant silence. The Tilkayat sat on a chair but everyone else was on the floor which was covered with rugs, except for a small area where I was to dance. It was of white marble. I noticed the three Maharaj from the Vitthalnathji Haveli seated near the Tilkayat, and the Tilkayat's two sons and their wives. Guru Purushottam was in the front row. With everyone watching, I walked to one corner and set up my make-up stand. I was uncertain about when to start. The Tilkayat's private secretary took charge of my cassettes and passed them on to a technician who had been hired to run the sound equipment. I walked over, prostrated myself in front of the Tilkayat, touched his feet and asked his permission to begin. A quick glance at Guru Purushottam gave me confidence. He appeared calm and proud and I too felt honoured to be taking part in the event. Whatever the views that might prevail elsewhere, there is no doubt that within the town I was experiencing the highest accolade that Nathdvara can bestow. I could imagine that, except for the fact that the music was on tape, the event differed in no significant way from performances that must have occurred many times over the centuries. Continuity is surely one of the strengths of the *sampraday*.

I began my recital with *Mangalacharan*, the traditional first dance in the Odissi repertoire. Entering the performing area holding flowers, I dropped them in front of the Tilkayat, to symbolize that I sought the blessings of mother earth and then mimed a prayer to the goddess. This was followed by dance intended to give an auspicious opening to the recital in which I invoked the eight guardians of the quarters (*dikpalas*), god, my dance teacher, and the audience. Only then was the recital fully commenced. The next dance was *Dasavatar*, from Jayadeva's *Gita Govinda*. I chose dances in three styles: Odissi, Bharata Natyam and Kuchipudi. I included the Sanskrit piece *Govardhanagiri*, in Bharata Natyam style, which was particularly appropriate as it relates the events surrounding the lifting of Mount Govardhan. The *Mandooka shabdam* is an amusing story about a maiden once cursed to live as a frog who becomes a queen. Other dances followed and I was careful to include both narrative and abstract dance. The room and the hall outside were packed, with over 150 people present which made the room very warm. The audience was largely silent, perhaps because no one raises their voice in the presence of the Tilkayat, but the applause at the end was warm.

Once my recital was completed I joined the audience to listen to Maharaj Kalyanray perform on *pakhavaj*. He had been well trained and he rendered his recital in a lively and animated fashion. Several *khyal* singers followed. I did not stay until the end, but left at about 11.30 p.m., as I wanted to be up by 4 a.m. to attend *Mangal darshan* the next day. Several people stopped me in the bazaar later and were enthusiastic over the previous evenings events. With so many persons in the audience, I had no idea who was there.

That evening, Uma Sharma, the well known Kathak dancer, danced in the courtyard below the dance school for the *mundan* ceremony.

The next morning, prior to *Shringar darshan*, she also performed in the *darshan* room (*doltivari*) before Shri Nathji, accompanied by *tabla* and harmonium. Because of the narrow space available on the risers in the audience chamber, movement was very restricted and she confined herself to presenting *abhinaya* (gestures and expressions) to songs (*thumris*) which she sang. She also performed a few of Guru Purushottam's special rhythmic compositions which Tulsi Narayan, one of his students whom he had taught in New Delhi, played on the *pakhavaj*, having just accompanied her on *tabla*. Neither the songs nor the rhythmic dance were part of the temple repertoire, but belonged to the secular court tradition (Hein 1972).

Some visiting musicians use their presence in Nathdvara to give public concerts in the large audience hall in the compound of one of the larger rest houses (*dharamsala*), or in the newer rest house complex known as Vallabh Cottages. In some cases these musicians were officially attached to other Krishna temples in Vrindavan, Porbandar and Calcutta, while in others they were professional musicians who earned their living on the concert stage. In several instances this led to further engagements for them in the large urban centres from which devotees had come. Such concerts allowed the musicians to reach a large audience because, as was pointed out earlier, the pre-*Shringar* recitals are open only to a very limited audience and most devotees are unaware of them. The regular passage of outside musicians also helps to keep the Nathdvara musicians in touch with the world of art music and the concert stage.

SPECIAL STATUS OF VISITING MUSICIANS

Playing or dancing in front of the image by visiting artists always precedes *Shringar darshan*; a curtain then hides Shri Nathji while he is being dressed. Only those with special permission from the Tilkayat may watch and listen to the visiting artist; the maximum number I have seen present is twenty. Most of the *kirtankars* come; occasionally one of them provides accompaniment on *sarangi*, harmonium, or even *tabla*, which is never played during regular *darshan*.

Visiting musicians are accorded greater status than those in the regular employ of the temple. Muslims are normally forbidden to enter the *haveli* except on specific occasions such as during an eclipse of the moon, after which elaborate purifying procedures take place (Jindel

1976: 17). Nevertheless, Muslim artists are granted dispensation if they wish to play during the pre-*Shringar* period and many have taken this opportunity. In March 1985, I heard a violin recital by Shri Satyadev Pawar (an All India Radio, Delhi artist) accompanied by Shri Faiyaz Khan, a Muslim, on *tabla* (also All India Radio, Delhi artist). They performed at the designated time, just prior to *Shringar darshan*. Only musicians and music connoisseurs were present. We sat on the steps of the *darshan* room facing the niche which houses Shri Nathji (*nij mandir*). While the musicians played the image was being decorated and was concealed from our view by a bamboo and cloth curtain.

The music recital lasted for about twenty minutes with the musicians from the Shri Nathji temple making requests and signifying approval by the customary "vah vah". At intervals the priests would peek out at us. Just before the curtain was opened to reveal Shri Nathji, the steel bar which separated us from the sanctuary was raised to allow the temple musicians to move very quickly forward and take up their appointed places. They began playing immediately just as the devotees began to rush in from our left. The visiting musicians picked up their instruments and we all took *darshan*. To have been caught sitting would have risked being trampled (see also Jindel 1976: 96).

The late Dagar brothers, Zahiruddin and Faizuddin told me that they had sung *dhrupad* in the Shri Nathji Haveli. For them, the occasion had great spiritual significance. They saw no conflict in offering their art at a Hindu shrine. Zia Moinuddin Dagar's father used to tell him, "In life you are a Muslim but when you sing you are a Hindu" (Rita Joshi 1989: 62).

Visiting musicians normally in the employ of another temple, or belonging to one of the families of professional temple musicians join those musicians who play regularly in the temple, entering with them and singing or playing while *darshan* is taking place. To do this they must wear the required dress of *angarkhi* (jacket), *dhoti* (cloth tied as pants) and *pagri* (turban). I have seen only male musicians participating during the *darshan* singing, but artists of both sexes may sing in the period before *Shringar darshan*.

Guru Purushottam was usually called upon to organize dance and music for all the Tilkayat's family celebrations. This was because he was regarded as the senior musician, being the only one who has received national awards. Latterly he was assisted by his grandson, Prakash. The resident musicians attend the Tilkayat's concerts, usually just to listen, but sometimes to accompany the visitors and occasionally to sing or play. When I have attended such events those *haveli* singers who performed usually chose to sing *khyal*, which they regard as more refined and more suitable for such gatherings. *Khyal* as well as *dhrupad* and *thumri* may be sung during the *Shringar* pre-*darshan* periods, but during *darshan* only *haveli sangit* is acceptable. Music performed during this pre-*darshan* period therefore has elements of the *durbar* situation. In particular the audience which was usually composed of other musicians and persons knowledgeable or interested in music had gathered specifically to listen to it.

CONCLUSION

The musician community has always been composed of distinct groups, with little or no interchange occurring. The musicians of the *haveli* and the *naubat/naqqara khana* do not inter-marry or interact socially. Nor do the musicians of the *haveli* have any connections to those of the Tilkayat's bodyguard. For all the musicians their family heritage is important in securing a post in the *haveli* and seniority is often determined by the position held by a family member. The preference of the Tilkayat is, however, still paramount.

The *haveli* musicians have three different, but overlapping repertoires: music that is played daily, music that is played on festival occasions and music that is played in the concert or *durbar* situation. There is nothing unusual in this; most concert musicians are also familiar with popular and folk styles. The important thing, in the context of the Nathdvara tradition, is that the musicians maintain a competence in classical styles, and see themselves as part of a broader artistic community, as well as being servants of the temple. This allows them to maintain a pride in their art which sets a certain standard for the music.

The sheer abundance of performance in the temple situation often dilutes the artistry applied. Musicians must perform on demand, whether sick, fatigued, or stressed by the press of events. These constraints are hardly likely to promote great music. Nevertheless, away from the hurly-burly of *darshan*, most of the musicians were able to give a competent recital. Some of the most inspired and sweetest music I have heard has been sung and played in off-hours in the music school in Nathdvara.

NOTES

1. Carnatic is another way of spelling Karnatic. The latter is used more often in 1990.
2. The names of other communities for musicians in other temples vary. For example in Kankroli in the Dvarkadhishji Haveli the musicians stated that they belonged to the *ghandharva* community and in Ahmedabad to the *nayak* community. See chapter 12.
3. Most *Brajvasis*, including Prakash's father Damodar, have concentrated their musical training on singing *haveli sangit*. Prakash has become a *pakhavaj* player which is unusual for *Brajvasis*.
4. Ganeshlal's father, Brijlal (*jalandhara* division), was the brother of Channulal whose sons were Damodar and Kanhaiyalal,
5. For further details about *sarangi* and dancing girls at the court of Udaipur see Sorrell 1980 and for *sarangi* and dancing girls in general Bor 1987.
6. Neuman (1980: 114, 124) comments on the classical status of *shahnai* music. Since the late 1980s the caste restrictions have changed in the Shri Nathji temple.
7. See Baily (1980) who mentions both *naubat/naqqara khanas* and military bands in Afghanistan at the beginning of the twentieth century.
8. See also Gaston 1991a for a discussion of patronage in the southern dance traditions.
9. The tradition of dancing in Nathdvara differs from that described by Hein (1972) in Vrindavan where it was a regular part of the ritual activities. Hein observed in the 1950s the activities of a Kathak dancer Nand Kishore who presented his dance as *seva* in the Anandibai temple in Vrindavan. "The dancing place was the floor of the veranda across the courtyard from the open shrine, in a direct line of vision from the images" (Hein 1972: 34). Hein was unaware of the cultural explosion that had already begun in Indian dance which was about to transform the dance (Hein 1972: 47).
10. This was shown in the film made in 1985, *Given to Dance: India's Odissi Tradition*. It is part of the contemporary South Asia film documentary series, available at the Centre for South Asian Studies, University of Wisconsin, 1269 Van Hise Hall, Madison Wisconsin. 53706, USA.
11. The Dagar family were converts from Hinduism to Islam around the nineteenth century (Owens 1983).

Plate 7.1: Guru Purushottam playing the pakhavaj in one of the dharamsalas

An informal musical evening held in 1983. Guru Purushottam is playing the *pakhavaj*. Shyamlal is providing the *laya* for Guru Purushottam on the harmonium. Shyamlal will play the *tabla* later. This event was held in a large hall in one of the *dharamsalas* known as Vallabh Cottages.

Plate 7.2: Mulchand Playing the pakhavaj in one of the dharamsalas

An informal musical evening held in 1983. Mulchand is playing the *pakhavaj*. Guru Purushottam seated behind is listening intently.

Plate 7.3: The musicians of Nathdvara c. 1911

SEATED IN THE CENTRE: Guru Purushottam Das

FRONT ROW: *Binkar*: Manu/Matu (see also Plate 11.1), Shri Nathji Haveli; *tanpura*; Ghanshyam, father of Guru Purushottam Das; holding child: Jaikrishna, Kirtankar Mukhiya, Navnitpriyaji Haveli

BACK ROW: Jamnadas holding the *jhanjh* (cymbals). He later became the *Binkar* in the Shri Nathji Haveli. Jamnadas adopted his brother Gokuldas's son, Vallabhdas, and trained him in *bin*. Vallabhdas succeeded Jamnadas as *Binkar; sarangi* player Parasuram and Raghunath, father of Radhakrishna, and grandfather of Bhanvarlal II, *Kirtankar Mukhiya* in the Navnitpriyaji Haveli.

Plate 7.4: Detail of Plate 7.3

Plate 7.5: Four Kirtankars in the outer courtyard of the Vitthalnathji Haveli (1985)

FROM LEFT TO RIGHT: the late Radhakrishna, *Kirtankar Mukhiya*, Vitthalnathji Ḥaveli (*jalandhara* division), Brijlal (*haveli* singer in the Shri Nathji Haveli, *Mandalia* division), Guru Purushottam Das (honorary *Pakhavaji* in the Shri Nathji Haveli, *kakatiya* division) Shyamlal (*Pakhavaji*, in the Shri Nathji Haveli, *mandalia* division).

The four *kirtankars* are seated in the courtyard of the Vitthalnathji Haveli beside the shop run by Shyamlal and Ramchander (*haveli* singer in the Shri Nathji Haveli). The painting on the wall is in the traditional style and illustrates the celebrations for Govardhan *puja*. The cows are decorated with peacock feathers, red hand marks and bells. The cowherds too dress in elaborate *dhotis* and carry a rattle which they shake to make the cows run. "Cowplay" is an important feature of Govardhan *puja* and is still performed.

Plate 7.6
Playing the pakhavaj, jhanjh and singing haveli sangit
Kanhaiyalal I, Kirtankar, Madanmohanji Haveli, 1985

The Madanmohanji Haveli employed one *kirtankar*, Kanhaiyalal I, (*jalandhara* division) in 1985. He sang and provided rhythmic accompaniment for himself on *pakhavaj* and *jhanjh*. He is wearing the required dress for temple musicians and servants of *angarkhi* and a turban.

Plate 7.7: The Tilkayat Damodarlal and Hamsa (*c.* 1934)

The Tilkayat Damodarlal is shown with his children by his legal wife. He is accompanied by Hamsa, the Kathak dancer sitting at his left.

FROM LEFT TO RIGHT: Damodarlal's older daughter, Gabla Betiji (partially seen) and who is currently(1988) in charge of another *haveli* in Baroda, Damodarlal's son, Shri Shri Govindlal, the present-day *Tilkayat.* Gabla Beti's son Baban who in 1987 was the personal secretary to the Tilkayat Govindlal. At the far end is Durga, Hamsa's maidservant. Servants are standing behind.

Plate 7.8: The Ras Lila in Nathdvara (c. 1930)

FAR LEFT: Mohanlal holding cymbals: Maganlal (*haveli* singer in Navnitpriyaji Haveli); *pakhavaj*: Balkrishna (s/o Ramnarayan); *sarangi*: Gokuldas (*jalandhara* division); *gopis*: Shyamlal and Ratanlal

ON RIGHT SIDE FROM BACK TO FRONT: Damodar, Parmanand (father of Mulchand and Ratanlal); harmonium: Radhakrishna

LOWER FAR RIGHT: Channulal (father of Damodar, Misrilal and Kanhaiyalal II)

Also present Balkrishna Thakur from Braj.

CHAPTER 8

Being a Musician in Nathdvara

THE IMPORTANCE OF THE TEACHER

Ghanshyam acknowledged in the *Mridang Sagar* the difficulty of trying to record in writing an essentially oral tradition. Although the book contains detailed notations of *pakhavaj* compositions he did not feel that it could replace actual experience:

> [The book] had its limitations and musical knowledge was essentially attained by practical skill ... only the person who has studied with an *ustad* (master musician), an *ustad* who performed frequently and was a full time musician ... only that person will be able to retain his expertise. Neither by listening nor stealing (copying musical patterns) can one attain the skill of real art. One will not get that dexterity. (MS: PV;6)

In fact, although he wrote an account of how to play the *pakhavaj*, only the sounds (*akshara*), and their various combinations (*matra*) were transcribed. For Ghanshyam it was important to practise and gain practical experience in combination with a good teacher. Only under such conditions will a musician be able to retain his expertise after his period of training is over. Ghanshyam stressed that a teacher must impart the knowledge and that there was no value in trying to obtain skill by imitation without the teacher's direct involvement. There is only so much that one can either pick up informally by listening, or reading books on the subject. He gives as examples the ability to distinguish sounds (*akshara*) and manipulate the mathematical divisions of the *laya* as "to some extent with him (the *ustad*)". In other words, the nuances are essential. James Kippen (1988) made similar observations about learning to play the *tabla*. These are the typical views of Indian master musicians and reflect the reality of learning an oral tradition.

The importance placed on the *ustad's* consent can also be viewed as a tactic designed to preserve monopolies over certain musical styles. There are numerous accounts of the lengths taken to hear musicians: "Sometimes when renowned artists came from outside the state to perform in the royal court, local artists would sit hidden behind curtains or lattice windows to hear them and learn their styles, techniques and texts" (Erdman 1985).

When tape-recorders were first introduced in India there was a great deal of resistance to their use.

> In the 1930s and 1940s the Maharana [of Udaipur, Maharana Bhopal Singh] ordered singers to record an eight hour set of favourite songs. But some musicians refused saying that they sang only for rulers and if recorded they could be heard by any foreigner who does not understand the *sangit*. Thus an early recording of the Dagar's *dhrupad* was denied (Erdman 1985: 40).

Unfortunately the aversion to recording has meant that there is nothing tangible with which we can evaluate the so called "good old days" with their "higher standards". This is in contrast to today when nearly every minor cultural event is being recorded and preserved on tape and film. Much more than one could possibly see or hear in a lifetime is being preserved for posterity.

Studying from a master is also important in demonstrating the legitimacy of particular knowledge and artistic expertise. In India, not only in music, but in all forms of traditional teaching, mere knowledge is not considered sufficient; the knowledge must come by direct transmission from the teacher to have its full effect.[1] Ghanshyam used the Urdu word *ustad* for a qualified performing artist. In contrast today only Muslim artists and teachers are known as *ustad*; Hindu artists and teachers are referred to as *pandit* or *guru* (Misra 1985).

THE TRAINING OF THE PRESENT MUSICIANS

Guru Purushottam and all the present musicians, reported receiving most of their training from their own fathers. Nevertheless, as they were very mobile from a young age, often travelling to other centres of the *sampraday*, they also reported significant input into their training from other musicians, not resident in Nathdvara. Another factor that appeared to be very important in their musical life was the constant presence of visiting musicians in Nathdvara (chapter 7). Many musicians reported exchanging information on musical techniques and generally cordial relations with the visiting musicians. Ghanshyam in the *Mridang Sagar* describes a music conference that was precipitated by the fact that several musicians were visiting Nathdvara simultaneously. More details are given in chapter 11, but probably there has always been an infusion of musical ideas from the outside.

Guru Purushottam received some training in *dhrupad* but he never gave a vocal recital. His family were *Pakhavajis* and all his relations, via the male line (*kakatiya* division), had worked as *Pakhavajis*. The same applied to his nephew, Sohanlal. All the other musicians could sing *haveli sangit* as well as play an instrument. Shyamlal, *Pakhavaji* of the Shri Nathji Haveli, received training in both *Pakhavaj* (from Guru Purushottam) and singing (from his father, Mannalal, *vanavadiya* division). Shyamlal had worked as both a singer and a *Pakhavaji*.

Most of the musicians from the older generation currently serving in the temples reported that by the age of ten they had started performing in one of the smaller *havelis*. Because the number of musicians employed by the Nathdvara *havelis* has been reduced, their sons no longer have the same opportunity to serve in the lesser temples. Consequently, work in the *haveli* is increasingly seen as appropriate, and possible mainly for the older members of the *kirtankar* community.

At present music is taught in Nathdvara in the *haveli*, in the music school attached to the *haveli*, and in some instances in the home. The opening of the music school has brought about several significant changes in the teaching of the Nathdvara musical tradition. First of all, the younger generation is now able to study on a regular basis with members other than their own family. Secondly, there has been some attempt to systematize teaching, with periodic evaluations. These changes have prompted some people from non-hereditary families to study music. None of the non-hereditary students, however, are likely to become temple musicians: it is not a financially viable way of life; even more importantly, any vacancies are almost certainly to be filled by members of *kirtankar* families.

THE MUSIC SCHOOL, SHRI NATHJI SHIKSHAN KENDRA

The music school, the Shri Nathji Shikshan Kendra, is attached to the Shri Nathji Haveli and is situated inside its walls, beside the Tilkayat's residence. The activities of the school have to conform to the Shri

Nathji's timetable because, except for the late principal, Guru Purushottam, and the then secretary, his grandson Prakash, all the staff were also employed as musicians in the temple. Consequently the hours of instruction were established as 2-4 p.m. and 7-9 p.m. so that they did not conflict with temple duty. On numerous festival days, with their extended hours and their various other duties, the teachers had to fit in their teaching as best they could.

The Tilkayat is the nominal head of the school, and he in turn reports to the temple board, which is administered by a Central Government officer who resides in Nathdvara. The music school has been running for twenty years, but there are no accurate written records concerning its administration. The first principal was Ramdas, the present *Kirtankar Mukhiya* (1988) of the Shri Nathji Haveli, who held this post during 1966-73. The next was Mulchand, the present harmonium player who held it during 1973-82. He was replaced by Guru Purushottam. While the musicians are rewarded in kind for their service in the temple, those who taught in the music school in 1988, received a fixed salary. This varied from one hundred and fifty rupees per month for the teachers to eight hundred rupees for the Principal.

TABLE 8.1 THE STAFF OF THE MUSIC SCHOOL IN 1988

PRINCIPAL:		Guru Purushottam (*kakatiya*)	
SECRETARY		Prakash Chand	(*jalandhara*, Guru Purushottam's grandson)
TEACHERS:	Singing	Bhanvarlal II	*Kirtankar Mukhiya* VNJ (*jalandhara*)
		Kanhaiyalal II	*Haveli sangit* NNP (*jalandhara*)
	Pakhavaj	Mulchand	harmonium SNJ (*mandalia*)
	Tabla	Shyamlal	*pakhavaj* SNJ (*vanavadiya*)

Vacant posts: *Kathak*: sometimes taught by Kanhaiyalal II

Instruction they would like to offer: *sitar*, *khyal*.

No convincing explanation was given for not teaching *khyal*. Everyone acknowledged its importance.

All the staff at the music school have always combined working as a musician in a *haveli* and teaching. *Haveli sangit* was taught by Radhakrishna until 1986 when he suffered a stroke. He was replaced by his son, Bhanvarlal II, as both *Kirtankar Mukhiya* in the Navnitpriyaji Haveli and *haveli* teacher in the school. On account of his duties as *Kirtankar Mukhiya* he was sometimes late for his teaching duties. The versatility of the musicians is evident from the fact that several of them are employed by the temple for a skill different from the one that they teach in the school. For example, Shyamlal plays the *pakhavaj* in the Shri Nathji Haveli but is employed to teach *tabla* in the school, while Mulchand plays the harmonium in the Shri Nathji Haveli but teaches *pakhavaj* in the school. Guru Purushottam also taught *pakhavaj* and in 1988, two of his students, his grandson Prakash, and Balmukund, Shyamlal's son, had Government of India scholarships to study the instrument with him.

From 1983 to 1986, there were twenty-five students in the music school but the numbers fluctuated, particularly during school examination time. The most popular subject was *haveli sangit* and "general singing", as it was termed, with eighteen students enrolled. The next most popular was *tabla*, for which there were six students, and then *pakhavaj*. Only one girl chose to study Kathak dance.

SCHOLARSHIPS

Three types of scholarships were available for students to study at the school.

1. Centre of Cultural Research Training (CCRT), Delhi. For this the student must be below age fourteen. One student, Murli, a relation of Guru Purushottam held that scholarship in 1985. Murli's grandfather, Dayalal, was Guru Purushottam's nephew and his father, Balmukund, a supervisor and temple board worker. Murli had to go to Delhi for an interview for the scholarship, which amounted to approximately fifty rupees per month.

2. The Shri Nathji Temple board gave fifty rupees per month scholarship on the recommendation of the Principal of the music school. In 1985 five students had this scholarship: Manoj Tripathi, a *brahmin* boy aged twelve and the son of a school teacher; Gopal Gorva,

a Brajvasi brahmin aged twenty-one; Ashok Kumavat, aged fourteen, the son of Sohanlal, *Pakhavaji* in the Navnitpriyaji Haveli; Krishnagopal Sanchiar, a *brahmin*, aged twenty-two; and Hemlata, aged 10, daughter of Vallabhdas (*Binkar* in the Shri Nathji Haveli). Manoj Tripathi and Gopal Gorva were learning *haveli sangit* with Bhanvarlal II; Ashok Kumavat and Krishnagopal Sanchiar were learning under Guru Purushottam, the former *pakhavaj*, the latter, *tabla*; and Hemlata had a scholarship to learn Kathak which she was doing with Kanhaiyalal II until a qualified professional teacher could be found for the school. In 1987 a Kathak teacher from Bhilwara,a nearby town, was coming to the school on Sundays.

3. A scholarship of two hundred and fifty rupees per month was awarded by the Sangeet Natak Akademi in New Delhi. Two of these scholarships had been awarded to study *pakhavaj* with Guru Purushottam. Both the recipients were related to him: Prakash, his grandson and Balmukund, his nephew.

All the students combine learning music with some other activity, either studying at school or college, helping out in the family shop or, as in the case of Prakash Chand, working as the secretary for the school. For the younger students the scholarship of fifty rupees was a welcome bonus for their families' income, but Prakash and Balmukund, both young men in their twenties, and married, needed to supplement their stipend. It was generally accepted that no matter how modest, scholarships gave some recognition and provided important incentives for the recipients.

THE *KIRTANKAR'S* CHILDREN

In 1987 approximately half of the students studying music at the music school came from *kirtankar* families. This fact seems to indicate that training from non-family members is now accepted. Because they must combine studying music with academic education their artistic education must be obtained outside classroom hours and in a classroom situation rather than as apprentices on the job. The hours of work in the temple conflict with school. Nevertheless on festivals and holidays, a few children of hereditary musicians participate in temple music, thus obtaining on the spot training.

The atmosphere provided by the school is different from that in which their fathers trained. The older generation probably learned a great deal by listening to music in the temple and in their home. Today, very little instruction is given in the homes of the Nathdvara musicians. Their hours of work in the temple are long and, out of economic necessity they are often engaged in other work. It would seem that this situation has been in existence for some time, as most of the musicians are actively engaged in some other type of economic activity. Children of musicians who wished to learn music could enrol in the music school; others accompanied their parents to the temple outside school hours. Their first experience was usually as a singer, and they practised simply by singing along. By and large, neither the children nor their parents saw a *kirtankar's* life as a desirable career. In Nathdvara it is possible to make a living only by combining several activities.

Amongst the older generation in the 1980s, Ramdas (*Kirtankar Mukhiya*) had taught his son Shyamlal II *haveli sangit.* Shyamlal II was then teaching music in a higher secondary school in Kankroli. None of the children of Mulchand (Harmonium SNJ) were working in the temple. While one studied music and had his own band, another was a medical doctor and the others were businessmen, or watch repairers. Those sons now in their twenties or younger had generally not completely severed their ties with music but earned their living making handicrafts. Tolaram (Singer SNJ) had one son, Brajesh, aged fourteen who studied *haveli sangit*, as well as making decorative items used for worship at home (*shringar* and *mukut*) and working in the family shop near the Vitthalnathji Haveli. Shyamlal (Pakhavaji SNJ), had seven sons and one daughter. All his sons made handicrafts (*shringar* and *mukut*) but only one, Balmukund also studied *pakhavaj* in the school. Vallabhdas (Binkar SNJ) had three sons and four daughters, all of whom made handicrafts. One son, Chandrakant was studying singing in the school and *bin* with his father. One daughter, Hemlata, was studying Kathak in the school. Amritlal's (Sarangi SNJ) son was a qualified art teacher. Only one of Damodar's (Kirtankar Mukhiya NNP) two sons, studied *pakhavaj.* Kisanlal's (Haveli NNP) children were much too young, but he said that he did not want them to learn music when they grew up. Similar was the case with Sohanlal's (*Pakhavaji* NNP) young children. One of his sons, Ashok, did study *pakhavaj* with Guru Purushottam for some time, travelling with him and acting as his assistant; but in 1987 he was working full-time in Mulchand's son's watch repair shop, having given up studying and practising the *pakhavaj.* Sohanlal's eldest son was running a tea stall just outside his home. Bhanvarlal I's son Daulal was a *Pakhavaji* in the

Vitthalnathji Haveli. Daulal's children were too young to study music. Except for Bhanvarlal II, a full-time *haveli* singer in the Vitthalnathji Haveli, the other children of the late Radhakrishna (Kirtankar Mukhiya VNJ) were too young to predict what their profession might be. Kanhaiyalal II (Singer NNP) had one son aged twelve who studied *haveli sangit*.

REMUNERATION

Musicians officially employed by the temples receive remuneration in kind (see also Jindel 1976: 106-12, 133). Their "salary" consists of a small amount of cash but the bulk of it comes as a portion of the *prasad*. *Prasad* includes the food offerings made that day: a wide variety of sweets, vegetable curries, rice, *chapatis*, fruit, milk and curd. Some of this *prasad* is consumed by the musicians' families, and the rest is handed over to local shops which sell it to pilgrims and townsfolk. Such a salary, given in kind and then sold, is known as *neg*. Once a month the musicians collect a percentage of the selling price. This fluctuates considerably, as more *prasad* is prepared on festival days. The amount that the musicians eventually receive varies from one hundred and eighty rupees to eight hundred rupees.

Musicians are only one of several groups of temple employees who are paid in *prasad* (Jindel 1976). Some employees are paid entirely in cash. Because the costs of raw materials have been rising, the temple administration has been trying to change the system to one of universal cash payment, but the workers are reluctant to accept this. Although they do not get much from selling the *prasad*, at least the price paid by pilgrims can be expected to rise with increasing prosperity. The temple is not regarded as generous with wage increases. There is no entrance fee to enter any of the Vallabha Sampraday *havelis* and take *darshan*. If, however, pilgrims want *prasad* it must be purchased.

The *neg* system of payment to temple employees gives a large number of people a stake in the continued sale of the *prasad*, and this in turn may help to maintain the quality and the numerous preparations for festival days. As Nathdvara continues to be esteemed for its traditional cuisine, the preparation of food can be regarded as another traditional art nurtured by the temple.

Although music is not a lucrative activity in Nathdvara, the temples continue to maintain a high level of activity. This situation contrasts sharply with that found in nearby Udaipur, where the traditional temple musicians, formerly dependent on patronage from the palace, now receive negligible remuneration. Consequently, music has disappeared from most of the city temples. The situation is variable in the other *havelis* of the *sampraday*. Most *havelis* have some music, however perfunctory. Some give their musicians a meagre stipend, while others rely upon musicians giving their music as *seva* (chapter 12).

Some of the Nathdvara musicians earn additional money and acquire some artistic satisfaction by playing on All India Radio. Among the musicians who play in the Shri Nathji and Vitthalnathji temples, several have contracts to play monthly. Those who play outside the temple situation report little difficulty in shifting from one venue to the other. Not surprisingly they find more scope for musicianship on the radio but they feel that playing in the temple allows them to be in touch with the music daily.

SICK LEAVE AND HOLIDAYS

The *kirtankars* work long hours for very small remuneration and there is no job security. If a musician is sick, or required to be away for personal business, it is his responsibility to get someone to stand in for him. Mulchand, the harmonium player in the Shri Nathji Haveli, was frequently ill, so his brother Ratanlal came from Bhilvara as a substitute. Although Ratanlal normally earned his living as a watch-repairer he had received training in *haveli sangit*, *pakhavaj*, *bin* and harmonium. I have, on many occasions, seen him assist with his many musical talents playing harmonium for one *darshan*, *bin* during a pre-*darshan* period, and *pakhavaj* for yet another pre-*darshan*. His flexibility allowed him to fill in for several musicians.

Sohanlal, the *Pakhavaji* of the Navnitpriyaji temple, sometimes handed over his duties to Kanhaiyalal II, one of the singers. On such occasions Kanhaiyalal II sang and played *pakhavaj* simultaneously. Most of the *haveli* singers have had some rudimentary training in *pakhavaj*, which gives them this flexibility. Except for the two *pakhavaj* players, Guru Purushottam and Sohanlal, all the musicians have, at some time in their careers sung *haveli sangit*. This is because the basis for Indian instrumental music is the vocal tradition.

MUSIC AS *SEVA*

Donating artistic talent, manual work, or indeed any type of service to Shri Nathji is considered to confer great merit on the donor. As honorary *Pakhavaji* of the Shri Nathji temple, Guru Purushottam donated his services by playing the *pakhavaj* in the temple. From 1982 onwards he played at least twice a day, usually at *Raj Bhog* and *Bhog darshans*. I never saw him go to the temple just for *darshan*; if he went to the temple it was to play. Several other musicians also played in the temple from time to time as *seva* for Shri Nathji. But if they were filling in for a permanently employed musician, they would receive the *neg* normally given to the absent musician.

Seva was acceptable in the temple situation but when singing, playing or dancing before the Tilkayat, remuneration was sought. In this sense musicians differentiated between his secular and religious roles, interpreting his private pleasure as separate from that of Shri Nathji.

HOURS OF WORK

An enormous amount of rich food is offered to Shri Nathji seven times a day. Both food and music are extremely important as ritual offerings. The quality and quantity of the food is of utmost importance to the temple, in that it provides an important source of income. This is in contrast to music which serves only a ritual purpose and has no resale value; it has little intrinsic value beyond that of embellishment.

Because music accompanies most activities in Shri Nathji's daily routine the musicians are intimately aware of each activity taking place within the *nij mandir*, where Shri Nathji resides. They get their direction and cue from the priests. Knowledge of the ritual significance of each temple activity is as important to their position as knowledge of the music itself. They must know what to play and when to play it, as well as how to do so in an acceptable manner. Waiting and being on call is very much part of their daily routine and they must be able to anticipate for just how long they can leave the *haveli* at any particular time. As they reported, "There are no fixed timings". Hence, if I wanted to obtain an accurate record of their work, I had to sit with them in *kirtankar gali* while they either waited or played. I recorded their account of Shri Nathji's activities, as his daily routine defines the whole purpose for their music.

Each *darshan* may be considered the culmination of the real work of that particular segment of the day, which consists of the preparatory rituals performed by the priests. Pilgrims taking *darshan* see the Lord and share his presence. *Darshan* helps to publicize the *sampraday* and to attract devotees, who provide the cash and enthusiasm for maintaining and running the temple. My account of their daily programme of *darshan* is a synthesis of the accounts of several musicians. I am particularly indebted to Guru Purushottam, Shyamlal (*Pakhavaji*, Shri Nathji Haveli), Pannalal (*Haveli* Singer, Shri Nathji Haveli) and Vallabhdas (*Binkar*, Shri Nathji Haveli). The latter has the most important musical responsibility because he is present during all *darshans*. If music was to be played for Shri Nathji, Vallabhdas was always there. He would either play the *bin*, or sing *haveli sangit*, occasionally accompanying himself on the *tanpura*.

Music must be played for all *darshans* and also during the period while the *svarup* is being prepared beforehand, and afterwards when the deity is eating. The normal order of events includes eight *darshans* per day, coupled with eight pre-*darshan* periods, and one post-*darshan* period at the end of the day, making a total of seventeen times when music is required. Usually seven of the eight *darshans* are open to the public;[2] none of the pre-*darshan* periods are.

Except on festival days, *darshan* periods are short, the longest being *Raj Bhog*, which usually takes forty-five minutes to an hour. On festival days, such as *Chhappan Bhog* (the festival on which fifty-six varieties of food are offered), *Raj Bhog darshan* can take up to two hours; on such days, the musicians are required to play for a longer period. On normal days, even when *darshans* are not taking place, all musicians are required to be on duty in the temple from about 7.00 a.m. to 11.30 a.m., beginning with playing before the second *darshan* (pre-*Shringar*) in *kirtankar gali*. There is a long break in the middle of the day. In the afternoon the musician's hours are approximately from 4.00 to 5.30 p.m. All these times are approximate and are generally much longer during festival days.

The *Kirtankar Mukhiya* and the *Binkar* in the Shri Nathji temple have longer hours. In the morning, their duty begins with pre-*Mangal*. Depending on the season, they begin any time between 3.00 and 4.30 a.m. in the winter and slightly later in summer. Their afternoon sessions begin around 3.30 p.m., with pre-*Utthapan*.

Vallabhdas, the *Binkar* of the Shri Nathji temple, recounted his duties for September 14, 1984. At about 3.00 a.m. a temple servant arrived at his home to wake him. He walked to the temple where, at 4.00 a.m. he played *bin* in *doltivari* to wake Shri Nathji, as is his daily custom. For this he stood on the right hand side of the entrance, the doors to the *nij mandir* being closed. During *Mangal*, the first public *darshan* of the day, he and Ramdas, the *Kirtankar Mukhiya*, presented two songs in *mani kota*, the usual place where musicians stand during public *darshans.* By 7.00 a.m. all the musicians had gathered in *kirtankar gali.* There, before *Shringar*, three songs composed by Surdas, Kumbhandas and Parmananddas (all *ashtachhap* poets), were sung in *kirtankar gali.* At the same time, Vallabhdas played the *bin* in the *darshan* hall. During *Shringar darshan*, only one song, by the poet Vitthal, was sung. After *Shringar darshan*, when the doors were closed, Ratanlal, the brother of the harmonium player Mulch and, sang a song in *kirtankar gali* for the pre-*Gval* session. It was not his duty that day, but he did so because he had free time. It was, however, his responsibility that day to sing for *Gval*, the next *darshan*; for which he sang only one song, though he said he could have sung two or three.

Gval is important in the early stages of a musician's career. Many younger musicians reported having their first musical performance experience at that time, either singing or accompanying. Guru Purushottam reported that from the age of eighteen to twenty-five, before he became the official *Pakhavaji* of the Shri Nathji temple, he accompanied singers at this *darshan* to get experience, practice and exposure in accompaniment.

After *Gval*, *bin* and *pakhavaj* were played in *kirtankar gali* for about twenty to twenty-five minutes. This is the period (pre-*Raj Bhog*) during which Shri Nathji eats his main meal of the day. *Raj Bhog* (11.30-12.00 noon), the fourth *darshan* of the day, is the most elaborate. On that day, when all the musicians had assembled in front of Shri Nathji, they sang only one song. After *Raj Bhog*, the musicians received their portion of the *prasad* (*neg*). The temple was then closed and the musicians went home to have their midday meal and rest.

By 3.30 in the afternoon, the *Binkar*, and *Kirtankar Mukhiya*, assembled again for *Utthapan darshan*. Their duty then was to wake Shri Nathji with the music of *bin* and *haveli sangit.* The *pakhavaj* is never used on this occasion, or indeed at any time when Shri Nathji is being roused from sleep. By 4.30 p.m. all the musicians assembled again for *Bhog darshan*. On that day they sang one song in *kirtankar gali* and one in the presence of Shri Nathji. For *Shayan darshan* at 6 p.m. only the *bin* was played.

I was present during *Shayan darshan* for the festivals of Chhappan Bhog, and Annakut in 1985. On these occasions all the musicians including the *Pakhavaji* played. This was a very important occasion as it marked the visit to Nathdvara of two of the other *svarups*, Balkrishnaji from Surat and Dvarkadeshji from Kankroli (Tod 1829: I.437; chapter 11). On these occasions a temple servant holds a large flaming torch in *ratan chauk*, beside the door closest to the *darshan* room, where the ladies enter. It is important that this medieval custom is continued because the electricity supply in Nathdvara is very erratic and the temple could be plunged into darkness at any moment (see also Jindel 1976: 66).

MUSIC AND RITUAL

To be a musician is to be intimately linked with the most important components of temple ritual. I have therefore transcribed their observations of what is going on while they are playing music, in particular the events surrounding the presenting of *prasad*. This material is of a more general nature and is intended to complement the detailed description given above of a single day in the life of Vallabhdas. Festival celebrations alter the daily routine which is either expanded or contracted, depending on the intent of the festival and the funds that have been made available. Each festival highlights certain aspects of Shri Nathji's daily activities with a variety of artistic offerings: more donations bring greater opulence.

For all of the art forms there are certain underlying rules governing their presentation which depend on such factors as the season and the time of day. Aesthetic considerations seem to be; the appropriate type of music for Shri Nathji's activity (ordinary or special); which instruments play: *bin* and vocal being considered soothing, *jhanjh* lively and festive. Festival days require more instruments and in particular those that are of the *shikaram* or struck variety. The rules differ somewhat among different *havelis*, apparently because of the personal predilection of the individual Maharaj. For instance, in the Natvarlal Haveli in Ahmedabad the *pakhavaj* has become an accepted part of *Mangal darshan* whereas in the Shri Nathji Haveli the drum is never played for this *darshan*. This exception could be because the head of the Natvarlal Haveli, Maharaj Purushottamlal, is an excellent *pakhavaj* player.

The account that follows lists the regular accepted practice in the Shri Nathji Haveli with comments on those special touches that are added for *Radhashtami*, the festival that commemorates the birth of Radha. I have chosen this festival as it was celebrated two days after the day for which I recorded normal daily activities. Once again, in those instances where I could not be present, I have depended mainly on the account of the *Binkar*, Vallabhdas.

Vallabhdas stated that he generally reported to the temple about 3 a.m. and, as above, a temple servant came to wake him. It was his duty to play the *bin* and then blow a conch to awaken Shri Nathji. After this he played the *bin* while Shri Nathji enjoyed some light refreshment (*Mangal Bhog*). This included one *dubara* (a liquid measure) of milk and curd, twenty-two *thor* (a large round sweet, about eight inches in diameter and made with butter and sugar, one *katori* (a solid measurement) of pickles and two *pan*.

Fortified with this light refreshment, Shri Nathji is ready to greet his devotees and *Mangal darshan* is opened to the public. Shri Nathji appears in the garments in which he has spent the night. In winter he is completely covered in *angarkha* (short jacket) made to look very much like a quilt (*razai*), in summer a loin cloth (*araband*) and during the rest of the year an *araband* and a long scarf draped over the shoulders (*uperna*).

As soon as doors open for *Mangal darshan*, one song is sung by the *Binkar* and *Kirtankar Mukhiya*, without the percussion accompaniment of *pakhavaj* or *jhanjh*. Although Jindel (1976: 64) reported that music accompanies *arati* (waving of a lighted lamp) my observations, supported by the testimony of Vallabhdas, were that unless one were among the first to enter the *darshan* hall, it was possible to miss entirely the short musical offering for this *darshan*. The music usually finished well before *arati* and the custom was always for *arati* to signal the closing of *darshan*.

I was often present for *Mangal darshan* and I noticed that although they were not on duty, most of the musicians also took *Mangal darshan* along with the main body of devotees, before starting work. They would then take up position in *kirtankar gali* where they sat on the stone floor (this could be very cold in winter). The musicians kept a few pieces of sacking to protect them from the cold floor, and when I sat with them I found it useful to carry a shawl. By then it was about 6 a.m. and most of us were only half awake. The daily routine was to sing two songs while Shri Nathji was being adorned. As described above, the *bin* played in the *darshan* hall (*doltivari*) at the same time.

All instruments were played, including *sarangi* and *pakhavaj* but only on festive days would *jhanjh* be included. On a normal day the two required songs would be completed in about ten to fifteen minutes but during Radhashtami and other festivals the songs would have to be longer as the ritual of dressing Shri Nathji took longer. Vallabhdas reported that on many festival days, and in this particular case as it was Radhashtami, prior to being dressed, Shri Nathji would be bathed in *panchamrit* (nectar of five ingredients: sugar, honey, milk, ghee and curd).

There was usually a break before *Shringar darshan* opened, at which point all the musicians would rush out, either to their homes, or to a nearby cafe, for a cup of tea or coffee. Some went to check up on their shops which sold religious articles for pilgrims, others to collect pilgrims that they had offered to guide. I usually went with a different musician each day, to the coffee shop on Vitthalnathji Gali (lane), or to the tea shop run by a distant relation of Guru Purushottam (which was not far from the Madanmohanji Haveli), or, along with the rest of the pilgrims, bought a rich milk sweet (*ravadi*), which had been part of Shri Nathji's breakfast.

We often had to wait at least an hour before *Shringar darshan*. All the musicians returned to *kirtankar gali* within half an hour to be ready to play one song in front of Shri Nathji as soon as *Shringar darshan* opened. All instruments would play except the *bin*. The musicians would leave well before *Shringar* closed, and again many would dash out of the temple, estimating the length of their absence by the number of pilgrims waiting to get in for *Shringar*. The more pilgrims, the longer the *darshan* stayed open, and hence the more time they had to complete their private business. Once *Shringar darshan* was closed the musicians again gathered to play as Shri Nathji ate for the second time. They reported, "Shri Nathji eats many varieties of sweets after *Shringar* but he does not eat *thor*". Those sweets he does consume were *mathari* (thirty-five), *laddu* (thirty-six), and one full *dubara* of white *ravadi*. There were in addition to a *dubara* of milk, curd, *masunti*, and saffron as well as *shikaran*, pickles, *vasonti* and small *pan*.

Before *Gval darshan* opened Shri Nathji drank some milk. This activity was accompanied by one song accompanied by *pakhavaj* in *kirtankar gali*. As discussed earlier, this pre-*Gval* period was the time when many of the inexperienced musicians were given a chance to play or sing, usually with one of the more established musicians. *Gval* is the one *darshan* in the Shri Nathji Haveli that is not always accompanied by music. The Navnitpriyaji Haveli, however, does include music for this *darshan*. Many of the musicians leave after *Shringar darshan* and do not report back until pre-*Raj Bhog* which begins as soon as *Gval* is closed.

The period between the closing of *Shringar* and the opening of *Raj Bhog* generates considerable activity. Normally this is between approximately 8.30 and 10.30 a.m. All the pilgrims will have attended at least one *darshan* by then, having had the choice of *Mangal*, *Shringar* and *Gval* and all would be eagerly anticipating the culmination, *Raj Bhog*. During this waiting period, religious fervour is the highest. Some pilgrims take time to shop in the many small stalls that are located both inside and just outside the temple compounds. Nothing is very far in Nathdvara so others take this opportunity to visit the smaller *havelis* of the *sampraday* as their *darshans* are always later than those of the Shri Nathji Haveli. A guide was absolutely essential if one wanted to take the maximum number of *darshans*, which included those in minor temples. The latter were difficult to locate and the times for their *darshans* were erratic. Several musicians acted as guides for tourists. After *Shringar*, some musicians once again rushed off to attend to their shops, while others sang at the other *havelis*, or did minor chores associated with those *havelis*, such as purchasing raw materials to be used to make *prasad*, or flowers to decorate the image. For such work they received some small remuneration. Kanhaiyalal II reported that he served in this capacity, buying articles for the *darshan* preparations in several of the smaller *havelis*.

During the pre-*Raj Bhog* period, Shri Nathji was presented with a huge midday meal. This included rice, *chapatis*, curries (of spinach, etc.), *puri*, *khir*, and curd. At that time four songs were usually sung in *kirtankar gali* to the accompaniment of all musical instruments except the *bin*. At the start of *Raj Bhog darshan* one song was sung. On Radhashtami two songs were sung as it was a special festival and *Raj Bhog* remained open for a much longer period to accommodate the extra pilgrims. As soon as *Raj Bhog* was closed the *haveli* was cleared and locked. Many of the pilgrims and townsfolk did not eat until after Shri Nathji had eaten his lunch, and they had greeted him at *Raj Bhog darshan*.

Shri Nathji was awakened at about 4 p.m.from his afternoon nap by *bin* played alone for the pre-*Utthapan darshan*. The pilgrims could enter only at the beginning of *Utthapan* at which time the *kirtankars* sang a song. Immediately after the closing of *Utthapan* Shri Nathji received an afternoon snack of fruits and a special sweet; there was no musical accompaniment. Music for *Bhog darshan* may include *bin* accompanied by *pakhavaj*, *sarangi* accompanied by *pakhavaj* or songs accompanied by *bin* and *pakhavaj*. As soon as *Bhog* closed Shri Nathji had another snack of eleven *thor*. This was the fifth time that Shri Nathji had received food and at this time *bin* and *pakhavaj* accompanied his meal.

After *Bhog darshan* all the musicians sang and played to announce the opening of *Sandhya/Arati*. The *bin* was optional. As soon as *Sandhya/Arati* had closed Shri Nathji was presented with food for the sixth time, including lentils (*daal*) and rice, curry, spinach (*sag bugana*), *puri, laddu,* and a *dubara* of *basonti* and milk.

Before retiring for the night Shri Nathji received another substantial snack. At that time four songs, intended to induce sleep, were sung, usually accompanied only by the *tanpura*. On festive occasions, however, a full complement including *pakhavaj* and *jhanjh* were added. In 1988, on Radhashtami, an additional song was sung by Brijlal in *patal ghar*, the lane parallel to and behind *kirtankar gali*. Finally, the last *darshan*, *Shayan*, which was not open to the public, included one song, sung by the *kirtankar mukhiya* in *patal ghar*. This was followed by three pieces played solo on the *bin* by Vallabhdas, seated in *kamal chauk*, underneath *dhruvari,* the small window said to allow Shri Nathji to be illuminated by the North Star.

Shayan darshan is open to the public during Phalgun, and for fourteen days at Divali. When it is open to the public all the musicians play. For festival days and at other times considered appropriate, *jhanjh* were played to accompany *haveli* songs, but never to accompany instrumental music.

CURRENT TRENDS IN THE NUMBERS OF MUSICIANS

All the musicians reported that the importance of music in worship was declining. In 1985, two temples, the Madanmohanji and Banmaliji, employed only one musician, whereas twenty-five years earlier both employed two, one to sing and another to play the *pakhavaj*. In some temples music has virtually disappeared.

Two of the smaller temples, the Kalyanrayji and the Govindarayji, had informal arrangements for music, as they employ musicians who also worked in the Shri Nathji and Navnitpriyaji, where all *darshans* must have musical accompaniment. The Kalyanrayji Haveli used the services of Tolaram, who was also the *haveli* singer in the Shri Nathji temple, while the Govindarayji temple employed Bhanvarlal I, *haveli* singer in the Navnitpriyaji temple. As musicians working in two temples, they had to adjust their hours of work, rushing to the smaller temple between engagements at the larger. Consequently music was normally presented only once a day at the minor temples, most frequently at *Raj Bhog*. Solo musicians usually sang *haveli* and provided their own accompaniment by playing the *pakhavaj* and on festival days the *jhanjh* as well. Singing without rhythmic accompaniment is unknown, except when Shri Nathji is being woken or put to sleep. This emphasizes the importance of the rhythmic component of *haveli sangit*.

The training of the older musicians usually included a period of employment in the smaller, less well endowed temples, or training during less important *darshans*, such as *Gval*, in the Shri Nathji Haveli. Today, posts in the less endowed temples are occupied by older musicians. Twenty-five years ago, when there were more positions available, the musicians in these smaller temples were younger and less experienced. The Kalyanrayji Haveli employed two full-time musicians, Shyamlal (*pakhavaj*) and the late Radhakrishna (*haveli sangit*). Both of them received their training on the job, and were then able to move to more lucrative and prestigious temples. Shyamlal in 1985 was employed as the *Pakhavaji* of the Shri Nathji Haveli, and Radhakrishna left the Kalyanrayji temple to take up the post of *Kirtankar Mukhiya* of the Vitthalnathji temple, a post that he held until his death.

Today the children of the musicians attend school, or college and are not available at a young age to devote the same amount of time to playing in the temples (see also Erdman 1980). As a result the youngest musicians in active service in the temples of Nathdvara are in their early forties. With fewer positions available there is less opportunity for young artists to stay in the field while waiting for a professional musician's position to become vacant. Instead, most of the young men are working in shops where handicrafts are sold, some made by their own families and others by fellow *kirtankars*. It appears that more money is available for material goods than for nurturing and encouraging younger musicians to take up the profession.

All the musicians reported that their standard of living has fallen because of inflation. As a result, many of them have not taught their art to their children. While some children have joined the music school, the parents of the majority have encouraged them to join the professions, or seek other more secure ways of life. While the musicians may claim that they received more esteem and had a higher standard of living in the past, the most important reason for the changing aspirations of the younger generation is probably the increased opportunities provided by education and changes in the rigid structure of Nathdvara society. In the past they had no real choice, and they must have had to persevere with their calling whether or not times were bad (as surely often they were). "Inflation" and "lack of esteem" are universal explanations for hereditary professional groups abandoning their traditional calling. With this there is also a tendency to idealise the life they might once have led, while reaching for the greater flexibility and remuneration offered by employment outside the *haveli.*

CONCLUSION

Music as *seva* is still an important tradition in the temples of Nathdvara. All the musicians currently employed in the temples entered the Vallabha Sampraday and the musical profession by virtue of their birth. Even today, it is unlikely that anyone from outside the *kirtankar* families could obtain a position there as a temple musician.

The restrictions of caste and sect which continue in Nathdvara give the music continuity of purpose, and allow it to resist the changes and modernization occurring elsewhere. The musical and family links among members of this tightly-knit social group are the kind of social structure that must have been typical of Indian musical traditions in the past, but which is becoming increasingly obscured in the modern context by the mobility of artists and the breakdown of caste restrictions that once determined who could join the profession (Gaston 1991a).

Studying a traditional system that is still operative is of considerable historical interest, because many of the artistic traditions of present-day India cannot claim to be more than re-creations of pre-existing systems. Those which ceased to be performed have been refashioned from descriptions in texts, carvings on temples, or paintings on walls, paper or palm leaves. The venues of performance have changed, and the audiences have been cultivated rather than absorbed as a way of life. Much of the art available to the outside world and to urban India is being packaged and "cleaned up" to make it more accessible. In this process, the balance has shifted from ritual to social and aesthetic values.

The music presented at *darshan* in the temples of Nathdvara is entirely in the hands of the musicians. The songs performed, their duration, and the type of accompaniment used are extremely flexible. In addition, music is liable to "break out" at other times and in other parts of the temple if the musicians feel disposed in the mood. This spur-of-the-moment attitude toward the music derives from their great familiarity with the entire establishment of the temple. Almost from birth, they became accustomed to the rituals of the temple, so that they never need to think about what should be happening. They are so much a part of the temple's functions that, within certain limits, whatever they consider appropriate is *de facto* correct. This freedom from strictly defined procedures may well be characteristic of hereditary traditions in which the general format of the art is absorbed at a very young age.

The music in Nathdvara *havelis* will continue as long as it is a recognized ingredient of *darshan* and is considered an important part of *seva*. Nevertheless, the number of musicians supported by the *havelis* is declining, and only three continue to support more than one musician. Whether music will continue to be regarded as an occupation with sufficient status and remuneration to attract talented recruits is questionable. Already, many of the musicians' children have chosen to enter other professions. The fact that some of the young people were studying *pakhavaj* was probably a measure of Guru Purushottam's reputation, rather than an indication of a general revival of interest. For *bin* and vocal, there did not appear to be any seriously committed students in the twenties age group.

The decline in the importance of music in the temples, which almost all the musicians perceived, might eventually lead to a dilution of the Nathdvara tradition and a falling off of standards. On the other hand, the musical success of Guru Purushottam gave great encouragement to those who aspired to become good musicians. His presence at the music school lent the profession of music at Nathdvara a greater prestige than before. As a result, visiting musicians were more likely to perform there, knowing they shared a platform with an acknowledged master. This may have created greater enthusiasm for the art within the community.

Yet the music of Nathdvara, which depends entirely on the patronage of the temple, is not likely to be exported elsewhere. Its flavour is bound up with the Vallabha Sampraday faith, rituals and setting. I am reminded of two Ras Lila recitals by the same troupe of traditional actors, one in Vrindavan in 1983, the other in London in 1984. The London recital at the Commonwealth Institute did not make the intended impact; the actors looked disaffected, the costumes garish, and the audience was either unable to interact, or felt it improper, even though their spiritual head, Purushottam Gosvami, was present. In Vrindavan, by contrast, when viewed by devotees in Purushottam Gosvami's home and with him in attendance, the same performance had purpose and meaning, generating atmosphere and involvement.

The music of Nathdvara, lacking the ingredients for a lasting concert stage presentation, is entirely dependent on the temples for venue and patronage. Should this support be withdrawn, it would lose its purpose, as well as its financial basis. In the final analysis, it is the attitude of the temple hierarchy, particularly the Tilkayat, towards the standard of musicianship within the temple retinue, which is likely to determine the fate of Nathdvara's *haveli sangit* tradition.

NOTES

1. Powers (1979: 17) makes the same point.
   In 1987 I visited a Bhutanese *lakhang* (temple) accompanied by a reincarnate lama. Two nuns resident in the *lakhang*, asked him to read a text written by his former incarnation. They also knew the text by heart but he explained that only after hearing it from him, was the power of the teaching fully available to them. Ghanshyam's statement about "stealing or taking" musical ideas reflects a similar attitude.
2. *Shayan* is the exception, open to the public at some times and closed at others.

Plate 8.1: Guru Purushottam on the balcony of the music school

The music school was located in the compound of the Shri Nathji Haveli until 1985. Moti Mahal, the Tilkayat's palace is in the background.

Plate 8.2: Guru Purushottam teaching his grandson, Prakash

Plate 8.3: The music school

The author playing the *pakhavaj* in the music school with the musicians. Playing the harmonium, Radhakrishna, *haveli* singer and *Kirtankar Mukhiya*, Vitthalnathji Haveli, Guru Purushottam Das, Mulchand, Shyamlal, playing the *tanpura*.

BACK ROW: Misrilal, Prakash Chand and the female caretaker.

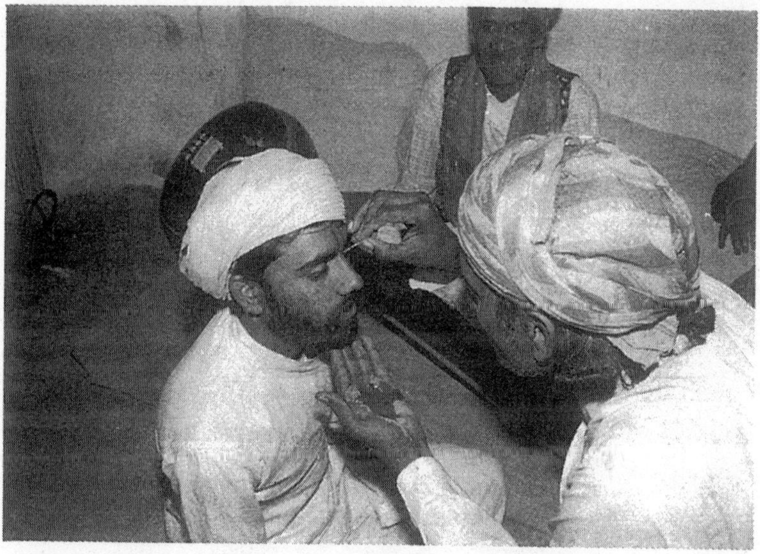

Plate 8.4: Kanhaiyalal II (jalandhara division) drawing the bindi on his nephew, Prakash. Kanhaiyalal II's elder brother Misrilal is in the background

Plate 8.5: Guru Purushottam Das with his great nephew Balmukund and grandson Prakash Chand

All of them are from different divisions of ***kumavats***: Guru Purushottam (***kakatiya*** division); Prakash Chand (***jalandhara*** division); Balmukund (***mandalia*** division).

Balmukund's father is employed as the *Pakhavaji* in the Shri Nathji Haveli, but Prakash Chand, the son of Guru Purushottam's daughter Radha has been adopted as Guru Purushottam's legal heir. No one was able to state who would succeed Shyamlal.

Plate 8.6: The four Pakhavajis of Nathdvara (1985)

LEFT TO RIGHT: Ratanlal, a trained *Pakhavaji* who plays occasionally in the Shri Nathji Haveli; Radhakrishna, *haveli sangit* teacher and at that time *Kirtankar Mukhiya* Vitthalnathji Haveli; Guru Purushottam Das, *pakhavaj* teacher and principal of the school;Prakash Chand, Secretary of the school, learning *pakhavaj*; Mulchand, *pakhavaj* teacher, harmonium player Shri Nathji Haveli; Misrilal, music teacher at the local girls' school; Shyamlal, *tabla* teacher, *Pakhavaji* in the Shri Nathji Haveli; missing Sohanlal, *Pakhavaji*, Navnitpriyaji Haveli.

Plate 8.7: Prasad in Nathdvara

Prasad being carried through the streets to the various shops and the places where pilgrims stay. The carriers are wearing the required dress of ***angarkhi*** and ***dhoti***.

Plates 8.8 and 8.9: Prasad being sold in Nathdvara

Various vendors are selling the ***prasad*** after ***darshan***. They are wearing the required dress of ***angarkhi*** and ***dhoti***.

CHAPTER 9

Making Ends Meet: Other Economic Activities of the *Kirtankars*

Being a musician in a Nathdvara *haveli* generally involves a variety of skills beyond that of actually performing music. This has probably been true for several generations. One notable exception is Guru Purushottam and those members of his family recorded in the *Mridang Sagar*. The reasons for this diversification are economic. It is very difficult, if not impossible, to support a family on what the temple provides. Whereas Guru Purushottam and his family found patronage from princely courts and obtained remuneration from performing on the concert stage, other musicians looked elsewhere for supplementary income. In those instances where they continued their hereditary association with the *havelis* as *kirtankars*, they chose jobs that allowed them to combine both activities. Other than teaching in the music school, which is attached to the *haveli* and which has hours that are compatible with their temple duty, they were left with few options for employment requiring fixed hours. Consequently most looked for self-employment in cooperation with other family members. With increasing education and mobility, their options are expanding. Several of the younger generation have joined the professions and hence removed themselves from dependence on the *haveli*.

Other than employment in the temples, *haveli* singers have limited options for earning a living through music. Two of the hereditary *kirtankars*, Misrilal (the middle brother of Damodar, Kirtankar Mukhiya NNP, and Kanhaiyalal II, singer, NNP) and Shyamlal II (son of Ramdas, Kirtankar Mukhiya SNJ), teach music in government high schools. Besides the temple, this is the only outlet for regular paid employment in their field.

Most of the Nathdvara musicians supplement their income from music with some additional work, usually concerned with some aspect of the temple. Maduro (1976) made a similar observation concerning the traditional brahmin painters of Nathdvara. Within the two groups of brahmin painters that he studied, only one, the Jangiras, were diversifying their occupation and encouraging their children to look beyond painting. The other group, the Adi Gaurs were actively discouraging their children from diversifying. In 1987, when I spoke to several of the same families included in Maduro's study, they confirmed that this trend persisted. Those who were staying in the tradition were proud to acknowledge that they would continue to be painters.

Unlike the painter community which was divided, all of the *kirtankar* families were encouraging their children to help supplement the family income, either by repairing watches, working in the administration of the music school, or making and selling articles of decoration that serve to enhance the worship of Shri Nathji. In the latter capacity they were still very much a part of the religious life of the town.

CRAFTS

All of the artistic life of musicians, painters and crafts people in Nathdvara revolves around Shri Nathji. Music, painting on canvas and paper, painted and embroidered *picchvai*, jewellery and other articles of decoration, are all created to enhance his worship. Many of the musicians supplemented their income by making, and/or selling religious articles. These include items used in household shrines as well as those used in the various *havelis*. In both instances they are bought by pilgrims; the small items are kept for their own use and the larger ones are donated to the temple.

Miniature dresses, jewellery and crowns used to decorate replicas of Navnitpriyaji are constantly made. They are relatively inexpensive, so pilgrims buy a lot of these items. They can be assembled by almost anyone and the demand for them seems unlimited. Most pilgrims wish to purchase a complete set (*saja*), which includes a small metal image of Krishna as Navnit ('lover of butter'), and a seat or throne with bolsters on which he is placed (*simhasana*). The image must have several changes of dress, which includes *angarkhi*, various crowns and necklaces. The decorative elements are referred to as *shringar* [including necklaces (*mala*), earrings, bracelets and collars] and a wide variety of crowns (*mukut*) which include *kulai* (one kind of turban), *tipara* (a type of crown), *feta*, *pagadi* (turban) and *dumala* (double crown). Some enamel work (*minakari*) is also carried out. Most pilgrims like to add to their collection of jewellery and decorative crowns, so that they can change the adornments of their household shrine. The demand for these smaller items is so great that their making is often sub-contracted to village women who live nearby. They are then marketed by various *kirtankars.* Until 1987, I had not seen any miniature replicas of Shri Nathji sold, although paintings of him in every conceivable dress were one of the commonest items on sale. A carved Shri Nathji, about ten inches high, in black stone, was recently introduced and is proving to be of interest to pilgrims.

Other items used in worship, of a more specialized nature, are not always as readily available, but can be made to order. These include peacock feathers secured on the end of a long stick with silver ropes (*morcchal*). This device is held towards the image and rotated in front of it by twisting the wrist. The *morcchal* is used mainly in the cooler months of winter. Its ritual importance lies in keeping the image auspicious by removing any evil influences; it also has the practical use of getting rid of flies. In the summer, fans and fly whisks (*chamara*) are used. Traditionally, yak tails were used to make *chamara* but in Nathdvara the hair from a cow's tail is used.

The larger and more impressive objects used in temples, and on occasion in private homes, have been developed and refined by particular *kirtankar* families and are made only by them. These are just a few of the many items used in worship that are purchased by pilgrims for use in shrines, both at home, and in Vallabha Sampraday Havelis in Nathdvara, and throughout India, and abroad. The export market is growing, particularly to the Gulf states and the UK (Skelton 1973: 23-5).

PICCHVAI

Among the arts of Nathdvara the best known is the art of making *picchvai* (Skelton 1973; Talwar and Krishna 1979). The practise of hanging a *picchvai* on the back wall of the *nij mandir* behind the main image was introduced into the Vallabha Sampraday by Vitthalnath in the sixteenth century, while still based in Braj (Barz 1976). According to Talwar and Krishna (1979), the Radha Vallabha sect in Vrindavan uses *picchvai* in a manner similar to the Vallabha Sampraday. It seems that with this exception the use of *picchvai* is unique to the Vallabha Sampraday. The use of *picchvai* has been said to mimic the splendour of the Mughals, who used wall hangings in their tents and palaces, or to imitate Buddhist *thanka* (*Marg* 1980: 117). As objects of beauty, they found their way into the worship of a sect which specialised in honoring its deity with beautiful things. All of those illustrated in Talwar and Krishna (1979) and *Marg* (1980) that relate to worship in Nathdvara are dated to the late nineteenth and early twentieth century. They show clearly that worship today continues to be very much as it was then.

Picchvai may consist of narrative scenes, showing the life of Krishna, or may be covered in floral, animal or geometrical motifs. They are made in a variety of ways. The most famous are those painted directly on cloth.

The making of painted *picchvais* is reserved for a group of professional painters (Maduro 1976). Although previous writers have devoted most of their attention to the painted *picchvai*, in my experience, this type of *picchvai* is not often used in the Shri Nathji Haveli. Those made with embroidery or applique are used in the *havelis* more frequently. This is supported by Talwar and Krishna (1979: 12), who observed that the Shri Nathji Haveli and "the other major *gaddis* use mostly brocaded, or embroidered *picchvais*. The painted ones are used only on the less important holidays of the smaller temples of the sect". The *picchvais* made by the *kirtankar* community are often of high quality. Yet, although the art of the *picchvai* forms the main theme in the work of both Skelton (1973) and Talwar and Krishna (1979) and to some extent that of Maduro (1976) on the painters, none of them refer to the role of the musician community in this industry. One explanation may be that since the traditional work of the community involves music they therefore identify themselves as musicians (*kirtankars*) despite being engaged in other types of work. At the same time, their supplementary income is essential for them to be able to continue as musicians.

ART AS A HISTORICAL RECORD OF EVENTS IN THE *SAMPRADAY*

Narrative *picchvai* may be painted, embroidered, or made with applique (patchwork). Because much has already been written on the art of *picchvai* I do not intend to deal with them at length. Nevertheless, an aspect of these *picchvai* that has been insufficiently emphasized and which is important to my theme, is the extent to which the subject matter derives from actual events enacted within the *haveli.* In that context the fact that some of the work is done by the musicians is significant, because they are actually present and participate in most of the celebration depicted.

I compared my observations to events depicted by *picchvai* in the collection of the Calico Museum, Ahmedabad,[1] illustrated in Talwar and Krishna (1979), and in the private collection of Amit Ambalal illustrated in *Krishna as Shri Naṭhji* (1987), and found them to be still an accurate record of how the festivals take place. For example, I attended the festival of Nandotsav on 28 August 1986, which re-enacts the joy of Krishna's parents, Nanda and Yashoda after his birth. The festival is celebrated one day after the birth of Krishna (Janmashtami). On the occasion of Nandotsav, two of the priests dress up as Yashoda and Nanda. They sit beside a cradle holding the Navnitpriyaji image which acts as a surrogate because the Shri Nathji image is too large. During the *darshan* they rock the cradle and amuse Shri Nathji by shaking silver rattles and spinning tops. Replicas of these toys can be purchased in the market. Growse, writing in 1883, noted that they were made in Braj, near Gokul and used during the rituals of the Vallabha Sampraday temples in the area.

NANDOTSAV CELEBRATIONS

In the other Vallabha Sampraday temples in Nathdvara the same ritual of playing with toys is repeated. One particularly delightful part of the Nandotsav celebrations in the Vitthalnathji temple was when all of the devotees, myself included, joined in a circle and danced with Nanda, Yashoda and other temple servants dressed as milkmaids and cowherds (*gopa*). We did this in front of the image of Vitthalnathji. In the Shri Nathji Haveli, where there were considerably more devotees, the dancing was in *kamal chauk* which had been decorated with petals from roses and other flowers. Later, more temple servants dressed like cowherds arrived carrying pots of curd mixed with turmeric. They proceeded to flick the contents with their fingers onto the crowd. As the curd became well spread underfoot, they began to push one another playfully so that they slipped on the slick stone floor. Throwing curd spread to the street and it was impossible to escape as the lanes were so narrow. Everyone who came participated directly in the play.

All of these activities associated with Nandotsav are faithfully represented in the *picchvai* illustrated in Talwar and Krishna (1979: plate 15) and correspond with celebrations today. The *bin*, *pakhavaj* and *jhanjh* (cymbals) depicted in the *picchvai* were still being played, although the *bin* and *tanpura* illustrated in the *picchvai* were played while standing, something that I have never seen in the Shri Nathji Haveli. Other differences in 1986 were the presence of two additional instruments, a *sarangi* and harmonium. Because *picchvai* record the exact way in which temple festivals are conducted they provide a constant reminder of the traditions of the sect, which presumably helps to preserve them largely unchanged.

The painted *picchvai* are made by a few Brahmin families dedicated only to this art, and to the production of miniatures of Shri Nathji in his different seasonal costumes (Maduro 1976: 50-4). Most of their output is sold to pilgrims, but some are then donated to the temple. Studies of the painters of Nathdvara report that in 1980 there were fifty artists painting *picchvai* (*Marg* 1980: 123). While the themes of both painted *picchvai* and miniature paintings are similar, *picchvai* are larger than miniature paintings as they are used as backdrops. Both are important sources for documenting the cultural activities of the temple and the sect, in particular the numerous festivals. It has been my experience that scenes in the paintings are still being faithfully reproduced when festivals are celebrated. Those festivals which have inspired the most *picchvai* are Ramaṇavami, Nandotsav, Dana Ekadasi, Sharada Utsav and Annakut.

EMBROIDERED *PICCHVAI*

Embroidered *picchvai* are made by two *kirtankar* brothers, employed in the Shri Nathji Haveli—Pannalal, *haveli* singer, and Vallabhdas, *Binkar*—and their families. The two brothers cooperate closely; the fact that Vallabhdas was brought up in a different household, having been adopted by a paternal uncle, Jamnadas, who had no son of his own, has not affected their relationship. The making of applique *picchvai* is a recently imported tradition. Apparently, the biological father of these three brothers, Gokuldas, acquired the expertise during his stay at Dwarka (Gujarat) where he worked for a time as a musician in the *haveli* there.

All of Pannalal's family is involved in making items for sale. His four sons, four daughters-in-law and one of his numerous grandsons all make *picchvai*. Lakshmi, Pannalal's wife, did not know embroidery work before she married, but was taught this skill, and until her eyesight began to fail, was very much involved in making *picchvai*, and other articles. Her own father had been in construction work the other main occupation for *kirtankar* families and had been a specialist in putting mirrors on buildings.

This family also makes applique or patchwork *picchvai*, as well as cradles, swings, and *bangala* (small replicas of houses). These *bangala* may be made of wood embedded with mirrors or pearls and silver; they are considered appropriate for more temperate seasons. In the summer, a *bangala* of a particular type of grass (*khas*) is considered cooling. *Bangala* vary in size and I have seen several as much as fifty feet long, and ten feet deep. They are made in sections, which makes them portable and easy to store. They are made in the *kirtankar's* homes which are small; and at the Shri Nathji complex, though it is large, storage space is at a premium. The favourite spot for a *bangala* to be reassembled is in front of the main entrance to the large room that houses Navnitpriyaji. As part of the ceremonies Navnitpriyaji is brought out and enthroned in the *bangala*. The raised platform of this area is ideal. Pilgrims either donate a new *bangala* for the temple or make a sizable donation to the temple for one to be erected.

All major items, such as *bangala* and *picchvai*, must be ordered, and the materials paid for, before work is undertaken. The *kirtankars* report travelling to Bombay and Surat to purchase materials. At this time they make contact with old customers and try to initiate new business. I was told that one way of helping to finance a trip was to bring fresh *prasad* from the temple. Distant devotees will pay a premium to have it delivered to them.

Pannalal's sons market many of the crafts made by Vallabhdas' family that are not made on special consignment for a particular customer. Vallabhdas, as the *Binkar* of the Shri Nathji Haveli, is far busier with his musical commitments than his brother Pannalal (see chapter 8). Vallabhdas' sons and daughters make the craft items whereas Pannalal's three sons run two shops as well as travel extensively to get orders from customers and purchase materials. This leaves the daughters and daughters-in-law at home to make the craft items. As both have very large families, the impact these brothers have on the manufacture of craft items is considerable. The families co-operate extensively. I was present on several occasions when Pannalal's sons came to pick up goods at Vallabhdas' home.

Two other brothers who are of importance to the crafts are Pyarelal, who has abandoned his hereditary profession as a musician to concentrate on making, designing and selling craft items and his brother Manaklal. Manaklal was adopted, albeit informally into the family of the Maharaj of Jamnagar, and was brought up separately from his brother in Jamnagar (chapter 12). Their elder brother, Bhanvarlal I, also made craft items, but was only trained in sewing and was not as enterprising as the other two.

INFLUENCES ON THE CRAFTS OF THE *SAMPRADAY*

The stylistic influences exhibited by the arts and crafts of Nathdvara can be traced to Braj, Gujarat and Rajasthan. Because of the active *havelis* in these centres, regional influences on the manner in which religious objects are made are important.

One reason for the great diversity of styles exhibited is that devotees have been largely drawn from the merchant class in Gujarat, who in turn were influenced by the arts, not only from their own region, but from China and Europe (*Marg* 1980: 94). This is particularly evident in the techniques used for decorating textiles.

The history of the cult is interwoven with that of the coastal cities of Gujarat, such as Surat, which played an important role in the export of painted and printed calicos. The tradition of embroidery work, which is still used to decorate the *havelis* of the Vallabha Sampraday, was recognized as of such fine quality that it was exported by the Portuguese as early as 1522 (*Marg* 1980: 94). Chinese merchants who later settled in the coastal towns of Gujarat introduced certain patterns and methods of embroidering with silk on silk that are still used in Nathdvara today. Additional Mughal influence both in Braj and in Gujarat also reached the arts of Nathdvara (Irwin and Hall 1972: 100).

Another very important influence is the mobility of the artists themselves. The musicians who have travelled for various periods of time to serve in other *havelis* of the *sampraday* have absorbed bits of local culture and imported techniques and artifacts from Gujarat and elsewhere. In some cases they have started to make, or adapt ways of making, various objects that have caught the eye of those in charge of decorating the *haveli*. Some of these innovations are now accepted as part of the tradition, although in fact they are relatively new. The activities of Pannalal and Vallabhdas, whose father resided in Dwarka for some time, and of Manaklal and Pyarelal, with their connection to Jamnagar, provide examples of channels by which outside influences have entered the crafts of Nathdvara. The increasing ease of travel can only accelerate this process.

The *Mridang Sagar* gives an account of a visit paid to Nathdvara by the Maharaj of Jamnagar in 1854, accompanied by a *Pakhavaji*, and another musician (MS. Jivani: 4.MV:3; chapter 11). Such travels seem to have been commonplace. Certainly all the *havelis* and their servants appeared to keep in touch. Many of them looked to Braj and Nathdvara for musicians or temple servants when vacancies became available. Thus the combination of mobility, ability to innovate, and the reluctance and inability of most of the musicians to rely solely on their income from temple service or musical engagements has generated new artistic ideas.

PRODUCING AND MARKETING THE CRAFT ITEMS

The goods that the musicians make to supplement their income are sold to the pilgrims, either in shops run by the musicians themselves, or in other shops specializing in religious souvenirs. Shyamlal I and Brijlal own one jointly, Pannalal and Pyarelal each have their own. Selling handicrafts has become so lucrative that only one of Pannalal's sons has studied vocal music and none of them perform *seva* in the temple. Instead they are fully employed running and supplying their three shops, one in *ratan chauk* in the Shri Nathji Haveli, one just inside the Gopallalji temple, and the other in the covered market near the Banmaliji Haveli. In addition, they supply numerous special orders.

The whole of Vallabhdas' family is also involved in making *picchvai* and other items. Vallabhdas' adoptive father Jamnadas, was previously the *Binkar* in the Shri Nathji Haveli. His adoptive-mother, Chotibai, lives with him and still assists in making *picchvai*, as do Vallabhdas' daughters, daughter-in-law, and three sons. Vallabhdas' father-in-law had been in construction work and his daughter-in-law's father sold lottery tickets, so both women learnt the craft after marriage. The male members of these families travel as far afield as Bombay, Madras and Calcutta to sell goods. Manaklal also is well known for his artistic creations; his contribution is described in chapter 12 under the Jamnagar Haveli.

Ramchandra, from another *kirtankar* family, worked and studied with Gokuldas, Pannalal and Vallabhdas' father. He restricts his own products to *shringar* and *mukut*. Shyamlal, the *pakhavaji* of the Shri Nathji Haveli, was taught *shringar* and *mukut* by his brother, Ramchandra and both of them run a shop in the compound of the Vitthalnathji Haveli. They also employ Shyamlal's son, Balkrishna, and the son of Bhanvarlal I. As mentioned above, Bhanvarlal I has never taken up the making of embroidered *picchvai*. He mainly sews clothes and other articles for Shri Nathji. Although I made no attempt to assess the economic value of the handicraft work carried out by the *kirtankars*, it was apparent that those families engaged in this business were generally more prosperous than the rest of the community.

Pyarelal was fortunate to have developed his skills as both a producer of articles of worship and an entrepreneur. Refusing to transfer from the post of *haveli* singer in the Navnitpriyaji Haveli to one of the smaller *havelis*, the Madanmohanji (chapter 7), he concentrated on his shop (just inside the first gate of the Vitthalnathji Haveli), where he sold *shringar* and *mukut*.[2] Although he made some of the items, his extensive network in the villages round about supplied him with a good deal of the smaller handicrafts. Indeed his business appeared so prosperous that it was difficult for me to imagine that he had sung in the Navnitpriyaji Haveli for any reason other than his desire to perform *seva*. His family tradition was no doubt important as well. His father, Mohanlal, had served as *haveli* singer in the Shri Nathji Haveli and his uncle, Raghunath, as *Kirtankar Mukhiya* there. Raghunath's two sons Radhakrishna and Tolaram were both musicians. The former in the Navnitpriyaji and latter in the Shri Nathji.

VERSATILITY OF MUSICIANS

Apart from those involved in the pilgrim crafts industry, some *kirtankars* supplement their incomes by acting as guides for pilgrims. Because they are well acquainted with the various rituals and the working of the *havelis* they can provide an excellent entrée for the pilgrims. Another important profession is watch repairing, an activity which, by virtue of the manual dexterity required, is not far removed from the delicacy required in the making of *shringar*. One musician also works part time in a betel shop.

Most of these tasks tend to be shared between the male family members. Females, although they perform *seva* in the *haveli*, do not act as guides and are never (at least in Nathdvara) employed as musicians. Their economic contribution is therefore limited to tasks they can perform in their own home. All the crafts are done at home, and in this area it appears that women make a substantial contribution. There is one instance of the art of making *picchvai* being introduced into a family via the artistic skills of the new wife.

The whole livelihood of the musicians, from selling *prasad* to making souvenirs, is obtained through the economic activities of the *sampraday*. Hence, the musicians are completely dependent upon Shri Nathji, either through the support of their ritual function in the temple, or through their sales or services to pilgrims. When I first visited Nathdvara, I assumed that members of traditional communities associated with the temple were locked in a timeless backwater of history, engaged in the routine performance of long-established tasks. I assumed their virtues to be those of conservative people, averse to risk or change. My investigations convinced me that my early assumptions were far from true. While the activities within the temple walls remain fixed, and still demand an enormous investment in time, the ancillary trades practised outside of their ritual duties are a fertile field for innovation and entrepreneurship. The role of *kirtankar*, though not lucrative, may confer additional benefits in ensuring the musicians a close relationship with the centres of patronage within the sect. It is surely no coincidence that several of the *kirtankar's* shops are situated within temple precincts.

I conclude that their constant involvement with ritual activities dictated by tradition has not robbed the *kirtankars* of ambitions to better themselves and their families. I was impressed by the energy and initiative exhibited by people whose whole lives have been led within boundaries narrowly defined by caste and sect.

NOTES

1. During my visit to the Calico Museum I was impressed by the *haveli* that has been constructed within the grounds of the museum.
2. Pyarelal estimated that his salary was reduced from about four hundred rupees to two hundred rupees. He was able to give up working as a *kirtankar* because he was not entirely dependent on his temple earnings.

Plate 9.1: Crafts (picchvai)

This small *picchvai* was made by Bhanwarlal I (*kirtankar* Navnitpriyaji Haveli, *devatval* division) and Bhanwarlal II (*Kirtankar Mukhiya* Vitthalnathji Haveli, *jalandhara* division). These men stand in front of their work which could be used in a household shrine or as decoration. The *picchvai* is made embroidered silver sequins on velvet.

Plate 9.2: Crafts (picchvai)

The *picchvai* on the left is embroidered in silver threads on velvet and is of the pot and foliage motif. The composition is Mughal but was adapted by many Rajasthani royal houses.

Plate 9.3: Crafts (picchvai)

The *picchvai* on the right is held by one of Pannalal's sons who helped to make it. It is embroidered with coloured threads and was made for export to Bahrain. There is a healthy trade in *picchvais* and other articles, both religious and secular between the Gulf States and Nathdvara.

Plate 9.4: Nandotsav (mid-eighteenth century)

The image of Navnitpriyaji is placed in a swing in front of Shri Nathji. One of the priests is dressed as Krishna's father, Nandraya, and another as Yashoda, Krishna's mother. The devotees and Gosvamis dance for joy. The cowherds that work in the cowsheds in Nathdvara as well as other temple servants dress as *gopas* and pour milk and curd mixed with tumeric on the devotees. The circle dance shown here in which five Maharajs are dancing is still an important activity. This painting reproduces what I saw and experienced during the celebrations of Nandotsav. This painting is in the collection of Amit Ambalal.

Plate 9.5: Nandotsav (mid-eighteenth century; detail of Plate 9.4)

Plate 9.6: Shop in Nathdvara

A brahmin painter, Mr Sharma, in his shop cum studio. Note the painting of Vallabha behind and the various other paintings of Shri Nathji in a variety of dresses.

The photograph illustrates a shop where religious articles are sold. Some of the craft items could have been made by musicians and their families.

CHAPTER 10

Festivals

In many ways, life in Nathdvara revolves around the celebration of festivals and the townsfolk will recommend that it is only on festive occasions that Shri Nathji's splendour can be fully appreciated. On festival days Shri Nathji, as the maharaj of gods, receives both his subjects, and on certain occasions, his fiefs. These are the lesser deities of the Vallabha Sampraday who come to see him and pay homage. Festival displays are the stimulus for a profusion of artistic activity that more than anything else in my experience still faithfully recreates the past. To be in Nathdvara while a festival is being celebrated is to feel that at every turn another picture from a history book is being projected before you. We know this for certain because many such scenes have been faithfully recorded in miniature paintings (Skelton 1973; Talwar and Krishna 1979; Ambalal 1987).

While each festival is intended to mark a particular event, the celebrations are not limited to a single location or activity. Activities may go on simultaneously in different places within the Shri Nathji Haveli and in other *havelis.* Consequently, to appreciate fully the theatrical, multi-dimensional nature of these events one must celebrate a festival on several different occasions. This also makes description complex. Just as one festival has many events associated with it, it also heralds the events that are associated with the anticipated festival. At times both occasions are simultaneous, which can make participation difficult.

Devotees reported that watching and participating in the theatrical events of festivals gave them a "feeling of oneness with Krishna". Such personal experiences help them to become intimately associated with the events in Krishna's life. While many of the festivals celebrated in Nathdvara are shared with Hindus in general, some are unique to the *sampraday*, and some are celebrated only in Nathdvara. Certain festivals occur on a regular basis, others are less frequent. It is difficult to predict when some will be celebrated. These festivities, which occur from time to time, mark the occasion when the importance of Shri Nathji as the supreme *svarup* must be reasserted. This event is usually in conjunction with another festival. From Tod's account, miniature paintings (illustrated in Ambalal 1987 and Aman Nath 1987), and my own experience, I know of three festivals that have been combined with the visits of several *svarups* to Nathdvara: Nandotsav, Annakut, and Chhappan Bhog.

THE OTHER *SVARUPS* PAY HOMAGE TO SHRI NATHJI

The first recorded gathering of the original *svarups* of the *sampraday* was arranged by the Tilkayat Giridhar (1633-67) in 1666 in Satgharam, Mathura. In 1739 the Tilkayat Govind (1729-74) organized a similar gathering in Nathdvara, as did the Tilkayat Damodar II/Dao (1797-1826) in 1820. Tod, the British Political Agent in Udaipur at the time, was called to Nathdvara to supervise, and made the following comments:

> I contrived no small degree of favour with the supreme pontiff of the shrine of Apollo (Krishna) and all his votaries for effecting a meeting of the seven *svarups* in 1820. In contriving this I had not only to reconcile ancient animosities between the priests and the different shrines, in order to obtain a free passport for the gods, but to pledge myself to the princes in whose capitals they were established, for their safe return: for they dreaded lest bribery might entice the priests to fix them elsewhere, which would have involved their loss of sanctity, dignity and prosperity. It cost me no little and still more anxiety, to keep the assembled multitudes at peace with each other for they are as outrageous as any sectarians in contesting the supreme power and worth of their respective forms (*rupa*). Yet they all separated, not only without violence, but without even any attempt at robbery, so common on such occasions (Crooke 1920: 639).

Friction between the different branches of the sect may explain why a similar assembly in 1933 attracted only five *svarups*. It was attempted again in 1966 by the present Tilkayat, Govindlal, on the occasion of Nandotsav, the annual festival commemorating the celebration of Krishna's birth held by his foster father, Nanda. Once again, because of differences among the leadership of the *sampraday*, only five attended: Dvarkadeshji (Kankroli), Gokul Chandramaji (Kamvan), Mukundrayji (Kashi), Vitthalnathji (Nathdvara), and Shri Nathji

(Nathdvara). In order to have the required seven *svarups* the Tilkayat raised the status of two other images, Navnitpriyaji who is permanently housed in Nathdvara and Natvar Prabhuji from Ahmedabad who was visiting Nathdvara for the festival. Once again the gathering ended with disputes over precedence (Jindel 1976: 73).

In 1985, during the Annakut and Divali celebrations, I was present when Balkrishnaji from Surat and Dvarkadeshji from Kankroli visited Shri Nathji with much pomp and splendour. The festivities on that occasion were conducted without friction. Miniature paintings illustrate that Annakut has, on several occasions, attracted at least one or two *svarups* from outside Nathdvara (Ambalal 1987).

DIVALI, GOVARDHAN PUJA AND ANNAKUT

The festivals of Divali and Govardhan Puja/Annakut follow each other. The festival days are calculated by the lunar calendar and occur some time in October/November. Nathdvara then teems with pilgrims and accommodation is at a premium. My husband and I were fortunate to get accommodation at Vallabh Cottages, one of the guest houses operated by the Shri Nathji temple board.

Devotees try to be in Nathdvara not only to join in the festivities but also to meet their spiritual leaders. The Tilkayat, as well as the Maharaj of the Vitthalnathji Haveli are always in Nathdvara for these festivals. So too are other Maharaj, if the *svarup* under their protection is visiting Nathdvara. Consequently, many devotees make a habit of taking their holidays in Nathdvara around this time. An added bonus is the pleasant weather around this time of year; sunny during the day and cool at night.

Festival days invariably alter the daily routine in the *haveli*, mainly because the decorations are more elaborate and more food must be prepared. The *darshans* must be open longer to the public than usual to accommodate the increase in pilgrims. As every *darshan* must be celebrated, time is saved by not opening all of them to the public.

DARSHAN DURING DIVALI

Divali is a pan-Hindu celebration but in Nathdvara it takes on special significance because it is followed by the major festivals of Govardhan Puja/Annakut. On November 12, 1985 during the Divali celebrations,

I attended all four *darshans* that were opened to the public: *Mangal*, *Shringar*, *Raj Bhog*, and *Shayan*. For *Mangal*, Shri Nathji was still covered with a quilt (*razai*), as the nights were then becoming cool. There was no *picchvai* behind the image, which *Mangal darshan* usually had. Although only two musicians are required to be on duty for *Mangal darshan*, I noticed that, like most of the townsfolk, the other musicians liked to attend it along with other devotees and begin their day with Shri Nathji's blessings. By 5.46 a.m. all the musicians had gathered in *kirtankar gali* to sing for the pre-*Shringar* period. As is the custom on Divali, a *picchvai* made of embroidered gold and silver threads and sequins (*zari*) was displayed in both the Shri Nathji and the Navnitpriyaji Havelis from *Shringar darshan* onwards. Shri Nathji was adorned with diamonds, pearls, rubies and emeralds—all real—and a heavily ornamented dress (as in Ambalal 1987: 30).

Even before the Divali celebrations were concluded, preparation had begun for Govardhan Puja/Annakut. As described earlier, the mythological events of both Govardhan Puja and Annakut are interrelated: the worshipping of mount Govardhan by offering mountains of food (*anna* food, *kut* mountain) and the raising of Mount Govardhan to shelter the villagers from the torrential rains when the jealous storm god Indra threatened to drown them for having changed their allegiance to Krishna.

"COW PLAY"

On the afternoon of Divali about two hundred cows were corralled in a small area of interconnecting streets leading to an open area outside the gates of Vallabh cottages, which is one of the guest houses (*dharamsala*). The enclosure in which they were kept is normally reserved for parking cars and tour buses. It is essentially a walled compound with a gate that can be closed at night. The movements of the cows and the clanging of their bells could be heard from the guest rooms within.

The cows were dressed for the occasion with head-dresses of coloured cloth and peacock feathers, daubed with red and green colours and their horns were painted. They were honoured by being fed with "thuli", a kind of grass which the pilgrims donate. The young cowherds were dressed up in traditional dress, very much as depicted on the walls of the temples, and on houses and in miniature paintings.

They were in their element and seemed to enjoy every minute that they were "on stage".

The arrival of the cows was described to me as heralding "cow play". The "playing" consisted of harassing these normally docile milk machines in a variety of ways to encourage them to chase their herders. They were poked or hit with sticks; rattles were shaken in their faces or their young calves were teasingly dragged away. A few with bells tied to their forelegs were singled out particularly. The tormented beasts tossed their heads at their tormentors and made feeble rushes, much to the delight of the huge crowd. The whole spectacle is a far cry from the Spanish *sports des toros.*

On the evening of Divali some of the decorated cows were herded into Govardhan Chauk, within the Shri Nathji Haveli. A cow, supposed to be descended from one of Krishna's father's[1] herd was worshipped and requested to return the next day for Annakut with the other cows (Ambalal 1987: 30). Also, a *hatadi*, or small shop of mirrors (usually called a *bangala* or house by the musicians) was erected in Ratan Chauk and the *svarup* of Navnitpriyaji, after being carried in a palanquin, was seated inside it. The *hatadi* recalls the one which Krishna set up during Divali in Vrindavan when he tried to sell various articles and thereby attracted the attention of the *gopis* (Ambalal 1987: 31; Jindel 1976: 77). That night the decorated cows remained outside the Vallabh Cottages, their bells clanging throughout the night. To get to our room we had to make our way through them. Some of them tossed their heads in annoyance; their horns looked larger and sharper from close quarters.

GOVARDHAN PUJA

Govardhan Puja, celebrated in many parts of India, it takes on a special significance in Nathdvara because Shri Nathji is represented with one hand held aloft. This symbolizes the raising of Mount Govardhan (Growse 1880: 278). The arrival of the decorated cows heralds this festival and the cow play in the streets is an integral part of the celebrations. Later, some of the cows were driven through the town and into Govardhan Chauk in the Shri Nathji Haveli. There, a huge pile of cow dung was decorated with stumps of banana trees. A rock from the original Govardhan Hill was placed on top of the simulated mountain. Offerings were made to the mountain and worship took place. Ambalal (1987: 106-7, 153) illustrates a painting circa. 1800 that faithfully represents the scene as it is created today with the decorated cows, the Tilkayat, visiting Maharaj and the musicians. The only minor change that I noticed was that the musicians in the painting were wearing the long full Mughal dress rather than *angarkhi* and *dhoti* which is their usual attire today. The only instruments present were a *pakhavaj*, played standing, and two varieties of cymbals: large ones known as *jhanjh* and the smaller variety.

ANNAKUT, BALKRISHNAJI AND DVARKADHISHJI[2] VISIT NATHDVARA

In 1983, when I first attended Annakut in Nathdvara, there were no other *svarups* present. For the 1985 festival, two *svarups*—Balkrishnaji and Dvarkadhishji—visited Nathdvara. The *svarup* of Balkrishnaji, who normally resides in Surat,[3] visited Nathdvara for about fifteen days along with the Maharaj of his *haveli* and many of his personal servants. They had travelled by bus. Balkrishnaji, who is approximately one inch high, was installed in the first courtyard, just below the music school. Various curtains were used to block off particular areas and thus a functioning *haveli* was created so that the visitor, Balkrishnaji, could live quite independently of Shri Nathji. There were occasions when various servants and musicians had to be borrowed from both the Shri Nathji and Navnitpriyaji Havelis. Sometimes the children of the musicians played for Balkrishnaji's *darshan*. In particular, Shyamlal II, the son of Ramdas, *Kirtankar Mukhiya* Shri Nathji Haveli, often sang and played the harmonium for Balkrishnaji. So did Ashok, the son of the Navnitpriyaji Pakhavaji, Sohanlal. In addition, the regular *kirtankars* from the Navnitpriyaji temple often played during Balkrishnaji's *darshan*.

All the *darshans* for Balkrishnaji were held after those of Shri Nathji and Navnitpriyaji to enable devotees to attend them all. The time-lag between each was, however, rather short which meant that pilgrims had to be alert if they were to take all the *darshans*.

Similar events concerning musical matters and the gathering of the Maharaj and *svarups* in Nathdvara are discussed in chapter 12. In 1985 Guru Purushottam was engaged to teach *pakhavaj* to the son of the Surat Maharaj. He subsequently visited his *haveli* in Surat, for a month to continue the tuition.

The *svarup* of Dvarkadhishji, from nearby Kankroli[4] was also present for Annakut in 1985, arriving at around noon on the day of the festival. Though Dvarkadhishji has his own permanent guest house attached to the Shri Nathji Haveli, he returned to Kankroli around 3 a.m. after the celebration of a 'feast' hosted by Shri Nathji. The menu consisted of a huge mountain of rice and various vegetable preparations. Like Balkrishnaji, he and his entourage, which included musicians and other servants, travelled by bus and truck. Perhaps because the visit was very brief, his retinue was much smaller.

THE TRIBAL PEOPLE AND ANNAKUT

On the same afternoon that the celebration of Govardhan Puja is taking place, Bhils and Minas, the tribal people from the areas around Nathdvara, arrive in the town. Just as the arrival of the decorated cows heralds the celebration of Govardhan Puja, the arrival of the Bhils is in anticipation of Annakut. On this occasion the tribals have the privilege of being allowed to 'loot' the mountain of food prepared for Shri Nathji. Again miniature paintings give accurate rendering of the events even as they occur today (see Ambalal 1987: 141).

The Bhils and Minas, as tribal people are generally very poor. They live away from the local people and rarely come into Nathdvara. Occasionally a few girls[5] who come to town for selling metal utensils. The women are colourfully dressed, with red skirts and are heavily bedecked with ornate silver jewellery on their wrists, ankles, upper arms, neck and waist. Much freer and more open than the local women, they stride along confidently in contrast to the housewives of Nathdvara who are rarely seen outside the home except on specific errands. The local women tend to keep their *saris* well down over their heads, covering most of their faces.

On the occasion of Annakut, the tribal people, both men and women, arrive in great numbers. They gather in small groups in the lanes around the temple and dance. By and large they give the appearance of being poor. Most of them are thin, and smaller in stature and frame than the residents of Nathdvara. Their numbers continue to grow throughout the day and around eight o'clock, just after dark, they begin assembling in the open courtyard between the outermost door of the Shri Nathji Haveli (*lal darvaja*), and the main gate below the *naubat khana*. This area, although within the outermost wall of the *haveli*, is surrounded by shops and open to anyone.

At about the same time those townsfolk and pilgrims who wish to be able to see the tribals "looting" the *annakut* from the *haveli*, start assembling along the roofs and balconies that overlook the square. The only way to get a good vantage point is by scrambling up walls over roofs, and jumping across terraces. In 1983 we managed to clamber onto the roof of one of the shops that surround the square. We were perched precariously, along with scores of others. The roof moved occasionally when we shifted our weight. It was rather like being in a crowded lifeboat; weight distribution was all important if the roof was to remain intact.

Looking down, the *chauk* seemed like an amphitheatre. The stars sparkled in the clear desert sky as we settled down to wait and watch. As the darkness settled in, it began to get cold and those of us with shawls shared with others as we huddled waiting for the show to start. Below us, the tribal men, wearing only a *dhoti* and a cotton bed-sheet slung across their chest were mainly seated cross-legged. By about ten o'clock, a dense mass of them had gathered and the *jhapatiyas* at the doorway of the temple, armed with branches, made them sit, and tried to control the periodic surges that they made towards the gate. Occasionally the main gate into the *haveli* would open a crack, and all the tribals would surge forward, only to be turned back. This seems to have been deliberate teasing by the temple authorities, or perhaps by those manning the gate. The procedure appeared to me to be similar to that used when *darshan* was about to close—but on a much grander scale. The atmosphere also was reminiscent, in a more frantic and elemental manner, of the seemingly unnecessary haste during *darshan*.

More and more men, both tribals and townsfolk who wished a better view, crammed into the square. As we waited, the *naubat khana* played non-stop. Once again the crowd surged and then remained still. My husband, seeing a photo opportunity, climbed onto an even more precarious tin roof. We watched him take up position, which was certainly much better than ours, fully expecting that the structure, intended to bear no more than a few crows, and now supporting about fifteen persons, would collapse at any minute.

As midnight approached the mob became even more densely packed. When the gate leading into Govardhan Chauk was finally thrown open, the men surged forward and there was an intense struggle to enter first. Several nimble fellows were able to climb up on the backs of the others and, starting from the back of the crowd, run forward to the front on the packed bodies of their rivals. These opportunists received fond cheers from the crowds which numbered several thousand on every available rooftop and balcony. The *jhapatiyas*, holding tree branches, slashed right and left, but the tribals kept coming forward. No one appeared to be hurt and all the competitors exhibited great good humour. Finally, like a cork coming out of a bottle, the blockage in the gateway melted away and the flood of perspiring men swept into the temple.

Each was equipped with a huge bed sheet, which was strung across his bare chest and was used to carry steaming hot rice that was looted from the temple. I marvelled at how none of them seemed to get burns from it, as I could see that much of it fell directly on their skin. As well, they filled the sheet with the various vegetable curries, even more liquid than the rice. Jindel (1976) described the sight of tribal people covered in sticky rice, and vegetables as "odious". They certainly were well covered, with rice and vegetables sticking on their body and in their hair. I would estimate that each assault on the temple yielded at least an amount equivalent to what would fit into a normal three gallon bucket, so not only was it hot but it must have been very heavy to carry. Plenty of rice spilled onto the ground to be scavenged later by dogs, pigs and cows.

The looting took place for several hours, ending at about two in the morning. Once the looting was over the tribal people left Nathdvara or retreated to the outskirts; none were to be seen on the streets the next morning.

Except for the fact that the looting has dramatic theatrical potential, and forms a contest among the men to be first inside the *haveli*, it is not clear why the looting is quite so wild. Most contestants returned several times to refill their pouches, after transferring the loads to the female and younger family members stationed nearby. Once the first crush was over, passage in and out of the *haveli* was fairly quick. It appears that the tribal men are competing not only for the food, but also for the favour of the deity. The whole event is part sport, part theatre, part religion, and no doubt part the enticement of a huge meal. Shri Nathji's food is considered remarkable for its excellence.

TAKING *DARSHAN* OF THE *ANNAKUT*

In 1985, I went inside *doltivari* to see the *annakut* placed before Shri Nathji and his guests, Balkrishnaji and Dvarkadhishji. There were only two *darshans* on that day, mainly because there was an enormous amount of work involved in preparing the food. To take *darshan* of the Annakut I entered via the back lane which opens out near the

Vitthalnathji Haveli. The soldier had some reservations about allowing me past but I showed the necklace given to me at the time of initiation (*kanthi*). I hurried past, crossed *kamal chauk*, through *hathi darvaza* into *ratan chauk* and joined the huge queues of pilgrims waiting to enter and take *darshan* before the doors would be closed and the looting by the tribal people take place.

Baskets of food were piled up in front of Shri Nathji and in front of him were the four images of Navnitpriyaji, Balkrishnaji, Dvarkanathji, and Vitthalnathji. All the images were decorated. It seemed to me that the only special additions to Shri Nathji's decoration on that day were additional flowers and a red ribbon.

All devotees were obliged to walk past, stopping only momentarily in the space normally reserved for ladies which is at the front of the *darshan* hall. This was because the men's *darshan* space was piled high with rice. The area just in front of the image (*mani kota*), where the musicians usually stand, was full of huge pots containing, what appeared to be various curries.

All the musicians plus a few extras were on duty when I went through at 2.20 a.m. They stood in *mani kota* and continued playing until the looting took place. The music from the *naubat khana* played non-stop throughout the entire celebration. On both occasions I was struck by the medieval quality of the event. Ambalal (1987: Plate 141) illustrates an excellent portrayal of the looting dated at early twentieth century. The only differences are that the *picchvai* in Ambalal's painting is black with gold flowers, in a Mughal pattern, whereas when I viewed the event it was a plain saffron one. Also the tribal people shown in the painting do not resemble the tribals, as though the artist was familiar with the scene inside the *doltivari*, but not with the people themselves. In addition, the scene seems too orderly—I can imagine that there is much more of a scrum while the actual looting is taking place. I base this on the sheer confusion and chaos in the outside courtyard as the tribals emerged, and re-entered, to loot again, and again.

In 1985, having taken the decision to see the mountain of food (*annakut*), it was impossible to secure a place in the courtyard to view the surging mob as it pressed against the door and tried to enter the *haveli*. As in 1983, there were thousands of people who had assembled hours before and viewing places were occupied on the basis of, first come, first to get a good place. I presume that events were much the same outside as I saw in 1983. It was certainly a wonderful spectacle inside.

HOLI

Holi, the festival of colours, heralds the Indian spring. It is celebrated during the Hindu month of Phalgun. Klostermaier (1969:12) remarked that it was celebrated for a week in Vrindavan. Growse, in 1874 noted however, that it was celebrated in Braj for the whole month, as it is today in Nathdvara.

To celebrate Holi in Nathdvara is to experience all of the poetic metaphors assigned to spring—the colourful flowers, the bees buzzing around them, the nesting birds, all allegories of love and sexual union. Central to this festival is the throwing of *gulal* or coloured powder and in Nathdvara this occurs after *Raj Bhog darshan* for the whole month prior to Holi. As a spring festival, celebrating Holi includes activities with erotic overtones. Interpreting some of them has provoked various responses. Mulji was critical of the throwing of *gulal*, an activity synonymous with celebrating Holi. He believed that the Maharaj took licence with their female devotees, aiming specifically at their breasts, and in this way inviting them to engage in more serious love sports. Mulji dwelt at length on this:

> The Maharaj would throw *gulal*, a red powder, made of a certain wood ground down; but this is done only in the spring, and upon high festivals. In throwing this powder, which is often made into small balls, the Maharaj aims chiefly at the breasts of females. It is also customary for him to project a yellow extract obtained from flowers, from a syringe,[6] at the worshippers, and particularly at the females (Mulji 1865: 105).

I did not observe this specific type of activity. During *Phalgun*, the month in which Holi is celebrated, at the end of *darshan*, the Maharaj or the *mukhiya* threw *gulal* that had been tied up in a small handkerchief. The dust was choking but I did not observe him specifically aiming at the breasts of the devotees as described by Mulji. In the Shri Nathji Haveli the sheer crush of the crowd would hardly allow for such accuracy.

In 1985, I tried to avoid the throwing of the coloured powder, although I must admit a couple of times I did leave it rather close. Most of the musicians shared my desire to leave quickly after *darshan*; Guru Purushottam, as one of the senior musicians, would often leave early. This powder is believed to have a cooling effect, considered beneficial by some because in the middle of the day it can become quite hot. A concurrent belief was that it caused respiratory troubles. Certainly most of the musicians had colds. No one, however, seemed to consider the possibility that Shri Nathji might suffer similar effects. In 1985 on Holi at *Raj Bhog darshan*, Maharaj Kalyanray and his brothers played the *pakhavaj*, and all the musicians from the Vitthalnathji temple were present for some part of the *darshan*, demonstrating their respect for Shri Nathji as pre-eminent amongst *svarups* of the Vallabha Sampraday.

The forty-day period before Holi is also celebrated in a similar manner in Bhattaji's temple in Vrindavan.

> A daily *samaj* is sung during that entire period in the courtyard of Bhattaji's temple, while the *pujari* creates beautiful designs with coloured powders on a white cloth backdrop within the sanctum sanctorum ... led by Krishna Chaitanya Bhattaji on the harmonium, the devotees join in singing the verses of the great poet saints of the *bhakti* renaissance sixteenth-seventeenth century (Shapiro 1987: 100).

There are similarities in the creation of the beautiful designs on the white backcloth or plain *picchvai*[7] but there are differences in that the head of the temple takes direct control over the music and the devotees actually join in. Such celebration is known as *samaj*, a practice that I did not see in Nathdvara.

The week during Phalgun that I spent in Nathdvara was truly one of the finest aesthetic experiences of my life. Round every corner it was as if miniature paintings had come to life, with flowers and decorations and musicians in traditional dress playing everywhere. Everything was arranged in the most artistic fashion: musicians perched on the stairs that lead to Moti Mahal; others, in traditional dress were seated in the various courtyards amidst a backdrop of vegetation brought in to decorate the *haveli*. The celebrations often spilled over into the garden[8] beside the palace of the Maharaj, where an elaborate forest had been created. Braj had come to Nathdvara.

Jindel (1976), despite being generally unenthusiastic about the practices of the *sampraday*, also appears to have been moved by Holi in Nathdvara. She commented particularly on the influence of Braj which can be traced to the *rasiya* songs. Growse (1874), in *Mathura, A District Memoir*, also noted the prominence of these songs in the Holi celebrations in the land of Krishna from whence Shri Nathji originated. Like the *kirtankars*, the *Rasiyas* (those who sing the *rasiyas*) wear *dhoti*, and *angarkhi*, with a piece of cloth tied at their waist. They tie their turbans in such a way that the two ends of the turban hang on each side of the face like pigtails. They also add a few peacock feathers and bells. Jindel noted that in 1976, Ras Lila was a popular entertainment during the Holi celebrations. I did not see any, but the photograph of several of the *kirtankars* taking part in Ras Lila celebrations is evidence that it was performed at one time there (plate 7.8).

SANJHI

Although it is not as well known as the *picchvai* tradition, *sanjhi*[9] is another important genre of narrative art. There are several types of *sanjhis* and all appear to be part of festival celebrations. Whereas *picchvai* are hung vertically behind the image *sanjhi* are placed on the ground in a variety of centres throughout the temple. This horizontal art form is created either by sprinkling coloured powders through stencils onto water[10] or making cut-outs with paper or plantain leaves. Both traditions exist in Nathdvara (Jindel 1976) and depict scenes from the life of Krishna.

During the forty-day period before Holi,[11] the *kirtankar*, Bhanvarlal I, makes the cut-out for a variety of *sanjhis*. This tradition comes from Braj, where there are two types of *sanjhi*: folk or popular and the temple tradition of *sanjhi*. The temple tradition in the "new temples" of Barsana and Vrindavan is described by Shapiro: "The folk tradition may be an ancient ritual, but the temple tradition which I now describe is not more than five hundred years old" (Shapiro 1987: 88).

Shapiro describes the temple tradition in two temples in Braj: in both cases the *sanjhi* is laid out in front of the *nij mandir* in which the deities are enthroned and the *sanjhi* is in line with the embossed silver doors which, when opened allow the deities to view it. Each day the arrangement of the *sanjhi* is begun after *Raj Bhog* to "allow its worship in the evening after the *Sandhya/Arati darshan* of Radha and Krishna".

I mention the tradition in Braj because in Nathdvara it is kept alive by one of the musicians, Bhanvarlal I. *Sanjhi* is important for disseminating the myths and legends surrounding Krishna worship. Persons from a variety of backgrounds continue the tradition. In the Junagarh Haveli one of the *jhapatiyas* made the *sanjhi*, and when I visited there in 1988, he proudly showed me his master designs or models which he kept in a folder. In Braj the *gosvamis* or hereditary brahmin religious leaders make it (Shapiro 1987: 96). The musicians in Braj complement the *sanjhi* by singing songs relating to the episodes that it depicts. Apparently the *sanjhi* in Nathdvara were prepared previously by Adi Gaur brahmins (Jindel 1976: 169), but the family concerned has ceased to maintain the tradition. Bhanvarlal I told me that he had made *sanjhi* for many years, but I could not discover the origin of this tradition within the *kirtankar* community. It appears to be another manifestation of their strong identification with the traditions of the *sampraday.*

CHHAPAN BHOG

The preparation of fifty-six different varieties of food is done in all the centres of the *sampraday.* On the occasion when I saw it at Nathdvara, all the food was later assembled in the barred open rooms that surround Kamal Chauk. The sweets were either white or brown and of various shapes. My favourite was *ravadi*, which is of the consistency of custard pudding. Like Shri Nathji I often ate it first thing in the morning, usually purchasing it from a shop where some of the servants of the *haveli* sold it as part of their *neg.* These shops are all located just outside the gates of the *haveli.*

A remarkable Chhapan Bhog is recorded in a nineteenth century miniature painting illustrated by Aman Nath (1987: 171). It depicts the celebration of Chhapan Bhog at Kankroli in A.D. 1886 on the thirteenth day of the bright half of the Hindu month of Bhadrapada. The seven *svarups* have assembled. According to the caption this included Shri Nathji as well as Govinddevji, who was then in Jaipur, Mathureshji from Mathura and Giridharji from Vrindavan as well as others unnamed. Each of these *svarups* was offered fifty-six varieties of food, with no two receiving the same type, making a total of three hundred and ninety-two varieties.

JANMASHTAMI

Janmashtami, Krishna's birthday, is one of the most important festivals for Vaishnavites all over India and it is celebrated with great enthusiasm in Nathdvara. Krishna's birthday falls in the month of Bhadon (August-September). In 1986 Janmashtami was celebrated in Nathdvara at midnight on August 26. When *Mangal darshan* closed that day most of the devotees who attended stayed to clean up afterwards.

Many were given brooms for this task and a mass *seva* took place. I recognized many of the musicians also taking part in what, during the normal course of events, was a task undertaken by temple servants hired for this activity. Mulchand and some of the other *kirtankars* stored their brooms in Kirtankar Gali, near their instruments, and used them later in the day. A visiting Bombay school-teacher who had taken a particular interest in music, participated and I too was urged to join in, but there were not enough brooms to go round. The work was completed quickly and *doltivari* cleared, and the doors locked so that stragglers could not remain for the pre-*Gval* activities. The evening before the birth was also marked with many festivities and began with several events intended to remind devotees of what was to come.

I attended *Arati/Sandhya darshan* that day and noticed that Rakesh and Rajiv, the sons of the Tilkayat, were seated on either side of Shri Nathji looking out into *doltivari*. The full *kirtankar* orchestra was present, including *sarangi* and *pakhavaj*. The *haveli* singers played *jhanjh*. Six of the musicians were seated on Shri Nathji's right, the others on his left. Two priests held fly whisks and another a fan.

After *darshan* the Shri Nathji Haveli was closed and I went to take the same *darshan* in the Navnitpriyaji Haveli. As usual this little temple was exquisitely decorated. That day a silk parrot, of the type suspended over a baby's cradle, was hung above the image. The musicians sat in front of the image and played while the devotees, including myself, sat behind. It was often the custom for devotees to be seated in the Navnitpriyaji Haveli. There was no rush.

Fortunately, after the *darshan* in the Navnitpriyaji Haveli was closed, I returned to Kirtankar Gali. That night was one of the rare occasions on which the full *kirtankar* orchestra moved to the alley behind Kirtankar Gali and played for nearly an hour during *Shayan*. The *darshan* was closed to the general public but several devotees, including one from Bombay, were allowed in and given some *prasad*, perhaps as recognition for making a large donation to the temple. In a room adjoining the alley, huge quantities of food were piled and many servants carried food in and out while the music played. Vallabhdas, the *Binkar* sat facing the wall below *dhruvari* and played *raga behag* for about half an hour. At the same time, fresh flowers were placed in Kamal Chauk.

When I emerged from the temple it was about 8 p.m. and a painting of the baby Krishna was being taken in a cart in procession around the town. Several temple servants attended it and Prakash Chand, Guru

Purushottam's grandson, was in charge of making sure that any money thrown at the image was deposited in the box beside it. Several other children of the *kirtankars* also helped. The band of the Tilkayat's bodyguard accompanied the procession, and played vigorously, illuminated by kerosene lamps. The streets were densely packed and I was only able to get a good view by climbing up into a shop in Naya Bazaar which was about a metre higher than the street. Many townsfolk came out to view the painting which toured most of the streets joining the temple, as well as the main bazaars.

By about 10 p.m. all non-essential temple workers and devotees were ushered out of the inner temple and the door of Suraj Pol was closed. There was still access to Govardhan Chauk where many devotees had already gathered. I was told that the best spot to witness the announcement of the birth was in the *naubat khana*, overlooking Govardhan Chauk. I climbed up the winding staircase to find all of the *naubat khana* musicians present, as well as some other visitors who had also come to get a better view. In the large open windows of the *naubat khana*, with their scalloped arches, one drummer played the *naqqara*, a *shahnai* player sat on a ledge and played facing out towards the street, while another played facing the other way, standing with one foot on the ledge while looking out over Govardhan Chauk. In a corner, another temple servant called through the microphone, urging devotees to be ready for the coming of Krishna.

Soon after 11 p.m. the band of the Tilkayat's bodyguard arrived in Govardhan Chauk. They played one or two tunes and then were silent. The soldiers with muskets stood still and more and more devotees arrived. Other soldiers with muskets raised stood poised to fire a twenty-one gun salute. Several of the *naqqara khana* musicians slept, but the head musician kept a watchful eye both on his watch for the magic hour of midnight and on the door of the temple to see if it opened. The music from the *naqqara khana* continued until about 11.30, with the musicians taking turns. Often two *shahnai* players played and several drummers. Some stood with one leg propped up on the low window sill, while others sat cross-legged.

I was told that at that time only the ritual *Mukhiya*, Gangadas, the Tilkayat and his two sons were present in the *nij mandir*. As midnight approached silence descended. Both the musicians in the *naqqara khana* and the Tilkayat's band stopped playing and the crowd hushed; the tension and expectation was palpable, as we listened for the sound of the conch that would be blown in the *nij mandir* to announce the birth. The anticipation was heightened by the fact that the expanse of Govardhan Chauk, normally busy and bustling, had never been so still. I can still see the *naubat khana* musicians, with arms raised, ready to strike their drums: *naqqara*, *dhumsas* and *dhols*. The *shahnai* players, elbows bent, held their instruments a few inches from their mouths. The soldiers below stood ready to fire their muskets into the air while the Tilkayat's band held their instruments poised to play.

When the moment arrived the music and the twenty-one gun salute of the muskets, all happened simultaneously. I never heard the conch, but it may have been drowned by the instantaneous response of the musicians and soldiers. It looked to me as if the actual signal had been given by the door to the temple being opened slightly. As soon as the signal was given pilgrims began to rush in, each wanting to be the first to greet the newborn babe. I waited until the crowd had subsided somewhat and then entered. Shri Nathji was dressed in a south Indian type of *dhoti* and cloth was tied around his shoulders. His hair was tied in a knot. He was dressed in the same way for the *darshans* the next day.

Thus was the baby Krishna's birth celebrated; the birth of god and king. The *tali*, a metal plate was struck, the traditional symbol that a son has been born, and the world rejoiced. My experience mirrored that of Klostermaier (1969) who witnessed Janmashtami in Braj:

> It was August 6 1963, but no Christmas has made me understand better the mystery of the coming of God". Klostermaier's friend explained it thus: "He has come", said Gopal. We must look for him. He only hides so that our impatience may grow and our love be purified—so that we do not seek our pleasure, but his. He does not come to ease our life on earth, he comes out of his divine will, to teach us his love (Klostermaier 1969: 86).

There are some moments when, even as an observer, one is totally drawn into the spirit of the event. Certainly the midnight of Janmashtami was for me, such a moment.

NANDOTSAV

The festival of Nanda (Nandotsav) is celebrated the day after Krishna's midnight birth. On that day *Mangal darshan* was not held until about 9.30 a.m. This was to allow the baby Krishna to sleep in after the post-midnight *darshan*. Unfortunately I missed *Mangal darshan*. On that particular day, the only way into the temple was from the lane behind

Vitthalnathji Haveli. Unaware of this I chose the usual route of the front door.

On Nandotsav, as during many other festival days such as Holi, the *kirtankars* played in various locations around the temple. When I eventually did reach Kamal Chauk I could hear that the *kirtankars* had already begun to play in Ratan Chauk, the *chauk* further inside the temple. The door connecting Ratan Chauk and Kamal Chauk was locked but when it finally opened, temple servants dressed as cowherds emerged throwing curd mixed with turmeric. The events surrounding this celebration were described in chapter 9.

Having missed *Mangal darshan* in the Shri Nathji Haveli I was fortunate to catch it in the Navnitpriyaji Haveli. In both temples the image was bathed in five nectars (*panchamrit*) which included a mixture of milk, honey, ghee, curd and sugar. In the Navnitpriyaji Haveli the younger son of the Tilkayat waved a fan over the image while the elder son circled a lamp (*arati*). Then the younger poured the five nectars into the conch held by the elder brother who then poured it over Navnitpriyaji. There was brocade on the wall behind Navnitpriyaji and a brown coloured material inset with red was behind the image. Later the Tilkayat's younger son poured the *panchamrit* on the image while the Tilkayat's grandson, a child about three years of age, peeked from behind. During this activity the *kirtankars* sang and played. On a festival day it is essential to have a full compliment of musicians. On that day the regular *haveli* singer, Bhanvarlal I was absent so Chandrakant, the son of the *Binkar* Vallabhdas, sang in his place.

As *Mangal darshan* had been late, *Shringar darshan* for Shri Nathji followed almost immediately. I was anxious to attend, as it was one of the rare occasions when the *meghnad pakhavaj* would be played. I was fortunate to be able to enter with the musicians via Kirtankar Gali. It being a festival day, a great many pilgrims were gathered by the public entrance and with the ensuing crush it was possible that I would not have got in. As usual I rushed in with the musicians who were carrying their instruments; Shyamlal the *Pakhavaji* carried the *meghnad pakhavaj*.

The high point of the *darshan* came when the Tilkayat, who is about six feet tall, reached forward and placed a *tilak* on Shri Nathji's forehead. In doing so he did not have to reach up, and the width of the image was not greater than the length of his arms. The *meghnad pakhavaj* was played as the *tilak* was applied, two conches were blown and a tray bearing betel and two candles were shown to Shri Nathji. One of the sons of the Tilkayat performed *arati* and placed betel beside Shri Nathji. The *picchvai* was plain red and Shri Nathji was highlighted with blue behind; the division between the two colours was marked with a gold border. Shri Nathji wore a yellow skirt in the Mughal style and the whole of the Tilkayat's family, including the wives, stood to the right of Shri Nathji. The younger son placed a beautiful pink flower in Shri Nathji's hand.

CONCLUSION

There is obviously a tremendous amount in the celebration of festivals at Nathdvara that I have not recounted. One person cannot hope to experience even a small part of what is going on. I can imagine that many of my experiences such as during Nandotsav at the Vitthalnathji Haveli, when we danced and were showered with curd (chapter 9), was to some extent serendipitous, and that other interesting events must have occurred elsewhere without my knowledge. The continuation of one festival into another, as in the celebration of Janmashtami and Nandotsav somehow epitomizes events in Nathdvara, with its endless cycle of joy and celebration in sharing Krishna's life.

A striking feature of the festivals was their flexibility. They exemplified and perhaps amplified the impression that I was constantly given in Nathdvara, of confusion deliberately created to increase the element of spontaneity in worship. Through this technique the devotees experience by proxy the elusiveness of Krishna. As Klostermaier's (1969) informant affirmed, "He does not come to ease our life on earth, he comes to teach us his love".

NOTES

1. Nandraya is Krishna's stepfather and Yashoda his step-mother (see O'Flaherty 1975: 209-17; 205-25).
2. In the seventeenth century both these *svarups* were controlled by one family. Entwistle (1987: 183) gives an account of the circumstances that brought this about. Growse (1882) relates that the various images associated with the sect in Braj visited each other.

3. Balkrishnaji was removed from Gokul and installed in Surat in 1670 (Entwistle 1987: 183).
4. Dvarkadhishji was removed from Braj in 1670 and first installed in a village near Kankroli and later in 1719 installed in his own mansion in Kankroli (Entwistle 1987: 184).
5. For a photograph of a Bhil girl see Nath (1987: 109).
6. Ambalal (1987: 97,152) shows a painting with these syringes (*pichkari*) placed on the platform in front of Shri Nathji. These are used in Braj and shown in symbolic gesture in north Indian dance traditions when spring is portrayed.
7. These designs are illustrated in a miniature painting illustrated by Ambalal (1987: 97,152).
8. The garden was built over in about 1987. Ambalal 1987: 98,152 includes a painting of Vitthalnathji in his garden.
9. There is also a folk goddess called *Sanjhi* who is worshipped by unmarried girls over a wide area of India. *Gosvamis* make *sanjhi* in the Bhatjika Mandir (Entwistle 1987: 303,404).
10. Some temple musicians in Udaipur produce *sanjhi* on water.
11. Entwistle (1987: 412) refers to *sanjhi* for other festivals.

Plate 10.1: Looting the Annakut
(early-twentieth century; from the collection of Amit Ambalal)

Plate 10.2: Navnitpriyaji Haveli during Divali, Navnitpriyaji in a hatadi (mid-eighteenth century)

In the evening of the Divali festival celebrations, Navnitpriyaji is installed in a *hatadi* or bungalow/shop made of mirrors. It is here that devotees take *darshan*. All the usual rituals take place and music is played. Three of the musicians are seated, two of the vocalists play *jhanjh*; there is one *Pakhavaji*. One of the vocalists stands and plays the *jhanjh*. The devotees are seated on the left. Two of them are keeping time by clapping (putting the *talam*). On the far left, a *jhapatiya* is represented holding a whip. Inside the *hatadi* beside Navnitpriyaji there are six attendants. One of them is holding a *morchhal* made of peacock feathers, and three of them are holding flywhisks. They are not identified but one of them could be the head *Mukhiya* and the others visiting Maharaj who are in charge of the numerous *havelis* of the *sampraday*. Except for the exaggerated size of Navnitpriyaji (the actual image is no more than ten inches high), the scene represented in this miniature painting simulates worship today. I was present during the Divali celebrations in 1983 and 1985 and on both occasions the arrangement of the *gosvamis*, their dress, jewellery, hair style, and physical features are the same as here. The same is true for the musicians except that they are much older, and have not grown the same type of moustache

Plate 10.3: Navnitpriyaji Haveli during Divali, Navnitpriyaji in a hatadi (mid-eighteenth century; detail of Plate 10.2)

Plate 10.4: Govardhan Puja (mid-nineteenth century)

The celebration of Govardhan Puja re-enacts the first Annakut or food offering given to Mount Govardhan. The mountain is created with cow dung and is decorated with plantain leaves, flags and a stone from the actual Mount Govardhan brought from Braj. The cow are decorated with peacock feathers and red hand marks and the cowherds (*gopas*) dress up and lead them into this outer courtyard of the temple, known as Govardhan Chauk. The image of Navnitpriyaji is brought from his temple within the compound in a palanquin and placed near the steps leading up to Suraj Pol. The musicians who play during *darshan* accompany the party as it moves in procession, stopping at various spots before reaching Suraj Pol. The musicians include a *Pakhavaji*, on the left and a *jhanjh* player. Another musician, also on the left holds a small pair of cymbals. Most of the details were identical when I saw this festival in 1985. This painting captures the essence of the festival. It is in the collection of Amit Ambalal.

Plate 10.5: A painting of the Govardhan Puja celebrations on the wall of the outer courtyard of the Vitthalnathji Haveli

Plate 10.6: The cows decorated for Govardhan puja

Plate 10.7: People of Nathdvara watching the cows running through the streets

CHAPTER 11

The Family History of Guru Purushottam Das

In presenting the history of Guru Purushottam's family I have attempted to place their careers in the context of other events that were happening at the same time. The history of the family illustrates the close connection between courtly and religious music, because they found employment in both these centres of patronage. Although there were very few musicians of Guru Purushottam's stature who continue to combine a career in both secular and religious venues, actual Hindustani music continues to reflect both influences. This is particularly true in view of the recent trend for professional musicians to revive traditions which are perceived to be older and 'purer' styles of music (pers. comm. Ashok Ranade). Hence the temple repertoire is sometimes also performed on the concert stage. This trend may relate to the need to infuse performances with greater variety to satisfy the eclectic taste of modern concert-goers (Ashok Ranade 1984: 95-100).

The *Mridang Sagar* (MS: 1911) and *Mridang Vadan* (MV: 1982) document the unbroken musical career of Guru Purushottam's family in the royal courts of Jaipur, Jodhpur, and Baroda and finally in the main religious centre of the Vallabha Sampraday, the Shri Nathji Haveli in Nathdvara. Some important historical events are, however, only briefly discussed in the *Mridang Sagar* and *Mridang Vadan*. The weakness of these two works as historical sources is that the authors were so deeply a part of the tradition and the performance that they describe, and patrons and the musical world were so much a part of their daily life, that they did not feel it necessary to elaborate on many aspects that might have been of great interest to us.

Guru Purushottam was employed for many years by the temple, and played for several rulers of princely states. Nevertheless his career was only marginally dependent on royal patronage because during his lifetime the princely purses were abolished. He therefore looked for his livelihood to areas which have become commonplace for today's musicians: All India Radio, foreign tours, teaching in a music school in a large urban centre, and the concert stage.

The intimate association between Guru Purushottam's family and the religious head of the Vallabha Sampraday, the Tilkayat, from the nineteenth century onwards gives us some insight into the musical world in Nathdvara of that period. Guru Purushottam's family traces its working association as *Pakhavajis* in the Shri Nathji temple from 1802, when Vallabhdas, Guru Purushottam's great-great grandfather, was invited by the Tilkayat Damodar II/Dau (1797-1826) to leave his post as a musician at the court of Jodhpur. Since then, the family has made Nathdvara its home, except for the brief period between 1820 and 1824 when Vallabhdas was employed by the Gaekwad of Baroda.[1] Vallabhdas' son, Shankar, was born in 1829.[2] He succeeded his father as *Pakhavaji* in the Shri Nathji Haveli on his death in 1849. Shankar's son, Ghanshyam, succeeded his father in the same post as did Guru Purushottam, Ghanshyam's only son.

All of this information has been documented by Purushottam's father, Ghanshyam, in the *Mridang Sagar* (1911). The book confirms the close association of their family with religious and courtly music over many generations.

THE COURT OF AMBER AND JAIPUR

The history of Guru Purushottam's family, as recorded in the *Mridang Sagar*, begins in the early part of the seventeenth century. At this time three brothers were forced by the ravages of war to leave their small village, Kekutkhera, on the outskirts of Jaipur in Rajasthan, to live as wandering musicians, performing devotional music. Eventually, one of them, Halu, settled at the court of Amber. Halu was the only one to have sons: Swami and Chabaldas. Of these two, only Chabaldas had children and four generations later, his descendant Rupram was still at Amber, serving as a court musician. The family retained its link with the Jaipur area and Ghanshyam recorded that at the time of writing, "even today many of our relatives have some land which the Raja bestowed on our family" (MS. Aparna Patrika: 1). When Jaipur was founded in 1727 by Maharaja Sawai Jai Singh, replacing Amber as the capital, Rupram accompanied the court there. Eight years later he received an invitation from Maharaja Abhay Singh requesting him to join the court of Jodhpur.

JODHPUR COURT

Numerous miniature paintings attest to the fact that Abhay Singh (1724-50), the Maharaja of Jodhpur (Crooke 1920: 1035), like many other rulers, enjoyed music and encouraged musicians (Topsfield 1980). Besides being a patron of the arts, he appears to have been a connoisseur. Although he is described as "full of the art of music", he also used art for his own purposes: "King Abhay Singh propagated his own reputation through artistic activities. He enjoyed singers *Pakhavajis Binkars, Sarodiyas*, and Kathak dancers" (MS. Jivani: 1).

Most Rajput rulers of the time were patrons of music, as artistic activity was highly regarded and talented artists enhanced their courts (Bhattacharya 1979; Erdman 1985; Neuman 1980: 18).

Abhay Singh could afford to be generous, because his state's income was augmented with booty carried off from as far away as Gujarat. Even before he had ascended the throne, he established himself as a great warrior, fighting alongside the combined forces of his father, Ajit Singh, ruler of Jodhpur (Crooke 1920: 1033), and the royal houses of Mewar and Jaipur, in an attempt to rid the area of the Marathas (Crooke 1920: 496-535). Abhay Singh became the ruler of Jodhpur in 1731. After establishing Jodhpur as a strong, independent state he returned to the capital to live a life of ease and refinement (Tod 1829: 75-83). His invitation to Rupram can be seen as a result of his more settled phase, once the kingdom of Jodhpur was secure.

When Rupram arrived at the court of Jodhpur in 1735, another Pakhavaji, Pahar Singh, was already in residence. Pahar Singh must have been a very accomplished musician, for even Ghanshyam in the *Mridang Sagar* acknowledges him as an authority alongside his grandfather Rupram, whom he describes as, "a master of *tandavà parans* [vigorous rhythmic passages]", and whose playing was "magical" (MS. Jivani: 2). These *parans* were intended to mimic the sounds of the ankle bells of various deities such as Shiva, Krishna and Parvati as they danced:

Rupramji was ordered to show his skill in playing the *pakhavaj*.... He gave a demonstration which made the Raja happy. Rupramji knew [how to play] the *parans* of the gods, the *tandava* dance. The same ones they danced with their lotus feet and *gunghurus* (ankle bells). He spoke these *parans* and played the same sounds (MS. Jivani: 2).

These comments give us a glimpse of court performance; the Raja ordering his musician to play, and the musician responding with music that claimed divine inspiration; religious art in a secular court from which it received patronage. Ghanshyam includes some of these *parans* in the *Mridang Sagar*. Guru Purushottam has recorded several, but not all of them are in his repertoire.

When Abhay Singh died in 1750, Rupram stayed on as a *Pakhavaji* at the court, serving Abhay Singh's successor, his uncle Bakhat Singh (r. 1750-53) and Bakhat Singh's son Bijay Singh (r. 1753-93). Ambalal (1987: 152, Plate 102) illustrates Maharaja Bijay Singh, *c.* 1772 taking *darshan* in Nathdvara. Shri Nathji is being attended by the Tilkayat, at that time Tilkayat Govind (1729-74), and his son Giridhar (1769-1807). A *Pakhavaji* is playing during the *Shringar darshan* on a summer day that they are attending. As it was often the custom for musicians to accompany their patrons it seems possible that Rupram may have visited Nathdvara. It might have been as a result of such contacts that Rupram's son Vallabhdas later came to be invited to Nathdvara by Giridhar in 1802.

Pahar Singh, the other *Pakhavaji* mentioned in the *Mridang Sagar* continued to be attached to the Jodhpur court after Rupram was also hired. Rupram's son Vallabhdas was born in 1769. Pakhavaji Pahar Singh also had a son, Johar Singh, and these two were trained by their respective fathers. While Vallabhdas was also taught by Pahar Singh, no mention is made of Johar Singh receiving instruction from anyone other than his own father. The fact that Pahar Singh seems to have been prepared to share his knowledge equally with Vallabhdas is unusual, because true knowledge is normally reserved for blood relations.[3] The comments of Ghanshyam also confirm the well-established fact that most musicians are reluctant to part with their knowledge:

Wise people say, if you teach someone the secret of your trade you only teach your son, and if you do not have a deserving son, keep the trade secret in your heart. This is because many students come who are ungrateful, who strike at your position in the trade, and dislodge you from your employment (MS. Jivani: 1).

Mention is made in the *Mridang Sagar* of Vallabhdas' devotion to his teacher (*guru*), but even in the orthodox teaching system[4] this is not necessarily enough to obtain advanced instruction. We must assume that Vallabhdas' talent was also a factor in Pahar Singh's generosity. This candid quotation from the *Mridang Sagar* introduces two very important ingredients in the teaching situation: "Vallabhdas was able to flatter Pahar Singh and learnt many *parans* and *talas* from him, and his son Johar Singh. But Vallabhdas was not ungrateful to his teacher and he considered his teacher always better than himself"[5] (MS. Jivani: 2).

The fact that, three generations later, Ghanshyam in the *Mridang Sagar* acknowledged that some of his family's knowledge came from a non-relative, provides further evidence of Pahar Singh's importance and the honesty and humility of the family. It is customary for musicians to forget these "transfusions" from other families.[6] Ghanshyam reports that each of his ancestors relayed this to their sons: Vallabhdasji told Shankarji and Shankarji told Ghanshyam who wrote it down. Vallabhdasji took Pahar Singh as his real guru and he remained loyal to him and was not among those students who were ungrateful. He was distinct from others. This fact Vallabhdasji related to his son Shankarji, "Whatever musical knowledge which is extra from the knowledge I received from my own family, it was from Pahar Singh and I am grateful to him" (MS. Jivani: 2).

Unfortunately the *Mridang Sagar* only mentions that Pahar Singh played the Delhi style and does not elaborate on his family's musical lineage. Although no mention is made of *Pakhavajis* at this time also playing in temples, this seems highly probable. Even if the musician's activities were limited to the palace grounds, most palaces had at least one temple within the complex. Today, within the compound of the City Palace, Udaipur, there are musicians who play in the temple and some of them report having also played for the previous Maharana in the palace.

In 1790, at the age of twenty-one, Vallabhdas took over his father's post as court musician serving under Raja Bhim Singh (r. 1793-1803, Crooke 1920: 1077) until 1802. The period of twelve years prior to 1803, when Raja Man Singh emerged as Maharaja of Jodhpur (Crooke 1920: 1080), was marked by palace intrigues and, no doubt, considerable uncertainty for those dependent upon the patronage of the ruler. This might well have been one of the factors that persuaded Vallabhdas, in 1802, to accept an invitation from the Tilkayat Giridhar

(1769-1807) (Ambalal 1987: 106,153) to leave Jodhpur for Nathdvara. Vallabhdas apparently considered himself fortunate to obtain the job (MS. Jivani: 3). He may have felt differently soon afterwards, because Nathdvara had to be abandoned in the face of invading Marathas.

NATHDVARA, THE MARATHAS, AND THE REMOVAL OF SHRI NATHJI

In 1802, the year in which Vallabhdas was summoned to Nathdvara, the Maratha army under Holkar was finally defeated at Indore by Raja Scindia of Gwalior. Holkar's huge army retreated. When it arrived in Nathdvara, Holkar himself entered the Shri Nathji Haveli, an event recorded by Tod:

> It was here this active soldier first showed symptoms of mental derangement. He upbraided Krishna (Shri Nathji), while prostrate before his image for the loss of his victory; and levied three lakhs of rupees on the priests and inhabitants, several of whom he carried to his camp as hostages for the payment (Crooke 1920: 529).

The new Tilkayat, Damodar II, decided that it was prudent to move the image of Shri Nathji to Udaipur, as yet still free from Maratha control. He received the protection of the army of one of the sixteen nobles on whose land Shri Nathji's property was located, the Chauhan chief of Kotaria. When these soldiers returned home to Kotaria after safely depositing the image in Udaipur most of them were slaughtered by Holkar's troops. The image remained in Udaipur for six months. When it was clear the Marathas also had designs on Udaipur, the Tilkayat Damodar II removed the image to Ghasiyar, a small village about halfway between Udaipur and Nathdvara, in a hilly region near Haldighat. Damodar then proceeded to visit the minor shrines of the *sampraday* which were nearby, no doubt to reassure the devotees that Shri Nathji was safe (Crooke 1920: 529). To do this he was guarded by four hundred cavalry. Damodar's role as a warrior and expert horseman are recorded in a painting of him on horseback illustrated in Ambalal 1987: 65.

Damodar's intuition that Udaipur was not safe proved to be correct. Holkar eventually invaded Udaipur and exacted very heavy tribute from its inhabitants. The devastation of Udaipur is described by Tod who led the British army:

In the spring of 1806, when the embassy (British) entered the once fertile Mewar, ... nothing but ruin met the eye—deserted towns, roofless houses and uncultured plains. Wherever the Marathas encamped, annihilation was ensured; it was a habit; and twenty-four hours sufficed to give to the most flourishing spot the aspect of a desert (Crooke 1920: 545).

Trouble flared up again and in 1809, the Marathas threatened to demolish the temple of Eklingji, the important Shaivite shrine halfway between Nathdvara and Udaipur, unless the Rana of Udaipur paid them tribute of eleven lakh rupees. The Rana was unable to pay the full amount, so the Marathas stayed in his capital, Udaipur. The Marathas did not destroy the shrine of Eklingji, which houses the deity that confers the right to rule on the royal family of Mewar. They did, however, continue to plunder. By 18ll the situation throughout all of Mewar had deteriorated further: "Mewar was rapidly approaching dissolution, and every sign of civilization fast disappearing; fields laid waste, cities in ruin, inhabitants exiled, chieftains demoralised, the prince and his family destitute of common comforts" (Crooke 1920: 547).

Still worse was to come and it was only some time after the signing of the treaty with the British in 1817, giving them control over the area, that it was alleviated.

The capital was to serve as a specimen of the country. Udaipur which formerly reckoned fifty thousand houses within the walls, had now not three thousand occupied, the rest were in ruin, the rafters being taken for fire wood. The realization of the spring harvest of 1818, from the entire fiscal land was about four thousand pounds! Grain sold for seven seers the rupee, though thrice the quantity was procurable within the distance of eighty miles. Insurance from the capital to Nat'hdwara (*sic*) (twenty-five miles) was eight percent (Crooke 1920: 555).

It seems that the Marathas showed no mercy. They brought the ruling family in Udaipur, the House of Mewar to their knees, something the Mughals had not been able to do.

The Kotaria chief, whose ancestors are immortalized for fidelity, had not a horse to conduct him to his prince's presence ... All were in ruins; and the Rana, the descendant of those patriot Rajputs who opposed Baber (*sic*), Akber (*sic*) and Aurangzeb, in the days of Mogul splendour, had not fifty horse to attend him, and was indebted for all the comforts he possessed to the liberality of Kotah (Crooke 1920: 555).

When Vallabhdas was summoned to Nathdvara by the Tilkayat,

Maharaj Shri 108 Shri Giridhar (1769-1807), to take up the post of *Pakhavaji* in the Shri Nathji temple, he could hardly have anticipated these events. Vallabhdas stayed in Nathdvara for eighteen years, yet the *Mridang Sagar* does not relate the events surrounding the removal of Shri Nathji from Nathdvara. It seems likely, however, that he accompanied the image to Udaipur and Ghasiyar. By 1807-8 (Jindel 1976: 23; Ambalal 1987: 64), Shri Nathji and his retinue had returned to Nathdvara. Although the *Mridang Sagar* does not record the end of the upheavals caused by the Maratha invasion, everything must have been back to normal well before 1820. In that year a gathering of the eight *svarups* was held in Nathdvara (Crooke 1920: 639; chapter 10). This event is overlooked in the *Mridang Sagar*. Nor does the *Mridang Sagar* describe where and when Vallabhdas, or indeed any of the musicians played regularly. There is only one reference to music being played near the image. The term used in the *Mridang Sagar* for the spot was *sanadhi* (a Sanskrit term, to describe an area near the deity) whereas the normal term for the area where the musicians stand is *mani kota* ("diamond square"). The picture referred to above (Ambalal 1987: 102) gives an excellent illustration of the relationship between the musicians, the priests, the Tilkayat and members of royal families. This picture dated at *c.* 1772, shows Maharaja Bijay Singh of Jodhpur, Vallabhdas' former employer taking *darshan*.

THE BARODA COURT

In 1820 Vallabhdas accepted an invitation from the Gaekwad of Baroda,[7] Shri Siyaji Rao, to join his court. Before leaving for Baroda, Vallabhdas invited his teacher from Jodhpur, Pahar Singh, to take over his duties in the Shri Nathji temple. The convention that musicians at Nathdvara arrange for their own replacements is still followed today. Vallabhdas' letter in which he tries to encourage Pahar Singh to accept the appointment in Nathdvara is interesting:

> You have spent your whole life playing musical instruments before Rajas and Maharajas and you have only pleased them. If you had played for the Lord (Shri Nathji) he would have enabled you to cross this material world. If you look at the enchanting image and play at his lotus feet and offer your skill of playing as a service to the lord this will enable you to cross the material world (MS. Jivani: 3).

Vallabhdas' letter is somewhat contradictory, and reveals that, while the religious setting was not without its rewards, at that point he preferred to be based in the secular art world. No mention is made of Vallabhdas combining his official post as court musician to the Gaekwad with temple service in Baroda. It seems highly likely that he would have done so, as there are still many Vallabha Sampraday Havelis in Baroda, some of which employ musicians and encourage visiting artists (chapter 12).

Although the Gaekwad was very fond of music (Wade 1984: 187) there is a hint that he was not very generous. Fortunately for Vallabhdas, a fellow Jaipuri, Vishnudas, was the personal assistant to the Gaekwad and was able to intercede on his behalf: "Vishnudas got the best salary arrangement of three rupees. With great honour they got Vallabhdas to agree to stay".

This last comment implies that from the beginning Vallabhdas had no intention of making his visit permanent. In fact, when he wanted to leave, he had some difficulty in doing so, and his departure required the intercession of the Tilkayat: "A little later Vallabhdasji wanted to return to Nathdvara but the Gaekwad did not give permission. When a letter (from the Tilkayat Damodar) to the Gaekwad reached Baroda he sent Vallabhdasji back to Nathdvara and gave him clothes and ornaments" (MS. Jivani: 3).

THE RETURN TO NATHDVARA

In 1824,[8] after receiving these honours from the Gaekwad, Vallabhdas returned to Nathdvara, where Damodar II/Dau was still the Tilkayat (MV: 2). We may conclude that Vallabhdas was liked by the Tilkayat and must have been a very accomplished *Pakhavaji* to have been allowed to come and go freely. Furthermore, it seems that the post of *Pakhavaji* at Nathdvara was a fairly prestigious appointment, to have attracted Pahar Singh, a very senior musician, away from the Jodhpur court. Pahar Singh left for Jodhpur when Vallabhdas returned, and there is no further mention of him in the *Mridang Sagar*.

Vallabhdas was fifty-five when he finally took up permanent residence in Nathdvara. The arrival of Vallabhdas in Nathdvara from the court of Jodhpur and his subsequent return to Nathdvara, after a short stay at the court of Baroda are important landmarks in the history of *pakhavaj* music in Nathdvara, because it is from this time that the family made the town their permanent home.

Vallabhdas had three sons: Chaturbhuj, Shankar (born 1829) and Khem (born 1832). The eldest, Chaturbhuj, moved to Udaipur and is not mentioned further (MS. Jivani: 4-5). The other two became *Pakhavajis* and their descendants are still serving in Nathdvara in the Shri Nathji and Navnitpriyaji Havelis. While Shankar was able to get employment in the Shri Nathji Haveli in 1849 after his father's death, Khem remained unemployed for a long period, a situation that is still common today among musicians in Nathdvara.

Instead of taking other employment, as many musicians today have done, Khem, who lived in a joint family with his elder brother Shankar, started work on the *Mridang Sagar*: "For the purpose of making progress in the art of music and musical instruments he looked into old books ... and looked at the difference between *matras*, their numbers ... and made a collection of *talas*. He busied himself studying old books that were available at that time" (MS. Jivani: 4).

While the initial work on the *Mridang Sagar* was begun by Khem, perhaps with some input from his elder brother Shankar, it was completed by Shankar's son, Ghanshyam, to whom it is attributed. Ghanshyam received instruction in the *pakhavaj* from Shankar, and Ghanshyam in turn taught his son Purushottam. Guru Purushottam has had no sons of his own but he taught several of his relatives: his grandson Prakash, his great-nephew, Balkrishna, son of Shyamlal, the present *Pakhavaji* in the Shri Nathji Haveli, and Ashok, son of Sohanlal. Sohanlal, the sixth generation descendant of Khem, in 1988 occupied the post of *Pakhavaji* in the Navnitpriyaji temple in Nathdvara. Sohanlal was taught by his father, as were each of his forbears, tracing an unbroken tradition back to Khem. The hereditary component of the Nathdvara *pakhavaj* tradition continues.

THE MAHARAJ OF JAMNAGAR VISITS NATHDVARA

In 1854, one of the religious leaders, Shri Brajnath, the Maharaj of Jamnagar, of the Vallabha Sampraday visited Nathdvara for Shri Nathji's *darshan*. He is described as having had "a great passion for the art of music", and for this reason he was accompanied by a *Pakhavaji* (MS. Jivani: 4; MV: 3). The *Mridang Sagar* records that the visitors were highly impressed with Shankar's *pakhavaj* playing during *Raj*

Bhog darshan and this prompted their discussion of various musical technicalities with Shankar, Khem and the Tilkayat, Giridhar (MV: 3). One may conclude that these discussions took place near the image because there alone are the musicians, the Tilkayat and visiting religious heads, found in close proximity during *Raj Bhog*. This convention continues today. When the other titular heads visit Nathdvara they join the Tilkayat near the image, just in front of the musicians.

Their discussions must have not only been very animated, but possibly controversial[9] as well, to prompt Maharaj Brajnath to suggest that, "... all knowledgeable people come after *Raj Bhog arati* the next day, at which time they can discuss this subject in a leisurely manner" (MS. Jivani: 4). The gathering escalated into a festival for connoisseurs, held in the guest house for Dvarkadhishji, which is attached to the Shri Nathji Haveli.[10] The Shri Nathji Haveli is closed for about three hours during mid-day after the *arati* at the time of *Raj Bhog*. The musicians are able to attend to various errands or, as in this case, get together for discussion. The original group was joined by more musicians: two from the Shri Nathji temple—the head musician (*Kirtankar Mukhiya*) Daulat Ram, and a *Binkar*, Ghanshyam and Ramnarayan/Rancchor, *Pakhavaji*, from the Navnitpriyaji Haveli. The *Mridang Sagar* names him as Rancchorji but the Nathdvara musicians refer to him as Ramnarayan. Note that Rancchor was in the Ambalal painting (1987: 134) playing the *sitar*. He was the son of Devkisan, *Sarangiya*.

Other singers from Nathdvara included Sundardas, to whom Radhakrishna (the late *Kirtankar Mukhiya*, of the Vitthalnathji temple in Nathdvara) and Tolaram (in 1988 the assistant *Kirtankar Mukhiya*, of the Shri Nathji temple) were related. Sundardas compiled a song book that is still consulted by the musicians. It was particularly moving in 1987 to witness Radhakrishna, while recovering from a stroke that left his right side paralysed, singing songs from this book in his small room. Words cannot describe the happiness, and the contentment that radiated from him as he sang.

The *Mridang Sagar* includes three more singers: Giridhar, Sivlal and Balkrishna (Ambalal 1987: 134). Other musicians who were present were: Rajeshwari from somewhere south of Nathdvara (unspecified), Balmukund, Biharidas from Kota,[11] and Haridas from Jhansi. Jhansi was a princely state in Uttar Pradesh, and so naturally several musicians would be attached to this court. Once again it illustrates the importance of the shrine for musicians while on tour.

Unfortunately Ghanshyam does not mention why so many musicians were in Nathdvara then. I suspect that it was either for the celebration of a major festival, such as Divali, Annakut, or Holi. Crooke's description of Annakut would support this:

> ... almost all Rajput princes; Rana Arsi of Mewar, Raj Bijay Singh of Marwar, and Rana Gaj Singh of Bikaner and Bahadur Singh of Kishengarh... were in Nathdvara during Annakuta. Rana Arsi Singh presented to the god a *tora*, or massive golden anklet-chain set with emeralds: Bijay Singh[12] a diamond necklace worth 25,000 rupees and other princes according to their means (Crooke 1920: 638).

Another reason for so many musicians and important people gathering in Nathdvara could be that the event coincided with a birth, marriage or anniversary within the Tilkayat's family. I have taken part in such festivities on two occasions and both times many musicians and dancers assembled.

The re-convening of the discussion and the gathering of so many musicians also suggests that it was regarded as a chance for musicians to demonstrate both their theoretical and practical skills.[13] The musical profession appears to have been highly competitive[14] during this period, for the *Mridang Sagar* noted that Maharaj Brajnath, after listening to the *Pakhavajis* discuss *talas* and *matras*, blessed the two brothers, Shankar and Khem. We may infer that they were probably given presents in cash or kind, and in the future could feel free to approach the Maharaj of Jamnagar for help, should they ever be in need (MS. Jivani: 5).

The *Mridang Sagar* lists some of the Maharajas, both religious and secular, who honoured Shankar by presenting him with ornaments, clothes and cash. The Maharaja Thakhat Singhji, of Jodhpur, and the Maharaval[15] of Dungarpur, Raja Prithvi Singh of Jhalrapatan, and Maharanas Svarup Singh (r. 1842-61) and Shambhu Singh (r. 1861-74) of Mewar (MS. Jivani: 5,6). In any biography of a musician it is customary to list prizes obtained from high ranking persons as it helps to confirm their expertise and status.

The Maharaval of Dungarpur[16] seems to have been particularly generous. He was so moved by Shankar's playing during *darshan* that Shankar was summoned to the Maharaval's lodgings[17] in Nathdvara where he was complimented. After presenting him with gold lion-faced bangles and clothes the Maharaval requested that Shankar wear them when he was playing for Shri Nathji: "According to his orders

Shankarji did this for *Raj Bhog* and those that saw this are still living" (MS. Jivani: 5-6).

The presence of so many heads of princely states and smaller kingdoms confirms the importance of Nathdvara as a centre of pilgrimage for rulers and is further support of Richardson's (1979) suggestion that the heads of the *sampraday* made every effort to cultivate the rich and powerful. The *sampraday* was particularly attractive to such people, and this in turn has helped it to flourish financially.

THE COURT OF UDAIPUR

In 1876 the Maharana of Udaipur, Sajjan Singh sent for Shankar to accompany the vocalist, Kale Khan,[18] in a musical evening he held at Govardhan Vilas, a palace resort two miles south of Udaipur. This palace was originally built by Svarup Singh (r. 1842-61) and was a popular venue for music recitals and other entertainment (MS. Jivani: 6).[19] Shankar played both *pakhavaj* and *tabla* (MS. Jivani: 6) making it possible for him to accompany *dhrupad* as well as *khyal*. *Khyal*, which is accompanied by *tabla*, would have been considered a more popular style of music, even at that time.

Two other singers, Saddu Khan (Owens 1983: 185) and Ava (sic) Danji, also sang in the same programme. The Maharana, pleased with Shankar's playing, later invited him to take part in the wedding celebrations for one of his relations that was to be held in Kishangarh,[20] another Rajput state. Shankar writes, that because the Maharana would be attending:

> ... the head of the palace servants ... gave an order that someone from Udaipur was going to marry someone from Krishnagarh (Kishengarh) and Shankarji had to play. The servant said that the best arrangements would be made for my father to travel to Krishnagarh ... Shankarji was very enthusiastic to attend such an auspicious occasion (MS. Jivani: 6).

Shankar, who was in the employ of the Tilkayat, asked for and received permission from the Tilkayat. Shankar, with his son Ghanshyam, on the back of his horse, and his brother Khem on another, set out for Nathdvara. When they reached the Shaivite temple of Eklingji, roughly half way, heavy rain and thunder storms assailed them. Shankar and Khem fell ill and returned to Nathdvara. Shortly afterwards in about 1876, Khem and his son Shyamlal died (MV: 3). Ghanshyam commented that "Shri Nathji did not wish my father to go to Kishengarh" (MS. Jivani: 7). The tragedy of the death of his uncle Khem and his cousin Shyamlal inspired Ghanshyam to ponder: "Only those who have experienced such a sorrow can realize what it is like ... One must accept God's will without complaint"

Shankar, however, was unable to be so detached. He became very depressed and in 1877, seven years after Khem's death, "my honourable mother requested my father to go on a *tirthyatra* (religious pilgrimage)" (MS. Jivani: 7; Eck 1983: 34-6).

SHANKAR GOES ON PILGRIMAGE

Accompanied by his family, and in search of peace of mind, Shankar visited various holy cities: Pushkar,[21] Prayag/Allahabad, Kashi/Banaras,[22] and Gaya (Eck 1985: 39). He went to three locations specifically to bathe: in the lake in Pushkar, Rajasthan, in the river Yamuna which flows through Braj and the city of Mathura, and the confluence of the three rivers: Ganga, Yamuna and Saraswati rivers at Prayag/Allahabad. In all three places, "according to his ability, he gave alms" (MS. Jivani: 8).

In Gaya he offered the *pind shraddh* ("offerings to the ancestors", Babb 1975: 95-97; Eck 1983: 215-16) to his dead relatives. Once again another patron, referred to as Guru Shyamlal, who was probably another Maharaj from the Vallabha Sampraday, called him to play for him in his palace. After he had played several solo *pakhavaj* pieces (*paran*, *podar*), and spoken the rhythmic syllables (*bols*), Shyamlal said he wanted to reward Shankar with "prizes". Shankar, however, after considering the matter, felt it improper to accept these gifts and instead replied: "Your *ashirvad* (blessing) itself is too much" (MS. Jivani: 8). This exchange illustrates the custom of presenting gifts to a Maharaj or spiritual teacher, a debt Shankar paid with his music, thus leaving both parties feeling comfortable. This was just one of the several contacts Shankar made while travelling. It is still customary to give gifts to a Maharaj when one visits, as I have observed on numerous occasions. Whenever I have visited the Tilkayat, and other Maharajas, pilgrims would offer presents, some in kind such as music or poetry, some in cash.

The *Mridang Sagar* recounts several other incidents of good fortune that Shankar encountered during his travels. The first was while he was returning from Gaya to Mittapur station when he heard the station master playing *sitar*. Shankar offered to accompany him on *tabla*. The station master was impressed and sent a telegram to his immediate superior, who was also a music connoisseur. After hearing them play, the station master gave Shankar a free second-class ticket to Patna (Ms. Jivani: 8). There were three classes in those days and a second class ticket was considered luxurious.

In Patna, Shankar's luck continued. There he met a good singer, Navnit Babu, who along with others was impressed with Shankar's playing. From Patna, Shankar went to Banaras and took the *darshan* of Maharaj Jivanlal head of the Vallabha Sampraday Haveli there. Maharaj Jivanlal was an old acquaintance who had previously visited Nathdvara and discussed the intricacies of *pakhavaj* with him and his late brother, Khem. As an accomplished *Pakhavaji,* Maharaj Jivanlal was only one of the many Maharaj who took an interest in developing and perfecting their own artistic skills, a tradition which continues to this day (chapter 3). In a painting dated 1876, Maharaj Jivanlal is shown in the Mukundrayji Haveli in Kashi (Ambalal 1987: 132-3). I was reminded of the interchange between these *havelis* when in 1988 the only musician serving in one of the Jamnagar Havelis was Dau Diyar, a brahmin from Braj, who had two years earlier served as a musician in the Mukundrayji Haveli for twenty years (chapter 12).

I can attest to the professional calibre and earnest commitment of the Maharaj of the Vitthalnathji temple in Nathdvara/Indore (who play *pakhavaj* and *sitar* and sing *khyal* and *dhrupad-dhamar*), the son of the Maharaj in Baroda who plays *pakhavaj,* the Maharaj of Ahmedabad who plays *pakhavaj* and the grandson of the Surat Maharaj, who in 1987 began his training with Guru Purushottam. Guru Purushottam travelled to Surat and stayed in the *haveli* for one month in order to initiate him into the art. There are many others and their artistic activity varies from recording songs, to writing poetry and studying music (chapter 3).

While in Banaras, Shankar accompanied a *Binkar,* Varas Ali, and a *Sitariya,* Ganesh Singh Bajpai. On the latter occasion he probably played *tabla,* as *pakhavaj* is not normally used to accompany *sitar*. From Banaras, Shankar continued his pilgrimage to Ayodhya, Lucknow, Mathura, and Kishengarh, finally returning to Nathdvara. He mentions getting presents from a wealthy merchant in Mathura and from the ruler of Kishengarh (MS. Jivani: 8), leaving the impression that while on pilgrimage he was able to combine acquiring religious merit with gathering musical honours, and social status with some financial remuneration.

The pilgrimage lasted six months and on his return Ghanshyam, his only son, was married to Ramibai. Her father, Tekchand, was a construction worker, a common occupation for members of the *kumavat* community to which the majority of the Nathdvara musicians belong. In 1887, Shankar was invited to Asavare, near Ahmedabad, on the occasion of Chhapan Bhog, to play in the presence of the *svarup* normally resident in Ahmedabad. It had been moved to Asavare for this celebration (Jindel 1976: 42). He then travelled to Baroda to play for another religious leader there, Gosvami Gopallal who is reported to have given "good gifts in front of all" (MS. Jivani: 9). Once again he does not limit his performances to religious leaders, as he mentions that in Baroda he was also rewarded with presents by Jamnabai, the wife of the late Gaekwad. Certainly wives of the nobility often played an important part in giving patronage to the arts. He singles out two other excellent musicians who were then in Baroda, another *Pakhavaji*, Nazir Khan and a *binkar* Mola Baksh and both of them "praised Shankarji" (MS. Jivani: 9; MV: 3).

Although the following statement was made in jest it tends to suggest that court musicians were more highly regarded than those who were employed in the temple: "The *binkar*, Maula Baksh[23] asked my father (Shankar), "where do you dwell?" ... it seems you are from Lanka or beyond, otherwise the Gaekwad Maharao would have been your patron" (MS. Jivani: 9).

In fact, the Gaekwad had been his father's patron before he chose to return to Nathdvara. The musicians must surely have been aware of this, which raises a question concerning the actual circumstances under which Shankar's father chose to leave the Gaekwad's court. Wade (1984: 186) mentions Maula Baksh as a singer at the Baroda court and relates an instance where he got himself into trouble with the Gaekwad. He seems to have been an outspoken musician.

SHANKAR'S RETURN, HIS DEATH AND THE APPOINTMENT OF GHANSHYAM AS *PAKHAVAJI*

From Baroda, Shankar went to Surat and Bombay, both cities with *havelis* and Maharaj of the Vallabha Sampraday. He does not, however, mention specific occasions, or persons, that he encountered. Before returning to Nathdvara he performed at Udaipur for Maharana Fateh Singh[24] who rewarded him with "prizes" (MS. Jivani: 10). This was the last time Shankar was to leave Nathdvara, for as Ghanshyam stated: "After that my father could not go anywhere as he was too old. In the last stages of his life he felt he should serve only the lord" (MS. Jivani: 10).

Shankar died in 1893 and the Tilkayat, Govardhanlal[25] appointed Ghanshyam, at the age of twenty-four, to be his father's successor as *Pakhavaji* in the Shri Nathji temple. The *Mridang Sagar* includes two *pakhavaj* compositions which include a text, intended to be recited rhythmically (*parans*), composed by Shankar in honour of his two important patrons: the Maharana Fateh Singh Paran (MS: 11) and the Guru "Paran" (MS: 11) dedicated to the Tilkayat Govardhanlal.

Although Ghanshyam was the author of the *Mridang Sagar*, the book is not autobiographical and he recorded very few details about himself. He gives, however, some indication that his life was not easy, describing it as "full of agony", because his father was often ill. This presumably refers to his father's depression over the untimely death of his brother Khem and nephew Shyamlal. Both Ghanshyam and Guru Purushottam one generation later are emphatic that their only teachers were their fathers. Ghanshyam does not appear to have taught anyone else, whereas Shankar taught at least four other students, the brothers: Parasuram, Tikamdas, Ramnarayan and Gangadas. Tikamdas later played in the Chandramaji temple in Udaipur. The family connection was maintained by the marriage of Shankar's grandson, Guru Purushottam, to one of Tikamdas' daughters, Gulab. It is their grandson Prakash who has become Purushottam's chief disciple and musical heir. Guru Purushottam, however, taught many other students while employed as *pakhavaj* teacher in New Delhi (MV. 4). Ramnarayan later became a *Pakhavaji* in the Shri Nathji Haveli, until Guru Purushottam was old enough to take up their families' post. Ramnarayan taught his son Balkrishna, who played *pakhavaj* in the Navnitpriyaji temple, but none of Balkrishna's children became musicians. The relatives of Shankar's other two students Parasuram and Gangadas have abandoned the profession.

GURU PURUSHOTTAM DAS (1907-1991)

Guru Purushottam Das was born on July 7, 1907 in the same house where he lived until his death. It had been in his family since his great-grandfather, Vallabhdas, first arrived in Nathdvara in 1802.

Situated in Naya Bazaar, it is well appointed for making frequent visits to the Shri Nathji Haveli. Naya Bazaar (New Bazaar), now deep in the heart of town, is a reminder that one hundred and fifty years ago Nathdvara must have been less than half its present size. Guru Purushottam's street, "Tambaku Gali" (Tobacco Lane) is also a remnant of the past. The tobacco merchants that the name commemorates are no longer there. Not much has changed otherwise; there are still the narrow cobblestone lanes, hardly a metre wide, with water running freely down both sides in open drains, and typical Mewari designs of decorated elephants ridden by turbaned Rajputs painted on the whitewashed walls are reminders of times past.

Most of the buildings in the old town are at least three storeys high, enclosed within the walls that once served to protect the inhabitants from marauders. The rooms are laid out around a tiny square courtyard space that runs vertically like a mine shaft and lets air and light in. The light filters through small shuttered windows opening on to the courtyard, but most of the rooms are deeply shadowed, except for those opening onto the roof. As the weather is hot most of the year, the windows provide ventilation. They are unglazed but are crossed by steel bars which deny entry to intruders, including the langur monkeys which abound in the town. The importance of this precaution cannot be exaggerated as these monkeys are almost entirely dependent on what they can scavenge from *Homo sapiens*. They are quick to snatch food, or anything else that might attract their attention, before bounding off over the roofs to safety. An uneasy peace exists between these two groups of primates who, despite their constant battles for territory, may also derive pleasure from watching each other.

Because of the warm weather, much of the daily life of the inhabitants takes place outside on terraces open to the sky. In the summer, families sleep outside, and in the cooler months, they gather mid-morning to bask in the warmth of the sun. Living outside, and in close proximity to each other, leaves family life open to public scrutiny.

Guru Purushottam's home was like most of the traditional dwellings in Nathdvara. The house itself was a tall building, decorated with white stucco, seemingly squeezed between adjacent houses. There was charm, simplicity, and a feeling of privacy in these tiny rooms stacked together and linked by winding staircases. Such staircases are typical of Nathdvara homes, and even when he was over eighty years of age, Guru Purushottam was very nimble on them, moving up and down with great speed, even in the pitch dark during the frequent electricity cuts. The living quarters were on the second and third storeys. At the top of his house were two rooms. One was set aside for worship, and contained pictures of Shri Nathji, Vallabha and Shiva. Another room commemorated his father, Ghanshyam, and contained memorabilia, such as a large oil painting of him. Here Guru Purushottam also kept his instruments, a *pakhavaj* and an old pair of *tabla*. With the exception of some electric light sockets, and a table fan, there was nothing in his home that could place it in the twentieth century. Indeed, so modest were his possessions, that it contained little to place it in any century.

Guru Purushottam began his musical training at the age of five, and early photos attest that he was frequently present when his father practised, played in public, or attended any musical event. After his father's death, Guru Purushottam was taken under the tutelage of the Tilkayat, Govardhanlal, the present Tilkayat Govindlal's grandfather. He was given an allowance of nine rupees per month until he was twenty-five years old and took up the post of *Pakhavaji*. He continues to be grateful to the Tilkayat's family for the encouragement given to him to pursue his studies of the *pakhavaj*. Like most musicians of his generation, his formal schooling was sporadic, although he says he studied up to the seventh standard.[26]

Guru Purushottam's mother was dependent upon him for support[27] after his father's death. His sisters, who were considerably older, were already married. During the early period, he could not afford a *pakhavaj* and practised what his father had taught him by beating his fingers on the sides of a wooden box.[28] He was unclear as to what happened to his father's instrument, but presumably it was sold. Another reason why he was forced to use a box, was that he preferred to practise at night, or in the early morning and this sound did not disturb the neighbours. He later claimed that being forced to play on a box was a blessing in disguise. It aided him in developing the crisp, clear sounds, which are characteristic of his playing. The box technique also proved very effective when he was teaching in Delhi: he would illustrate the exact sound he demanded from his students by beating his fingers against the sides of the harmonium.[29] Guru Purushottam also remembered practising at night in a lonely farmhouse away from the city so that the deep sonorous sounds, so characteristic of the *pakhavaj*, would not cause disturbance to others.

Guru Purushottam stated that although he had some instruction from his father during those early years, after his father's death, he relied heavily on the music recorded in the *Mridang Sagar* as a teaching aid. The question arises whether the material in the *Mridang Sagar* is really representative of the music played by Guru Purushottam's father, Ghanṣhyam, and his great-uncle Khem. We shall probably never know the answer, but one thing is clear; most of the pieces notated in the book are intended for solo performance of the *pakhavaj*. In contrast, most of the music played in Nathdvara today is as accompaniment for *haveli sangit*. Only Guru Purushottam, whose career took him away from the influence of the temple for many years, had the opportunity to develop a really extensive solo repertoire. As the *Mridang Sagar* was compiled over a period of time by percussionists who played in many settings, we may assume that the authors made a deliberate attempt to collect a variety of *pakhavaj* compositions. Some of those included may never have been part of the frequently performed repertoire.

When he was twelve, Guru Purushottam recalled, "some persons became jealous" of his progress.[30] Two events stood out in his mind. The first was when the farmhouse[31] where he kept his instrument was broken into and his harmonium and *pakhavaj* were smashed; the second was his contrived disgrace before his patron, the Tilkayat Govardhanlal, who had summoned him to accompany *dhrupad* at a festival. Up to this point Guru Purushottam had always practised alone and so was feeling somewhat nervous. When he started to play, some members of the audience created a disturbance which affected his performance. Guru Purushottam, "was not able to perform well" and "was asked to leave the concert". Heartbroken, he went to the river Banas and seriously considered suicide.[32] Fortunately some friends found him and dissuaded him. During this difficult period his mother inspired him, and two years later he played at a similar occasion. This time he left the audience with no doubt that he would uphold the family tradition of *pakhavaj* playing (MV: 4).

At the age of fifteen he began to play in the Shri Nathji temple at pre-*Gval darshan*, learning accompaniment by playing with the singers on duty for the day. Most of the present-day Nathdvara musicians recall playing at this time when they first began their musical careers. Guru Purushottam continued this for eight years, practising particularly with Harnath Sanadya, a specialist in *haveli sangit*. Harnath did not train his own children as musicians and his family is no longer associated with music in Nathdvara. On a visit to Nathdvara in 1988, I met one of Harnath's children, who will be retiring soon as a railway official. He has begun to attend all *darshans* in the Shri Nathji Haveli to "sing along" and intends to take up singing regularly after he retires.

In 1925, at eighteen years of age, Guru Purushottam spent one month in Udaipur with Parasuram, a singer in the Gokulchandramaji temple. Although employed as a singer, Parasuram, as well as his three brothers, Tikam (later to be Guru Purushottam's father-in-law), Gangadas and Ramnarayan, all studied *pakhavaj* with Guru Purushottam's grandfather, Shankar. Guru Purushottam said that he chose Parasuram over Tikam because he played better, and it was Parasuram who taught him the best sounds on the *pakhavaj* to complement vocal accompaniment and instrumental music.[33] He reported that this resulted in a great improvement to his mastery over maintaining a steady tempo (*laya*), a prerequisite for accompaniment. Parasuram taught Guru Purushottam one rhythmic composition (*paran*). Since Guru Purushottam's grandfather, Shankar, had taught Parasuram there was no question of payment[34] and Guru Purushottam stayed as a guest in the family. He later married Gulab, Tikam's daughter as mentioned above.[35]

On Ghanshyam's death the post of *Pakhavaji* in the Shri Nathji Haveli went first to Govindrao of Burhanpur (MV: 4).[36] According to Guru Purushottam even though Govindrao of Burhanpur was a very accomplished *Pakhavaji*, he was told from the beginning that his appointment would only be temporary. The post was designated as the hereditary tradition of Guru Purushottam's family and would be filled by Guru Purushottam in due course. Govindrao stayed only a year, and was replaced by Parmananddas. His son Mulchand teaches *pakhavaj* in the Music School attached to the *haveli* (Shri Nathji Shikshan Kendra). One year later, Ramnarayan, Shankar's other student, was appointed to the post, which he occupied for fifteen years. Ramnarayan was several years older than Guru Purushottam; it was apparently he who set up the latter's disgrace and near-suicide. Ramnarayan taught *pakhavaj* to his son, Balkrishna, who assumed the post of *Pakhavaji* in the Navnitpriyaji temple, but the latter did not teach his own children.

The same year (1925), as well as studying *pakhavaj* accompaniment with Parasuram in Udaipur, Guru Purushottam studied *tabla* from Ganpatlal, who had come to Nathdvara from Kota to perform for the Tilkayat. He stayed for a month. During that time Guru Purushottam took *tabla* lessons from him. Guru Purushottam has taught *tabla* but I have never heard him play *tabla* in a concert. Four years later, when a Kathak troupe was invited by the Tilkayat to come to Nathdvara, Guru Purushottam again took *tabla* lessons, this time from a member of the troupe, Bikaner Mohan, who played in the style of the Banaras *gharana*. The troupe stayed for about five years and during that period another *tabla* player, Balmukund replaced Bikaner Mohan (see chapter 7).

In 1932, at the age of twenty-five, Guru Purushottam was officially employed in the Shri Nathji Haveli, a post he held until 1957, when he was invited to Delhi to teach *pakhavaj* at the Bharatiya Kala Kendra Music Academy. Nazir Aminuddin Dagar had heard Guru Purushottam on the radio, and/or in Udaipur, and it was on this basis that he recommended him. In the 1980s Guru Purushottam still accompanied him at various *dhrupad* festivals. It is interesting to note that the Dagar family, the most famous exponents of the *dhrupad* style of music, has been associated both with the Jaipur court, where the home of their ancestor Behram Khan (Wade 1984: 228-9) is still maintained, and with the Udaipur court, where Nazir Aminuddin's father's cousin was employed as a court musician. Very early in his career Nazir Aminuddin sang for the Udaipur Maharanas.[37] Guru Purushottam's family has also been connected with both these royal courts. Hence there was periodic contact between these two musical families, the Dagars for the music of vocal and *bin*, and Guru Purushottam's for rhythmic accompaniment, for several generations.

In 1947 Guru Purushottam auditioned for All India Radio,[38] Delhi and was given a B grade in the All India Radio classification (Neuman 1980). The audition was arranged by Hanuman Prasad, a Kathak dancer who had met Guru Purushottam while in Nathdvara, performing for the Tilkayat. It was Guru Purushottam's radio recordings that eventually resulted in his being appointed *pakhavaj* teacher at the Bharatiya Kala Kendra. He was given this opportunity by Dr Nirmala Joshi, at that time Assistant Director of All India Radio, and also an officer of the Bharatiya Kala Kendra. Both of them had gone to Nathdvara in search of talent for the school. Only Guru Purushottam was chosen and he attributes the appointment to the recommendations of both Dr. Joshi and the *dhrupad* singers Nazir Moinuddin Dagar and Nazir Aminuddin Dagar who were then teaching *dhrupad* at the Bharatiya Kala Kendra, the institution that hired him.

In 1957, when Guru Purushottam moved to Delhi, he was placed in the All India Radio grade A. In 1980, after he received the Sangeet Natak Akademi Award (1979), All India Radio recognized his talent and placed him in the highest category, top grade A. Every year until about 1986 he played four or five times on the radio, both as a solo artist, and accompanying eminent vocalists and instrumentalists. He also presented an hour-long recital on the 'National Programme', an honour awarded to very few percussionists (Neuman 1980).

Aside from radio broadcasts, Guru Purushottam did very little performing while he lived in Delhi, mainly because there was little music being performed publicly in the *dhrupad* style. This situation started to change in the mid 1970s. With the sudden resurgence of interest in the style, several *dhrupad* festivals were organized in centres such as Vrindavan, Banaras, Bhopal, Rampur and Nathdvara. Some of these have become annual events. While the central and state governments often give money towards them, they rely on the help of volunteers and other enthusiasts (Erdman 1985). The festivals attract performers from all over north India. They often include artists not specifically invited, but who arrive, and by custom, are allowed to participate. The result is that the gatherings (*mela*) have a relaxed and impromptu format. They can last anywhere from three days to one week. There is usually virtually non-stop singing, instrumental music and *pakhavaj* playing, all in the *dhrupad-dhamar* tradition. Recently *haveli sangit melas* have been organized as there is a resurgence of interest in *haveli sangit* being performed on the stage and on the radio. Guru Purushottam attended and participated in many of the *dhrupad-dhamar melas.* Like other masters, he used their forum to introduce his grandson, Prakash, to the discerning gatherings. I myself played *pakhavaj* in the Jaipur *Dhrupad Mela* in 1982. Guru Purushottam assisted me by keeping the *tala* and his grandson played *layra* on the harmonium.

In 1962-63 Guru Purushottam toured Nepal, the Soviet Union Germany and Japan on government-sponsored exchanges (MV: 4), along with the brothers Nazir Moinuddin and Nazir Aminuddin Dagar. In 1964 he was invited to Sri Lanka on a similar exchange.[39]

Although married three times, Guru Purushottam has only one surviving child, Radha, who was born to his first wife Gulab. Radha married Damodar, currently the *Kirtankar Mukhiya* in the Navnitpriyaji temple and they have five children: three girls and two boys. Their eldest son Prakash Chand came to Delhi in 1979 to join the Kathak Kendra as a student of *pakhavaj* under his grandfather. Before this, Prakash studied at the Government Art College in Nathdvara and had not taken formal *pakhavaj* lessons. From the time that he joined the Kathak Kendra, Prakash assumed the position of general assistant and chief disciple to his grandfather. In 1981, when Guru Purushottam retired from the Kathak Kendra at the age of seventy-four, Prakash returned with him to Nathdvara and both took up posts with the music school, the Shri Nathji Sangit Shikshan Kendra. In 1984, Guru Purushottam officially adopted Prakash and arranged for his wedding. Prakash will also be Guru Purushottam's musical heir.

By maintaining his connection with the musical tradition of Nathdvara, Guru Purushottam was able to retain the strictly traditional style of his ancestors. At the same time, through his association with national institutions of music and his performances and broadcasts he was also able to infuse some of this tradition into the current mainstream of Indian classical music. It was with great sadness that I read his grandson Prakash's letter to me:

> Respected Anjali,
> Your Guru, Padma Shri Purushottam Das, Pakhavaji
> expired on 21-1 91.
> Prakash Kumavat,
> Nathdvara, 25 January 1991.

I had lost a teacher and friend and Nathdvara and India had lost a great musician.

CONCLUSION

The *Mridang Sagar* and *Mridang Vadan* establish the musical credentials of Guru Purushottam's family. Like many musical families, they began as itinerant musicians (Neuman 1980; Wade 1984). By the 1700s, they were settled at the court of Amber as *Pakhavajis*, a profession they have followed ever since. Such historical documentation is important for any family, if their musical lineage is to be taken seriously (Wade 1984; Neuman 1980; Sorrell 1980).

As well as long association with music, the family's having a place in musical history is also defined by the importance of their patrons. Consequently, the *Mridang Sagar* gives full details of the patronage which the family received. After working in the Jaipur, Jodhpur and Baroda courts, the family finally made their home in Nathdvara. The stability and permanence given by employment in the Nathdvara Haveli gave the family a firm basis from which to work. Their periodic movement to other centres was always undertaken with the blessings of the Tilkayat, giving them the opportunity of playing in both temple and court situations. Whatever else they did, the link to Nathdvara remained unbroken.

The *Mridang Sagar* demonstrates that a keen interest in music has typified many Maharaj for several generations. The interest shown by the Maharaj of Jamnagar, Gaya and Banaras, in the playing of Shankar attest to this. Indeed the *Mridang Sagar* credits the Maharaj of Kankroli with reviewing an entire draft of the book before publication (MS. PR: 1). This sustained and detailed appreciation of music among the Vallabha Sampraday and its senior priesthood is a notable characteristic. It further emphasizes the important role that music plays in its religious celebrations.

The influence of the Tilkayat is felt in all of Ghanshyam's comments. As his patron and eventual publisher of the *Mridang Sagar,* Ghanshyam naturally records his gratitude. The pervasive influence of the Tilkayat appears throughout, most particularly with reference to the necessity of obtaining permission for any absence from Nathdvara, which in turn would mean not performing his *seva* in the *haveli.* For example, Shankar has to return from Udaipur to Nathdvara to ask if he can accept the Rana of Mewar's invitation to play at the wedding in Kishengarh. We might have expected the Maharana's wishes to have had more weight. As the virtual leader of the Rajputs, the Rana of Mewar was no minor prince. Yet, Shankar travelled thirty miles to Nathdvara to obtain the necessary consent.

The *Mridang Sagar* sheds light on another aspect of the north Indian musical tradition in its account of Shankar's relationship with the unrelated *Pakhavaji,* Pahar Singh of Jodhpur. The account makes it clear that such a transmission of important material from one family to another was most unusual and worthy of comment even several generations later. Otherwise the *pakhavaj* tradition of Nathdvara places great emphasis on the concurrence between blood lines and those of musical transmission. All the same, the prolonged period of teaching by Guru Purushottam in New Delhi, at both the Bharatiya Kala Kendra, and Kathak Kendra, has meant that his family's tradition is now widely disseminated among younger *pakhavaj* players in north India. It was a measure of Guru Purushottam's sincerity as a teacher that he appears to have held nothing back from his students. Hence, one of the traditional areas of north Indian music became accessible to the broader musical community. His role in infusing the *pakhavaj* tradition of Nathdvara into the mainstream of north Indian music is, perhaps, Guru Purushottam's most important legacy. Guru Purushottam's students came from a wide variety of backgrounds, both socially and educationally. They are now making use of their training in a variety of ways. Consequently, some distant echoes of the music performed for Shri Nathji may be heard as far afield as the Kathak Kendra's dance productions, and in music performed on concert stages across India.

It must have been a great change for Guru Purushottam's generation to teach in a school, with fixed hours, to pupils supplied by the institution, with evaluations, examinations, and the possibility of scholarships for the most deserving. All this was very different from the close community, and limited access and demand for training found in Nathdvara. The tradition may be seen to be changing under the onslaught of the twentieth century. Change, however, is not something new. The *Mridang Sagar* details many events that may have led to changes in the family's musical heritage: the interaction with Pahar Singh in Jodhpur, Vallabhdas' experiences in Baroda and other places

TABLE 11.1: *PAKHAVAJIS* OF THE SHRI NATHJI HAVELI FROM 1802

1802-20	Vallabhdas, Guru Purushottam's great-grandfather
1820-24	Pahar Singh
1824-69	Vallabhdas, Guru Purushottam's great-grandfather
1869-93	Shankar, Guru Purushottam's grandfather
1893-1914	Ghanshyam, Guru Purushottam's father
1914-16	Govindrao of Burhanpur
1916-17	Parmananddas (Mulchand's father) Mulchand was employed to play the harmonium in the Shri Nathji Haveli
1917-32	Ramnarayan
1932-57	Guru Purushottam Das
1957-81	Ramchandra is currently (1989) employed as a singer in the Shri Nathji Haveli
1981-present	Shyamlal (Ramchandra's brother)
1982-91	Guru Purushottam Das (honorary *Pakhavaji* in addition to Shyamlal)

on his travels, Khem's deliberate attempt to collect material from different sources, and Shankar's experiences on pilgrimage and elsewhere. All of these events may have led to modifications in the family's music and hence to changes in the Nathdvara tradition. Such evolution is natural and occurs in all living artistic traditions. Nevertheless, *haveli sangit* remains a distinctive musical genre by virtue of the peculiar circumstances under which it is played. Irrespective of the events and changes proceeding outside Nathdvara, within the *haveli* the music continues day in and day out—a resilient thread in the rich fabric of Indian music.

NOTES

1. Wade 1984 and Jariwalla 1973 describe the Baroda Court.
2. Vallabhdas had three sons: Chaturbhuj, Shankar and Khem.
3. Comments by those who have had to overcome this are given by Allaudin Khan in Bhattacharya (1979) and Ramnarayan in Sorrell (1980: 16-17), Bhimsen Joshi in Nadkarni (1983) and Owens (1983) with reference to the Dagar family.
4. The method whereby an oral tradition is handed down is usually called *guru-shishya* (teacher-student) *parampara* (tradition) or the uninterrupted acquisition of knowledge from one generation to the next.
5. There are numerous accounts of a teacher later being upstaged by a student.
6. See Owens (1983: 164) who records such a transfusion into the Dagar family. Very often it is only the most famous teacher who is acknowledged, although many professionals have studied with several teachers and go on to develop their own style. Neuman (1980:43-58) deals with this in a very general way. See the biographies of Bhimsen Joshi (Nadkarni 1983) and Allaudin Khan (Bhattacharya 1979).
7. Wade (1984: 9) states that the Gaekwad of Baroda employed singers trained in a variety of musical traditions (*gharanas*) so that Baroda was not associated with one particular style. From Wade's remarks we may conclude that the Gaekwad was open to new forms (see also Jariwalla 1973).
8. The miniature painting of Tod (1782-1835) illustrated in Aman Nath 1987: 163, presenting his credentials to Maharana of Udaipur, Bhim Singh II (1778-1828), suggests that Vallabhdas might have seen Tod as this was the period when Vallabhdas was serving in Nathdvara. In the *Mridang Sagar*, Tod is mentioned as an important source to consult regarding the history of Nathdvara and Rajasthan.
9. See Jariwalla 1973: 92-8 for an account of just how tense such encounters can become.
10. The *Mridang Sagar* states that the conference was held in the Dvarkanathji

temple (*mandir*) but that is in Kankroli. I have therefore interpreted it to mean the guest house for Shri Dvarkanathji. It would have been a convenient spot to meet as it is beside the Shri Nathji Haveli.

11. Kotah was one of the princely states whose rulers were staunch devotees. See Ambalal (1987: 67) and Richardson (1979) for the influence that the Vallabha Sampraday had on the art of Kotah and other princely states of Rajasthan.
12. Ambalal (1987: 102,152) illustrates Bija Singh taking *darshan* in Nathdvara.
13. Bhattacharya (1979:53-8) recounts such events in which another musician Allaudin Khan participated.
14. There are numerous accounts of the competitive nature of musical gatherings. For example in Guru Purushottam's own experience he was driven to contemplate suicide, as was Allaudin Khan (Bhattacharya 1979: 28).
15. Crooke (1920: 356). Raval is the term of address for the head of Dungarpur State.
16. See Aman Nath (1987: 83) for an illustration of nineteenth century decorative motifs in the Dungarpur palace.
17. It was no doubt customary for the various heads of state to keep a house in Nathdvara so that they would be accommodated in comfort. Today in Nathdvara wealthy devotees have built "cottages" or made a substantial donation to one such building so that whenever they are in Nathdvara they can stay in Vallabh cottages. During the rest of the year these are rented out to pilgrims. They are self-contained units with a kitchen and several bathrooms. One must, however, supply one's own stove and cooking utensils. Banaras, Vrindavan, and other religious centres boasted palaces of the Maharajas set up for their own use.
18. There were two singers named Kale Khan active at that time. One from the musical tradition of the Kirana *gharana* was at both the Bharatpur and Baroda courts in 1894 (Wade 1984: 185-7). He had two sons, Abdul Karim (b. 1872) and Abdul Haq; Abdul became more famous than his father. As another professional singer living at this time, Mira Baksh (d. 1920) adopted the name of Kale Khan. It is impossible to know which of the two was accompanied by Shankar. See also Jariwalla (1979: 28).
19. A miniature painting in Cimino 1985, dated 1859 shows a picnic scene at Govardhan Vilas. An illustration of Govardhan Vilas is in Purohit Dev Nath (1938).
20. Richardson (1979: 98 fn11) states that Krishnagarh and Kishengarh are the same place. The *Mridang Sagar* states that they are to travel to Krishnagarh. Crooke (1920: 638) confirms that the ruler of Kishengarh was also a devotee of Shri Nathji. This has had a great deal of influence on the miniature paintings in the Kishengarh style.
21. Pushkar is in Rajasthan and is sacred to Brahma. It has a very holy lake.
22. Hanuman Ghat is considered to be the spot where Vallabha was born. The Mukundarayji *svarup* is installed in Banaras (Jindel 1976: 73; Barz 1976: 55; Eck (1983)).
23. Owens (1983) spells Mola Baksh as Maula Baksh and describes him as a

Dhrupadia and *sarangi* player, an outstanding non-family student of Behram Khan.

24. Aman Nath (1987: 85) illustrates Shiv Niwas palace built in the late eighteenth-early nineteenth century by Fateh Singh.
25. Ambalal (1987) describes Govardhanlal as a generous patron of the arts who was also very interested in them.
26. Jariwalla (1973: 20) states that earlier education was not as important as musical knowledge. Owens (1983: 184) confirms this: "Aminuddin Dagar was the product of an upbringing which placed all types of education second to the acquisition of performance skills" (See also Wade 1984).
27. Owens (1983: 175) gives an example of another musician, Moinuddin Dagar, supporting his family at an early age.
28. Many *tabla* exponents have deliberately practised on wood. In southern India it is customary to begin *mridangam* training by playing on wood.
29. Although a *sarangi* player was usually present in the class, Guru Purushottam would play the harmonium while teaching how to maintain a strict tempo (*laya*).
30. See also Bhattacharya (1979: 28) who gives examples from Allaudin Khan's life.
31. Owens (1983: 183) describes Behram Khan of Jaipur maintaining a house outside the city so that students could practise in a peaceful spot.
32. Bhattacharya (1979) relates an incident that caused Allaudin Khan to consider suicide. See also Shankar (1968).
33. See Bhattacharya (1979) who describes how the sounds of the percussion instrument should complement the music. Also Gaston (1983b, 1984).
34. Payment in kind was the accepted method. This is an example of musical knowledge being "returned" to a family. There are many examples of this when the hereditary exponents died young and their children were dependent on others.
35. There are many examples in the musical world of a student marrying into his teacher's family. For example Ravi Shankar married Annapurna, the daughter of his teacher, Allaudin Khan.
36. Burhanpur is in the state of Madhya Pradesh but the *haveli* there has kept close ties with Nathdvara. During the Radhashtami celebrations the *dhari* comes from there to dance with the *dharan* from Nathdvara. Prem Lata Sharma (1988) refers to the *Pakhavaji*, Govindrao from Burhanpur. For a photograph of Govindrao see the photographic archives in the Sangit Natak Akademi, New Delhi.
37. See Owens (1983: 170); Sorrell (1980: 14) describes the *sarangi* player Ramnarayan.
38. Owens (1983: 193) remarks on the importance of radio programmes for musicians.
39. He has also toured other countries as he has shown me a photograph of himself outside the Parthenon in Athens, which was taken while on tour. He had no recollection of having visited Greece, which indicates that it was probably an exhaustive tour that included many countries.

Plate 11.1: Darshan during the eclipse (1883)

The musicians are identified on the back of the painting are: Shankar playing the *pakhavaj*, Jamnadas *kirtankar* (singer), Devkishan playing the *sarangi*, Matu playing the *bin*, Jelaniya playing the cymbals, and Rancchor/ Ranchod the *Sitariya*, playing the *tanpura*. Ranchod is the only musician also mentioned by Ghanshyam in the *Mridang Sagar*.

Matu *Binkar* did not have any children. The position of *Binkar* passed into the family of Jamnadas.

This subject of this painting documents three events: the eclipse, the playing of music as an auspicious offering during this potentially inauspicious time, and the initiation of three young men, probably from gosvami families. There are two gosvamis present: Gopallal and Kalyanray as well as the Tilkayat which suggests that the event was important.

Tilkayat Govardanlal is seated on the left with a rosary bag on his hand. Shri Nathji's dress indicates that the weather was warm. Comparing this miniature painting with the photograph 1914 (Plate 7.4) tends to suggest that with the exception of Guru Purushottam's family who have held the post as *Pakhavaji* in the Shri Nathji Haveli the other posts have passed into various other families. This painting is in the collection of Amit Ambalal.

Plate 11.2: Detail of Plate 11.1

Plate 11.3: Shri Nathji, Shringar on a summer's day (c. 1772)

This painting shows Tilkayat Govind (1729-79) and his son, Giridhar (1779-1807), standing in the Nij Mandir on Shri Nathji's right. Maharaja Bijay Singh of Jodhpur is outside the Nij Mandir.

The influence of the Tilkayat over the princes of the various Rajasthan states is considerable. In 1772 the rulers of Mewar, (Ari Singh), Jodhpur (Bijay Singh) and Bikaner (Gaja Singh) and Kishengarh (Bahadur Singh) visited Nathdvara to ask the Tilkayat to settle a dispute between the Rana of Mewar, Ari Singh and the Maharaja of Jodhpur, Bijay Singh.

Five musicians are present. The *Binkar* stands on one leg, supporting his *bin* on the knee of his bent leg, the *Pakhavaji* squats and the other three musicians are keeping time by clapping. The musicians are not playing *jhanjh* which would indicate that it is not a special festival. When Giridhar became Tilkayat he invited Vallabhdas to become one of his musicians. It is possible that Vallabhdas accompanied the son of the then Maharaja of Jodhpur, Bijay Singh, during the visit to Nathdvara depicted here.

Shri Nathji is shown wearing light clothing and temple servants are pouring water on the floor which evaporates and cools the temperature. Tilkayat Govind, and his son Giridhar, both carry fans to fan Shri Nathji. This painting is in the collection of Amit Ambalal (1987: 102,152).

Plate 11.4: Guru Purushottam Das (1907-91) and his father Ghanshyam Das Pakhavaji (1869-1916), Shri Nathji Haveli (c. 1911-14)

Plate 11.5: Guru Purushottam Das, his wife and daughter Radha, now married to Damodardas, Kirtankar Mukhiya, Navnitpriyaji Haveli

Plate 11.6: Guru Purushottam Das receiving the Sangeet Natak Akademi Award (1979)

Plate 11.7: Guru Purushottam Das keeping the tala

CHAPTER 12

Other Centres of the *Sampraday*

BAITHAKS

Baithaks are important centres of worship and visitation for the Vallabha Sampraday. There are said to be eighty-four *baithaks* or shrines all over India which commemorate an incident in the life of Vallabha or his successors. They have been established by members of the Vallabha Sampraday in places visited by Vallabha or some other important spiritual teacher of the sect. The reason for their visit may have been to preach, go on pilgrimage or write a religious work. Other reasons for establishing a *baithak* are to commemorate the spot where a miracle was performed or a leader displayed his superiority over other philosophers (Entwistle 1987: 264).

There are twenty-two *baithaks* in Braj, which pertain to Vallabha. Others are located in other centres, especially Gujarat. Vallabha's son Vitthalnath has twenty-eight *baithaks*, of which seven are in Braj. Vitthalnath's sons also have *baithaks* maintained in their name. Two *baithaks* are for Vallabhdas' main disciple Damodardas. Shri Nathji himself has about ten to mark the various spots where he and his entourage rested when he was taken from Braj to Nathdvara.

HAVELIS

The number of *havelis* must certainly run into hundreds.[1] Some are very small and may only be known to local people: a complete inventory would probably not be possible. The Vallabha Sampraday is very strong in Gujarat and it is a reasonable assumption that every city and most towns in the state have at least one *haveli* each. This is not surprising when we consider that Vitthalnath, Vallabha's son, visited most of the major cities and towns in Gujarat (Entwistle 1987). Parekh (1943) noted than Vallabha's initial travels were to holy places while his tours to Gujarat were to attract followers: "What he did in this province (Gujarat) was more in the nature of spreading his church than a pilgrimage proper" (Parekh 1943: 76).

Gujarat was particularly suitable as it has had a long history as a major mercantile centre. Because the enjoyment of wealth is considered acceptable after it has been offered to Krishna, Pocock concluded that: "More than any other sect in Gujarat, the *pustimarga* provided an arena in which the wealthy merchant classes could display their wealth and earn at once distinction and merit" (Pocock 1973: 117).

Another factor that assisted in the growth of the sect in Gujarat and Rajasthan was that most of the *svarups* and minor deities of the Vallabha Sampraday were taken there after they were removed from Braj during the reign of Aurangzeb (Entwistle 1987: 184). Like Shri Nathji, most of them have been moved at various times and installed in several centres for varying periods (Entwistle 1987: 183-5). Three of them have, in the last century been returned to Braj, where they are located today (Entwistle 1987: 222-3; see Table 2.1).

Each of the seven major centres of the *sampraday* are known as a *gaddi*, which literally means a cushion but in practice is interpreted as a dais or throne. While these were administered and founded by the seven sons of Vitthalnath, many of the younger grandsons founded junior lines (*upagriha*, Entwistle 1987: 221). Most of the various Maharaj will have at least two, if not more, *havelis* under their control. Generally one *haveli* is in a large city and one or more are in smaller cities and towns. These function as centres for the Maharaj and his family to stay. They also help to direct the loyalty of the various devotees living there towards his family. This personal contact is important to both attract and maintain the support of followers. Although Maharaj are not evangelical, in the fashion of certain Hindu *gurus*, they must be prepared to travel extensively, on what may be seen as 'pastoral tours'. Consequently most of the Maharaj, along with their entourages, are constantly on the move. Their activity has resulted in an almost endless number of *havelis*, and any attempt to catalogue them would be a monumental task.

Despite their wandering, all the Maharaj and the Tilkayat have established patterns which assure devotees that they will be able to celebrate certain festivals in their presence. For instance, the Tilkayat is always present in Nathdvara to celebrate Divali and Annakut. When I was in Nathdvara for these festivals, in 1983 and again in 1985, I was constantly meeting families from Bombay that every year organized their holidays around being in Nathdvara at that time. The women usually engaged in very long hours of *seva*, rising early, bathing in the *haveli* compound and then working in various departments of the *haveli*. By and large the men did not, and reported that they had come mainly to accompany their womenfolk.

Another group of devotees who are now making a strong economic impact on the activities of most *havelis* are expatriate Indians. On one occasion I was standing outside the Shri Nathji Haveli waiting to deposit my sandals, when I struck up a conversation with a girl in her early twenties, wearing jeans. She turned out to be from Canada (Brandon, Manitoba) and visiting Nathdvara with her family. The meeting proved very useful to me, as she later included me in their party for a particular ceremony. The family had come to give thanks to Shri Nathji on the successful completion of the marriage of one of their sons to a girl from Baroda. The younger, unmarried daughter of the party provided an interesting interface between the Eastern and Western life-styles. Although initiated into the Vallabha Sampraday, she had made some concessions to life abroad, and these had to some extent reduced what she could do in the *haveli*. In particular, only her mother performed *seva* in the *haveli*. The daughter confessed to having on occasion, eaten hamburgers, which is strictly forbidden by the *sampraday*. "Somehow all that seems quite different outside India", she remarked.

TAKING *DARSHAN* IN *HAVELIS* OUTSIDE NATHDVARA

I made no attempt to be exhaustive in my enquiries outside Nathdvara, but I particularly wanted to visit a few centres that I knew to have links with the *kirtankar* community of Nathdvara. Consequently, in January 1988 I spent two weeks visiting selected cities and towns in Gujarat, talking to musicians, Maharaj and their relations, and ordinary devotees of the Vallabha Sampraday. I also attended *darshans* in some of the *havelis*.

Generally speaking, I found far less difficulty in entering these local *havelis* than I had initially experienced in entering the Shri Nathji

Haveli. Although I usually showed my *tulsi mala* and informed people that I had been initiated by the Tilkayat, I would probably have been allowed to take *darshan* in some *havelis* without any credentials. Most people were simply surprised to see me. Unlike Nathdvara, the lesser *havelis* had probably not been visited by many foreigners before, and people were just as interested in me as I was in them. If there is one outstanding impression it is of being welcomed into a community, almost a family. Everywhere the devotees showed an intense desire to ensure that I had a good position to take full advantage of the *darshan*.

UDAIPUR AND NATHDVARA

The courts and temples of Nathdvara and Udaipur have a long history of sharing musicians. Evidence for this is recorded in the accounts of Ghanshyam in the *Mridang Sagar* given in chapter 11. The connection with Udaipur, the royal family, and the temples of the city, has been continuous. In 1986 I met the musicians in Udaipur who worked in seven temples, which are probably all those where music is still performed regularly.

SHRI NATHJI TEMPLE, UDAIPUR

When I arrived at the Shri Nathji Haveli in Udaipur for *Raj Bhog darshan*, about thirty devotees were waiting. The women welcomed me. I sat outside with them until the *darshan* finally opened. There was no rush to enter. Instead, people entered in orderly fashion. The women then sat in front gazing at the image, which was black, and dressed in hot pink, one of the favourite colours of the *sampraday*. The music lasted longer than is usual at the Shri Nathji Haveli in Nathdvara but that may have been because I was there and they knew that I was a disciple of Pakhavaji Guru Purushottam.

There were two musicians employed in the Shri Nathji Haveli in Udaipur, a singer, Basantilal Sharma and a *Pakhavaji*, Chiranlal II. Basantilal was a Paliwal brahmin whose family originally left Braj to serve as *kirtankars* in the Shri Nathji Haveli in Nathdvara. His family moved to Udaipur when one of his ancestors, Devkrishna Paliwal, was invited by Mahrana Swarup Singh in 1847, to serve in the Jagatsiromani temple. Basantilal had only recently taken up the post of musician after retiring as headmaster of a higher secondary school in Kilvada, Kumbhalgarh. He held an M.A. degree and both his two sons were also teachers. Basantilal's father had been a *kirtankar* in the Udaipur Shri Nathji temple and had taught him music, but he had not taught his own sons. As a retired teacher, with a pension of seven hundred and fifty rupees per month, Basantilal was singing mainly as *seva*, and to fulfil his families' traditional role. He explained:

> My father sang in the *haveli*, but I did not take it up as a profession because it does not pay. Besides, there is no one to encourage us. For those reasons I did not teach my sons.
>
> Because the working hours in the temple are so long it is impossible to do anything else. We are fond of our job so we do it, but not for the money. We can't even earn enough for tea. Since our parents did it, we are doing it, in the hereditary spirit.

Basantilal also sang in the Vitthalnathji temple in Udaipur.

The hereditary association of Basantilal's family with the Jagatsiromani temple was being maintained by Basantilal's elder brother, Bhanvarlal III, who was also academically educated and worked as a head clerk in a government office. He also sang in the Shyamsundar temple. I had

TABLE 12.1: LINEAGE CHART OF UDAIPUR MUSICIANS

Paliwal Brahmin
Dolatram
(*H. sangit*, SNJ Nathdvara)
|
Devkrishna
(*H. sangit*, Jagatsiromani, Udaipur)
|
Nathu
(*H. sangit*, Jagatsiromani, Udaipur
|
Purushottam
(*H. sangit*, Jagatsiromani, Udaipur)
(*H. sangit*, Shri Nathji, Udaipur)

Bhanvarlal (clerk, later *H. sangit*, Jagatsiromani Shyamsundar, Udaipur)	*Basantilal* (school principal, later, *H. sangit* Shri Nathji, Vitthalnathji Udaipur)

met Bhanvarlal previously in the Shri Nathji Haveli in Nathdvara. He visited Nathdvara often, as did the other Udaipur musicians. In Nathdvara I heard him sing in *kirtankar gali* during pre-*Gval darshan*. He was accompanied by Ramchandra, who was employed by the Shri Nathji Haveli as a singer but who also played *pakhavaj*.

The other musician in the Shri Nathji Haveli, Udaipur was Pakhavaji Chiranlal II. He was related to Guru Purushottam (*kakatiya*), through his mother, Rukmini. Rukmini was the daughter of Vitthal, one of the sons of Khem, Guru Purushottam's paternal uncle (Table 7.1). His father, Madanlal, was from the *devatval* division of *kumavats*. Madanlal had played *pakhavaj* and sung in the Shri Nathji temple in Udaipur but had supplemented his income as a painter. Chiranlal described his father's work: "He was an excellent painter. He specialized in painting elephants on either side of the doorway, which is the custom during marriages".

Maduro (1976) in his study of brahmin painters in Nathdvara, noted that some of them also engaged in this type of painting. This was remarkable because painting on homes, and in particular outside homes, was not regarded as a high status occupation by the brahmin painter community. This suggests a division of space considered appropriate for the two communities.

Chiranlal was the youngest of three brothers: his eldest brother Giriraj Singh had trained as a tailor, his second brother Laladhar had trained as a welder and Chiranlal had trained as a draftsman. He was the only one who studied music with his father. Chiranlal stated that in 1946 at the age of thirteen he began to study in the Udaipur Shri Nathji Haveli and very occasionally at home. Chiranlal had taught his two sons, Satyanarayan and Lalitkumar, who took turns playing for various *darshans*. Satyanarayan worked in his own watch repair shop. Lalitkumar was studying in school but planned to train in some trade or profession. As well as the Shri Nathji temple in Udaipur, they also played in the Gokulchandramaji temple. For their services to the temples the family received a cash payment of one hundred and twenty rupees. The only payment in kind was twice a month when they received sweets—two large (*laddus*), each worth three rupees. This family regarded it as their duty (*dharma*) to continue their musical tradition.

At the Vitthalnathji Haveli in Udaipur, there was another musician, Hathiram, who lived in the *haveli*. He played the *pakhavaj* and sang. At the time of my visit he was in Braj, leading a bus tour of pilgrims.

Besides working in the Vitthalnathji Haveli, Hathiram also served in the Bananath temple in the City Palace Udaipur, along with another musician, Mannalal. The latter, who also sometimes played in the Jagatsiromani temple, identified himself as being a *pujari* and not a *kumavat*. Thus neither of the musicians who worked in the Jagatsiromani temple (Mannalal, Bhanvarlal) was a *kumavat*, the community that dominates music in the Nathdvara Haveli.

Mannalal also maintained a small room in his home, which was a temple, the Govardhanathji ka Mandir. It had been founded by one of his ancestors about one hundred and twenty-five years ago, after a small image of the mother goddess had been found in Udaipur city and installed there. He reported singing songs composed by Surdas, Mirabai, Tulsidas and several of the *ashtachhap*. Mannalal's father Ratanlal had also been a musician and it would appear from a photograph that I was shown, that he was rather prosperous. Mannalal played *tabla*, and a very rudimentary *pakhavaj*, which he had studied from his father from the age of six. He reported that the pay for musicians was declining. Some years before he had received four hundred rupees per month, but at the time of my visit, his combined income from working in the three temples was three hundred and fifty rupees. He received two hundred rupees from the Bananath temple and one hundred and fifty rupees for playing in both the Jagatsiromani and Shyamsundar temples. He said that in the old days there were more singers in the Bananath temple, but all had left except him, and Hathiram, who sang while Mannalal played *tabla*.

Mannalal's work began at nine o'clock in the morning and ended at seven in the evening. He was engaged as follows: in the morning from 9-11 he played at the Jagatsiromani and Shyamsundar temples, and then from 11 a.m.-12 noon at the Bananath temple; he played again in the evening from 5-7 p.m. at both the Jagatsiromani and Shyamsundar temples.

Like Chiranlal's family, Mannalal and his sons alternated their duty in the temple. His eldest son, aged thirty (1986), worked for the municipality and played *pakhavaj* when his father could not be present. The second son, aged twenty-five, had not shown any aptitude for music and worked in a betel shop. His third son was more interested in painting than music. Nevertheless he was studying *pakhavaj* with his father. Mannalal was also a painter. The technique he used was putting coloured powder on water.

As befits their close proximity to Nathdvara, the *havelis* of Udaipur are active and maintain a modest musical tradition. The families involved appear to be more diverse than those of Nathdvara, although one family is related to the Nathdvara *kirtankars* from the *Devatval* division of *kumavats*. My impression was that the decline of professionalism among the musicians in Udaipur had led to a falling off of standards; the ritual importance of music, however, appears undiminished. With constant contact and movement of musicians to and from Nathdvara, the Udaipur temples clearly constitute an outlying fragment of the Nathdvara musical tradition.

BARODA: BAITHAK MANDIR

There are several *havelis* in Baroda. According to sectarian literature it was during Vallabha's third tour that he visited Baroda; thus there is a Baithak Mandir in Baroda (Parekh 1943: 82). I visited it in January 1988 to attend *Shringar darshan*. The image, Dvarkadhishji, was completely covered so it was impossible to see anything except a black face. It was also very small, certainly no more than ten inches high. The deep orange *picchvai* behind the image was made of brocade and silk, this heavy material being considered appropriate for the time of year. The ceiling was decorated with a yellow cloth. There were five musicians playing that day, as it was part of the festival celebrations for Makarsankranti (Crooke 1920: 697). Not all the musicians wore the customary traditional dress of *angurkhi* and *dhoti*; western trousers and shirts were in evidence, something completely forbidden in the Nathdvara Shri Nathji Haveli. Three were regular musicians. The other two described themselves as "occasional *sevaks*", thereby meaning that they came on occasion to offer their music to the deity.

The three musicians who served regularly in the Baithak Mandir were brothers from the Gandharv community and they affirmed that all their relations had been musicians. The eldest, Suresh, was fifty-six and was paid one hundred and fifty rupees for his services. He played the harmonium and sang. The other two were considerably younger, playing only from time to time; they received no remuneration. Bhagwati Prasad, aged twenty-four, played the *pakhavaj* and harmonium and sang, Sarad, aged twenty, sang. He was also learning the *pakhavaj* and had just completed his high school.[2] Bhagwati Prasad had a B.A. in music, and sometimes played on All India Radio, but earned his living as an accountant.

After the *darshan* we went to the private apartments of Maharaj

Brajesh Kumar, which were adjacent to Baithak Mandir. On learning that we were interested in music, the Maharaj was anxious that we hear his second son, Dvarkesh, play the *pakhavaj* and summoned him from across town to perform for us. Although only in his twenties (1988), Dvarkesh administered his own *haveli*, called the Kalyanrayji. We had to wait some time for Dvarkesh to arrive, and during that time we sat on the floor while the Maharaj greeted his devotees. After receiving his blessings they presented him with various gifts, mainly in the form of small amounts of cash. This was not unlike many of the occasions on which I visited the Tilkayat, his sons and their wives in Nathdvara. Like most of the Maharaj, Brajeshkumar was of large build, about six feet tall, and weighed about one hundred and eighty pounds. Physically he resembled most of the Maharaj depicted in miniature paintings, slightly portly, a high forehead, receding hairline and a large moustache. Tod's description in the nineteenth century of the Tilkayat Damodar corresponds with my own observations of most of the Maharaj:

> The present pontiff is now about thirty years of age. He is of benign aspect, with much dignity of demeanour: courteous, yet exacting the homage due to his high calling: meek, as becomes the priest of Govinda, but with the finished manners of one accustomed to the first society. His features are finely moulded, and his complexion good. He is about the middle size, though as he rises to no mortal, I could not exactly judge of his height (Crooke 1920: 642).

Also Pocock's description of Vrajbushanlal, Maharaj of Kankroli could apply equally to most of the Maharaj,[3] that I have met.

> He is a tall, well-built man in his mid-fifties, very fair and fresh complexioned ... he also allowed me to sit as often and as long as I liked at the foot of the *murti*, and watch the ritual. What stands out most clearly in my memory of him is the very jollity, I can think of no better word, which he brought to these acts. Whatever he was doing, whether feeding the god, giving him a toy, or the most solemn moment of the day, offering him the evening incense, *arati*, the almost irresistible illusion was that here was a father performing services for a loved son, whose every need and movement was a source of delight to him (Pocock 1973: 113-4).

The reception rooms of every Maharaj that we saw appeared very similar,[4] being approximately twenty by thirty feet. The walls were covered with framed pictures of their ancestors as well as a variety of descriptive paintings illustrating Krishna's pranks. The furniture tended to be elaborate, of Victorian style. Ambalal (1987: 135, 159) includes a miniature painting of two Gosvamis seated on a Victorian sofa. It looks identical to the sofa on which the Maharaj of the Vitthalnathji

Haveli, Nathdvara, sat in front when I photographed all three of them in 1985 (Plate 3.1). In that *haveli* all the chairs and the three-seater settee were made of ornately carved wood and upholstered in very heavy brocaded material. In Baithak Mandir, Baroda, there was a rug on the floor on which I sat along with twenty or so devotees who had come to take *darshan* of the Maharaj, and the musicians who had been summoned to await the arrival of Gosvami Dvarkesh. The number of devotees fluctuated. There was a constant coming and going both from the doors on one side which led to the temple, and the doors on the other side which led to more rooms in the private apartments of the Maharaj. We faced the Maharaj who was seated on a raised platform covered with pillows.

After about one and a half hours Gosvami Dvarkesh arrived. He was dressed in the traditional manner of spotless white *kurta* and *dhoti*, a little tuft of hair hanging at the back of his head (*choti*). He had the vertical Vaishnavite marks, worn by all Maharaj and devotees, drawn carefully on his forehead. Without much fanfare, after tuning his *pakhavaj*, he began to play solo. His technique was good, and like Maharaj Kalyanray of the Vitthalnathji Haveli in Nathdvara, he remarked that he liked to play the *pakhavaj* in the *haveli* during festivals. After playing solo for about twenty minutes he accompanied *haveli* songs rendered by the three musicians.

According to the musicians there has never been more than one official musician for Baithak Mandir. His duties were typical of those found in smaller *havelis* which require music at various times both before and during the specific *darshans*. In this case it was for six of them—three in the morning (*Mangal*, *Shringar* and *Raj Bhog*), and three in the afternoon (*Uthhapan*, *Sandhya/Arati* and *Shayan*). During all the pre-*darshan* periods they sang in an area known as Jag Mohan, as there was no specific area designated as Kirtankar Gali. As in the Nathdvara Haveli, music during the pre-*darshan* periods was a private affair. The musicians stated: "We sing to tell Dvarkadhishji that he should eat this sweet food. At that time the doors are closed and the *mukhiya* puts a *tulsi*[5] leaf in each portion of food".

AHMEDABAD, NATVARLALJI HAVELI

Ahmedabad supports several *havelis*. I visited the most central, the Natvarlalji Haveli, where the *svarup* reputedly comes from Chaupasni in Rajasthan. In the early evening, when I visited, unfortunately just seconds after *Shayan darshan* closed, it was busy with devotees. Maharaj Purushottam, who was also present, was elegantly attired in a spotless white *kurta*, exquisite earrings, diamond choker necklace, perfumed, and with *kohl* around his eyes. He was chewing betel, which always gives a fresh smell.

Although I did not hear Maharaj Purushottam play the *pakhavaj*, from all accounts he is very accomplished and encourages his musicians. Unfortunately our meeting was brief, as he was anxious to celebrate the final hours of the *Makarsankranti* festival by flying the customary kites from the roof of his palace which was located on the upper floors of the *haveli*. He did, however, invite me to attend the special birthday celebrations[6] for his late father, Ranchorlal which would take place the next day, when he would sing and play the *pakhavaj*, and his devotees would dance the *garba*, a semi-classical dance style peculiar to Gujarat. This dance is performed in a circle and is intended to represent the *ras* dance performed by Krishna and his milkmaids.

The musicians in the Natvarlalji Haveli lived away from the *haveli*, so I was fortunate to be able to speak with them after the last *darshan*. One, Purushottam C. Pandey, was a Rajasthani brahmin from Bhilvara (Rajasthan). His caste accounts for the fact that his father, Chaganlal had been the ritual *Mukhiya*. Purushottam was known affectionately as "Pusey". His legs had been crippled by polio when he was young. He could play the *pakhavaj* and harmonium and received two hundred and fifty rupees from the *haveli*. He had completed high school and earned his living as a typist. The other singer, Vishnu Bai Mehta, a Gujarati had been a clerk in a film theatre, but was by then retired. He received three hundred rupees for his musical services. The third musician, Ghanshyam Nayak did not receive any remuneration. He was the son of Champaklal, the noted authority on *haveli sangit* who has written several books in Gujarati on the subject. I met Champaklal on several occasions, in his home and in the *haveli*.

The Natvarlalji Haveli had only three *darshans* a day open to the public—two in the morning: *Mangal*, which took place between 7 and 8 a.m., and *Raj Bhog* which took place between 9 and 10.30 a.m.; and one in the afternoon, *Bhog/Arati*, which took place between 4:30 and 5 p.m. No doubt this was because Ahmedabad is a large city and it is difficult for devotees to travel across town on days when they work. "Pusey" reported that he had started to play the *pakhavaj* at the age of seven and all his training had been in the *haveli*. He had started when Ranchorlal had been Maharaj. According to Pusey, there had been three excellent musicians in service: the late Mangaldas, the late Chunnilal and the late Gopaldas, and it had been his good fortune to train with them.

JAMNAGAR: MADANMOHANJI HAVELI

Jamnagar is an old port city which, like many others in Gujarat, used to be the capital of a small state of the same name. According to sectarian literature, Vallabha visited Jamnagar during his second tour (Parekh 1943: 82). We visited the main *haveli*, the Madanmohanji. The Maharaj, Brajbushanlal, who traces his descent to the sixth son of Vallabha, divides his time between the Madanmohanji Haveli in Jamnagar and another *haveli*, the Shyam Manoharlalji, in Chaupasni, Rajasthan (Entwistle 1987: 184).

From Ghanshyam's account in the *Mridang Sagar* it seems that music and artistic concerns were especially important to the Maharaj of Jamnagar at that time, Shri Vrajnath, whom he described as having "a great passion for the art of music" (MS. Jivani: 4; MV: 3). Like his ancestors, the father of the present Maharaj of Jamnagar was keenly interested in music. He took a personal interest in the upbringing of one of the *kirtankars*, Manaklal, whose father and uncles had served as musicians in the Shri Nathji Haveli. Until recently Manaklal served in the Madanmohanji Haveli. Navnitlal, the son of the present Maharaj, whom I met while in Jamnagar also plays the *pakhavaj*, although I did not hear him while I was there.

I had especially wanted to meet Manaklal, as I was well acquainted with his brothers, both musicians, in Nathdvara. Luckily I was able to locate him easily, as he ran a shop that sold craft items and decorative articles for home worship, close to the *haveli*. When Manaklal was very young he received musical training in the Nathdvara Haveli and then was sent to Jamnagar as a young boy and brought up by the Maharaj, Brajbhushanlal. He continued his musical training in Jamnagar, singing and playing the *pakhavaj* in the Madanmohanji Haveli. He also visited Nathdvara from time to time and sang in the Shri Nathji Haveli where his father Mohanlal was employed. His father also spent considerable time in Jamnagar. Manaklal's musical expertise has been given recognition in Baroda. In 1985 on the invitation of the Maharaj Brajeshkumar (described above), his *haveli sangit* music was recorded for him there.

THE INFLUENCE OF MUSICIANS ON THE CRAFTS OF THE *SAMPRADAY*

Just a generation ago, three brothers from the *devatval* division of *kumavats*: Mohanlal, Madanlal and Gokuldas, were all musicians in Nathdvara (Shri Nathji Haveli) and Udaipur. They appear to have simultaneously introduced certain innovative elements into the making of decorative backdrops (*picchvai*). They also perfected some other techniques which had already been developed. Today in Nathdvara and Jamnagar, their descendants are carrying on the same work, as well as making other innovations.

Manaklal, Mohanlal's son, as mentioned above, had been adopted by the Jamnagar Maharaj and had, until 1985, been employed as a musician in the *haveli*. Perhaps because Manaklal had been trained and lived in Jamnagar from age eleven, his salary from the *haveli* of one hundred rupees per month plus a daily glass of milk, was never raised. Manaklal gave this as the main reason for his resignation from the position of *kirtankar* in 1985. Interestingly, the new *kirtankar* who was hired by the *haveli* could only be attracted to this job by a salary of eight hundred rupees.

Manaklal was somewhat ambivalent about his resignation stating that it was for several reasons besides money. First of all he would rather devote his time to making craft items and selling them in his shop just opposite the *haveli*. Also, he lived far from the *haveli*. Reaching the *haveli* early in the morning was difficult. Also since he could not go home for lunch, it meant that he was on call for nearly twelve hours. This is a recurring problem for temple musicians as cities sprawl outward and affordable housing is available only far from the centre.

According to Manaklal, his father, Mohanlal, invented the making of the net *picchvai*; involving applique scenes on net material against a black background. The idea may have come from some European source, via Gujarat, as these *picchvai* look very much like the narrative lace curtains that were popular in Europe during the same period. Mohanlal perfected the cutting techniques and later taught two other *kirtankars* from the *kumavat*, *jalandhara* division, Gokuldas and Jamnadas. Mohanlal also developed the art of applique *picchvai*; cutting out the main figures and sewing them onto a plain piece of cloth. The end result of both techniques is similar, in highlighting the narrative except that the net *picchvai* are all in one colour, whereas the applique type are often made with a variety of colours. Gokuldas' sons Pannalal and Vallabhdas (who was adopted by Gokuldas' brother, Jamnadas) and their mothers, wives and children now carry on this tradition.

Manaklal's own contribution to making craft items was considerable. As an innovator his story is remarkable. The other crafts that he produces are esteemed by several *havelis*, which have commissioned him to make articles for them. He specializes in items made out of food, that then becomes *prasad*. Manaklal described swings (*jhula*) and *bangala* studded with cashew-nuts, almonds, raisins and pistachios. These food structures are used in the cold weather. He reported creating several for the Maharaj of Jamnagar. His most important creation was in 1987 when he constructed a cradle (*palna*) of pistachios and raisins for the birthday of the wife of the late Maharaj of Junagarh, Purushottamlal, who presided over the Moti Haveli in Junagarh. The intent of the cradle was to assist in providing the Maharaj with a male heir, who already had four daughters. The ploy was not successful. When I visited Junagarh and met the new Maharaj, I learnt that he had been adopted into the family on the death of Purushottamlal.

Another special creation, which Manaklal showed me a photograph of, was a cashew-nut *bangala* that had been created during the month of Purushottam, a month that occurs only every three years according to the Hindu calendar. The use of a special type of grass (*khas*) to make *bangalas* and swings was undertaken by Manaklal, and the families of Pannalal and Vallabhdas. If water is poured on *khas* it absorbs it; the evaporation during the hot season produces a cooling effect, and a pleasant smell.

Manaklal also described another specialty that was unique to him; a three-dimensional wooden tableau of an artificial mountain of wood, with a cutout showing Shri Nathji inside and a wooden cow on top of the mountain releasing milk onto the image. This is in effect, a working model showing how the image of Shri Nathji was discovered and appeared at Govardhan in Braj.[7] Manaklal was confident that he had pioneered this, and he was the only one who could make such models (Plate 12.2). I have not seen or heard of such models of Govardhan in Nathdvara. He also showed me photographs of other tableaus very reminiscent of nativity scenes made in the West at Christmas. The literal nature of these constructions is important in making devotees familiar with the mythology and history of the *sampraday*. I have also seen mechanical devices used to provide special effects during presentations of Ras Lila staged in Vrindavan. One such event, held in the Shri Chaitanya Prem Sanstan, Jai Singh Ghera, Vrindavan in 1984, included artificial rain from a sprinkler system over the stage, and tape recordings of spring sounds and other special effects, which formed an important part of the production. This is but one example of the impact that technology is beginning to have on methods of worship.

According to Manaklal, the Madanmohanji Haveli in Jamnagar owns several painted *picchvai*. One that illustrates Govardhan (by the painter—*Chitrakar*—Motilal) is used as a backdrop when his model of Govardhan and the cow that gives real milk is on display. Additional *picchvai* illustrate Krishna's other *lilas* (*Ras*, *Dan*, Annakut, *Chiran*).

Manaklal was unusual in that in the course of his temple duty he had met a lady Psychology lecturer, a brahmin, who spent a great deal of time performing *seva* in the flower department of the *haveli* (*phul ghar*). After they had known one another for some time they decided to marry, arranging it themselves with the blessing of the Maharaj. Such an event was perhaps more likely in a cosmopolitan coastal city in Gujarat than in the more tightly knit community in Nathdvara, where marriages are still, almost exclusively, arranged by parents who choose persons of the same caste. I had no evidence of out-of-caste marriages among the Nathdvara musicians. Manaklal's wife, though a graduate herself, was enthusiastic about the artistic skills of her husband, who had no formal schooling. All the same, they were not encouraging either their son or daughter to pursue music.

In Jamnagar there is considerable activity selling religious objects for home worship. Many of these are supplied from Nathdvara. As well as Manaklal, I also met three others from Nathdvara who were associated with the activities of the *sampraday*: a young Brajvasi *gujar* who was working in the *haveli* and two more shopkeepers who go regularly to Nathdvara to purchase supplies and make contacts with pilgrims. One had a shop near Manaklal's, the other's shop was some distance away, near another Vallabha Sampraday *haveli*, the Dauji temple, where Maharaj Brajbhushanlal's daughter presides. I did not visit this *haveli*, but it is common in most cities in Gujarat for more than one *haveli* to be active.

MADRAS: SITA BHAVAN

The members of the *sampraday* in Madras were almost entirely from north India, an interesting feature considering that Vallabha, the founder of the *sampraday* was from the southern state of Andhra Pradesh. Nevertheless, as he spent most of his life in northern India and as the image of Shri Nathji was found in Braj, the sect has been active mainly in the north. The younger son of the present Tilkayat married Rajeshwari, the daughter of one of their distant relatives who was living in the south. As I mentioned in chapter 1, I danced at their wedding which was held in Mathura.

I visited the Madras Haveli in August 1989 on the occasion of Janmashtami, Krishna's birthday. The *haveli*, known as Sita Bhavan was near the central railway station. It was six storeys high and built around a courtyard. It was constructed twenty years ago by Jawarmal Champal to commemorate the death of his son-in-law. The entrance to the building is occupied by about ten cows and I had to push them aside to enter. Inside there is a large room about seventy feet across. Previously guests had stayed in the many rooms that overlooked the central courtyard, but, as Madras had been suffering a severe water shortage for many years, their well had dried up and this was no longer possible.

All the worshippers and the persons involved in the running of the temple were from north India: Braj, Gujarat and Rajasthan. Those in the employ of the temple wore the same type of dress, *angarkhi*, *dhoti*, and a coloured scarf, in this case orange, as in the Shri Nathji Haveli. The temple manager was from Gujarat, the ritual *mukhiya* was from Govardhan, in Braj. The temple manager's son-in-law earned his living reciting the *Bhagavata Purana* and was present that day to do this on behalf of a man whose wife had died. The proceedings were being recorded on cassette.

The Shri Nathji Haveli in Nathdvara has separate rooms for the various departments that prepared the materials used at *darshan*, but in Sita Bhavan several departments were located in the main room so that it was possible for the female devotees preparing the flowers to be seen. The food was prepared in a separate room by a male from Braj and some helpers. As it was a festival day they prepared fifty to one hundred *puri*, spinach curry, and various sweets: *thor*, *mumtal*, *barfi* and *laddu*. They told me that they presented eight of each of these sweets to the image. Afterwards all of the food presented to the image was to go to the home of the founder. To celebrate Janmashtami, during *Mangal darshan*, the image was bathed in the five elements *panchamritsnan*: honey, curd, milk, ghee and sugar. This is the usual practice.

I arrived just after *Mangal darshan*. The *Bhagavata* specialist had begun chanting and the audience responded. Some had their own books, while others appeared to know the hymns by heart. When it was time for *Shringar darshan* several men left the *Bhagavata* group and went and took *darshan*. The *darshan* area was directly opposite where the *Bhagavata* readings were going on. The image, wearing a Mughal style of dress, was about two feet high, free-standing and was modelled after Shri Nathji. The reading from the *Bhagavata* continued, and as it was being held beside the *darshan* area, it was possible to take *darshan* while listening to the discourse. The *darshan* opened at about 10.30 a.m. After about fifteen minutes a curtain was drawn in front of the image, thus closing *Shringar*. About seven men and fifty women came to take *darshan*. Most of them stayed to listen to the discourse.

There are no musicians in the permanent employ of Sita Bhavan. Instead the women, many of whom had gathered for *seva*, sang. I was told that this was the usual practice. The most important *darshan* is *Mangal*, which is held between 7.15 and 8.15 a.m. This is followed by *Shringar* at 10-10.35 a.m., and *Raj Bhog* at 11.30 a.m.. The evening *darshans* are *Bhog/Arati* at 4.30-5.00, and *Shyan* at 5.45-6.

There are many such *havelis* all over India, which maintain the traditions of the *sampraday* with *darshan*, food, clothing and songs in *Brajbasha* or other north Indian languages. The *Bhagavata Purana* remains the central focus, and the performance of music continues, although sung in many cases by members of the congregation, rather than by professional *kirtankars*.

PORBANDAR: GOPINATHJI HAVELI

Porbandar has several *havelis*, of which I visited four. On January 15, 1988 I attended *Raj Bhog darshan* in the Gopinathji Haveli, which is situated in a large walled compound near the centre of the town. Four musicians sang, all of them were Gujaratis. Parbutbai was a fifty year old Gujarati Patel. He had studied up to the seventh class and was then employed in the *haveli* to play the harmonium and sing. He said he had learnt singing by listening and singing along in a temple in Gokul,

Braj.[8] Another singer, Lalbai, was also from the Patel community in his late forties. Mangalbai, from the Lohana or farmer caste, was a grain merchant. Educated to the tenth standard he was thirty-five years old. Kisandas was a brahmin who also taught music in a school. He usually played the harmonium but on festival days played the *pakhavaj*. The musicians stated that none of them were from hereditary singing families (*parampara*) and all of them performed as *seva*. They seemed to have a rota system established. That day Lalbai arrived at 7.15 a.m. He sang two songs during *Mangal darshan*, this was followed by two more songs before *Raj Bhog* and two during *Raj Bhog*. Later, Lalbai rested while a further two songs were sung by Mangalbai and Parbutbai. In the afternoon Parbutbai sang one song before, and one song during *Sandhya/Arati*, followed by two songs before *Shayan*. Finally, at 6 p.m. he sang one song during *Shayan*.

PORBANDAR: RANCHORJI HAVELI

One of the most active *havelis* in Porbandar during my stay appeared to be the Ranchorji Haveli, situated beside the birthplace and home of Mahatma Gandhi,[9] who was also, by birth, a member of the Vallabha Sampraday. When I arrived there to attend *darshan* a fire (*homa*) ritual was going on attended by the two sons of the Maharaj, Chandragopal and Sharadkumar. Their father was reported to be at one of his other *havelis*, which include the Banmaliji in Nathdvara, and another important one in Viraval, Gujarat. He also administers the Daoji Haveli in Calcutta, the Madanmohanji in Surat, Gujarat, and the Banmaliji in Jodhpur, Rajasthan.

The Ranchorji Haveli had one *kirtankar*, A.J. Bakshi, a Gujarati aged forty-five. He was from the Baniya community and also worked in a bank. He received some *prasad* from the *haveli*, but no cash; he regarded his job as *seva*. His father Jamnadas, who had been the *kirtankar* before him, now lived in Viraval, and sang in the *haveli* there which was administered by the same Maharaj. Jamnadas had been self-taught and also had another job, with the railways, his father had not been a singer.

I also visited the Madanmohanji Haveli to attend *Mangal darshan*. No *kirtankar* had arrived when the *darshan* opened. Instead the twenty women present sang, sitting while the ten men hummed along, standing. During the *darshan* the *kirtankar* arrived, and made his way to the front of the crowd. While one of the sons of the Maharaj performed *arati*, the singer sang a song by Surdas in *Lalit raga*. He was unsure of the name of the *tala*. He said: "I am not a trained musician. I just come and do *seva*. In Nathdvara they get paid for singing in the temple, here it is just *seva*. Because I have other work I can only come for *Mangal* and *Shayan*".

On holidays,, however, he sings for all the *darshans*. He stated that the *haveli* is open for six *darshans*, three in the morning—*Mangal* at 7, *Shringar* at 9.30, *Raj Bhog* at 11.30—and three in the afternoon—*Bhog* at 4.30, *Arati* at 5.30 and *Shayan* at 6. The *picchvai* in this *haveli* are sewn by tailors and there is only one mother of pearl *bangala* which was made by carpenters. I noticed a very plain wooden swing as well.

I attended *Raj Bhog* at the Govardhannathji Haveli. There was no regular *kirtankar* and the women in the congregation sang instead. The *pichvai* was a piece of simple cotton cloth. The Maharaj who administered this *haveli* resided in Bombay.

JUNAGARH: MOTI HAVELI

There are at least six *havelis* in Junagarh. I visited three of them in mid-January 1988. Although each Maharaj traces his descent to a different son of Vitthalnathji the lineages are not necessarily by direct descent. In the absence of sons, adoption[10] from within the extended family is often practised. Such was the case in Moti Haveli, where the previous Maharaj, Purushottamlal died without a son. He was succeeded by Maharaj Kishorechand. The families of Purushottamlal and Kishorechand both trace their descent to Vitthalnath's sixth son, Giridhar. Kishorechand's elder brother administers his own *haveli* in Manvi, Kutch, Gujarat. Maharaj Kishorechand had occupied his present position for eight months prior to our meeting.

In the Moti Haveli there are two images of Krishna: Madanmohanji and Damodarji. I attended two *darshans* and listened to music during two pre-*darshan* periods. I also met Maharaj Kishorechand and the two regular *kirtankars*. These were Yedunanda, the brahmin *Kirtankar Mukhiya*, and Ramjibai, a *jhapatiya* from Braj, who also assisted in various artistic activities associated with the *seva*. Both these men had directly experienced the traditions of Nathdvara and Braj.

The musical presentations in the Moti Haveli, while not as elaborate as those in the Shri Nathji Haveli, were still very much an integral part of the ritual and *darshan*. I saw and heard *tanpura*, harmonium, and *pakhavaj* being played. *Jhanjh* were hanging on the wall, to be used during festivals.

Yedunanda Sharma was a Tailang brahmin from Andhra Pradesh, the same community as Vallabha. He had married the daughter of the late Maharaj Purushottamlal, the head of this *haveli*. All his children had been trained in music and took part in playing and singing music in the *haveli*. His caste gave him considerable status in the temple and he often served as the ritual *Mukhiya*, officiating when the Maharaj was out of Junagarh. Thus he combined the two roles of ritual and music specialist. Indeed, this seemed to be quite often; while I was there the Maharaj departed for Bombay after only a few days in residence. Like the other Maharaj, he appeared to be very mobile and unwilling to be away from the large centres where most of the devotees and potential devotees were living.

Yedunanda had played the *pakhavaj* and sung in the *haveli* for over twenty years and devotees described him as "singing sweetly". His training linked him to the present Nathdvara tradition, having trained in *haveli sangit* with Pannalal, the present *haveli* singer in the Shri Nathji temple. This had been while Pannalal was serving as a musician in Porbandar. Both Yedunanda's son and daughter sang and played the *pakhavaj* in the *haveli* during *darshan*, a rather unusual role for a female, and the only instance that I came across. The only *jhapatiya*, Ramjibai was from Braj, but had also had some contact with Pannalal at the same time, picking up certain craft skills from him. Ramjibai could also make *sanjhi* and he played the *pakhavaj*. The influence of these mobile musicians is extensive particularly as many have served in several *havelis* which has given them the opportunity to both learn the crafts of that area, and transmit their skills.

It appeared that this *haveli* was willing to give funding to musicians: as four others came occasionally. All of them were Gujarati, from a variety of castes, and with varying degrees of musical skill. One of them, Vitthaldas, a carpenter (*sutar* caste), worked with All India Radio Bhavnagar, and sang in Moti Haveli on occasion. The others were listed as Gokuldas, a blind singer, also from the *sutar* caste. Another, Narsidas, had died just before my visit. He was from the *kasar* caste (maker of utensils). Two of the older musicians appeared to be performing strictly as *seva*, having had no particular training. Nandlalbai, aged sixty-five, had been a goldsmith. Harjeevandas, aged eighty, also from the *kasar* community, had been a silversmith. He was a self-taught *Pakhavaji*, but was apparently teaching his son Dakubai, aged thirty-five, very well.

As with all other *havelis* Brajvasis were very much in evidence serving in the Moti Haveli: in this case there were fifteen to twenty. Some of the decorative objects used to embellish *darshan* had been made in Nathdvara by the *kirtankars* there. According to Ramjibai, the Moti Haveli in Junagarh had two *bangala*: one of *khas*, the other of pearls. Both of them had been made by one of the *haveli* singers employed in the Shri Nathji Haveli, Pannalal.

DARSHAN IN THE MOTI HAVELI, JUNAGARH

The *darshan* in Moti Haveli was much more orderly than in Nathdvara and devotees waiting for it to open spent their time chatting with friends. Men and women were separate, as is also the custom in Nathdvara. Also music took place during the pre-*darshan* periods. I wrote after my first visit on January 15, 1989:

> During the *darshan* the spectators move forward to the front where each has a few seconds to see the deity. They are then pressed to the side. There they bow to touch their head on the floor, or prostrate themselves. The *darshan* is for ten minutes but the music lasted only for about five.

The *picchvai*, which was hung on January 15, was cotton and on January 16 it was a red background covered with gold sequins (*zari*). These elaborate *picchvai* are considered appropriate for the winter season. I was fortunate to see two examples because apparently the *picchvai* here are changed only every few days, unlike the Shri Nathji Haveli in Nathdvara where changes are usually made daily.

CONCLUSION

My travels took in only a very small sample of the *havelis* of the *sampraday*, and I spent only a short time at each. I was mainly interested to see what role was played by music in these smaller centres. My impression was that great importance is attached to the presentation of *haveli sangit*, in even the smallest *haveli*. Where resources are not available to maintain full-time musicians, the *havelis* rely on amateurs contributing *seva*. These may be members of hereditary musician families who have been forced to seek a living elsewhere, but who continue the family tradition as a spare time pursuit. They may also be people from other walks of life who have chosen to train in music without any family background in the field. In extreme cases there may be no specialists, and the music may be rudimentary, but it is almost invariably presented and *darshan* is apparently incomplete without it.

I found the atmosphere at *darshan* in the smaller *havelis* much less frenetic than in Nathdvara. People knew one another, were familiar with their *haveli* and had developed a relaxed style of worship. The pre-*darshan* gatherings outside the *haveli* seemed to function mainly as a social club, bringing together members of the *sampraday*. The fact that *darshans* are brief and unpredictable means that such congregations are inevitable, and the waiting period provides a more sociable forum than one normally encounters in those Hindu temples where worship can take place through most of the day.

NOTES

1. Talwar and Krishna's map (1979) is somewhat misleading in showing only sixteen centres for the *sampraday*.
2. Clearly this family exhibits all the expectations discussed by Kippen (1988) with regard to academic education assuming priority over musical education.
3. See Ambalal (1987: 140, 159) for Tilkayat Govardhanlal (1862-1934); also Balkrishnalal Maharaj (1868-1917) (Ambalal 1987: 146-47, 160), in an early 20th century portrait and another from that same period Gosvami Devkinandacharya (1859-1903) (Ambalal 1987: 142-160).
4. These were almost a carbon copy of the private apartments of another Maharaj described by Mulji (1865).
5. The *tulsi* plant is sacred to Vishnu.
6. Birthday celebrations for the various Maharaj call for elaborate festivities. I danced in Moti Mahal on the occasion of the birthday of one of the sons of the Tilkayat. Ambalal (1987) records the special *shringar* of the deity on those days.
7. Entwistle (1987) records other images that were discovered in the same way.
8. He identified the temple as Chokiwalli Mandir but I did not find any reference to this temple in Entwistle (1987) or Growse (1874).
9. A shrine to Mahatma Gandhi has been created on this spot. One may still visit the small home where he grew up.
10. See also Entwistle 1987: 183,221.

Plate 12.1: A swing used in worship, Jamnagar: Craft items made by Manaklal, Kirtankar, Jamnagar Haveli

Plate 12.2: Craft item, a tableau

A unique tableau made by Manaklal *kirtankar*, Jamnagar Haveli. It re-enacts the legend which recounts a cow giving milk over the spot where Shri Nathji was found.

Conclusion

I have tried, above all, to describe the actual function of the musicians, their role in the *haveli* and their contribution to the artistic life of Nathdvara. Some variation may be found between my observations, the writings of previous authors, and the oral testimony of the musicians. For example, it is generally accepted that each *darshan* is accompanied exclusively by the music of a particular poet-composer (*ashtachhap*). The musicians, when asked will usually corroborate this notion. But when one actually attends *darshan*, and enquires what music is being performed, it is often a composition by a poet other than the one prescribed. Precept and practice are related, but they do not necessarily match exactly. As one whose principal association with the arts is through their practice, rather than theorizing about them, I have made practice my main concern and concentrated on what I observed occurring. Fortunately in the 1980s when my observations were made the music, and the way of life of the musicians of Nathdvara, were undoubtedly very much alive. They formed surviving relics of traditions which continued to nourish the rich heritage of India's art.

My approach was to deal with specific instances rather than to draw broad generalizations. I believe this provides the most concrete evidence of the situation as I found it. In future, the numbers of musicians and their activities could change radically. For that reason, these observations should provide a baseline against which to assess the direction, and magnitude, of change in the musician community. As I mentioned, I had no preconceptions about what I would find in the *havelis* nor within the internal working of the *sampraday*. The fact that many of my observations coincided with those of other writers and with scenes recorded in miniature paintings of that period, corroborates that many aspects of the ritual and the role of the musicians have remained unchanged. I adopted at the outset the view that I should accept the simplest explanation of my observations, wherever possible. Hence I tried to interpret the lives of the Nathdvara musicians and their role in *darshan* in a utilitarian manner, as a regular part of a daily routine, rather than as an esoteric form of behaviour. What the musicians did seemed to me to be second nature, the product of their family and economic circumstances, rather than the result of any deep philosophical or psychological tendencies. This attitude is wholly in keeping with the philosophy of the *sampraday* which places its emphasis on practical service to their *svarups*, and on the fervent rendition of their texts in song. *Seva* is the paramount means of salvation.

Pilgrims go to Nathdvara to see Shri Nathji during the seven to eight daily *darshans*. They in turn provide the financial support for both the *haveli*, and the town, which were created, and now exist, only for Shri Nathji. The various components of the *darshan* must be accompanied by music and there is hardly any religious observance of the *sampraday* that does not have its prescribed music. The flexible timing of *darshan* dictates that the musicians must be on call for most of the day and for long hours. As we have seen, much of the music cannot be heard by devotees. It is restricted to a very brief period if we consider the extent of time during which the *darshan* is open. Hence, it would be possible to overlook the role of music in the *sampraday*. Certainly it is possible to take *darshan* and be unaware that music is being played. As well as playing a part in ritual, music is used to summon the devotees. This music is played in the *naubat khana*, at the entrance of the *haveli*. Musically and socially the two groups of musicians are distinct. The *kirtankars* and the musicians of the *naubat khana* do not intermarry; their music is also distinct; also, none of the instruments are shared between the two areas.

The *sampraday* was founded in Braj and the link with that area in ritual practices and in personnel continues. Amongst the *kirtankars*, there were two families: one brahmin and one *kumavat* who traced their origins to Braj. The majority of *kumavats* traced their origin to Rajasthan. The Rajasthani connection was the one feature they shared with the *naubat khana* musicians. The family trees that I constructed show the extent of intermarriage within the group and the tendency for certain families to favour certain musical traditions.

Haveli sangit was not generally played in the courts but several musicians employed by the *haveli* also had a concert repertoire and technique which they played on secular occasions. In Nathdvara these occasions included playing in the pilgrims' guest houses, and in the palaces of the Tilkayat and of other Maharaj.

The history of Guru Purushottam's family provides an example of a family that enjoyed patronage from both courts and *havelis*. It contains many ingredients common to the lives of other musicians: work in courts and temples, the problems of learning, and of sharing artistic knowledge, the importance of the family in teaching, and the practical details of seeking and retaining patronage. Some elements are obviously particular to Guru Purushottam Das: the death of his father while Guru Purushottam was still young, the apparent loneliness of his early years and his drive to reach a high standard to regain the family's position as *Pakhavaji* in the Shri Nathji Haveli, his transfer to Delhi and the resulting national and international recognition. A young musician of Guru Purushottam's ability today would probably expect to travel more, as the classical arts have become concentrated in cities and are now popular abroad. Just as Guru Purushottam left Nathdvara to achieve recognition it seems unlikely that anyone today could hope to build a reputation as a classical musician based only in Nathdvara.

The political importance of the Tilkayat and his sway over the musicians and others in his employ was evident in many ways. So too was his secular role. In practice, the decisions of the Tilkayat appear to be paramount in more or less every activity of the *haveli*. Nevertheless, the deposition of several of the Tilkayats, the most recent being the father of the present Tilkayat, points to the limitations on their power. In 1962 the present Tilkayat also had his financial powers reduced. The last case illustrates the increasing tendency for government to exert control over major religious institutions.

Changing economic circumstances, and perhaps changing aspirations, have caused the Nathdvara musicians to supplement their living in a variety of ways. Guiding pilgrims may always have been an important supplementary activity, but the making and selling of craft items has probably expanded considerably in recent years. The versatility of the musicians in taking up other occupations with flexible hours has enabled them to keep their traditional posts. Their ability to supply many of the items needed for *darshan* and their ingenuity in creating new, and novel, religious articles stresses their artistic abilities and their close dependence on the *havelis* and pilgrims. Those who have been employed in *havelis* outside Nathdvara, whether in Braj, in Rajasthan, or in Gujarat, acquired additional skills and introduced them to their home town. In Nathdvara the emphasis of the *sampraday* on colour and visual dramatization of important events, both at festivals and during regular worship, lends itself readily to commercialization in the form of crafts and artwork. The role of the painter community has been frequently described.

The musical abilities and knowledge of some of the Maharaj was notable and music was considered worthy of their serious study. Such involvement with music began at the founding of the *sampraday*. My experience with music at centres outside Nathdvara gives some indication of the unity of the underlying aesthetic of ritual. The role of music, however, is most elaborately developed in Nathdvara. In the smallest centres elsewhere its presence may be regarded merely as symbolic.

Compared to secular music, the music played in temples today tends to be conservative in content and technique (N.P. Ahmad 1984; Srivastava 1980). Hence, it is not surprising that many of the older styles of vocal and percussion music have been preserved in temples, or in other religious contexts, long after they have disappeared from the repertoire of secular musicians. The practice of the Nathdvara *haveli sangit* tradition of using the *bin* as accompaniment, and the use of the *pakhavaj* as the standard percussion instrument, are examples of this phenomenon.

The history of Guru Purushottam's family indicates that musicians have always been part of the broader artistic community. The growing interest by concert musicians in temple music indicates that its status may be raised and the classical quality of its rendition will probably be augmented. Such music is now for sale on cassettes and CDs. The frequency of the music presentations in the *haveli* and the general confusion in the *darshan* situation have an effect upon how it is performed. It is louder, and more forceful than if it was rendered in a more settled situation.

Those knowledgeable about Indian music with whom I have discussed the music of Nathdvara, tend to dismiss it as falling outside of the classical canons. The sheer amount of music performed and the frequently inhospitable circumstances (it can be bitterly cold in Kirtankar Gali at 5 a.m. in January) can discourage quality. Nevertheless, the musicians identify themselves as artists and take every opportunity to perform in public. Their music is central to their lives and, within the confines of the *haveli* tradition, they have an enormous depth of knowledge. There can be few musical forms anywhere that have been performed for so long in unbroken tradition. The music itself (apart from the *pakhavaj*), I made no attempt to study; but it would provide a very fertile field for ethnomusicological analysis. A detailed study of Guru Purushottam's *pakhavaj* technique, compositions and approach to rhythm is being prepared for publication elsewhere. Already, in the few years since I completed my research, Guru Purushottam as well as several other senior musicians have died. Living embodiments of the Nathdvara musical tradition, they ensured that it was maintained. I hope that others have taken their place.

In Nathdvara in the 1980s there was always a sense of existing in the past. On the dusty road leading from the bus stand to the *haveli*, visitors passed through a time warp taking them back several centuries. It was a magical experience. The air of the past prepared us well for the ascendancy of tradition, and hereditary prerogative that still pervaded Nathdvara. What was more surprising, however, was the adaptability and entrepreneurial spirit shown by many of the *kirtankars*. The determination of Krishna's musicians to pursue their hereditary occupation was surely a major factor in the persistence of music at Nathdvara. Their particular solution to the challenges of the twentieth century was to combine new opportunities for economic betterment with the continuation of making music in the *haveli*. The lives of these musicians demonstrate the resilience of their tradition in the face of change.

APPENDIX

Lineage Divisions

LINEAGE CHART I

JALANDHARA 1

- Kishendas
  - Jadavdas
    - Bhagchand
      - Harchand
        - Shyamdas
          - Bhagwandas
            - **Ramchandra** 6 sons
              - **Laldas** MOVES TO Nathdvara 2 sons
                - Ramkishan
                  - Balkrishna (**Jalandhara.2**)
                - Sadaram
                  - Bandoji (no sons)
              - Jatiram no sons
              - Govardhan
                - **Raghunath**
                  - **Damodardas**
                    - adopted **Sundardas** (third son of Balakrishna)
                      - **Ganeshlal** *H.sangit* MMJ
                        - Murli no sons
                        - Govardhan no sons
                        - Brijlal no sons
                        - **Parmanand** *H. sangit*,MMJ
                          - **Kanhaiyalal I** *H. sangit*,MMJ
                            - Ganeshlal
                            - Liladhar
                          - Shrikrishna
                            - Kailash
                          - Babulal
                            - Ramesh
                      - Naisukh
                        - adopted **Raghunath** *H. Sangit* NNP (**Jalandhara.4**)
                      - Parasuram (**Jalandhara.3**)
              - Purushottam no sons
              - Tansen no sons
              - Khem no sons
            - Govardhan no sons

*= Musician employed in Nathdvara temples in 1988

LINEAGE CHART I

JALANDHARA 2

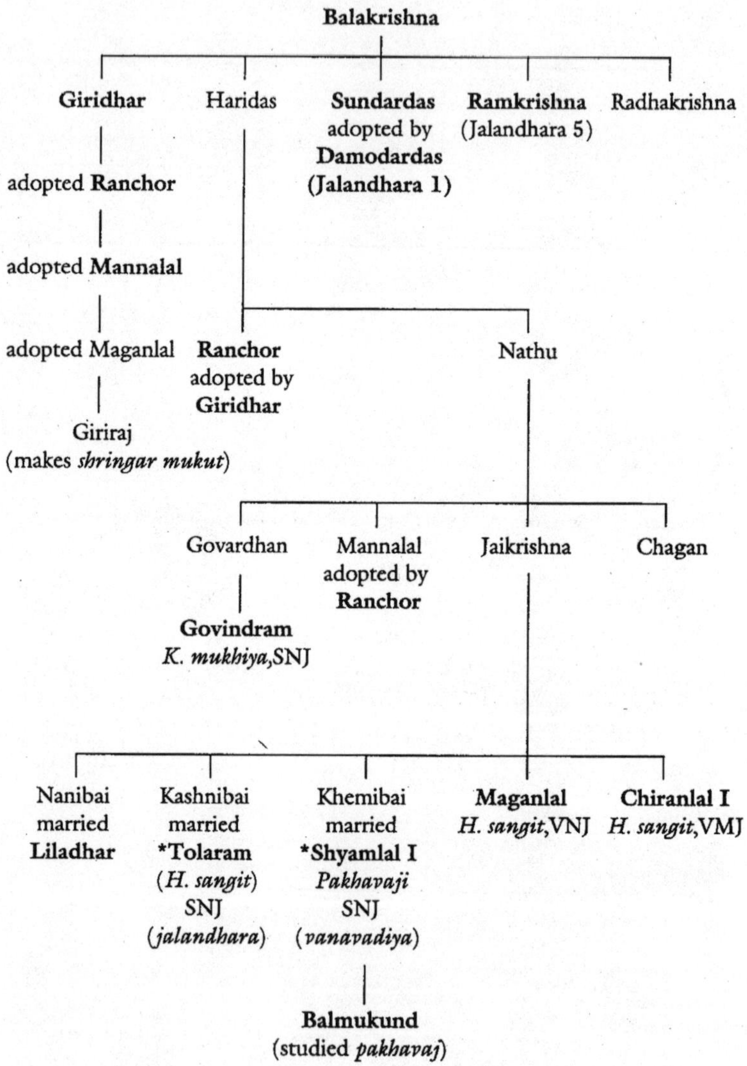

*= Musician employed in Nathdvara temples in 1988

LINEAGE CHART I

JALANDHARA 3

Parasuram

- **Raghunath** adopted by **Naisukh** **(Jalandhara 1)** [see below]
- **Jamnadas** *Binkar*,SNJ
  - married Chotibai/Vasanti d/o **Mannalal** (*H. sangit* SNJ) (*vanavadiya*) adopted, ***Vallabhdas** *Binkar*,SNJ
- **Gokuldas** *H.sangit*,SNJ married Lakshmi
- **Jaikrishna** *H. sangit* NNP

(father in crafts, and construction)

Children of Gokuldas:

- ***Pannalal** *H. sangit*,SNJ
- ***Vallabhdas** *Binkar*, SNJ adopted by **Jamnadas**
- Gopaldas Teacher, Govt. High School

Raghunath
H.sangit SNJ,NNP
Binkar SNJ

- **Radhakrishna** *K. mukhiya*,VNJ
  - ***Bhanvarlal II** *K. Mukhiya*,VNJ
- *** Tolaram** *H. sangit* SNJ
  - daughter
  - Brajesh (studied music)
- Dalibai married **Brijlal** *H. sangit*,SNJ
- Tamubai married **Narayanlal** *Pakhavaji*, NNP
  - *** Sohanlal** *Pakhavaji*, NNP
    - **Ashok** plays *pakhavaj*

*= Musician employed in Nathdvara temples in 1988

LINEAGE CHART I

JALANDHARA 4

- **Ramkrishna**
  - **Narayanlal** — *H. sangit*, NNP — married
  - **Ganeshlal** — adopted Lalram
  - Nandlal
- (Narayanlal married:)
  - **Channulal** — *H. sangit* at Bhindar
    - Bhagwandas (married Lakshmi daughter of **Guru Purushottam** (Kakatiya)
    - ***Damodar** — *K.Mukhiya*, NNP (married Radha daughter of **Guru Purushottam**(Kakatiya)
      - 3 daughters
      - **Prakash** Murli (*pakhavaj*) married Uttam
        - Pranou
    - **Misrilal** — Music teacher — 3 sons — 2 daughters
    - ***Kanhaiyalal II** — *H. sangit*, NNP — 1 son — 2 daughters
  - **Kishanlal** — *H. sangit*, NNP
    - Lalram — *H. sangit*, VMJ
    - Bhagwanlal
    - Mohanlal
    - **Brijlal** — *H. sangit*, VMJ
      - Ganeshlal (married **Shyamlal I's** sister, died in SNJ)
      - Hiralal (School teacher)
        - Raju (Govt job)
      - Fatehlal
  - Gatubai — married **Mathuradas** (*parihar*) *H. sangit*, MMJ
    - ***Ramdas** — *K. mukhiya* SNJ
      - **Shyamsundar** — *H. sangit*
    - ***Amritlal** — *Sarangi*, SNJ
    - Bansilal

*= Musician employed in Nathdvara temples in 1988

LINEAGE CHART 2

VANAVADIYA

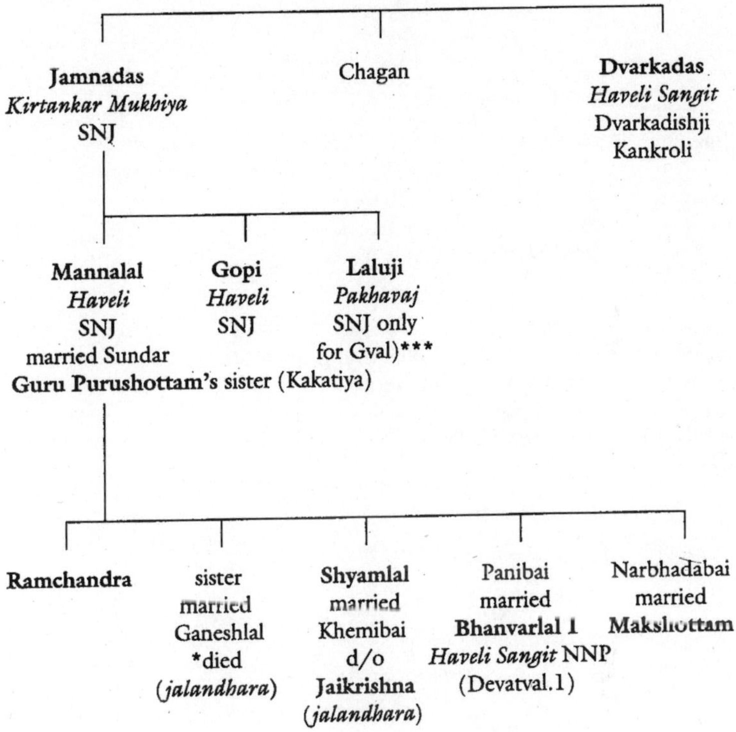

*= Musician employed in Nathdvara temples in 1988

LINEAGE CHART 3

KAKATIYA

Rupram (died 1790)

Vallabhdas(1769-1849)

Shankar 1829-1893)

Khem(1832-1876) **(Kakatiya.1)**

daughter

Ghanshyam (1869-1916) Married Ramibai, her father was Tekchand (construction worker)

Chandra married Mohanlal

Sundar married **Mannalal** *Kirtankar Mukhiya* SNJ (*mandalia*)

Hiralal died young young

Bansilal died

Guru (1907- 1991 **Purushottam** (*Pakhavaji*) SNJ married Gulab d/o **Tikamdas** *Pakhavaji* (Chandramaj,Udaipur) (*devatval*)

Radha married **Damodar** (*K. Mukhiya*) NNP. (*jalandhara*)

Prakash (1956- (*Pakhavaj*)

Pranou (1985-

daughter married SNJ

Ramchandra *H. Sangit* SNJ

Shyamlal *Pakhavaji* married Khemibai d/o **Jaikrishna** (*jalandhara*)

Bapulal

daughter married **Mohanlal** *Haveli* SNJ (*devatval*)

*= Musician employed in Nathdvara temples in 1988

LINEAGE CHART 2

KAKATIYA.2

- **Khem** (1832-1876)
  - **Vitthal**
    - **Narayanlal** (*H. Sangit*) NNP (*Pakhavaji*) NNP
      - **Sohanlal** *Pakhavaji* NNP
        - **Ashok** *Pakhavaji*
    - **Dayalal**(?) (*H. Sangit*) SNJ (*upang*)
      - Prabhulal married Shantidevi daughter of **Motilal** (*mandalia*)
    - Rukmini married **Madanlal** (*H.sangit*) (Udaipur) *devatval*
      - Giriraj
      - Laladhar
      - **Chiranlal II** (*Pakhavaji*) Udaipur Shri Nathji also draftsman
        - **Satnarayan** (*Pakhavaji*) Udaipur SNJ also repairs watches
        - **Lalitkumar** (*Pakhavaji*) Udaipur SNJ also repairs watches

*= Musician employed in Nathdvara temples in 1988

LINEAGE CHART 3

PARIHAR

Udairam

Nanuram

Kunjilal

Phatahlal
Haveli Daoji temple Chaupasni
Sangit

Krishnadas
haveli sangit Daoji temple
Chaupasni

Mathuradas
Kirtankar. Mukhiya
VNJ Nathdvara
2nd wife was
Gattubai sister of
Channulal
(*jalandhara*)

Ramdas
K. mukhiya
SNJ
married to Parvati(Paribai)
sister of **Mulchand**
(*harmonium*) SNJ (Mandalia)

Shyamsundar
teaches music in Kankroli
High School.

Amritlal
Sarangi
SNJ

son no music

Bansilal
adopted
by someone
from Jodhpur

*= Musician employed in Nathdvara temples in 1988

LINEAGE CHART 4

DEVATVAL
Jodhpur then to Udaipur
(Gokul) Chandramaji Temple

Parasuram	**Tikamdas**	**Gangadas**	**Ramnarayan**
HaveliSangit,Binkar	*Pakhavaji*	*Haveli.Sangit*	*Pakhavaji*
Chandramaji	Chadramaji	*Kirtankar Mukhiya* SNJ	SNJ
Devatval.1	Devatval.2	2 daughters	
[see next chart		married non-musicians	
for his children]			

*= Musician employed in Nathdvara temples in 1988

LINEAGE CHART 4

DEVATVAL.1 (cont.)

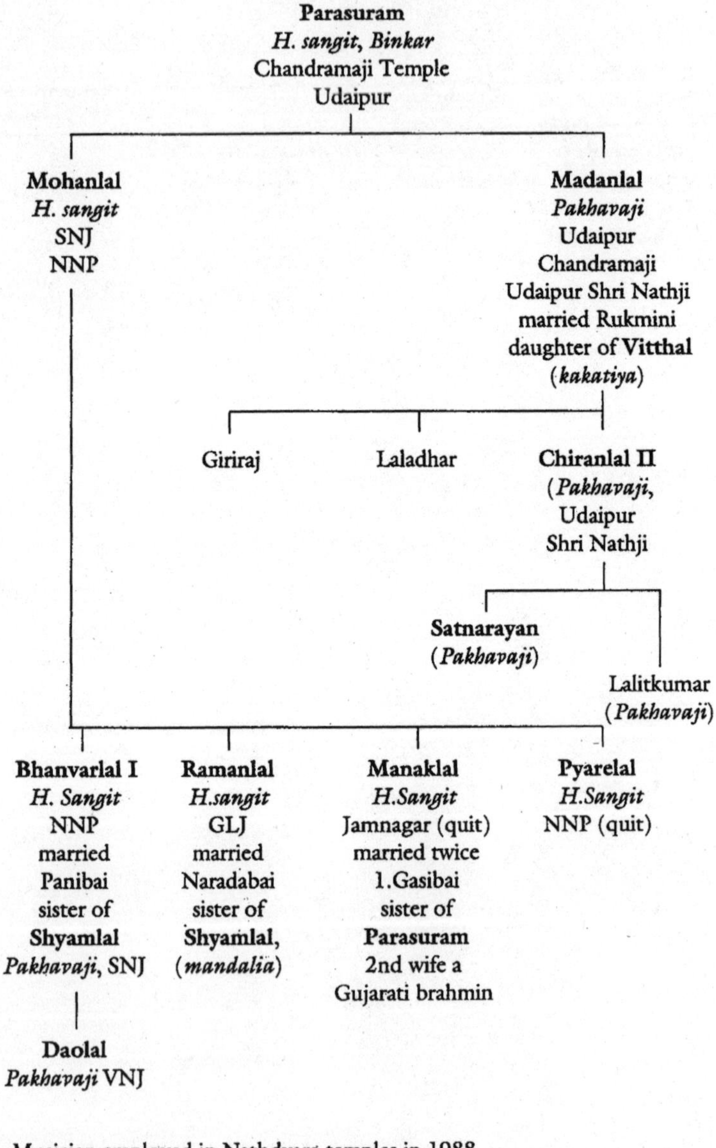

*= Musician employed in Nathdvara temples in 1988

LINEAGE CHART 4

DEVATVAL.2

Tikamdas
Pakhavaji

- Haribai married **Parmananddas** *H. Sangit* (*mandalia*)
- Suri married **Jaikrishna** *jalandhara*
- **Udailal** *Kirtankar* 4 temples in Udaipur
  - 3 sons all in construction
- Gulab married **Guru Purushottam** *Pakhavaji* SNJ (*kakatiya*)

DEVATVAL.3

Ramnarayan
Pakhavaji
SNJ

- **Balkrishna**
  Pakhavaji
  NNP
  - son
    Engineer

*= Musician employed in Nathdvara temples in 1988

LINEAGE CHART 5

SANADHYA

Family I

(Karhelavan)

Braj Tikam worked in
Shri Nathji ki Mukurtji, Karhelavan, Braj

Tikamdas had been invited to Nathdvara by the Tilkayat

Tikamdas
(*H. sangit*)

Balkrishna
H. sangit

Sundarlal
Government servant
returned to Braj

Makshottam

Kisanlal
(*H. sangit*)
NNP

Giridhar
studying music

Krishnakant
studying music

2 daughters

*= Musician employed in Nathdvara temples in 1988

LINEAGE CHART 5

SANDHYA, FAMILY II

From Mahaban, Braj

- Lalu
  - Kishore
Ritual *Mukhiya*
Kankroli temple
  - **Harnath**
(*haveli sangit*)
2nd *Mukhiya*, SNJ
at the time when
Govindram Jalandhara
was lst *Mukhiya*, SNJ
    - **Gopaldas**
station Master
learning *haveli sangit* to sing
after his retirement

*= Musician employed in Nathdvara temples in 1988

Glossary

abhinaya	the expressive aspect of dance; mime expressing the meaning of a song
Abhinayadarpana (AD)	a thirteenth century Sanskrit text on dramaturgy and dance
adarsha	ideal
akshara	"syllable", a single sound played on the *pakhavaj*; a single count
alap	development of the melodic line where the rhythm is apparently free
anagatam	starting a song before the *sam*
angarkhi	a long-sleeved jacket that fits tightly around the chest and falls loosely to waist level
Annakut	a festival celebrated in many places in north India, but particularly in Nathdvara where mountains of food are presented to Shri Nathji and then looted by the local tribals, the Bhils and Minas
anubhava	the aesthetic component which allows an emotion to be sensed; the *anubhavas* in ritual include flowers, colour, *picchvai*
Arati	"light", the circling of an oil lamp before the divine image, used to describe the entire sequence of offerings made to the deity, also the name of one of the *darshans*; it is an alternative name of the *Sandhya darshan*
archana	temple ritual
ashirvad	blessing
ashtachhap	"the eight seals"; eight poet-singers whose compositions form the core of the devotional music in many *havelis* of the Vallabha Sampraday;

	the *chhap* or name signature of the poet is incorporated into each verse, Vallabha is said to have initiated four of them to sing the praises of Shri Krishna: Kumbhandas in 1500, Surdas in 1511, Krishnadas in 1512 and Parmananddas in 1521; Vallabha encouraged singing in the first Shri Nathji temple on Mount Govardhan, which was completed in 1520; it was not until the Tilkayatship of his son Vitthalnath (1531-86) that singing became an important and regular part of the ritual
Avanaddha	a *vadhya* instrument in which the membrane is the primary sound-producing medium
bhagavata	devotee of God
Bhagavata Purana	a Sanskrit text written in A.D. 950 which describes the various exploits of Krishna. This text is important for the Vallabha Sampraday
bhajan	devotional song
bhakta	a devotee, literally one who "shares" with god
bhakti	devotion
Bharata Natyam	classical dance style that evolved from the earlier concert repertoire of the style of dance known as *sadir/dasi-attam* from southern India; the name Bharata Natyam was adopted in about 1933
bhava	"feeling" or "emotion", the basis of *rasa*
bhog	"food", the name of one of the *darshans* two *darshans—Bhog* and *Arati*—are often combined
bin	a north Indian stick zither; also called a *vina* but not to be confused with the south Indian instrument also called *vina*
Binkar	one who plays the *bin*
bol	rhythmic syllables; forming sequences of spoken sounds imitative of drum syllables, combinations of *aksharas*, used interchangeably with *matra*
brahmin:	the highest status group; the one which is believed to have the highest ritual purity
Brajbhasha	in use as a literary language from the sixteenth century to the nineteenth century; a dialect of Hindi
Braj/Vraj	the region associated with the playful life of Krishna now in the state of Uttar Pradesh
Brajvasi	a person from Braj

chamara	flywhisk
chapati	unleavened broiled bread
chauk	a public square
chhapan bhog	fifty-six varieties of foodstuffs which are presented to Shri Nathji during a festival of the same name
dakshina	"gift"; specifically the gift that is given in lieu of payment for knowledge imparted
daph/daff	a round circular drum with leather head.
darbari dhrupad	"court songs", the branch of *dhrupad* patronized by the courts
darshan/darsan	"seeing"; especially something sacred or special, a time when the deity is present to be seen
devadasi	"female servant of god"; the name for hereditary temple dancers; often used interchangeably with another caste name, *isai vellala.*
dharma	duty, righteous action
dhol	drum
dhoti	length of cloth tied at the waist to cover the lower half of the body
dhrupad	a medieval form of north Indian classical music; also the actual musical composition
dhrupad-dhamar	a classical style of north Indian music
Dhrupadiya	one who sings *dhrupad*
dhruvari/dhruvbari	a window in the Shri Nathji Haveli high on the wall which connects the hall of *darshan* (*dol tibari*) and Ratan Chauk.
dhumsa	a two headed drum
dipa	light
Divali	the festival of lights
doltivari/doltibari	hall of *darshan*
Dvarkadhishji	the name of one of the main *svarups* venerated by the Vallabha Sampraday; also the name of the *haveli* where the image of Dvarkadhishji is housed
Eklingji	"one *linga*", the name of a Shaivite temple located halfway between Udaipur and Nathdvara
kanthi	a necklace made of *tulsi* leaves
gaddi	"seat" or "throne", especially as the "seat" of a royal house or religious institution, one of seven centres of the Vallabha Sampraday, cushioned seat
gali	lane
gandharv	celestial musician, also the name of a community of musicians

gharana	"of the house"; a family tradition in the north Indian musical system
Gita Govinda	Sanskrit poem written by Jayadeva in the twelfth century; each of the twenty-four songs is known as an *ashtapadi* (octet) and concerns the relationship of Krishna with his mistress-consort, Radha
Gopallalji	a temple in Nathdvara
gopi	a cowherd lover of Krishna; one of the women of Braj.
Gosvami/Goswami/ Gosain	a term of address and often the surname for the descendants of Vallabha and other heads of Krishna sects; Gosvami and Maharaj are often used interchangeably
Govardhan Chauk	the first courtyard on entering the Shri Nathji Haveli; named after the mountain in Braj that Krishna lifted and held aloft
Govardhan	the name of a mountain in Braj which Krishna raised with his hand/ baby finger and held aloft as an umbrella to protect the people of Braj from a storm sent by the Vedic storm god, Indra
Govardhan *puja*	worship of the mountain Govardhan which Krishna raised
gulal	coloured powder thrown during the festival of Holi
Guru	term of address for teachers of traditional arts or a spiritual master
guru-kula	guru's household, especially as the basis for a traditional school
guru-shishya parampara	master-disciple succession of a tradition
gurukulavasa	traditional method of exchanging work for knowledge; usually the student lived in the teacher's home
Gval	"cowherd", the name of one of the *darshans*
harmonium	a small hand-pumped organ used to accompany singing in Indian music, originally brought to India by Christian missionaries
hasta/ mudra	hand gesture
haveli sangit/pushti-marg bhakti sangit	the genre of music sung or played in the *havelis* of the Vallabha Sampraday
haveli	a temple or place of worship of the Vallabha Sampraday; the term temple is often used interchangeably; a manor house

Hindi/Hindustani	an Indo-European language spoken mainly in north India
Hindustani music	the north Indian style of classical music from the region where Indo-European languages are spoken.
Holkar	a Maratha ruler
isai vellala	caste name given to hereditary temple musicians and dancers in south India, in particular Tamil Nadu
Jagannath/Jagannatha	an aspect of the Hindu deity Vishnu, especially as found in an important temple in Puri, Orissa.
Janmashtami	the festival which celebrates the birth of Krishna
jhanjh	cymbals
jhapatiya	"to pounce", men who control the crowds in the Shri Nathji Haveli
kalavant	hereditary musicians without dancing girls as relatives
Kama	the Hindu god of love
Kamal Chauk	"lotus square", an area in the Shri Nathji Haveli
Karnatic music	system of music followed in southern India, distinct from the northern or Hindustani style; it is indigenous to the region where Dravidian languages are spoken
Kathak	A dance style from North india
khyal	a classical style of north Indian music
kirtan	devotional song or devotional style of singing that involves repeating Krishna's various names.
kirtankar/kirtaniya	a musician in the *havelis* of the Vallabha Sampraday
Kirtankar Gali	"musicians lane", an area in the Shri Nathji Haveli where the musicians play music for some of the pre-*darshan* periods or wait before playing for *darshan*
Krishna	Hindu deity
Kuchipudi	classical dance style originating in the state of Andhra Pradesh; originally only performed by men who took female roles, it is now also performed by women
laddu	round sweet made of gram flour and sugar, a favourite of Krishna
kumavat	the caste name for some of the hereditary musicians who play in the Shri Nathji Haveli; there are seven divisions of *kumavats*, given in Table 7.1

kumbh	girth of a *pakhavaj*
laya vinyasa	rhythmic elaboration
laya	rhythm, tempo, speed
layakari	rhythmic manipulation, tempo control
lila	play
mahanta	head priest of a temple
Maharaj Gokulotsav	head of the Vitthalnathji Haveli, a position he shares with his two brothers, Maharaj Kalyanray and Maharaj Devkinand.
Maharaj	in some contexts a term of address for all of Vallabha's descendants; used interchangeably with Gosvami/Goswami
Maharaja	king; the title given to some secular rulers of princely states, in particular those from Rajasthan; the rulers of these various states also had titles unique to their own state: the ruler of the state of Mewar was called Maharana of Mewar, and the ruler of the state of Dungarpur was called the Rawal of Dungarpur
Maharana	the title given to the ruler of the former state of Mewar, one of the princely states of Rajasthan
Malayalam	A Dravidian language spoken in Kerala state
mandir	temple
Mangal	"auspicious", the name of one of the *darshans*
mangalam	"auspicious", the last song sung at the end of a Bharata Natyam recital
mani kota	"diamond square" the area in the Shri Nathji Haveli, in front of the image of Shri Nathji where the musicians play during the *darshans*
manodharma	artistic imagination
manoratha	"cherished desire"; a painting or other record of an important religious event
mantra	a mystical word or verse or sacred formula
matra	combination of *aksharas*; used interchangeably with *akshara*
maya	"illusion", that force by which Krishna conceals or distorts his true nature
meghnad	largest and most venerated of the *pakhavajs* in the Shri Nathji Haveli
mela	gathering, fair
melakkar	a group of hereditary musicians from south India
moja	socks
moksha	liberation

morchhal	a fan made of peacock feathers
Moti Mahal	"pearl palace", the official residence of the Tilkayat in Nathdvara attached to the Shri Nathji Haveli
Mridang Vadan	"drum playing", the title of the book written by Guru Purushottam Das and published in 1982
Mridang Sagar	"drum ocean", the title of the book written by Shankar and Khem and finally completed by Ghanshyam Das, Guru Purushottam's father, published in 1911
mridangam	two-headed drum played to accompany Karnatic music, both instrumental and vocal as well as those dance styles performed to Karnatic Music: Bharata Natyam and Kuchipudi; an older name for the north Indian barrel-shaped drum, the *pakhavaj*
mudra/hasta	hand gestures
mukut	decorative crown
mundan	tonsure ceremony
nagasvaram/ nagaswaram	reed instrument used in temple music and processions; the music is auspicious and is important at weddings; Hindu *nagasvaram* players generally belong to the *isai vellala* community
namaskaram/namaskar	reverential greeting
Nanda	Krishna's adoptive father; he is the chief of the cowherds of Braj
Nandotsav	"Nanda's festival", the festival which celebrates the birth of Krishna. Nanda is Krishna's adoptive father
naqqara	kettledrums
Natya Shastra (*NS*)	fourth-fifth century A.D. Sanskrit text which records the theory of drama, music, poetics, dance and general aesthetics
naubat	combination of *naqqara* (drums) and *shahnai* (reed instrument)
naubat/naqqara/khana	a room open on two sides located above the main entrance of the *havelis* of the Vallabha Sampraday where *shahnai dhol* and *dhumsa* are stored and played, also found above the main gates of palaces in Rajasthan
nautch	dance, north Indian term
Navnitpriyaji	one of the main *svarups* venerated by the Vallabha Sampraday; the name of the *haveli* where the

	image is housed (NNP)
nayaka	idealized hero
nayika	idealized heroine
nayika-nayaka-bhava	the emotions exchanged between a hero and heroine in love
neg	payment for service to the deity
nij mandir	inner shrine room of the Shri Nathji Haveli; niche where Shri Nathji is installed
Odissi	dance style originating from the eastern part of India, Orissa; a modern reconstruction of two traditions: the *mahari* or temple tradition and the *gotipua* tradition, danced by itinerant drama groups
pagri/pagha	turban
pakhavaj	double-conical-shaped drum with two heads; *mridanga* was the older name; differs in construction from the southern *mridangam*
Pakhavaji	one who performs on the *pakhavaj*
pan-supari	betel leaf folded into a cone, containing pieces of *areca* nut, lime paste and other fragrant ingredients
parampara	succession or tradition
paran	a *pakhavaj* composition
picchvai	backdrops that may be painted or embroidered; hung behind the image in the *havelis* of the Vallabha Sampraday during ritual
pind shraddh	"offerings to the ancestors"
pinda	the balls of rice and other grains used in rites for the dead, usually as offerings to nourish the deceased
podar	a *pakhavaj* composition
prasad bhandar	the room where the sanctified food is stored
prasad	sanctified food
puja	worship
Purana	books containing extensive sources of Hindu mythology, most having a strong sectarian bias; there are eighteen such collections of ancient (*purana*) stories which recount myths, legends, and rites
Pushkar	a holy lake in Rajasthan; an important pilgrimage centre
pushtimarg/pustimarg	"path of divine grace", an alternative name for the Vallabha Sampraday

Qawwali	Muslim devotional music sung at the shrine of a Sufi saint (Pir)
Radha	Krishna's most beloved *gopi*
Radhakrishna	*kirtankar* in Nathdvara
Radhashtami	festival celebrated by the Vallabha Sampraday honouring the birth of Radha, Krishna's consort
raga	a pattern of notes arranged in a specific way; the *raga* system of music is unique to both north and south Indian music; musical mode; the basis of melody in Indian music
Raj Bhog	"ruler's food", the name of one of the *darshans*
rakhi-bandan	festive occasion when *rakhis* (decorative wrist bands) are exchanged between brothers and sisters or friends
ras-lila	a drama depicting an episode from the life of Krishna
rasa	"juice, flavour"; mood; the essence of an artistic experience; in the context of aesthetics it is understood as aesthetic enjoyment, in the context of *bhakti* as devotional sentiment
rasika	connoisseur
rasiya	a genre of song heavy with erotic content; usually sung during the celebration of Holi; also the specialist who sings these songs
ratan chauk	a courtyard in the Shri Nathji Haveli
Raval	title given to the ruler of the state of Dungarpur, one of the princely states of Rajasthan
razai	quilt
rudraksha beads	beads worn by renouncers; generally by Shaivites
sadhana	penance, dedication, spiritual practice, means of realization, in the context of musical training complete devotion to training and practice
sadir	the name of the concert repertoire of dance performed by *devadasis*
sahitya	text
sakhi	female friend of Radha
sampraday/ sampradaya	an exclusive group that follows the teachings of a particular teacher such as Vallabha; an orally transmitted artistic tradition. the Vallabha Sampraday was founded in 1494.
samsara	term used to describe the ceaseless round of birth, death and rebirth; the world of change
sanadhi	a Sanskrit term describing an area in a temple

	near the deity; *mani kota* is the term used in the Shri Nathji Haveli
sanadhya	a brahmin community from the Braj area; some are hereditary musicians in the Shri Nathji Haveli
Sandhya	"evening", name of one of the *darshans*; an alternative name to *Arati darshan*
Sangitaratnakara	a thirteenth century Sanskrit text with details about music and dance attributed to Sarangadeva
sarangi	a bowed stringed instrument without frets
Sarangiya	person who plays the *sarangi*
sarod	lute-type stringed instrument without frets, with sympathetic strings, played by plucking with a plectrum
Sarodiya	person who plays the sarod
seva	service, performative acts
seva-vala	person who performs *seva*
shahnai	an oboe-like double-reed instrument
Shaivite	worshipper of Shiva
shastra	doctrine or treatise
Shayan	"lying, sleeping"; one of the *darshans*; closed for six months of the year during the hot season when Shri Nathji sleeps out of doors
shishya	disciple, pupil, student
Shiva	one of the Hindu deities
shringar/shringara/ sringar/sringara	erotic love, a term also used to describe the clothes and decorations which adorn images of the Vallabha Sampraday, and which is also the name of one of the *darshans*
shyahi	black spot on one of the heads of the *pakhavaj*
Sirnar	a village in Rajasthan which existed before Nathdvara was founded
sitar	a long-necked lute with gourd resonators and raised frets
Suraj Pol	"sun gate" one of the gateways into the Shri Nathji Haveli
svara	solfege syllable
svarup	"essential nature", an embodiment of the deity that appears fully formed
tabla	set of drums consisting of a wooden drum tuned to a specific pitch and a kettle-shaped metal drum of indefinite pitch
tala	time-cycle
tanpura/tambura	stringed instrument used as a drone

Thakurji	"Lord", a term used to address Shri Nathji, also a secular feudal landlord, master or chief
thumri	a style of light-classical north Indian music, the text of the songs expresses romantic themes
Tilkayat	title for the head of the Vallabha Sampraday
tirth yatra	"holy journey" to go on pilgrimage, the journey to a sacred place
tirtha	ford, crossing place, a place of pilgrimage
utsav	festival
Utthapan	"rising", the name of one of the *darshans*
Vaishnavite	worshipper of Vishnu
vina	plucked lute-type of stringed instrument with frets set in wax
viraha	the pain endured during separation from one's beloved
Vishnu	one of the Hindu deities
Vitthalnathji	the name of one of the main *svarups* venerated by the Vallabha Sampraday; also the name of the *haveli* where the image is housed (VNJ)
Vraj/Braj	the region associated with the playful life of Krishna now in Uttar Pradesh
vrata	A religious observance that is the fulfilment of a vow
Vrindavan/Brindavan/ Brindaban	a town in the state of Uttar Pradesh important in the mythology of Krishna because it is associated with Krishna's early life
yagna	sacrifice, especially the Vedic sacrifice
Yashoda	Adoptive mother of Krishna

Bibliography

Ahmad, Najma Parveen, 1984, *Hindustani Music, a Study of its Development in the Seventeenth and Eighteenth Centuries*, Delhi: Manohar.

Ahmad, Nasir, 1956, *Kitab-i-Nauras*, by Ibrahim Adil Shah, edited by Ahmad Nasir, Delhi: Bharatiya Kala Kendra.

Allami, Abu Al-Fazl, 1989, *Ain-i-Akbari*, trans. H. Blochmann, New Delhi: Motilal Banarsidass.

Altekar, A.S., 1962, *The Position of Women in Hindu Civilization*, New Delhi: Motilal Banarsidass.

Amarnath, Pandit, 1989, *Living Idioms in Hindustani Music: A Dictionary of Terms and Terminology*, New Delhi: Vikas.

Ambalal, Amit, 1987, *Krishna as Shrinathji*, Ahmedabad: Mapin.

Anand, Mulk, Raj, 1977, "Coomaraswamy's Holistic View of Art", *Marg*, Bombay.

Andres, Elizabeth, 1987, "Encountering Vrindavan", in *Vignettes of Vrindavan*, McDowell and Sharma (ed.), Delhi: Books and Books.

Appadurai, Arjun, 1981, *Worship and Conflict under Colonial Rule, a South Indian Case*, Cambridge: Cambridge University Press.

Appaswamy, Jaya, 1980, *Tanjore Paintings of the Maratha Period*, New Delhi: Abhinav.

Ashton, Roger, 1966, *Music East and West*, New Delhi: Indian Council for Cultural Relations.

Asian Music, 1976, Vol VII-2; 1988-89 Vol XX (1).

Atre, Prabha 1986, "Teaching Music at Institutions", *Sangeet Natak*, 79: 58-64.

———, 1988 "Modernity in Khyal: Some Notes", *Sangeet Natak*, 89-90: 16-23.

Ayyangar, R. Rangaramanuja, 1972, *History of South Indian (Carnatic) Music*, Madras: Rangaramanuja Ayyangar.

Ayyar, Ramakrishna, 1946 *Economy of a South Indian Temple, Annamalainagar.*

Ayyar, Jagadisa P.V.,1920, 22, *South Indian Shrines*, Madras.

Babb, Lawrence A., 1975, *The Divine Hierarchy: Popular Hinduism in Central India*, New York: Columbia University Press.

Bahura Gopal Narayan, 1974, *Literary Heritage of the Rulers of Amber and Jaipur*, Maharaja Sawai Man Singh II Museum, City Palace, Jaipur.

Baily, John, 1980, "A Description of the *Naqqarakhana* of Herat, Afghanistan", *Asian Music* IX (2): 1-10.

Balamurli, Krishna, 1984, "Tradition is What Survives", *Sruti*, Jan.-Feb., pp. 34-5.

Banerjee, Jayshree, 1986, "The Methodology of Teaching Indian Classical Music, A Statement on the Problem", *Sangeet Natak*, 79: 11-48.

Banerjee, P., 1978, *The Life of Krishna in Indian Art*, New Delhi: National Museum.

Banerji, Projesh, 1982, *Uday Shankar and His Art*, Delhi: B.R. Publishing Corporation.

——————, 1986, *Dance in Thumri*, Delhi: Abhinav.

Barz, Richard, 1976, *The Bhakti Sect of Vallabhacharya*, Faridabad: Thompson Press.

Beach, Milo, 1974, *Rajput Painting at Bundi and Kota*, Ascona.

Bennett, Peter John, 1983, *Temple Organization and Worship among the Pustimargiya Vaisnavas of Ujjain*, Ph.D. Thesis, School of Oriental and African Studies, University of London.

Bhagowalia, Urmila, 1980, *Vaisnavism and Society in Northern India: 700-1200*, New Delhi: Intellectual Book Corner.

Bhandarkar, R.G., 1913, *Vaisnavism Saivism and Minor Religious Systems*, Varanasi: Indological Book House (reprint of 1913 no date of new reprint)

Bharata Muni, 1967, *Natya Shastra*: trans. M Ghosh, Calcutta: Granthalaya.

Bhatkhande, V.N., 1972, *A Comparative Study of Some of the Leading Music Systems of the 15th, 16th 17th and 18th Centuries*, Baroda: Indian Musicological Society.

Bhattacharya, Joten, 1979, *Ustad Allaudin and His Music*, Ahmedabad: Prakashan.

Bor, Joep, 1975, "Raga, Species and Evolution", *Sangeet Natak*, 35: 17-48.

——————, 1987, *The Voice of the Sarangi*, Bombay: National Centre for Performing Arts.

Brown, Percy, 1965, *Indian Architecture* (Buddhist and Hindu Periods), Bombay: Taraporevala.

——————, 1975, *Indian Architecture, Islamic Period*, Bombay: Taraporevala.

Brown, R., 1965, *The Mrdanga: A Study of Drumming in South India*, Doctoral thesis, Middletown, Conn.:Wesleyan University.

Bryant, Kenneth E., 1978, *Poems to the Child God: Structures and Strategies*, Berkeley: University of California Press.

Burghardt, R. Arnold, 1976, "Indore as a Centre for Music; The Historical Background of Indore and the Sattelite Courts", *Asian Music*, VII (2): 51-58.

Calico Museum of Textiles n.d., *Textiles of the Vallabha Sampradaya*, Ahmedabad.

Chaitanya, Krishna, 1982, *Rajasthani Traditions*, New Delhi: Abhinav.

Chandola, Anoop,1977, *Folk Drumming in the Himalayas; A Linguistic Approach To Music*, New York: AMS Press.

Chandra, Pramod, 1975, *Studies in Indian Temple Architecture*, New Delhi: American Institute of Indian Studies.

————, 1983, *On the Study of Indian Art*, Cambridge, Mass.: Harvard University Press.

Chandra, Moti, 1973, *The World of Courtesans*, Delhi: Vikas.

Chari, V., 1980, "The Rasa Theory: Theology or Aesthetics" in *The Sacred and the Secular in India's Performing Arts*, V. Subramaniam (ed.), Delhi: Ashish, pp. 47-61.

Chatterjee, Chinmayi, 1981, *Studies in the Evolution of Bhakti Cult, with special reference to Vallabha School*, Part II, Calcutta: Jadavpur University.

Chaturvedi, Mahendra and Bhola Nath Tiwari, 1983, *A Practical Hindi-English Dictionary*, Delhi: National.

Chaudhuri, Buddhadeb, 1981, *The Bakreshwar Temple; A Study on Continuity and Change*, Delhi: Inter-India.

Cimino, R.M., 1985, *Life at Court in Rajasthan*, Florence.

Commissariat, M.S., 1938, *A History of Gujarat*, Bombay.

Cooper, Robin, 1977, "Abstract Structure and the Indian *Raga* System", *Ethnomusicology*, XXI(1): 1-32, Michigan, Ann Arbor.

Crooke, William, 1920, *Annals and Antiquities of Rajasthan*, edited version of the book by James Tod of the same name, reprint 1987, Delhi: Motilal Banarsidass.

Dallapiccola, Anna L., 1982, *Krishna: The Divine Lover, Myth and Legend Through Indian Art*, Delhi: B.I.

Damiya, Jasleen, 1965, "The Pechwais of Nathdvara", *The Times of India Annual* (Bombay), pp. 73-80.

Das, J.P., 1982, *Puri Painting*, Delhi: Arnold Heinemann.

Das, Ghanshyam, 1911, *Mridang Sagar*, Bombay: Subhodini Press, Bhagvallal Tribhuvan.

Das, Purushottam,, 1982, *Mridang Vadan*, Delhi: Sangeet Natak Akademi.

Das, Shyam, 1985, *Chaurasi Baithak*.

Dasgupta, S.N., 1959, *Hindu Mysticism*, New York: Frederick Ungar.

De, Sushil Kumar, 1942, 61, *Early History of the Vaisnava Faith and Movement in Bengal*, Calcutta: Mukhopadhyay.

Deleury, G.A., 1960, *The Cult of Vithoba*, Poona: Deccan College.

Delvoye, Francoise (Nalini), 1986, "Bibliography on Dhrupad (I)", *Dhrupad*

Annual, Vol. I, Banaras: Banaras Hindu University.

————, 1987a, "Sources of Materials For Critical Studies in *Dhrupad* Song-Texts, *Dhrupad Annual*, Vol. II: 35-50.

————, 1987b, "Bibliography on Dhrupad II", *Dhrupad Annual*, Vol II.

————, 1988, "Bibliography on Dhrupad III", *Dhrupad Annual*, Vol. III.

Deshpande, Vamanrao, H., 1989, *Between Two Tanpuras*, Bombay, Popular Prakashan.

Deva, Chaitanya, 1973, *An Introduction to Indian Music*, New Delhi: Director of Publications Division, Ministry of Information and Broadcasting.

————, 1974, *Indian Music*, New Delhi: Indian Council for Cultural Relations.

————, 1978, *Musical Instruments of India: Their History and Development*, Calcutta: Firma KLM.

————, 1987, *Musical Instruments of India, Their History and Development*, New Delhi: Munshiram Manoharlal.

Dhamija, Jasleen, 1985, *Crafts of Gujarat*, Ahmedabad: Mapin.

Dhond, M.V. n.d., *Evolution of Khyal*, New Delhi: Sangeet Natak Akademi.

Dumont, Louis, 1956, *Homo Hierarchicus*, London: Granada.

Dwivedi, Hariharaniwas, 1986, "The Dhrupad Dance of Gwalior and its Stage", *Dhrupad Annual*, Vol I.

Eck, Diana, 1983, *Banaras, City of Light*, London: Routledge and Kegan Paul.

————, 1985, *Darsan; Seeing the Divine Image in India*, Chambersburg: Anima.

Ellingson, Ter, 1980, "Ancient Indian Drum Syllables and Bu Stom's Pa Ta Ritual", *Ethnomusicology*, XXIV(3): 431-52, Michigan: Ann Arbor.

Entwistle, A.W., 1987, *Braj, Centre of Krishna Pilgrimage*, Groningen: Egbert Forsten.

————, 1988, "From Vraja to Braj", in *Rediscovering Braj*, London: International Association of Vrindaban Research, School of Oriental and African Studies.

Erdman, J.L., 1978, "The Maharajas Musicians: The Organization of Cultural Performance at Jaipur in the Nineteenth Century", in *American Studies in the Anthropology of India*, Sylvia Vatuk (ed.), pp. 342-67, New Delhi: Manohar.

————, 1980, *The Artist in Indian Society: Patrons and Performers in Rajasthan*, Ph.D. thesis, Department of Anthropology, University of Chicago.

————, 1985, *Patrons and Performers in Rajasthan: The Subtle Tradition*, Delhi: Chanakya.

Erskine, Major K.D., 1908, *The Mewar Residency*, Vol. II, Rajputana Gazetteers, Ajmer: Scottish Mission Industries Company.

Fowke, Francis, 1865, "On the *Vina* or Indian Lyre", S.M. Tagore (ed.) *Indian Music*, Calcutta, pp.193-97.

Fox Strangeways, A.H., 1914, *The Music of Hindostan*, New Delhi: Oriental Books Reprint Corporation (1975).

Fuller, C. J., 1984, *Servants of the Goddess: The Priests of a South Indian Temple*, Cambridge: Cambridge University Press.

Gadon, Elinor W., 1984, "Iconographical Analysis of the *Balagopalastuti*: Early *Krisnabhakti* in Gujarat", Ph.D. thesis, Chicago: University of Chicago.

Gaeffke, Peter and David A. Utz,, 1984, *Identity and Division in Cults and Sects in South Asia*, Philadelphia: University of Philadelphia, South Asian Studies.

Gangoly, O.C., 1989, *Ragas and Raginis, A Pictorial and Iconographic Study of Indian Musical Modes based on Original Sources*, New Delhi: Munshiram Manoharlal.

Ganguli, Kalyan Kumar, 1983, *Cultural History of Rajasthan*, Delhi: Sundeep Prakashan.

Ganhar J.N., 1973, *Jammu, Shrines and Pilgrimages*, New Delhi, Ganhar.

Gargi, Balwant, 1966, *Folk Theatre of India*, Washington: University of Washington Press.

Gaston, Anne-Marie, 1980, "The Place of Indian Classical Dance in Traditional Indian Culture", in *The Sacred and the Secular in Indian Performing Arts*, V. Subramaniam (ed.), New Delhi: Ashish, pp. 62-85.

——————, 1983a "The Effect of Changing Patronage on Indian Performing Arts", *Proceedings from the 10th International Congress of Sociology, Mexico City, 1982.* Sophia, Bulgaria:Institute of Culture: pp. 297-308.

——————, 1983b, *North Indian Drumming, the Pakhavaj Tradition of Guru Purushottam Das.* Report the Social Sciences and Humanities Research Council, Ottawa.

——————, 1984, "Research on the Music of Purushottam Das", ISTAR, (International Society for Traditional Arts Research), unpublished. New Delhi: American Institute of Indian Studies.

——————, 1989, "The Family History of Guru Purushottam Das, Hereditary Pakhavaji of The Sri Nathji Temple, Nathdvara, Rajasthan", *Dhrupad Annual*: pp. 16-57.

——————, 1991a, "Continuity and Re-creation in the Performing Arts in India, A Study of Two Artistic Traditions, D.Phil. thesis, Oxford University.

——————, 1991b, "Dance and the Hindu Woman, Bharata Natyam Re-Ritualized", in *Roles and Rituals For Hindu Women*, edited by Julia Leslie, London: Pinter.

————, 1991c, "Continuity of Tradition in the Music of Nathdvara", in Karine Schomer et al. (ed.) *The Idea of Rajasthan, Volume 1 Explorations in Regional Identity*, New Delhi; Manohar.

————, 1991d, "Bharata Natyam, A Classical East Indian Dance Style in Transition", in *South Asian Studies Journal*, (Cambridge).

Gautam, M.R., 1980, *The Musical Heritage of India*, New Delhi: Abhinav.

————, 1989, *Evolution of Raga and Tala in Indian Music*, Delhi: Munshiram Manoharlal.

Ghosh, Manomohan, 1967, *Natyasastra*, Calcutta: Granthalaya.

Gnoli, Raniero, 1956, *The Aesthetic Experience According to Abhinavagupta*, Rome.

Goetz, H., 1947, "Indian Painting in the Muslim Period", *Journal of the Indian Society of Oriental Art* (Calcutta), pp. 19-41.

Gold, Ann Grodzins, 1987, *Fruitful Journeys, The Ways of Rajasthan Pilgrims*, Berkeley: University of California Press.

Gold, Daniel, 1987, *The Lord as Guru, Hindi Sants in the North Indian Tradition*, Delhi: Oxford University Press.

Gombrich, R., 1971, *Precept and Practice*, Oxford: Clarendon Press.

Gonda Jan A., 1975, *A History of Indian Literature, Vedic Literature*, Wiesbaden.

Gosvami, O., 1961, *The Story of Indian Music, its Growth and Synthesis.* London: Asia.

Gottlieb, Robert, 1977, *The Major Traditions of North Indian Tabla Drumming*, Munchien: Musikverlag, Katzbichler.

Growse, F. S., 1874, *Mathura, A District Memoir*, Part 1 Northwest Frontier Provinces: Oudh Government.,

————, 1880, 2nd Edition

————, 1882, 3rd Edition

Hardy, Friedhelm, 1983, *Viraha-Bhakti, The Early History of Krsna Devotion in South India*, New Delhi: Oxford University Press.

————, 1978, "Ideology and Cultural Contexts of the Srivaisnava temple", in *South Indian Temples* Burton Stein (ed.), Delhi: Vikas.

Hardgrave, Robert L. Jr. and Slawek, Stephen M., 1988/89, "Instruments and Music Culture in Eighteenth Century India: The Solvyns Portraits", *Asian Music*, XX(1): 1-92.

Harle, James, 1974, *Gupta Sculpture*, Oxford: Oxford University Press.

Hawley, John Stratton, 1981, *At Play with Krishna: Pilgrimage Dramas from Brindavan*, Princeton: Princeton University Press.

————, 1984, *Sur Das, Poet, Singer, Saint*, Delhi: Oxford University Press.

Hawly, John Stratton, and Donna Marie Wulff, 1984, *The Divine Consort, Radha and the Goddesses of India*, Delhi: Motilal Banarsidass.

Hein, Norvin, 1972, *The Miracle Plays of Mathura*, New Haven: Yale University Press.

Higgins, Jon Borthwick, 1973, "The Music of Bharata Natyam", Ph.D. thesis, Wesleyan University, Middletown, Conn.

————, 1976, "From Prince to Populace, Patronage as a Determinant of Change in South India (Karnatic Music)", *Asian Music*, VII (2): 20-6.

————, 1983, "Balasaraswati's '*Tisram Alarippu*, The Musical Content", Bonnie C. Wade (ed.), *Performing Arts in India*, Berkeley: Centre for South and South East Asian Studies.

Hiralal, Maheshwari, 1980, *History of Rajasthani Literature*, New Delhi: Sahity Akademi.

Hobsbawm, Eric and Ranger, Terence, 1983, *The Invention of Tradition*, Cambridge: Cambridge University Press.

Huizinga, Johan, 1955, *A Study of the Play Element in Culture*, Boston: Beacon.

Irwin and Hall, 1973, *Indian Embroideries*, Ahmedabad: Calico Museum of Textiles.

Jairazbhoy N.A., 1971, *Ragas of North India*, London: Faber and Faber.

Jariwalla, S. Jayantilal, 1973, *Abdul Kharim Khan, The Man of the Times, Life and Art of a Great Musician*, Bombay: Balkrishnabuwa Kapileshwari.

Jha, Akhileshwar, 1980, *The Imprisoned Mind, Guru-Sisya Tradition in Indian Culture*, New Delhi: Ambika.

Jindel, Rajendra, 1976, *Culture of a Sacred Town, A Sociological Study of Nathdvara*, Bombay: Popular Prakashan.

Joshi, O.P., 1985, *Sociology of Indian Art*, Jaipur: Rawat.

Joshi, Rita, 1989, "The Dagars and Dhrupad", in *India Magazine*, 9 (May 1989) Delhi, pp. 60-4.

Kaemmer, John, E., 1980, "Between the Event and the Tradition: A New Look at Music in the Socio-Cultural Systems", *Ethnomusicology*, XXIV (1): 61-74.

Kalyanpurkar, Mohanrau, 1973, "Shambu Maharaj", *National Centre for Performing Arts*, December, Vol II. Bombay.

Khan, Inayat, 1974, *Inayat Khan*, London: Luzac.

Khandavalla, Karl, 1971, *Kishengarh Paintings*, New Delhi: Lalit Kala Akademi.

Khare, R.S., 1976, *Culture and Reality; Essays on the Hindu System of Managing Foods*, Simla: Indian Institute of Advanced Study.

Kinsley, David R., 1975, *The Sword and the Flute, Kali and Krsna, Dark Visions of the Terrible and the Sublime in Hindu Mythology*, Berkeley: University of California.

————, 1979, *The Divine Player: A Study on Krsna Lila*, Delhi: Motilal Banarsidass.

Kippen, James, 1988, *The Tabla of Lucknow; A Cultural Analysis of a Musical Tradition*, Cambridge: Cambridge. University Press.

Klostermaier, K., 1969, *Hindu and Christian in Vrindaban*, Bristol: SCM.

Krishnamoorthy, K., 1985, "The Evolution of Rasas in Indian Literature", *Sangeet Natak*, 75: 14-27.

L'Armand, Kathleen, and Adrien L'Armand, 1978, "The Urbanization of a Cultural Tradition", Bruno Nettle (ed.), *Eight Urban Musical Cultures, Tradition and Change*, Urbana Illinois: University of Illinois, pp. 115-145.

————, 1983, "One Hundred Years of Music in Madras: A Case Study in Secondary Urbanization", *Ethnomusicology*, 27: 411-38.

Lamarche, Manuel Peter, 1983, "Thumṛi in Historical and Stylistic Perspective", Ph.D. thesis, Los Angeles: University of California.

Lannoy, Richard, 1971, *The Speaking Tree: A Study of Indian Culture and Society*, Oxford: Oxford University Press.

Lath, Mukund, 1978, *A Study of Dattilam; A Treatise of the Sacred Music of India*. New Delhi: Impex.

————, 1978, "The History of Dhrupad: Plea for a new Approach", *Dhrupad Annual*, Vol II.

————, 1989, "The 'Modern', the 'Traditional', and Criticism in the Indian Musical Tradition", *Sangeet Natak*, 89-90: 5-15.

Lele, Jayant, 1981, *Traditions and Modernity in Bhakti Movements*. International Studies in Sociology and Social Anthropology. Leiden: Brill.

Lodrick, Deryck O., 1981, *Sacred Cows and Sacred Places*, Berkeley: University of California Press.

Losty, Jeremiah P., 1980, *Krishna: A Hindu Vision of God*, London: The British Library.

Luther, Narendra, 1980, "Urban Culture in the Performing Arts", *Sangeet Natak*, 58: 47-51.

MacGregor, R.S., 1984, *Hindi Literature from its Beginning to the Nineteenth Century*, Weisbaden: Harrassowitz.

Maduro, Renaldo, 1976, *Artistic Creativity in a Brahmin Painter Community*, Berkeley: Centre for South and Southeast Asia Studies.

Mandelbaum, David, G., 1984, *Society in India: Continuity and Change*, Vol. II, *Change and Continuity*, Bombay: Popular Prakashan.

Marfatia, Mrudula I., 1967, *The Philosophy of Vallabhacharya*, Delhi: Munshiram Manoharlal.

Marg, 1977a, *Homage to Jaipur*, XXX (4)

————, 1977b, *Coomaraswamy's Holistic View of Art*, Mulk Raj Anand.

————, 1980, *Treasures of Indian Textiles*, Ahmedabad: Calico Museum.

————, 1982, *Sivaji and the Facets of Maratha Culture.*

————, 1983, *An Age of Splendour—Islamic Art in India*, XXXV (2).

————, 1984, *Symbols and Manifestations in Indian Art.*

————, nd, *Patrons of Art, The Mughals and the Medici*, XXXIX (I).

————, nd, *Weavers and Dyers, Textiles of India and Persia*, XL (3).

Marglin, Frederique Appefel, 1985, *Wives of the God King*, New Delhi: Oxford University Press.

Massey, Reginald, 1976, *The Music of India*, London: Khan and Averill.
McDowell, Anna and Arvind Sharma, 1987, *Vignettes of Vrindavan*, Delhi: Books and Books.
Menon, Narayan, 1952, "About Indian Music", *Times of India Annual*, (Bombay), pp. 59-75.
———, 1988, "Tradition and Modernity" in *Sangeet Natak*, 89-90: 48-52.
Misra, K.C., 1971, *The Cult of Jagannatha*, Calcutta: Firma K.L. Mukhopadhyay.
Misra, Susheela, 1981, *Great Masters of Hindustani Music*, New Delhi: Hem.
———, 1985, *Music Makers of the Bhatkande College of Hindustani Music*, Calcutta: Sangeet Research Academy.
Mitra, Rajyeswar, 1986, "Reflections on Methods of Music Teaching", *Sangeet Natak* 79: 47-52.
Mokashi, D.B., 1987, *Palkhi, An Indian Pilgrimage*, translated from the Marathi by Philip Engblom and Eleanor Zelliot, Albany: State University of New York Press.
Morinis, Alan E., 1984, *Pilgrimage in the Hindu Tradition; A Case Study of Bengal*, Delhi: Oxford University Press.
Motivala, B.N., 1935, *Karsondas Mulji*, Bombay: Parbhudas Ladhabhai.
Mukherjee, Shri Bimalendu, 1986, "A Survey of Presentation of *Dhrupad* Style of Music Through Instruments", *Dhrupad Annual*, Vol. I.
Mulji, Karsondas, 1865, *History of the Sect of Maharajas or Vallabhacharyas in Western India*, London: Trubner.
Mutatkar, Sumati, 1987, "Dhrupad, Some Vignettes", *Dhrupad Annual*, pp. 11-13.
Nadkarni, Mohan Nad, 1983, *Bhimsen Joshi, The Man and His Music*, Bombay, Prism Communications.
Nag, Dipali, 1985, *Ustad Faiyaaz Khan*, New Delhi: Sangeet Natak Akademi.
Nagendra, Dr., 1979, *Suradas: A Re-evaluation*, Delhi: National.
Nath, Purohit Dev, 1938, *Mewar History; A Guide to Udaipur*, Bombay.
Nath Aman, Francis Wacziarg, 1987, *Arts and Crafts of Rajasthan*, London: Thames and Hudson.
Nayar, Sobhana, 1989, *Bhatkhande's Contribution to Music: A Historical Perspective*, Bombay: Popular Prakashan.
Nettl, Bruno, 1978, *Eight Urban Musical Cultures, Tradition and Change*, Chicago: University of Illinois.
———, 1985, *The Western Impact on World Music, Change, Adaptation and Survival*, New York: Schimer.
Neuman, Daniel, 1976, "Towards an Ethnomusicology of Cultural Change in Asia", *Asian Music*, Vll (2):1-5.
———, 1977, "The Social Organization of a Music Tradition, Hereditary Specialists in North India", *Ethnomusicology*, XX1 (2): 233-245.

———, 1978, "*Gharanas*: The Rise of Musical 'Houses' in Delhi and Neighbouring Cities" in *Eight Urban Musical Cultures, Tradition and Change*, Bruno Nettl (ed.), Urbana Illinois: University of Illinois, pp. 186-222.

———, 1980, *The Life of Music in North India: The Organization of an Artistic Tradition*, Delhi: Manohar.

New Grove Dictionary of Music and Musicians, 1980, Stanley Sadie (ed.), London: MacMillan, pp. 69-166.

O'Connell, Joseph T., 1985, *Bengal Vaisnavism, Orientalism, Society and the Arts*, Michigan: Asian Studies Centre.

O'Flaherty, Wendy Donniger, 1975, *Hindu Myths*, Harmondsworth: Penguin.

Owens, Naomi, 1983, "The Dagar Gharana; with special reference to Ustad Nasir Aminuddin Dagar", Bonnie Wade (ed.), *Performing Artists in India, Essays on Music, Dance, and Drama*, Berkeley: California, Centre for South and South East Asian Studies, pp. 158-70.

Pal, Bhishan H., 1969, *The Temples of Rajasthan*, Alwar, Jaipur: Prakash.

Pal, M.K., 1978, *Crafts and Craftsmen in Traditional India*, New Delhi: Kanak.

Parekh, Bhai Manilal, 1943, *Sri Vallabhacharya, Life Teachings and Movement (A Religion of Grace)*, Rajkot: Harmony House, Shri Bhagavata Dharma Mission.

Parimoo, Ratan, 1987, *Vaishnavism in Indian Arts and Culture*, New Delhi: Books and Books.

Parmar, V.S., 1987, "Temples of Gujarat; An Architectural Study", in *Vaishnavism in Indian Arts and Culture*, Ratin Parimoo (ed.), New Delhi: Books and Books, pp. 187-201.

Pocock, David Francis, 1973, *Mind, Body and Wealth*, Oxford: Oxford University Press.

Popley, H.A., 1986, *The Music of India*, Delhi: Award.

Powers, Harold S., 1979, "Classical Music, Cultural Roots and Colonial Rule: An Indic Musicologist Looks at the Muslim World", *Asian Music*, XII: 5-39.

———, 1980, "Language Models and Musical Analysis", *Ethnomusicology*, 1: 1-60.

Prajnananda, Swami, 1981, *A Historical Study of Indian Music*, Delhi: Munshiram Manoharlal.

Quinn, Jennifer, 1982, "Marathi and Konkani Speaking Women in Hindustani Music 1880-1940", Ph.D. thesis, Minneapolis: University of Minnesota.

Qureshi, Burckhardt Regula, 1986, *Sufi Music of India and Pakistan; Sound Context and meaning in Qawwali*, London: Cambridge University Press.

Rakesagupta, 1967, *Studies in Nayaka, Nayika Bheda*, Aligarh: Granthayan.

Ranade, Ashok D., 1984, *On Music and Musicians of Hindoostan*, New Delhi: Promilla.

————, 1986, *Stage Music of Maharashtra*, New Delhi: Sangeet Natak Akademi.

————, 1987, "Devotional Music in India", Sangeet Natak Akademi, 85-86.

————, 1988, "Music and its non-Music Uses", *Sangeet Natak*, 89-90: 24-9.

Ranade, G.H., 1938, *Hindustani Music; An Outline of its Physics and Aesthetics*, Sangli: G.H. Ranade.

Randhawa, M.S., 1971, *Kangra Valley Paintings*, New Delhi: Government of India,

Randhawa, M.S. and S.D. Bhambri, 1981, *Basholi Paintings of the Rasamanjari*, New Delhi: Abhinav.

Rao, Ramachanadra S.K., 1981, *Psychology of Laya*, Bangalore: Percussive Arts.

Reck, David, 1977, *Music of the Whole Earth*, New York: Charles Scribner's Sons.

Redfield, James, and Milton Singer, 1956, "The Cultural Role of Cities", in *Man In India*, 36 (3): 161-94.

Redington, James D., 1983, *Vallabhacarya on the Love Games of Krsna*, New Delhi: Motilal Banarsidass.

Richardson, Edwin-Allen, 1979, "Mughal and Rajput Patronage of the Bhakti Sect of the Maharajas, the Vallabha Sampraday, 1640-1760", Ph.D. thesis, University of Arizona: Department of Oriental Studies.

Roach, David, 1972, "The Banaras Baj; The Tabla Tradition of a North Indian City", *Asian Music*, III (2).

Rosenthal, Ethel, 1980, *The Story of Indian Music and its Instruments*, New Delhi: Oriental Books.

Rudolph, Lloyd I. and Susanne Hoeber Rudolph, 1984, *Essays on Rajputana, Reflections on History, Culture, and Administration*, New Delhi: Concept.

Sadagopala, V.V., 1970, "An Introduction to *Raga*", *Indian Music Journal*, VI (11-12).

Sangeet Natak Akademi, 1968, *Who's Who of Indian Musicians*, New Delhi: Sangeet Natak.

Sangita Ratnakara, *of Sarngadeva*, 1978, Text and Translation, Vol 1. R.K. Shringy and Prem Lata Sharma.

Sarkar, Jadunath, 1984, *A History of Jaipur, 1503-1938*, Hyderbad: Orient Longmans.

Saxena, Sushil Kumar, 1979, *The Winged Form, Aesthetical Essays on Hindustani Rhythm*, New Delhi: Sangeet Natak.

Schaffer, Stephen, 1987 "Revisiting Vrindaban", in McDowell and Sharma (ed.), *Vignettes of Vrindavan*, Delhi: Books and Books, pp. 139-47.

Sehgal, Rashme, 1989, "Bhimsen Joshi, The Master of *Khyal*", *India Magazine*, (February), pp. 83-8.

Sen, R.K., 1966, *Aesthetic Enjoyment, its Background in Philosophy and Medicine*, Calcutta: University of Calcutta.

Shah, Jethalal G., 1969, *Shri Vallabhacharya, His Philosophy and Religion*, Nandian: Pustimargiya Pustakalaya.

Shankar, Ravi, 1968, *My Music, My Life*, New Delhi: Vikas.

Shapiro, Alan, 1987, "*Sanjhi*, A Festival of Vraja", in McDowell and Sharma A. (ed.), *Vignettes of Vrindabam*, New Delhi: Books and Books, pp. 88-104.

Sharma, B.L., 1971, "Contributions of Rajasthan to Indian Music", *Journal of the Indian Musicological Society* (Baroda), 2 (2): 32-47.

Shepherd, F., 1976, "Tabla and the Benares Gharana", Ph.D. thesis, Middletown Conn: Wesleyan University.

Sheth, Noel S.J., 1984, *The Divinity of Krishna*, Delhi: Munshiram Manoharlal.

Siegel, Lee, 1978, *Sacred and Profane Dimensions of Love in Indian Traditions as Exemplified in the Gitagovinda of Jayadeva*, Delhi: Oxford University Press.

Shackle, C. and Snell, Rupert, 1989, *Urdu and Muslim South Asian Studies in Honour of Ralph Russell*, London: School of Oriental and African Studies.

Sharma, Dasharatha, 1966, *Rajasthan Through the Ages*, Vol. 1, *From the Earliest Times to 1316 A.D.*, Bikaner: Rajasthan State Archives.

Sharma, G.N., 1965, *A Bibliography of Medieval Rajasthan (Social and Cultural)*, Agra: Lakshmi Narain Agarwal.

Sharma, Krishna, 1987, *Bhakti and the Bhakti Movement*, Delhi: Munshiram Manoharlal.

Sharma, Prem Lata, 1969, "Manasollasa", *Indian Music Journal*, V (2): 103-111.

————, 1970a, "Rasakoumudi of Srikantha", *Indian Music Journal*, VI(11-12): 48-53.

————, 1970b, "Brhaddesi of Matanga", *Indian Music Journal*, VI (11-12): 54-57.

————, 1970c, "Music and Musicology", *Indian Music Journal* (VI).

————, 1980, "The History and Origin of Thumri with Special Reference to Gharanas and Style", in *The Sacred and the Secular in India's Performing Arts*, V. Subramaniam (ed.), New Delhi: Ashish, pp. 109-23.

————, 1986, "The Banaras Dhrupad Melas", *Dhrupad Annual*. I: 116-19.

————, 1987, "The Dhruva in Dhruva Pada", *Dhrupad Annual*, II.

———, 1987, "Editors Note", in *Dhrupad Annual*, II.

———, 1987, "Signature in Dhrupad and the Problems Arising Therefrom", *Dhrupad Annual*, II: 99-101.

———, 1988, "Musical Terms in Dhrupad Texts", *Dhrupad Annual*, III: 49-51.

———, 1988, "The History of Charatala or Chautal in the Talas of Dhrupad", *Dhrupad Annual*, Vol. III.

Silver, Brian, 1976, "The Evolution of a Gharana", *Asian Music*, 7(2): 27-50.

Singer, Milton, 1959, "The Great Traditions in a Metropolitan Centre, Madras", in *Traditional India, Structure and Change*, Milton Singer (ed.), Philadelphia: American Folklore Society.

———, 1966, *Krishna: Myths, Rites and Attitudes*, Westport Connecticut: Greenwood Press.

———, 1972, *When a Great Tradition Modernizes*, New York: Praeger.

Singh, Naina Ripjit, 1964, *Mushtaq Hussain Khan*, New Delhi: Sangeet Natak Akademi.

Singh, Yogendra, 1986, *Modernization of Indian Tradition*, Jaipur: Rawat.

Singh, Chandramani, 1981, "Performing Arts from Amber and Jaipur; a Study Based on Paturkhana and Naqqarakhana", in *Cultural Contours of India*: Dr Sarya Prakash Felicitations Volume, V.S. Srivastava (ed.), New Delhi: Abhinav, pp. 1-10.

Singh, Jaideva, 1976, "Prabhanda and Druvapada", *Journal of the Indian Musicological Society*, 7 (3).

Sinha, Purnima, 1970, *An Approach to the Study of Indian Music*, Calcutta: Indian Publications.

Skelton, Robert, 1973, *Rajasthani Temple Hangings of the Krishna Cult*, New York: American Federation of Arts.

Snell, Rupert, 1982, "Metrical Forms in *Braj Bhasa* Verse, the *Hita Caurasi Pada* in Performance", Paper presented at the Second Conference on Early Devotional Literature in New Aryan Languages, Bonn, March 1982, pp. 1-29.

———, 1989, "Rakshan the Neophyte: Hindu Perspectives on a Muslim Vaishnava", in *Urdu and Muslim South Asia Studies, in Honour of Ralph Russell*, C. Shackle (ed.), London: School of Oriental and African Studies, pp. 29-37.

Sorrell, Neil, 1980, *Indian Music in Performance*, Manchester: University of Manchester Press.

Spink, Walter M., 1971, *Krishna Mandala*, Michigan: Centre for South and South East Asian Studies.

Srivastava, Indurama, 1980, *Dhrupada: A Study of its Origin, Historical Development, Structure and Present State*, Delhi: Motilal Banarsidass.

Stein, Burton, 1978, *South Indian Temples: An Analytical Reconsideration*, New Delhi: Vikas.

Stern, Philippe, 1933, "The Music of India and the Theory of Raga", *Indian Art and Letters*, New Series, VII (1): 1-9.

Stewart, Rebecca Marie, 1974, "The Tabla in Perspective", Ph.D. thesis, Los Angeles: University of California.

Talwar, Kay and Krishna Kalyan, 1979, *Indian Pigment Paintings on Cloth*, Ahmedabad: Calico Museum of Textiles.

Te Nijenhuis, Emmie, 1974, *Indian Music, History and Structure*, Leiden: Brill.

Thomas, P., 1971, *Hindu Religion, Customs and Manners*, Bombay: Taraporevala.

Thoothi, N.A., 1935, *The Vaishnavas of Gujarat*, Calcutta: Longmans.

Tod, James, 1829, *Annals and Antiquities of Rajasthan*, 2 vols. (reprint 1978), New Delhi: M.N. Publishers. (1st edition, George Routledge and Sons, 1829).

————, 1920, James Crooke (ed.), 3 vols., New Delhi: Motilal Banarsidass.

Toomey, Paul Michael, 1985, "Food from the Mouth of Krishna: Sacred Food and Pilgrimage at Mount Govardhan", Ph.D. thesis, University of Virginia.

————, 1988, "Rediscovering Braj in the Anthropological Imagnation", in *Re-discovering Braj*, London: International Association of Vrindaban Research, SOAS.

Topsfield, Andrew, 1980, *Paintings from Rajasthan in the National Gallery of Victoria*, Melbourne: National Gallery of Victoria.

————, 1987, "Udaipur Paintings of the *Ras Lila*" *Art Bulletin of Victoria*, 28: 55-70, Victoria, Australia.

————, 1987, "Ras Lila", *Indian Miniature Painting*, Catalogue No. 41, London: Spink and Son.

Umrao Jan Ada, 1961, *The Courtesan of Lucknow*, trans. Khushwant Singh, New Delhi: Hind.

Van der Meer, Wim, 1975, "Cultural Evolution: A Case Study of Indian Music", *Sangeet Natak*, 35: 49-65.

————, 1980, *Hindustani Music in the Twentieth Century*, Bombay: Allied.

————, 1986, "Teaching Indian Music, Coping with a Changing Environment", *Sangeet Natak*, 79: 53-8.

Van der Meer, Wim and Joep Bor, 1982 *De Roep Van de Kokila*, Gravenhage: Martinus Nijhoff.

Vaudville, Charlotte, 1976, "Braj, Lost and Found", *Indo-Iranian Journal*, 1: 195-213, Holland: Dordrecht, Holland, Boston: Reidel.

————, 1980, "The Govardhan Myth in Northern India", *Indo-Iranian Journal*, 22:1-45, Holland: Dordrecht, Boston: Reidel.

Verdia, H.S., 1982, *Religion and Social Structure in a Sacred Town: Nathdvara*, Delhi: Research Company.

Wach, Joachim, 1948, *Sociology of Religion*, Chicago: University of Chicago Press.

Wade, Bonnie C., 1971, "Khyal: A Study in Hindustani Classical Vocal Music", Ph.D. thesis, Los Angeles: University of California.

————, 1979, *Music in India, the Classical Traditions*, New Jersey: Prentice Hall.

————, 1983, *Performing Arts in India: Essays on Music, Dance and Drama*, Berkeley: Centre for South and Southeast Asia Studies.

————, 1984, *Khyal, Creativity within North India's Classical Music Tradition*, Cambridge: Cambridge University Press.

Waghorne, Joanne Punzo and Norman Cutler, 1985, *Gods of Flesh, Gods of Stone, the Embodiment of Divinity in India*, Chambersburg, Penn.: Anima.

Widdess, Richard, 1981, "Aspects of Form in North Indian *Alap* and *Dhrupad*", in *Music and Tradition, Essays on Asia and other Music*, R. Widdess and R.F. Wolpert (ed.), Cambridge: Cambridge University Press, pp. 148-83.

————, 1990, "Involving the Performer in Transcriptions and Analysis: A Dialectic Approach to *Dhrupad*", paper given at the 11th European Conference on Modern South Asian Studies in Amsterdam, Holland, July 1990.

Williams, Raymond D., 1984, *A New Face of Hinduism: The Swaminarayan Religion*, Cambridge: Cambridge University Press.

Winternitz, Maurice, 1972, *A History of Indian Literature*, New Delhi: Oriental Books.

Index